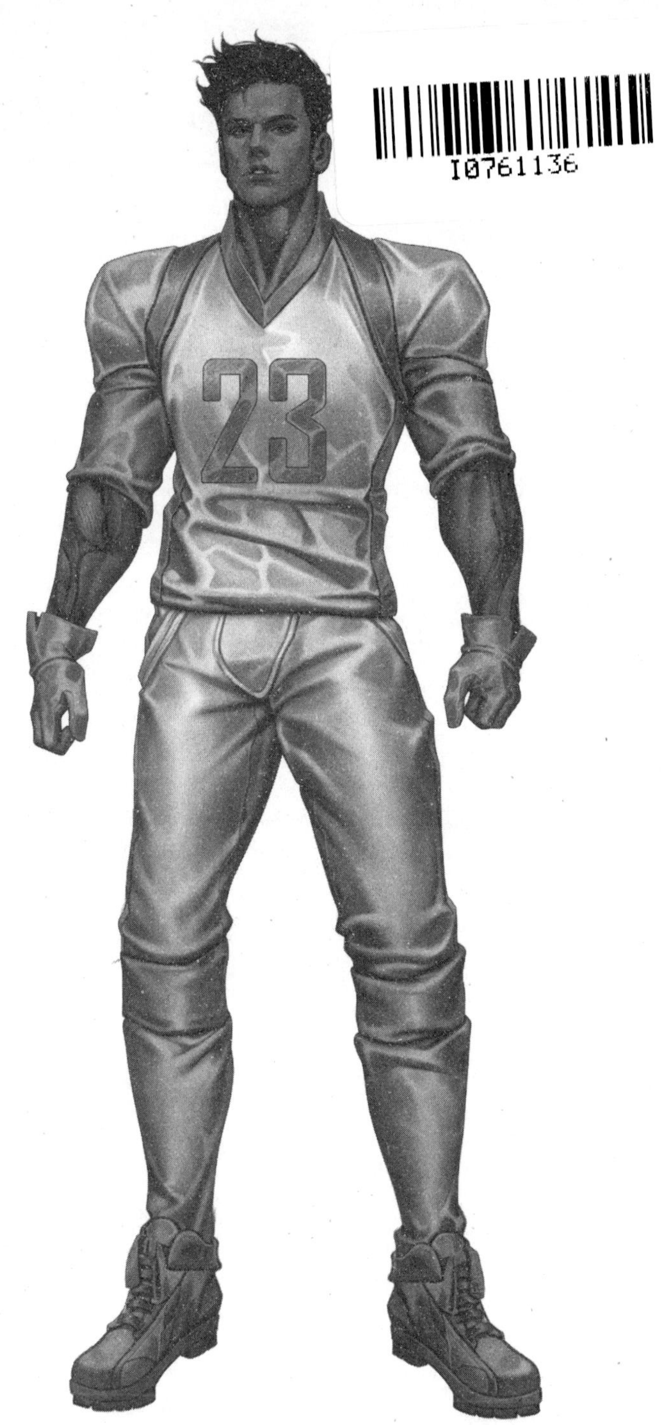
23

ALSO BY C.R. JANE

The Wrong Player Series

The Wrong Quarterback

The Wrong Play

Merry Me

The Wrong Catch

The Pucking Wrong Series

The Pucking Wrong Number

The Pucking Wrong Guy

A Pucking Wrong Christmas

The Pucking Wrong Date

The Pucking Wrong Man

The Pucking Wrong Rookie

The Spartan Flame Trilogy

Shadows of Sparta

The Wrong Made Men Series

Don't Say Mafia

THE WRONG CATCH

C.R. JANE

Podium

For the girl who was told she loved too much.
You weren't wrong—you were just ahead of your time.

Cover design by Emily Wittig
Photography by Michelle Lancaster
Editing by Stephanie H./Hannotek, Ink

ISBN: 979-8-3470-0430-0

Published in 2026 by Podium Publishing
www.podiumentertainment.com

Podium

Dear Renegades,

If you're holding this book in your hands, then you already know something dangerous about yourself.

You crave the stories that don't behave. The ones that bite back. The ones that whisper mine and don't pretend it's a metaphor.

This book was written for readers who don't flinch at obsession, who understand that love is not always gentle and that safety sometimes looks like teeth bared at the world. It's for the ones who find comfort in darkness, who recognize that being chosen, fiercely and without apology, can feel like finally coming home.

I write morally grey men because I believe devotion is a force of nature. I write broken, resilient women because surviving sharpens you, and wanting does not make you weak. I write love that is messy, consuming, a little unhinged, because neat love has never changed anyone.

You are not here by accident.

You are here because you like your romance intense, your heroes obsessive, your heroines strong enough to survive being loved that hard. You are here because you believe found family matters, because banter can coexist with violence, because laughter can live right next to longing. Because sometimes the fantasy is not being saved, but being seen and claimed anyway.

Thank you for trusting me with your heart and your nerves and your sleepless nights. Thank you for rooting for the characters who don't deserve grace and loving them anyway. Thank you for being loud, passionate, feral, and impossible to ignore.

You make these stories possible.
You make them worth writing.

Welcome to the madness.
Stay unhinged.

With all my love,

CR Jane

TEAM ROSTER

OFFENSE

QUARTERBACK:

Parker Davis | #12
Trent Maxwell | #07
Malik Harper | #16
Owen Matthis | #14

RUNNING BACK:

Garrett Harper | #22
Griffin Tillman | #30
Trevon Brooks | #29
Elijah Rivera | #33
Jordan Wright | #20
Marcus "Speedy" Hayes | #28

WIDE RECEIVER:

Jace Thatcher | #77
Hunter Manning | #63
Chris Jordan | #19
Caleb "Ace" Thompson | #11
Ethan Vance | #36
Isaiah Turner | #18
Brandon Holt | #17
Trey Anderson | #84
Quentin Scott | #89

TIGHT END:

Matthew "Matty" Adler | #23
Eric Simmons | #86
Logan Mendez | #80
Cam Richards | #82

OFFENSIVE LINE:

Hunter "Tank" Thompson | #67
Sam Carrington | #65
Connor Wright | #55
Chapman "Chappie" Cordell | #68
Derrick Morgan | #73
Connor Steele | #71
Blake McAllister | #75
Jared Foster | #54
Grayson Lee | #72
Noah Chambers | #74

TEAM ROSTER (CONT.)

DEFENSE

DEFENSIVE LINE:

Darwin Harrison | #90
Matt Santiago | #92
Elijah Reed | #99
Anthony Williams | #94
Jacob Tanner |#96
Jalen Fields | #69
Wyatt Cook | #98
Damien Ward | #91
Sean Little | #97

CORNERBACKS:

Tyrell Brooks | #24
Dante Jefferson | #66

LINEBACKERS:

Brandon Scott | Outside Linebacker | #44
Marcus Steadman| Middle Linebacker | #52
Andre Carter | Outside Linebacker | #41
Malcolm Spencer | #51
Aiden Cruz | #57
Cole Anderson | #53

SAFETIES:

Xavier Hawthorne | Free Safety | #21
Malik Greene | Strong Safety | #93

SPECIAL TEAMS

KICKER:

:han Collins | #3
Will Torres | #6

PUNTER:

Ryan Matthews | #2

RETURN SPECIALIST:

Chris Reddick | #46

LONG SNAPPER:

Colton Ramsey | #9

COACHING STAFF

HEAD COACH	Clint Everett
OFFENSIVE COORDINATOR	Dale Malone
DEFENSIVE COORDINATOR	Bryce Thompson
SPECIAL TEAMS COACH	Reggie Caldwell
STRENGTH AND CONDITIONING COACH	Travis Richards
QUARTERBACKS COACH	Evan Houston
WIDE RECEIVERS COACH	Trey Winston
RUNNING BACKS COACH	Nathan Grant
OFFENSIVE LINE COACH	Doug "Grizzly" Callahan
DEFENSIVE LINE COACH	Marcus Hayes
LINEBACKERS COACH	Jerome Brooks
DEFENSIVE BACKS COACH	DeAndre Moore

THE WRONG CATCH

PLAYLIST

THE FATE OF OPHELIA	TAYLOR SWIFT
YOU	JARED BENJAMIN
NO MERCY	AUSTIN GIORGIO
HANDS DOWN	DASHBOARD CONFESSIONAL
SLOW IT DOWN	BENSON BOONE
SAFE WITH ME	IKE DWECK
I'M YOURS	ISABEL LAROSA
LET THE WORLD BURN	CHRIS GREY
WORSHIP	ARI ABDUL
WILD HORSES	THE SUNDAYS
R U MINE?	ARCTIC MONKEYS
LOVE IS A BITCH	TWO FEET
WHISPER	CHANIN
NOW THAT I FOUND HER	GIO DARA
DON'T BLAME ME	TAYLOR SWIFT
DROWN (FEAT. CLINTON KANE)	MARTIN GARRIX, CLINTON KANE
AFTER DARK X SWEATER WEATHER	TOMMYMUZZIC, ZEDDMUSIQUE

LISTEN TO THE FULL PLAYLIST HERE

TRIGGER WARNING

Dear readers,

Please be aware this is a dark romance and as such can and will contain possible triggering content. Elements of this story are purely fantasy and should not be taken as acceptable behavior in real life.

Our love interest is possessive, obsessive, and the perfect shade of red for all you red flag renegades out there. There is absolutely no shade of pink involved when it comes to what Matty Adler will do to get his girl. There's also no shade of pink in what Ophelia Prescott will do to get her man . . .

Themes include football, obsessive stalking, self-harm, thoughts about self-harm, manipulation, dark obsessions, mental illness including anxiety and personality disorders, threatened breeding, confinement, forced marriage, emotional abuse (not by Matty Adler), parental gambling addiction, blackmail, and sexually explicit scenes.

There are no harems, cheating, or sharing of partners involved. Matty Adler only has eyes for her.

Prepare to enter the world of the Tennessee Tigers . . . You've been warned.

THE WRONG CATCH

“OBSESSION IS GONNA BEAT TALENT EVERY TIME.”

—Adam Sandler, *Hustle*

UTBallGirl411
@UTBallGirl411

Breaking News🚨: You guys...we’ve seen a lot of wild things on campus, but nothing like what just went down at Neyland. 🏈🔥 Star tight end Matty Adler scored, ripped off his helmet, and made a beeline straight for the Tigers’ mascot. Then, in front of 90,000 fans, cameras, and what we assume is a very confused opposing team...he kissed her in a full Tennessee meltdown. The internet is already in flames. Clips are everywhere. And sources (aka people who definitely shouldn’t be texting during the game) say the girl behind the mask might actually be his girlfriend. 👀 If that’s true, then Adler just turned into a full-blown campus legend. We’ll update you as this develops—because something tells us this love story just became the biggest catch of the season. 💋🐯
#AdlerHasAbs #Tigerlips #MattyAdler #CampusScandal

3:36 PM · Nov 22, 2025

53.4K Retweets **22.2K** Quote Tweets **110.7K** Likes

PROLOGUE

OPHELIA

Fourteen Years Old

I sat on the scratchy carpet just outside the door, my knees hugged to my chest so tightly they ached. The hall smelled like burnt coffee, and the air conditioner kicked on every eight minutes like clockwork, loud enough to almost drown out the voices behind the half-cracked door.

Almost.

"She says she *loves* him." My mother's voice sliced through the white noise, all edge and tension, like she was trying to cut the word out of her own mouth. "And not in a silly teenage crush way. She says it like she means it. Like she'd *die* for him."

My stomach clenched so hard I thought I might throw up right there on the beige carpet.

"Fourteen-year-olds have crushes all the time," the therapist commented gently.

"She doesn't just say she loves him," Dad cut in, his voice tight, like he hated being here but hated what I'd done even more. "She followed him home. She wrote him letters. She got into his locker somehow. This isn't a schoolgirl crush . . . It's obsession."

I wanted to disappear.

My fingers dug into the fabric of my jeans, trying to rip something—anything—to stop the memories from crawling out.

But they came anyway.

It was last Tuesday. I'd stayed late after class because I knew he always started his walk home fifteen minutes after the final bell. I waited behind the vending machine, pretending to dig around for a dollar I didn't have. When he finally walked out, alone and laughing at something on his phone, I followed.

Just a few steps behind.

He never noticed me. I made sure of it.

I knew where he lived. Of course I did. I'd memorized the map the first time I looked him up online. But that day . . . I just wanted to see if he went straight home. If he smiled when he walked in. If his mom hugged him.

Because I wanted to be that. The one he smiled at. The one he let in.

When he opened the door and turned around like he sensed me . . . I ran.

"Her behavior is escalating," Dr. Whitaker said then. Calm. Measured. Like she was reciting a grocery list instead of dissecting my soul. "We've spoken before about her diagnoses, but I think it's time to review. Obsessive love disorder is not officially recognized by the DSM-4, but the pattern is clear. She's exhibiting signs of borderline personality disorder, obsessive-compulsive disorder, and an attachment disorder."

The word *disorder* lingered in the air like the smell of antiseptic. I couldn't see them from where I sat in the hallway, but I could picture it—the way my mother would fold her hands in her lap, nodding too quickly, eager to prove she understood. My father's jaw tight, his eyes on the floor. Both pretending they hadn't already failed whatever test this was.

They would be acting as if they knew exactly what she meant, as if there was a neat bullet point in my file that could sum it up: *Age six, began exhibiting symptoms.*

Disorder.

They made it sound so small. Contained. A thing that could be boxed up, labeled, and filed away.

They called it when I first exhibited symptoms.

I called it the moment everything started leaking through the cracks.

I dug my nails into my palms, wishing I could claw the words out of the air before they reached me, before they reminded me of what I already knew . . . I was broken.

"She manipulates people to feel close to them," the therapist continued. "She imagines entire relationships that don't exist. It's not about the boy, really. It's about control. About filling the hole inside her."

I covered my ears . . . but it didn't work.

"I found her notebook," my mom said, and I could hear the sound of paper being shoved across a table. "Pages and pages of their names together.

'Ophelia plus Nico. Mrs. Nico Alvarez.' His schedule, his mom's phone number, even his little sister's birthday."

A tear slipped down my face as I pictured their hands on those pages, touching the parts of me I never meant to show.

They'd read it.

They'd *seen* it.

All those pages I'd filled in secret—every scrawl, every looping heart, every whispered fantasy that I thought would make the feelings smaller—now turned inside out under the fluorescent lights.

I could picture the therapist tilting her head, her lips pursed in clinical concern. My mother's hands quivering just enough to seem like she cared . . . my father sitting in frozen silence.

The panic was everywhere, swarming under my skin. My heart hammered so loudly I thought they'd hear it through the door.

I wanted to claw my own chest open and scrape out whatever made me *this way*.

The words in the office dissolved, replaced by the scratch of a pen.

I wrote it all in purple pen. The glittery kind that smelled like grapes.

I thought it was romantic.

I thought maybe if I learned everything about him, like his favorite gum flavor (cinnamon), the way he always tied his left shoe first, the fact that he always let girls go first in line . . . he'd see me. He'd realize I was the one who understood him best.

It wasn't stalking.

It wasn't.

It was love.

At least, that's what I told myself.

"She doesn't see anything wrong with it," my mom said, bringing me back to the present. And I could hear the way her voice shook with rage. "She thinks it's sweet. She told me last night she thinks he's her soulmate. Her *fucking* soulmate."

I pressed my forehead to my knees, squeezing my eyes shut so tightly it made stars burst behind my lids.

They weren't wrong.

They weren't wrong about any of it.

And that's what made it worse.

Because I had felt it. The second Nico smiled at me that first day of seventh grade—when he passed me the pencil I dropped and said "Here you go"—I'd felt it in my chest. That thud. That zing. That *connection*.

It wasn't just a crush. It was an obsession.

And I couldn't turn it off.

"Has she ever hurt anyone?" the therapist asked.

"No," my dad said quickly, too quickly. "But she's hurting herself."

"I think we need to consider a more structured environment. At the very least, intensive therapy. This isn't something she's going to outgrow."

My stomach twisted even more. The air seemed to leave the hallway all at once, replaced by a low hum that pressed against my ears. *Structured environment*. The words felt heavy, important . . . like they were supposed to fix me, even though I already knew nothing could.

It was my sentence.

I didn't know what a "structured environment" was, but it sounded a lot like a prison. And maybe I deserved it.

Because love wasn't supposed to feel like this.

It wasn't supposed to hurt this much.

The room blurred, and suddenly I was somewhere else again.

I stole Nico's hoodie once.

He left it in the locker room during gym, and I snuck in during lunch and slipped it into my bag. It smelled like his shampoo, minty and clean, and I wore it to bed for a week straight.

Every night, I pretended he gave it to me.

That he whispered I looked pretty in it.

That he missed me when I wasn't around.

But one day, Laura saw me wearing it. She was a girl in his friend group. She pointed and laughed and said, "Why are you wearing Nico's hoodie?"

I said, "He gave it to me."

She rolled her eyes. "You're such a freak."

I sucked in a breath like surfacing too fast, the pain in my chest blooming so violently I thought it might split me open.

I *was* a freak.

A broken, twisted, obsessive freak.

And I hated myself for it.

Not because I didn't believe in love . . . I did. I still did, even now, sitting outside this horrible office with my whole life exploding inside. But because I knew deep down he had never looked at me the way I looked at him.

He never would.

"I want to be clear," the therapist said then. "This isn't her fault. These are the symptoms of deeply rooted mental health disorders. With the right therapy, medication, and structure, she can learn to manage the impulses.

But she's going to need support. And patience. And for you both to stop reacting with disgust."

There was a pause.

"Right," my mom said flatly. "Support. Patience. For the daughter who makes up imaginary relationships with boys and calls it love."

That word again.

Love.

It made me feel like I'd swallowed glass.

Because what I felt . . . it wasn't cute.

It wasn't butterflies or blushes or locker notes.

It was hunger.

It was loneliness with teeth.

And now they were talking about *meds* and *structure* and maybe even *facilities*, like I was a problem to be managed. A bomb they were scared might go off again.

The therapist kept talking, and my mom's tone turned cold, precise. "We'll do whatever we need to," she said. "We can't live like this anymore."

My dad sighed, the sound of a man who was already done with the situation and wanted to leave.

But I didn't hear the rest.

Not really.

Not over the blood rushing in my ears and the echo of my own voice, remembered from just two nights ago when I told Nico I loved him. Not to his face, of course. I whispered it to the picture I'd printed off the school website. The one where he was mid-laugh on the soccer field, wind tugging at his hair.

I'd pressed my lips to it.

Called it our secret.

Now that secret felt diseased.

I jumped as my mom slammed the car door hard enough to make the frame shake. She didn't look at me, just stormed up the porch steps, her heels striking the wood like gunshots. My pulse tripped over itself, dread tightening my throat as I followed.

The keys jingled violently as she jammed them into the lock, muttering under her breath. I hesitated on the porch, glancing back at the car.

My dad was still in the driver's seat, hands slack on the steering wheel, his eyes fixed straight ahead. The engine idled softly, exhaust curling into the cold air. He didn't look at me. Didn't look at anything. Just sat there, like if he stayed still long enough, the whole day might erase itself.

I'd lost him. I could see that.

He'd been in my corner once. Not loudly, never that . . . but enough to make me believe I wasn't so bad. Now I could see the truth in the way he kept staring forward.

I was on my own.

My mom shoved the door open with her shoulder, the hinges groaning in protest. The sound made me flinch.

Inside, the faint smell of lemon cleaner clung to everything, unsullied and artificial, the way my mother liked it. She scrubbed the house until it gleamed, as if perfection could keep the cracks from showing. Lemon meant order. Lemon meant control.

It was obvious she had her own problem with obsession, though hers was the kind that got praised. Her addiction was perfection . . . and perfection never hurt anyone. Not the way mine did.

It burned the back of my throat.

I'd never smelled like lemon, no matter how many times she told me to clean up, straighten up, be better. I always carried something else on my skin: want, worry, the kind of wrongness she couldn't wipe away.

The smell made my stomach twist until I thought I might throw up.

She dropped her purse onto the table with a sharp *thud* and spun on her heel so fast I almost collided with her.

Her eyes found me, dark and gleaming with fury, and I knew the real punishment hadn't even started yet.

"You need more structure," she snapped, her finger pointed like a weapon. "That's what the therapist said, right? Well, I can tell you it's not going to be at your school. I'm done letting you drag this family down with you."

I didn't respond. I just stood there with my backpack still slung over one shoulder since I'd carried it straight from school to the therapist's office. The strap dug into my skin, and I felt small and stupid and sick all over again.

"You embarrassed us," she hissed, her lips twisting into a snarl. "You embarrassed *yourself.* You're lucky his parents didn't file a restraining order."

The term *restraining order* made something shift in my chest.

Something I didn't have a name for. Something rotten and soft, collapsing under its own weight.

The hoodie.

That was what had started today. The reason we'd been called in, the reason for the emergency appointment, the reason everyone looked at me like I was something that needed fixing.

I hadn't meant for it to be a big deal. It had just been his hoodie, soft and warm, still smelling like him.

But then Laura had noticed it. And she'd told.

And suddenly it wasn't comfort anymore . . . it was *evidence.*

My mother shook her head like she couldn't even look at me anymore, then turned and walked away without waiting for a response.

I went upstairs like I always did, one foot in front of the other, wooden and numb and not knowing what else to do. The afternoon light cut across the floorboards in neat, perfect lines, the kind my mother would've approved of. The edges of my mirror were taped with magazine clippings and sticky notes that didn't make sense anymore.

I shut the door quietly. Then locked it.

I dug through the bottom drawer of my desk, behind my old sticker books and bent-up gel pens, until I found the letter. The one I'd written to him and never sent. Pages of things I'd never say out loud: apologies, promises, and confessions I'd rewritten until the ink bled through.

It was attached to the picture I'd printed, the one where he was laughing in the sun.

I stared at it for a long time.

Then I tried to tear it.

But I couldn't.

I couldn't even *crease* it.

My hands shook as I held the edges, but every time I tried to rip it, something in me screamed. Something childish. Possessive. Broken.

I dropped it on the floor and then curled into myself on the bed.

The sob caught in my throat before I even knew it was coming. And then I was crying like a little kid, fists curled in my comforter, nose running, chest heaving—that kind of crying that doesn't have a shape or a reason or a place to go.

I didn't know how long I lay there.

But eventually the crying turned to silence.

To stillness.

To that familiar emptiness that always came after. The kind that whispered awful things in a soft, sweet voice.

You're pathetic. You're disgusting. You'll always be too much. Too intense. Too clingy. Too broken.

No one will ever love you back.

I sat up slowly and then got up and walked back to my desk.

The third drawer down, buried beneath a few books and my iPhone cord, held a safety pin I'd kept for emergencies. I couldn't even remember why anymore . . . maybe for a Halloween costume that never happened.

I took it out and unclipped it, turning the metal between my fingers until the point caught the light. Then I pressed it into the soft skin just below my waistband, where no one would ever see.

It wasn't deep. Just enough to sting. Just enough to remind myself that I could still feel something that wasn't shame.

For a second, the ache in my chest quieted. Not for long, but long enough to trick me into thinking I was okay.

The door slammed open somehow, even though I'd locked it, the handle hitting the wall like she expected to catch me doing something. I was just lying on my bed, staring at the ceiling, but I flinched anyway.

My mom stood in the doorway, arms crossed, car keys dangling in her hand. Her eyes swept the room, taking everything in like it was evidence.

"Get up. We're leaving," she said.

I blinked at her, pushing myself up on my elbows. "Where?"

My voice came out rough, torn up from tears that wouldn't stop. My brain was still scrambled from the last hour I'd spent crying.

She didn't answer right away. Her stare was pure disgust, like she couldn't believe she had to explain it.

"It's the place Dr. Whitaker mentioned as we were leaving," she finally said, her tone clipped, like this was logistics instead of my life. "When I told her we needed more . . . options than what she'd suggested. You knew this was a possibility."

I shook my head fiercely. "No," I whispered. "I didn't."

"You did," she snapped. "You sat in that office and nodded like you understood."

I hadn't understood.

I'd nodded to make the conversation end after they'd brought me into the room and made me feel like a monster. I'd nodded because no one had asked how it felt to be talked about like a diagnosis instead of a daughter.

"You're sending me away?"

The words scraped out of my throat before I could stop them. My chest felt tight, like all the air had been sucked out of the room.

She didn't answer right away, just looked past me, her jaw set, her eyes shiny but dry.

"I want to stay here," I blurted, panic clawing its way up my ribs. "I'll be better. I swear, I'll—" My voice cracked. The rest got lost somewhere between breath and pleading.

I wasn't sure what *away* meant yet, but every part of me knew it was bad. Bad in a way that changed you.

"It's not forever," she said, cutting me off as she turned away. "Just a few weeks. A reset."

A reset.

Like I was a busted machine. Like if they unplugged me long enough, I'd come back better. Easier.

"Let's go," she said over her shoulder. "You can bring a sweatshirt and your toothbrush. That's it."

Then she walked out. No hug or last look.

Just the sound of her boots hitting the stairs, one after the other. Measured, final, like punctuation at the end of something I didn't know was over.

I wanted her to turn back. To touch my hair. To tell me it wasn't as bad as it felt. One small gesture, something warm to hold on to before everything changed.

But of course she didn't.

It took me a second to drag myself off the bed because I was busy staring at the floor like maybe it would open up and swallow me whole.

Maybe that would've been easier.

Eventually, I stood and grabbed the photo from beneath the covers where I'd hid it.

The one of Nico.

Still perfect. Still smiling like he didn't know he'd ruined me.

I held it for a second, then tucked it into the inside pocket of my hoodie. Pressed it close.

If they were going to lock me up, I'd take him with me.

Even if I was the only one who ever believed it was love.

CHAPTER 1

OPHELIA

Senior Year

The glow from my laptop screen made everything else in the room look gray.

COMMON APPLICATION—FALL TERM ADMISSION

Click. Fill. Tab. Repeat.

I typed in my name, my address, my GPA. I'd done it so many times already for other places that they were all blurring together. Community colleges close to home that only offered two-year degrees. Schools you could drive to in half an hour. Safe choices. Predictable ones.

The kind of schools guidance counselors suggested for students with "transitional challenges."

That was the term they used when you'd been out of the real world for too long. When you had gaps in your transcripts and a résumé full of therapy sessions instead of clubs or sports.

When your "few weeks" away turned into two years, the world outside stopped feeling real.

I blinked, dragging my gaze from the blue glow of the screen.

But all I could see were the white walls of the place they'd locked me in.

They took my shoelaces first.

Then my phone and Nico's picture.

Then every piece of privacy I had left, one item at a time, until even the edges of me felt dull and padded and watched.

In exchange, they handed me a laminated daily schedule with color-coded blocks for group therapy, individual sessions, mealtimes, and "quiet reflection," along with a spiral-bound notebook I wasn't allowed to tear pages out of—just in case I tried to hide something inside. They even counted the pages before giving it to me, like trust was something that had to be measured.

"You'll be here for a couple weeks," my mom had said at intake in a tight voice, her mouth set in a line too firm to be comforting. My dad stood beside her, nodding along, his smile thin and grim, like he was trying to convince himself this was mercy and not surrender.

That was a lie, but I think she believed it when she said it.

It was a lie built from exhaustion and guilt and the desperate hope that someone else might be able to fix what she couldn't.

Two weeks blurred into two months.

Then six.

Then twenty-four.

I turned fifteen with a waxy cupcake from the cafeteria and a folded construction paper card signed by staff members I barely knew, written in that fake cheerful handwriting they all used when they didn't know what else to say.

By the time I left Northfield Psychiatric Wellness, I was sixteen.

My hair was buzzed to an inch of regrowth after a "therapeutic reset."

My file had been stamped with the word Stabilized *like it meant something.*

Like it meant safe.

Like it meant I was fixed.

I blinked hard, dragging myself out of the past and back to the glow of the laptop.

The screen had dimmed slightly, the cursor still blinking inside a blank field titled EXTRACURRICULAR ACTIVITIES/HOBBIES.

My fingers hovered over the keyboard, but nothing came.

No clubs. No sports. No volunteering. No late-night diner runs or beach trips or dumb inside jokes carved into yearbook pages.

Just . . . blank.

I hadn't done anything.

Not since I got back.

Before the facility, I'd at least had tumbling. Every afternoon and weekend were spent on the mats under harsh lights, chalk dust in the air, blisters on my palms, the sound of my breath syncing with each run and flip. The repetition, the rhythm . . . It used to be the one thing that could drown everything else out.

It helped me not to think. Not about what I'd done. Not about who I wasn't supposed to want.

I'd lived for that kind of forgetting, for the ache in my muscles, for the quiet that came when the music stopped and my head finally went still.

But when I came home, I didn't go back. The idea of mirrors and eyes on me made my stomach turn. The gym sent an email saying they missed me. I never replied.

While everyone else was building a life in high school, I'd been relearning how to eat lunch in a cafeteria without flinching. How to sit in a desk chair and not feel like I was being monitored. How to exist in a hallway full of people without breaking down from the noise.

I couldn't even fake it. There was nothing to write.

No "interests" that didn't feel like someone else's life.

After a long pause, I typed *None*.

Then I erased it and typed *Independent reading. Occasional drawing.*

Lies.

Sort of.

I read. But mostly articles about attachment theory or trauma recovery blogs I never commented on. I drew sometimes. Faces I'd never show anyone. Most of them looked like ghosts. Or boys I wished I'd never met.

I stared at what I'd written for another few seconds, then hit next.

INTENDED AREA OF STUDY

I'd been dreading this part, too.

My fingers hesitated over the drop-down menu as rows of majors scrolled by—Biology, Business, Communications, Criminal Justice . . .

Each one felt like a dare.

Pick something. Pretend you're someone.

But how do you choose a future when you've spent the last two years trying not to be a person?

There were days I couldn't even decide what to eat, when I couldn't choose between brushing my hair or curling into bed and pretending I didn't exist.

A major?

That felt like planning for a version of me that didn't exist yet.

That maybe never would.

I selected *Undecided* and moved on before I could think too hard about it.

I stared at the next section of the form, but the words started to blur.

Letters lost their shapes. My chest felt too tight.

I pushed back from the desk and stood, barefoot on the cold hardwood floor of my room, stretching like that would somehow knock something loose. Shake the numb off.

It didn't.

Nothing could.

I sat back down and let my fingers rest on the edge of the keyboard, not typing, not moving, just watching the little blinking cursor flash in and out of existence like it couldn't decide if it belonged, either.

Then—

POP-UP BLOCKED.

Click to allow content from www.utsportsnetwork.com.

An orange banner shoved its way across my screen before I could even think, bright and loud and everything I wasn't.

UNIVERSITY OF TENNESSEE FOOTBALL—RECRUITING EXCELLENCE

The bold white text was written over a looping video of boys in helmets slamming into one another, shoulder pads cracking, sweat flying.

I moved the cursor toward the little X in the corner, ready to shut it down and get back to pretending I had a plan.

But I missed the click.

The screen stuttered once, then fully shifted . . . loading an entire page I hadn't meant to see.

A highlight reel started playing automatically, filling my laptop with noise and motion. Blinding stadium lights. Orange-and-white uniforms. A sea of roaring fans. Pads colliding. Coaches shouting.

I reached for the back button, already annoyed . . . and then I stopped.

Because that's when I saw him.

Jersey #23.

Black hair.

Light blue eyes.

Tan skin, sun-warmed and stretched over lean, perfect, tattooed muscle.

He stood with his arms crossed, a smirk tugging at the corner of his mouth like he'd just scored and knew exactly what it did to people.

There were other people on the screen—players tackling, fans cheering—but my eyes locked on to *him.*

"Matthew Adler," I whispered. He was a tight end, whatever that was. A business major.

There was a video of him catching a pass, his feet leaving the ground in one fluid motion, arms outstretched, muscles tight, focus razor-sharp.

I didn't blink . . . or breathe.

I leaned closer to the screen. Not even consciously. Just drawn in like gravity didn't apply anymore.

He was *beautiful*.

I hadn't seen anyone like him in real life.

Not in the fluorescent lighting of group rooms. Not in the cold hallways of my high school. Not even in the magazines the other girls in the facility used to cut up and glue into collages during art therapy.

But now he was here.

Right in front of me.

And something inside me *shifted*.

Like the world had finally tilted into focus. Like *he* was what I'd been waiting to see through all the static.

My fingers moved before I'd even made the decision.

I clicked the Apply Now tab, and a new page opened, sleek and bright, the University of Tennessee logo stamped across the top like it was waiting for me all along.

I started typing.

Name. Birthdate. GPA.

The same mechanical details I'd filled in a dozen times for schools I didn't care about, schools that my parents preferred . . . what they would pay for. But here, those details took on weight. Like each keystroke was threading me to something I hadn't realized I'd been looking for.

I pasted the essay I'd written for the local schools into the application, my eyes skimming the words without really reading them. And then, halfway through, I stopped.

The tone was all wrong. It was too passive and soft, *not* like a girl they'd want to let in there.

And I *had* to be let in there. It felt like it was already a matter of life or death.

So I started editing.

I sharpened a sentence here. Reframed a paragraph there. Made myself sound clearer, bolder . . . like someone who had vision. Direction. Like someone who wasn't just surviving day-to-day.

Like someone who might belong in Tennessee. Someone who might deserve . . . him.

That was when it hit me.

He was in Tennessee.

And I was in Pennsylvania.

Almost six hundred miles between us, and somehow it felt less like a problem and more like a promise.

It was perfect.

It was far enough to leave everything behind—the house I barely spoke in, the town that never forgot, the whispers that still followed me through the halls of my school.

Far enough to be able to start over.

Because I didn't want to stay here. I *couldn't* stay here. Not in a place that only remembered who I used to be. Not in a place that reduced me to diagnoses and cautionary tales.

Tennessee felt like a clean slate. A new city, a new school, a version of me that wasn't broken or sick or shadowed by everything I'd been through.

I didn't know Matthew Adler, obviously.

But it didn't matter.

Something inside me had already decided . . . he was the point. The anchor. The reason all this had started to make sense.

I kept going.

Phone number. Graduation date. Emergency contact.

My fingers hovered over the field, the cursor blinking like it was waiting for me to lie.

It should've been my mom. It always had been for any other forms I'd needed to turn in.

But the thought of her name on this form, tethered to something she'd never approve of, something she'd try to shut down before it even began . . . It made my stomach twist.

I typed a fake name instead.

Someone who didn't exist and who wouldn't try to stop me.

My heart thudded, steady and loud-sounding, like something inside me had finally started to awake.

And I didn't care that my parents would refuse to help with the cost, because this wasn't about their approval anymore.

It was about *him*.

I'd find a way.

Loans. Grants. A job. Whatever it took.

Somehow, in the middle of an application I hadn't meant to open, with a stranger's face frozen mid-play on a paused highlight reel, I felt something shift inside me.

It wasn't logic. It wasn't hope.

But it felt like purpose.

Like direction.

Like maybe this—*he*—was the reason I hadn't completely unraveled yet. The reason the sky hadn't fallen in on top of me.

And yeah, I knew what it probably looked like. What they'd say if I brought it up in therapy.

Transfer of attachment.

That was the clinical term.

A new fixation. A different container for all the same brokenness. A new object to project everything onto—need, hope, desperation, fantasy.

But it didn't feel sick.

It didn't feel like an obsession, even though maybe it was.

It felt like *clarity*.

Like the sharp snapping into place of puzzle pieces that had never fit before . . . edges smoothing out into something that finally made sense.

Because I'd never been meant for the boys I used to chase. The ones I'd twisted myself into knots for, the ones who ran the moment they felt me coming too close.

I wasn't built for halfway love. Or maybe I wasn't built for love at all.

But I could be built for *him*.

For the man who looked like he belonged to a world I'd never been allowed into, but wanted so badly to touch. Who moved like gravity bent for him. Who smiled like he'd never suffered a day in his life.

I didn't know him yet.

But I would.

I wanted to know everything about him—where he lived, what he studied, the music playing in his ears as he walked across campus. I needed to learn what made him laugh, what kept him quiet, and what existed beneath all that effortless perfection.

What made him real.

I'd figure it out. I'd find a way to be near him, even if I had to build that way myself.

And maybe, if I got close enough, he'd see me.

Really see me. In a way no one else ever had.

CHAPTER 2

OPHELIA

Present Day

It always started with the sound of cleats.

That metallic *click* against the concrete . . . steady, unhurried, impossible to mistake. It sliced through the quiet parking lot like a warning bell, bouncing off car doors and metal bleachers until it felt like it was echoing inside my chest.

I froze. Then swore under my breath.

Shit.

The sound was getting closer.

I slouched lower in the driver's seat, fingers gripping the steering wheel, even though the engine wasn't on. Through the windshield, I saw them spill out of the athletic building exit one by one, jerseys half off, helmets dangling from their hands. And then there he was.

Matthew Adler.

His name felt dangerous even in my head.

He was laughing at something one of his teammates said, head tipped back, sun catching in his black hair. He looked too good, too perfect, too everything I wasn't supposed to want.

When his gaze flicked toward the parking lot—toward *my* car—I ducked so fast I hit my knee on the steering column.

"Damn it," I hissed, wincing, sinking lower until only my eyes cleared the edge of the dashboard. My pulse was a drum in my throat.

He couldn't see me. He couldn't *possibly* see me.

But for a second, it felt like he had.

I stayed like that until his voice faded into the noise of the team, until the cleats scattered and the lot emptied out again, leaving nothing but echoes and the quiet pressing in around me.

Only then did I breathe.

I was in the same parking spot as always—third row from the back, tucked between a dented pickup and a rusted-out sedan that hadn't moved all semester. I twisted the fraying hem of my sweatshirt between my fingers, pulling it tighter until the edge rubbed my skin raw.

Matthew *Matty* Adler.

I knew his nickname now. And what a tight end actually did.

I knew his stats. His schedule. The way his voice dropped when he was annoyed. The slight roll of his shoulder every time he caught a pass.

I knew the sound of his laugh, the slope of his handwriting, the scent of his laundry detergent when the wind caught it just right.

All of it—catalogued. Memorized. *Worshiped.*

And he still didn't even know my name.

I'd first seen him on my laptop screen. Back then, I'd thought that moment had ruined me.

But it was nothing compared to the first time I saw him in real life.

The heat clung to my skin as I walked past the row of off-campus houses, each one old and sagging but full of loud music. My shirt stuck to my back, and the air shimmered off the pavement, making everything feel slightly unreal.

I shouldn't have been there.

But I'd looked it up.

Weeks after my acceptance letter came, I couldn't sleep for three nights in a row . . . so I'd done some searching.

It didn't take much, just a couple deep dives into social media. A post from a party last spring that tagged the address, a zoomed-in photo of a porch with a jersey draped over the railing, and one of those stupid "house tour" TikToks his best friend and roommate, Jace Thatcher, had posted last semester.

His other best friend, and the star quarterback of the team, Parker Davis, lived at 321 Maple.

Matty and Jace were next door at 319.

I'd memorized it before I even packed to come to school.

And now I was here, walking slowly down the opposite sidewalk, pretending I had somewhere to be. Pretending I didn't feel my heart seize at the sound of a door creaking open just ahead.

Matty stepped out onto the porch of 319, wearing a black tank top and mesh shorts, a white towel slung over one shoulder. His skin gleamed, sun-warmed and sweat-damp, and his hair was a little too long, curling around the tops of his ears. Earbuds trailed down from his neck, the cord swaying with each step.

He was laughing at something Parker had called from next door, that southern drawl echoing between the houses. Jace followed behind, flipping a pizza box in one hand and doing a ridiculous dance as they headed down the walkway.

A couple girls across the street slowed their pace to stare. One of them actually giggled.

Matty didn't notice.

He walked right past them, right past me, like I wasn't even there. Which made sense, because I wasn't supposed to be there. I didn't live in this part of town. My dorm was across campus.

But I kept walking anyway, just slow enough to let my eyes track every detail. The way his shoulder blades shifted under his shirt. The slope of his neck. The lazy, careless confidence in his stride.

He and Jace turned into Parker's driveway, laughing about something I couldn't hear, and disappeared inside like they hadn't just changed everything.

I stopped at the corner and pretended to check my phone, my heart thudding like I'd just run a mile.

He hadn't seen me. Not when I lingered behind the corner of that porch, not when I crossed the street at the same time he laughed at something Jace said, not even when I paused just long enough to commit the turnoff to memory.

But I'd seen enough.

The way he moved. The sound of his voice. And his address.

319 Maple.

Burned into my mind now, tucked into that quiet space behind my ribs where everything that mattered went to live.

It was real.

Not some grainy image on a screen or a half-formed fantasy born of desperation.

Real. Possible. A door I'd seen with my own eyes.

And I would find a way back to it. To him.

Even if it took everything.

I blinked as I came back to the parking lot, the sound of faint whistles and yells from Matty's football practice drifting through my open window.

That day was when it had all started.

With just a glimpse.

Now it was my routine.

The lot was mostly empty now as practice neared its end, the sun dipping low enough that the metal bleachers cast long shadows across the asphalt. My phone screen glowed in the dim light of the car, the only thing keeping me company while I waited for practice to end.

I wasn't supposed to be here. I told myself that every time. But somehow, here I always was, watching, waiting for the same man.

My thumb scrolled automatically, muscle memory by now. I checked his social media hourly.

I didn't follow him, of course. That would be too obvious. But his page was public, and I knew every post, every caption, every photo like they were part of a textbook I'd been studying for years.

He didn't post often. Mostly team photos, all helmets and grins and adrenaline. A few stories with Parker and Jace and their girlfriends at parties—red Solo cups, neon lights, the kind of normal college life that looked like another planet to me.

I stopped at *the* post. The one that ruined me for days the second I saw it.

It wasn't even new. It was months old, buried halfway down his feed of him on the field, hair damp, the Tennessee sun turning the sweat on his skin into gold. A little kid perched on his shoulders, holding a foam finger too big for his hands. Matty was laughing, head tilted back, teeth showing. A laugh that felt like proof life could actually be that good.

I zoomed in until the pixels blurred so I could study the crease near his mouth, the faint smear of dirt on his cheek . . . the way his hand steadied the kid like it was the easiest thing in the world.

The caption was just a heart emoji. And that was all it took, as usual.

My breath hitched, like I'd been running.

He'd probably be a good dad. The man who'd show up to everything. Who'd never raise his voice. Who'd hold your hand in a hospital room, even if you were broken and bleeding and couldn't speak.

I knew what it felt like to be the one in that bed. To need someone who never came.

You sound crazy, a voice whispered in my head.

It wasn't loud, just steady, like someone stating a fact. The same voice that used to scold me when I lingered too long outside Nico's class, or when I memorized which lights in his house turned on first, or when I replayed his soccer interviews at night just to hear him laugh.

I tried to shove the voice down, the way I always did.

But lately, it had been harder to drown out.

It was getting meaner, louder in the parts of me no one else could touch, and maybe it was right. Maybe I was just living the same story again, only with different names.

"No. I'm not," I whispered fiercely.

But that sounded less true every day.

I stared at the picture until my phone screen dimmed. Tapped it back awake. Scrolled up. Back down. As if he were going to update his pictures while he was at practice.

I stared at it until my phone battery died.

A shout from the field cut through the stillness, loud enough to jolt me upright.

Somewhere along the way, it had gotten dark. The sky had turned deep blue, swallowing the edges of everything, and the floodlights around the practice field glared against it, harsh and artificial, humming softly like they were the only things keeping the world awake. The parking lot lamps buzzed, too, casting wide yellow pools across the asphalt.

I blinked, disoriented, the world rushing back in with the smell of asphalt and hot rubber and the metallic *clang* of a gate swinging open.

Then came the cleats again.

That sound I knew better than my own heartbeat by this point.

I shoved my dead phone onto the passenger seat and sat perfectly still, my breath caught halfway in my chest. One by one, they came into view, helmets tucked under their arms, the parking lot and practice field lights casting white halos over their sweat-damp skin.

And there he was.

His hair was darker now that it was wet with sweat, curling against his neck. He walked with the sort of ease that made people watch without realizing they were watching. Parker jogged beside him, throwing a water bottle that Jace caught behind his back with a grin.

Matty's laugh carried, low and warm, rolling over the distance between us.

I should have looked away. I knew that.

Instead, I leaned forward, palms pressed to the steering wheel, eyes locked on him through the windshield.

He reached up, running a hand through his hair, and for one terrible, breathtaking second, his gaze flicked toward my row of cars.

Straight toward *me*.

My whole body went still.

I didn't breathe. Didn't move. My pulse thundered in my ears.

Then Jace said something, Matty turned his head, and the moment broke.

I let out the breath I'd been holding, trembling.

The rest of the team began to scatter, some heading to the locker rooms, others toward the lot. Matty slowed down for a second when one of his coaches called his name. They slowly walked into the athletic building together, and I watched until I couldn't see him anymore.

Only then did I start the car.

The headlights flicked on, washing the cracked pavement in white. I gripped the wheel tighter than I needed to, palms slick. I told myself it was time to go. That this was enough for one day.

But I didn't move.

My gaze drifted back to the field where he'd been standing minutes ago. The spot looked smaller now, emptier, like even the light had followed him when he left.

The voice in my head was quiet again, for now.

That was the trick of it—it always went quiet after I saw him. Like he was the only thing that could hush it, could make everything inside me feel smooth for a while.

I sat there until the last of the players' cars pulled out, until the sky bruised purple and the first stars began to show.

Then I whispered it, barely audible, as if saying it aloud made it truer somehow.

"It's not like before."

My reflection in the windshield didn't argue, but I could almost hear the voice laughing anyway.

I put the car in drive, the tires crunching softly over gravel, and pulled out of the spot I'd claimed as mine weeks ago. The field lights blinked off behind me, one by one, until the lot was swallowed in darkness.

By the time I reached the main road, I was already calculating.

How long until the next practice.

What time he'd usually leave.

Tomorrow would be better.

Tomorrow, I wouldn't stay as long.
I'd go home before it got dark.
But even as I promised that, I knew it was a lie.
Because it always started with the sound of cleats.
And I didn't know how not to listen anymore.

CHAPTER 3

MATTY

"You might as well show him the pictures," Jace said, resetting the barbell on the squat rack. "It's a matter of national security . . . and it's his birthday."

I froze mid-rep like he'd just said nuclear launch codes were stored in my jockstrap . . . and shivered as the lowest point of my life came flashing back to me.

Jace had been gone less than an hour on whatever ridiculous task the secret society we were trying to get into had assigned, and I was already losing it.

He'd handed me his phone, made me download some app, rattled off instructions I only half listened to—because who the hell actually needed to track their friends—and then vanished into the night like it was just another Tuesday.

Except it wasn't just a Tuesday. It was a Sphinx initiation night.

Which meant when I finally went back, I was pacing the living room, staring at my phone like it was written in Greek, while worst-case scenarios scrolled across my brain like ESPN highlights.

Mauled by a wild dog.

Buried alive in some crypt.

Sacrificed in a candlelit ceremony by dudes in masks.

I stabbed at the screen again. "Come on, Jace. How hard can it be?"

The app blinked back at me, useless.

That's when the knock came.

The door swung open before I could answer, and in swept Darla, our terrifying next-door neighbor, wearing leopard print pants, a floral blouse, and enough patchouli perfume to fumigate the house. A Tupperware container of cookies was tucked under her arm like it was a baby.

"Evenin', Matty," she said sweetly, dropping the cookies on the coffee table. "Brought you boys a little treat."

I sighed, dragging a hand down my face. "Darla, it's midnight."

I appreciated Jace forgetting to lock the front door after he'd left. Real thoughtful of him to leave me accessible to home invaders, Girl Scouts, and the local population of aggressive cougars on the prowl.

"And?" She popped the lid off the cookies and shoved one into her mouth. "You look stressed, honey. Sugar helps."

I eyed the cookies. Then my phone. Then her.

Desperate times.

"Darla," I said slowly. "How are you with apps?"

She perked up instantly, like a cat hearing a can opener. Somewhere in the back of my brain, I vaguely remembered her mentioning she worked in IT. Or maybe she'd just said she was good with hardware. Either way, this was Jace's life we were talking about. I apparently had to gamble.

"Depends," Darla repeated, licking chocolate off her thumb. "What's in it for me?"

I narrowed my eyes. "What do you mean, what's in it for you? It's an app. You either know how to use it or you don't."

She leaned back against the couch, crossing her legs. The clash of leopard print and daisies burned my retinas, but at least she was wearing pants. She'd flashed her vagina at us a few times since we'd moved into the house, and the scars from that sight were never going to go away.

"Oh, I know how to use it, Matthew. Question is, how bad do you want me to?"

Fuck. She'd smelled my desperation. Or saw it, I supposed. I'd been pulling my hair out since I'd realized where Jace was going.

I groaned. "Jace could be dead in a ditch right now."

"Then you really want me to help, don't you?" she said brightly.

I raked a hand through my hair. "Fine. What do you want? Money? Cookies? You already brought cookies, so—"

"Pictures."

That stopped me cold. "Excuse me?"

Her grin widened. "Pictures. For my collection. Something tasteful. Something . . . cowboy."

My stomach dropped. "What?"

She was already digging in her tote bag, and when her hand came out, it was holding the ugliest, dustiest cowboy hat I'd ever seen.

And also . . . why had she been carrying that around in the first place?

At midnight.

To my house.

What was happening right now?

"You'll look perfect in this."

"Darla . . ."

"Shirt off," she said cheerfully, like we hadn't just crossed five lines of sanity. "Don't be shy. You've got the muscles for it."

I pinched the bridge of my nose. "Jace is going to die because you're trying to turn me into some kind of . . . playgirl rodeo clown."

"Briefs," she said as if she hadn't heard me. "Black ones. You know the pair."

My brain short-circuited.

"What the—How do you even—" I blinked at her, my words tripping over one another. "Are you tracking my laundry now? Do you have, like, a camera in my drawer? Because if so, I swear to—"

Darla just grinned like she'd won something.

I stepped back, scrubbing a hand down my face. "Absolutely not."

"Then I guess Jace is on his own." She turned the cowboy hat slowly in her hands, like she was auditioning it for a Western.

I stared at her. Stared at my useless phone. Stared at the clock.

Then I swore under my breath and stomped toward my room.

Ten minutes later, I was standing in the living room in nothing but my black briefs and the fucking cowboy hat.

"This is a violation of human rights," I muttered.

"Shh." Darla crouched low, holding her phone like she was Annie Leibovitz and not just some patchouli-scented menace in clashing prints. "Tilt your chin up a little. Think . . . desire. Think passion."

"I think *I'm going to be sick."*

She snapped three pictures. "Perfect. Now put one foot on the couch cushion. Power pose."

"Power pose? This isn't The Lion King, *Darla."*

"Confidence!" she barked. "Hand on your hip. No—your other hip. Yes! That's the one."

I slapped a hand to my hip, glaring at the ceiling like it might cave in and crush me. "If anyone ever sees these—"

"It's for my private collection," Darla said dreamily, snapping more shots. "I'd never show anyone. Oh! Give me a smolder. Think . . . seductive cowboy."

"I don't do smolders!"

"You do now."

She snapped another burst of photos, then gasped. "The briefs. Pull the waistband down just a tiny bit."

My eyes bulged. "Absolutely not."

"Do you want to find your friend or not?"

I groaned so loud it rattled the windows, then tugged the waistband down a fraction of an inch. "Happy?"

Darla squealed like Christmas had come early. "Yes! That's it! That's art."

"This is actually called blackmail."

"Art," she corrected, angling her phone. "Now, tip the hat forward. Just over your eyes. Mysterious cowboy. Brooding cowboy. Man who loves horses."

"I don't even like horses!"

"Pretend!"

Click. Click. Click.

By the time she was satisfied, I'd posed like a tragic cowboy, a sexy cowboy, a confused cowboy, and—her words, not mine—"a man who just lost his horse but still wants love."

I was sweating. I was humiliated. And I was praying Jace was at least getting waterboarded for this level of sacrifice.

Finally, Darla lowered her phone. "Okay, sugar. Let's get that app open."

She plopped down beside me, crumbs falling in between the couch cushions from the cookie in her other hand, and took my phone. Two taps, one swipe, and boom—Jace's blinking dot lit up on the screen.

"That's it?" I choked. "You made me do all that for two taps?"

She tucked her phone into her tote bag, smiling smugly. "Sometimes art requires suffering."

"How dare you bring that up at a moment like this," I snarled at Jace, coming back to the present as I racked my weights and sat up fast enough to see stars. "That wasn't part of the deal. That was a private moment in exchange for tech support to help your sorry ass."

Jace shrugged, all casual betrayal. "I feel like the American people have a right to know."

Parker glanced over from the dumbbell bench. "I have two questions," he said, pausing for dramatic effect. "Why is this a noteworthy moment for the American people? What pictures are we talking about? And why do I already regret asking?"

"That was three questions, big brain," I snapped. "Guess all that genius doesn't come with basic counting skills." He *was* basically a genius—honors program, perfect GPA, probably solving quantum equations for fun—but he liked to play dumb sometimes when it suited him.

Cough. Like to get Casey, his girl. Cough.

Parker huffed, wiping sweat off his forehead with the edge of his T-shirt. "I was being rhetorical, dumbass."

Jace smirked. "I'm still going to call him Big Brain despite his mistake," he said seriously. "Even if his brain doesn't come with an extra inch."

I groaned. Loudly.

Because of course he'd bring that up as well.

My one collective lapse in judgment—a drunken post-win "scientific" comparison that should've stayed buried in the hazy depths of tequila and bad decisions.

Jace was never going to let it go.

The stupid thing was, I didn't even know if Jace actually had the extra quarter inch he claimed. We'd been too drunk to see straight, too busy laughing to measure anything properly. It could've been a trick of the light. Or the angle. There was no way my hands had been steady while I measured.

Hell, we might've been the same damn size . . . or I could even be bigger than him.

Still, every time Jace brought it up, he got smug and I got annoyed, which meant it was basically tradition now.

I made a mental note that in the near future, we would be remeasuring.

For science, obviously. Not because I had any interest in seeing any more of my best friend's dick than I already did in the locker room.

But also for my fucking sanity because every time Jace brought it up, I was tempted to punch him.

And we couldn't have that.

Jace would complain about it for the rest of our days.

The man in question grinned, clearly proud of himself for steering the conversation straight into chaos. "I was talking about Matty's nudes, by the way. We got a little off topic there for a moment, so I'm going to bring us back in line."

A deep laugh cut through the weight room, far too amused for my liking.

Garrett Harper.

Of course.

The guy was leaning against the squat rack like he'd been there the whole damn time, a towel draped around his neck, dark curls plastered to his forehead, and that trademark smirk that had half the campus ready to throw themselves in front of him if he so much as blinked.

He was the team's star running back, quick and lethal and infuriatingly unbothered.

"Man," Garrett said, shaking his head, grin widening. "You miss one lift, and suddenly you're the last to know your teammate's dropping an OnlyFans."

Jace cackled. Parker just smirked.

"Mind your business, Harper," I snapped, grabbing the water bottle off the bench beside me.

Garrett lifted his hands in mock surrender, still grinning like he'd just been handed front-row seats to my humiliation. "Hey, I am minding it. It's not my fault that your business is so loud."

He turned to Jace, eyes glinting. "You got copies of the pics, right? For . . . research purposes?"

Apparently everyone in this weight room was interested in science right now.

Assholes.

I chucked my water bottle at Garrett and whirled around to face Jace.

"They were not nudes, Thatcher. I was dressed. Kind of. And they were tastefully shot."

"What do you mean, 'tastefully shot'?" Parker pressed, sounding way too intrigued. Which was exactly what Jace had been aiming for, the bastard.

"The fact that I know about this and you don't is one of life's great victories, Parkie-poo," Jace commented.

He hesitated for half a beat—just long enough for me to almost start to hope that he might finally shut up.

But then his grin widened, and my stomach dropped.

"You know . . . sometimes if I'm feeling cold at night, I think about the fact that you literally let Darla Pinswallow take pictures of you in a cowboy hat and briefs, and it warms me right up."

Everyone went silent for exactly one second.

Then Parker and Garrett both lost it. Parker laughed so hard he almost dropped the barbell on his own head, and Garrett had to steady the rack while wheezing, "Not the cowboy hat!"

I rubbed a hand over my face, wondering if there was a polite way to fake my own death mid-set.

Regret settled deep in my soul . . . the kind that made you reevaluate every decision that had led here.

Like choosing this school.

Or becoming friends with men who clearly had the collective emotional maturity of a wet sponge.

Hell, even being born started to feel like the wrong move.

"Mind your business, boys," I muttered, grabbing my towel and glaring at Jace.

Jace spread his hands like he was doing a PSA. "What? I'm just saying the world deserves to know the truth, Matthew. Transparency builds trust."

"Transparency?" I snapped. "You're the reason this happened!"

Parker blinked, wiping tears of laughter from his eyes. "Wait—*what*?"

Garrett straightened, eyebrows climbing. "Oh no. This is gonna be good."

I pointed at Jace. "He vanished on some secret-society bullshit, wouldn't answer his phone, and I thought he was dead in a ditch somewhere. I was losing my mind. So, when Darla showed up at the door with some cookies—"

Jace cut in, grinning. "The cookies were clever. I have to give it to Darla. Bring snacks, fix the app, collect nudes. Efficient."

I ignored him. "I asked her to fix the app Jace installed on my phone so I could track his location in case he was in a basement somewhere, dying. Except apparently, she didn't believe in free labor."

"I *could* have been dying in a basement," Jace said with a grin. "With six dudes in cloaks. That would have been very culty. You'd have loved it."

"You traded a thirst trap for tech support." Parker smirked.

Garrett bent over, laughing. "That's the most tragic barter I've ever heard."

"She said she worked in IT!" I shouted. "How was I supposed to know the *I* stood for *inappropriately* and the *T* for *thirsty*?!"

Jace put a hand to his heart and fluttered his eyelashes dramatically, obviously looking deranged while he did it. "And that's how I know Matthew Adler loves me."

"If you ever disappear again, I'm letting natural selection do its job," I hissed.

Jace smirked, unbothered as ever. "Relax, Daddy Darwin."

"That was actually a smart comeback, Thatcher," said Garrett, lifting an eyebrow and looking impressed.

"Why do you sound so shocked, Harper?" Jace growled. I stifled a laugh because Jace was touchy sometimes.

"That was a *compliment*," Garrett huffed. "I was saying it was borderline clever; what's bad about that?" he continued, because clearly he wanted a barbell to be thrown at his pretty face.

Jace clutched his chest. "*Borderline*? Excuse me, Harper, I'm a fucking scholar. Words are my art form."

Parker snorted. "Didn't you once write an essay in your high school English class titled 'Why I Shouldn't Have to Write This Essay?'"

"Yeah," Jace shot back, "and it still got a B-plus, so suck it, Hemingway."

I couldn't stop my laugh that time, and Jace whirled on me. "And you, you'd miss me too much if something happened, so let's not pretend otherwise."

I groaned, dragging a hand down my face. "Yeah, I'd miss you," I said. "Every time I would walk past a dumpster, I'd think, 'Didn't that used to talk?'"

"You two need couples therapy," commented Garrett.

Parker didn't even look up from the weights. "They'd make the therapist cry in the first five minutes."

"Yeah," Jace said cheerfully, clapping me on the shoulder. "But at least we'd give the therapist something pretty to look at. Brighten their day and all that."

I glared at him. "One more word."

Jace's grin turned . . . innocent. Which was always a bad sign. "Okay, one more. Perfect. Because I've got one."

I groaned, already bracing myself. There was nothing quite as terrible as Jace's jokes. And he seemed to not ever run out of them. "No. Absolutely not. That's more than one word. Which is against the rules. Whatever's about to come out of your mouth . . . keep it there."

Jace's grin only widened, eyes lighting up like he'd just been handed divine permission to ruin my life. "You don't even know what I'm gonna say."

"I *do* know," I shot back. "Because I know you. And every time you say 'one more,' I lose a year off my life expectancy."

"What's long," he started, dragging out the words, "hard, and full of seamen?"

Parker looked horrified while Garrett just looked intrigued.

Weirdo.

"If we don't look at him, maybe he won't finish," I whispered as I stared at the ceiling.

"Submarines," Jace finished proudly.

Parker groaned, and I just stared at Jace, deadpan. "You're proud of that one, aren't you?"

"Like a father at graduation," he said without hesitation.

At least he's not talking about Darla anymore, I thought.

As if he'd read my mind, Jace clapped me on the shoulder. "C'mon, *cowboy*, let's get started on your next set."

"That's not going to get old for you, is it?" I snarled.

Jace moved his eyebrows up and down obnoxiously. "Not a chance. You saddled up for this one, partner. I'm just making sure the rodeo never ends."

"Once the *hat* comes out, there's no putting it back in the box," Garrett added helpfully.

Parker groaned for the millionth time today, shaking his head. "Please stop saying *hat* like it's a metaphor."

Jace winked. "Who said it wasn't?"

Just then, the side door to the weight room creaked open. A couple of freshmen poked their heads in, caught sight of us, and immediately turned around.

"Probably heard the word *seaman* and ran," Parker said.

"Smart," I muttered.

"Speaking of stalkers," Jace added casually, even though we hadn't actually been talking about stalkers. "I noticed a certain car in the parking lot this morning."

My stomach did something stupid, but I kept my eyes glued to the bar I was lifting like it was the most important thing I'd ever seen. "Yeah, I saw," I finally muttered, trying especially hard not to think about the sedan that was omnipresent at this point . . . or the blonde-haired mystery girl that went along with it.

"Same car?" Garrett asked, stretching his shoulders.

"Same car," Jace confirmed, leaning back against the wall like this was his morning coffee conversation. "She's punctual, I'll give her that. And I swear I saw a flash of Tigers gear when I glanced over."

Parker didn't even bother to hide his grin. "You've officially entered legacy status, Adler. You know you've made it when someone's stalking you *and* coordinating it with team practice colors."

Garrett chuckled. "I bet she's got your calendar synced to hers."

Jace nodded solemnly. "Probably has a color-coded spreadsheet labeled *Matty's Movements*."

I rolled my eyes, finally setting the bar down and grabbing my water bottle. "You're all hilarious. Really."

Parker shrugged. "We try. But seriously, it's been, what, three months? What are you waiting for?"

Garrett blinked. "You haven't gone up to her car yet?"

I sighed. "No, I haven't."

"Why not?"

I rolled my eyes. "Because Parker and Jace are stalkers already. I don't need another one in my life."

Jace raised an eyebrow, not looking perturbed at all that I'd called him a stalker. Between the tracker he'd put in the weird friendship bracelet around my wrist and the fact that he'd done things that were illegal in every country to get his girl, Riley, there really was no arguing with me. He and Parker were, in fact, stalkers.

And I was still shocked about that fact every day.

"I really don't think it's that," Jace mused. "I think it's because you're scared she's going to be hotter than you expected, and then you would have to talk to her. And we all know how that would go."

"Shut up," I muttered. "I happen to be very good with the ladies."

He grinned. "You didn't say I was wrong about you being scared."

I scoffed and lifted the bar again, unable to *not* think about that car.

At first, I thought it was nothing. We've all got fans. Some cling harder than others. But she never approached, never called out, never left notes, or tried to follow me off campus. She just . . . watched.

And somehow, that was worse.

"You really don't want to know?" Parker asked, watching me like he already knew the answer.

"No," I said, too fast. Then, because Jace was already smirking, "Look, it's not hurting anybody. She's not showing up to the house, she's not interfering with games, she's just—there."

Garrett tilted his head. "There, like . . . quiet and creepy? Or there, like . . . comforting in a weird way?"

I shot him a look. "Why would it be comforting?"

He shrugged. "I don't know, man. Some people like being admired."

Jace leaned forward, grin spreading. "Yeah, like the guy who pretends he doesn't notice, but definitely looks for the car every time he leaves practice."

"I do not," I said automatically.

Except I did.

And we all knew it.

Parker laughed softly. "You so do."

I gritted my teeth as I tried not to drop the weights on my head. "You know what? Maybe I like consistency. Sue me."

Garrett smirked. "Consistency. That's what we're calling it?"

Jace whistled. "Sounds like you've developed a little *emotional attachment* there, Matty-kins. Sounds almost like looove."

"Don't start," I warned.

But they were already laughing.

And the thing was, I didn't even know why I hadn't done anything.

I could've gone to security. Or even just walked up and knocked on her window one day.

But I didn't.

Because something about it—the stillness, the silence—made me feel weirdly . . . seen.

Not in the fame sense. Not the autograph, camera, NIL contract kind of seen.

Something else.

Like whoever sat in that car wasn't looking at *Matty Adler, tight end for the Tigers*.

They were just . . . looking at me.

It was insane, and I knew it.

But every time I thought about walking up to that car, I froze.

Because I didn't know what I wanted to find— someone obsessed, someone dangerous, or someone who somehow saw something in me that even I didn't understand.

So instead, I did nothing.

It was easier to joke about it.

Easier to let Jace and the guys make their cracks and play along like it didn't get under my skin so I didn't *ever* have to admit that I wasn't sure if I was more freaked out by the idea that she was there every day . . . or by the idea of what it would mean if she suddenly wasn't.

"Earth to Matty-Daddy," Jace said, snapping his fingers in front of my face.

I blinked, dragging myself back. "What did you just call me? And why do you keep putting *Daddy* in with my name?"

He grinned. "Sorry, I was just workshopping that, but I think it's no good. I think we can all agree that the person in this group who has Daddy energy is me. And possibly Parker."

"I have Daddy energy," Garrett said.

We all snorted at that.

"Regardless, I wonder what you'll do when she finally works up the nerve to get out of the car," Jace continued as if Garrett hadn't said anything and we hadn't been talking about Daddies.

"Probably drop dead," I muttered.

Garrett smirked. "Could be worse ways to go. At least you'd die adored."

Parker rolled his eyes. "You three need professional help."

"Maybe," Jace said, leaning back with that smug, shit-eating grin. "But I'm still RSVPing for the wedding. Front row, open bar, tears of joy."

"Yeah," I said, standing up and slinging my towel over my shoulder, "you'll get that invite the same day I send you my obituary."

"Perfect," Jace said brightly. "I'll bring flowers to both. Maybe balloons, if I'm feeling festive."

I groaned but couldn't stop the laugh that escaped. That was Jace for you—turning every conversation into a sideshow.

And I welcomed it.

Because the truth?

That car haunted me.

Every practice. Every drive home.

Every night I told myself it didn't mean anything.

I thought about it every damn day.

And every damn day, I pretended I didn't.

CHAPTER 4

OPHELIA

"He's coming!"

I'd heard them before I saw him—two girls standing near the doors, whispering and giggling like they were sharing state secrets. His name slipped out between their laughter, soft and breathless. *Matty Adler*. They said it the way people talked about movie stars, not real men who took up space on the same campus.

I shifted on my bench, tucking one leg under the other and adjusting the straw in my iced coffee, pretending I wasn't listening, wasn't waiting. My pulse tapped out a rhythm in my throat anyway. The concrete under me was cold, the morning sun sharp against my skin, and I glanced down at my phone, even though I already knew what time it was.

9:14.

The door creaked open. A rush of voices spilled out, footsteps scuffing against tile . . . and then he was there.

I inhaled, sharp and involuntary, like relief, like oxygen after holding my breath too long. He was dressed in a gray Tigers hoodie and jeans that should honestly have been illegal, the ones that hung low enough to hint and fit tight enough to torture. A Tigers hat shadowed his eyes, and somehow, he still managed to look like he owned the entire damn world just by walking through a doorway.

I knew his schedule better than my own. Mondays and Wednesdays, he had sports psychology at eight a.m. I'd set up my schedule so I could sit outside that building those days, on the second bench from the door, iced coffee in hand, pretending I was waiting for someone.

At nine fifteen, he walked out.

Every time.

Sometimes he had his headphones in, lost somewhere far away in a world I'd never reach, probably listening to Dashboard Confessional, even though he'd never admit it to anyone. I only knew because once, when he'd taken his hoodie off after practice, his phone had lit up on the bench beside him, and the song title "Hands Down" had flashed across the screen.

After that, I started listening to them, too. I memorized every song, every lyric, every aching chord, like maybe if I learned the words he loved, I'd understand the parts of him no one else ever would.

Sometimes Jace was beside him, talking a mile a minute about who knows what while Matty just nodded along, half listening.

And sometimes he walked with girls, their laughter spilling across the sidewalk, light and easy. He'd smile at them, really smile, and it felt like something inside me cracked each time. Like I was watching him hand pieces of himself to people who didn't even realize how lucky they were.

He never looked at me as he passed.

Not once.

Today, thankfully, he was alone.

There was a frown tugging at his mouth, though, and it made me wonder what he was thinking, what could crease his face like that. He looked tired. Weighted. Human in a way he rarely did when he was surrounded by people chanting his name.

Matty walked past, close enough that the scent of his cologne brushed the air between us—clean, warm, unfairly good—and my pulse jumped. Before I even realized what I was doing, I was on my feet, falling into step behind him. I kept enough space between us, careful to stay hidden within clusters of students crossing the quad. I matched his pace, slowing when he slowed, quickening when he did, pretending I was just another face in the crowd . . . when really, I was orbiting him.

I tried to get his attention once. I got brave, or at least convinced myself I did.

That morning, I had stood in front of my mirror for nearly an hour, curling my hair into loose waves that brushed my shoulders and swiping on lipstick in the shade that was supposed to make my mouth look fuller. My hands shook when I slid into the short floral dress I'd bought just for him, the one that cinched at the waist and made my legs look longer. It wasn't me, not really, but that was the point. I wanted to be someone he might notice.

By the time I had gotten to the quad, my heart was a steady drumbeat in my chest. I picked the bench with the best view of the door, crossed my legs, and opened a book I wasn't actually reading. I tilted my chin up just enough to catch the light, pretending the sun felt good on my face, pretending I belonged there. Every few minutes, I turned a page I hadn't read, trying to look casual while sneaking glances from the corner of my eye, waiting for him to walk out and finally see me.

He didn't. He walked right past me, not even a flicker of interest, not one look.

And as the days slipped by, I was starting to hate myself for ever thinking he might.

A few yards ahead, a girl stepped out from the path leading to the library. Lane. I knew her from his classes. She always raised her hand and always laughed too loudly at something one of the guys said. She called his name flirtatiously and hurried toward him.

He stopped when she reached him, shifting his weight like he wasn't sure if he wanted to stay. When she touched his shoulder, his whole body went rigid. It was subtle, but I saw it. He didn't lean closer or smile; he just listened for a second, nodded once, and kept walking. She lingered for a moment, like she was waiting for him to turn around, but he didn't.

I shouldn't have felt good about that—but I did. The tightness in my chest loosened just a little, and something hot and trembling uncoiled inside me, a pulse of satisfaction I didn't want to name. He hadn't liked her touch. He hadn't smiled at her the way he smiled at his teammates.

Just as I was about to keep following him, he looked over his shoulder. My breath caught mid-step. For a split second, our eyes almost met . . . or at least I thought they did. He smiled, and I froze, every nerve lighting up with the wild, dizzy thought that maybe he saw me. Maybe he *finally* saw me.

But then Parker walked past me, dark hair gleaming in the sunlight, tall and golden in that effortless, all-American way that made everyone turn their heads when he walked by. His beautiful girlfriend, Casey, followed a step behind, her long black hair catching the light as she leaned into him. Parker's arm slid around her waist, pulling her close, and Matty's smile widened as he said something that made them both laugh.

The smile was for them.

The realization hit like a punch to the ribs. My chest hollowed, the air going thin as the warmth that had flooded me seconds before drained out completely. I felt stupid for thinking it, for letting myself believe even for a heartbeat that he'd been looking at me. My throat burned as the crowd flowed around me, students cutting through the quad, laughter and voices washing over me while I stood there, rooted in place. I couldn't make myself follow anymore. My legs wouldn't move.

It hit me then . . . how much I hated myself. How everything with him was a punishment I kept giving myself. Every glance that didn't land, every smile meant for someone else, it was like pressing on a bruise just to feel it ache. And I did it again and again, because maybe that ache was the only thing that made me feel real.

The thought lodged in my chest, raw and ugly. I stood there, surrounded by people who didn't notice me, either, wondering how I'd ended up like this—building my whole world around someone who didn't even know my name. I'd spent so long convincing myself it was love, but maybe it was something else. Maybe it was just loneliness wearing a prettier mask.

Still, a dark piece of me wanted him to find out. I wanted him to catch me watching, to see everything I'd tried to hide. I wanted him to get angry, to shout *What the fuck is wrong with you?*—because at least then, I'd be real to him.

At least then, I wouldn't be invisible.

At least then, I'd be seen.

Maybe anger would be better than invisibility.

Maybe being hated would hurt less than being nothing at all.

And maybe the worst part was knowing that, even after realizing all this, I'd still be back here on Wednesday. Same bench. Same time. *Same ache.*

Matty

The call came in just as I was walking across campus to my next class, worrying about the fact that my Sphinx trials hadn't even started yet and both Parker and Jace were already done with theirs. What did that even mean?

The late-morning sun was warm on my shoulders, my backpack digging into one side, and I was half listening to the chatter around me when my phone buzzed in my hand. I glanced down at the screen, expecting a text from the guys or a reminder about an assignment, but it was a call.

Dad.

Just that. No emojis. No "Pops" or "Old Man" saved in the contact. Just three letters and dread was settling heavy in my gut the second it lit up.

I wiped my hands on my jeans, my heart kicking up a notch as I stared at the name.

It rang again.

"Let it go to voicemail," I told myself.

But some part of me still wanted to believe . . . maybe this time would be different.

I hit accept.

"Hey," I said, lifting the phone to my ear.

"There he is. My big shot. My all-American. You got time to talk to your old man, or are you too busy signing autographs and bathing in money?"

His voice came through like a punch. Rough, tired, and a little too fast.

And just like that, I could see him. Clear as day. Reclining on that ratty armchair in the den that he always swore he was going to replace but never did. A beer sweating on the side table. The TV casting blue shadows over his face. Half watching a game. Half scheming. Always half something.

"So, tell me, Matty, how much did that new NIL deal really put in your pocket? Bet it's more than I make in a few years."

There it was. The signal. The real reason for the call.

The only reason he ever called, actually. Why I was still disappointed . . . I'd never understand.

I exhaled through my nose, shifting my backpack higher on my shoulder. "What do you need?"

"Straight to it, then, huh? Not even a how've you been?"

"You only call when you need something, Dad. I'm just trying to save us both time," I responded sarcastically.

A pause crackled over the line. Then, a forced chuckle. "Alright. Fair. You're a grown man now, I get it. But since you're asking, yeah, I could use a little help. My car broke down—"

I stopped outside the building where my next class was and leaned against the brick wall, my jaw tightening. "You already told me that. The last time I sent money, you said it was for the car."

"Did I say car?" he fumbled, his words tripping over one another. "I meant . . . the heater. Yeah, the water heater went out. Whole place was freezing. You know how it is. Things pile up."

My stomach twisted. *The water heater wasn't even for heat*, but I bit my tongue. He couldn't keep his stories straight anymore, the same excuses shuffled around like cards in a losing hand. And I was supposed to buy it. Again.

"You still there?" he asked when I hadn't said anything for a second.

"Is this about the heater or the sportsbook app?" I finally asked quietly.

Silence.

I closed my eyes, dragging a hand through my hair. "I told you the last time—I'm not enabling this shit anymore."

"Matthew."

Fuck, I hated when he said my name like that. Like I was five again, and he was still a man worth listening to.

"You think I don't know I screwed up? That I haven't been trying to do better? I just need a little help. A couple grand to get ahead this month. That's nothing to you now, right? I know what that deal with Under Armour is worth. You're rolling in it, son."

I flinched. "How do you know those details?" I asked, cursing the existence of social media and everything else that allowed my dad to know any details about my life.

"The whole internet knows. You think your little brothers don't shout it out every time you get mentioned on ESPN? You think the neighbors don't talk my ear off about it every time they see me? Everyone knows. You made it. You've got the golden ticket."

"You mean I *am* the golden ticket."

He scoffed. "That's not fair."

"Isn't it?" My voice was quiet, flat. "Every time you call, it's for money. You didn't even ask how classes are. Or how the season's going. Or if I'm okay."

"You owe us."

The words hit me like a punch.

"What?"

His voice hardened. "You think you got there on your own? You think those summer camps paid for themselves? Or the extra shifts I worked to afford your cleats? You think your mom didn't go without so you could have protein powder and a gym membership? We sacrificed *everything* for you."

Guilt twisted in my gut, ugly and sour.

"You think I wanted to take out that second mortgage? You think your siblings never noticed the lights getting cut off because we had to drive you to out-of-state tournaments? And now you're too good to help your family out when we're drowning?"

I started up the stairs of the building, only vaguely aware of the students that were passing by or the looks they were giving me. "It's not that I don't want to help. But I need to know it's actually helping. Not just going into another bet. Not just burning down with the rest of your excuses."

"You saying I'm a lost cause now? That I'm not even worth trying to save?"

"I'm saying I've been here before, Dad. Too many times. And I can't keep cleaning up after you."

"Wow," he said, his voice cracking just enough to make me feel like the asshole. "You forget where you come from real easy, don't you? All that money, and it makes you think you're better than us."

"That's not what this is."

"Then what is it? You too embarrassed of the poor family back home? You think your siblings want to keep eating ramen so you can live out your dreams? You think your mom doesn't cry every time your name comes up because she misses you so much and knows you won't call?"

I gritted my teeth. And of course, the second he said her name, I saw her. Sweet and small in the kitchen back home, still wearing her nurse's scrubs after a double, humming to herself while she stirred a pot of spaghetti that never seemed to stretch far enough. Her tired eyes lighting up every time she looked at me, like I was still her baby boy. Not the ghost who only called when he had to . . . because every call risked running headfirst into her asshole husband and his demands.

"Don't bring her into this," I snarled.

"She's in it, Matty. We all are. This family bled for your dream. And now that you're living it, we just want to breathe."

My hand was shaking by the time I stepped inside the doors.

"You think I don't carry that? Every day? That I don't lie awake at night wondering if I did the right thing leaving? Wondering if I should've quit and stayed home and gotten a regular job just to make sure you didn't drink away the mortgage again?"

His breath hitched, and I knew I'd gone too far.

But I couldn't take it back. Not now.

"Send the money or don't," he said finally. "But don't pretend you're better than us or that you're some kind of god who doesn't need to worry about his family struggling."

The call ended.

I stood there, phone in my hand, heart hammering like I'd just come off the field after a full game.

I wanted to throw the phone against the wall. I wanted to scream. But all I could do was stare.

Because as much as I hated it . . . he wasn't completely wrong.

They had sacrificed. They had scraped and clawed and pushed me toward this dream.

But somewhere along the way, it stopped being about the dream.

It started being about the payout.

And I didn't know how to fix that.

I just knew I didn't want to be the reason they drowned.

And I didn't want to be the reason I did, either.

I exhaled, long and hollow, a breath that felt like giving up and giving in at once. My thumb hovered over the screen, then moved. *Sending it now*, I typed, more because the motion steadied me than because it solved anything. I hit send before I could change my mind.

The three dots popped up almost instantly.

Dad: Knew I could count on you, son. You're a good kid. Don't forget who's always been in your corner.

I stared at the message until the words blurred. My phone screen went dark, reflecting my own expression back at me—jaw clenched, eyes flat.

"Hey, you good?"

Garrett's voice broke through the quiet. He was coming down the hallway, backpack slung over one shoulder, that easy grin on his face like nothing in the world could ever actually bother him.

"Yeah," I said. "Fine."

He didn't look convinced. "You sure? You look like you're about to fight a wall or something."

I let out an annoyed breath and started walking toward our class, and he fell into step beside me.

"Well," he said, his tone light, "maybe this'll cheer you up. Saw your little stalker again this morning. Girl's been getting bold—she was parked in the front row by the fieldhouse. And dude . . ." He grinned. "I actually got a closer look at her this time. She's hot. Like, *way* too hot to be that unhinged."

I stopped walking. Something twisted in my chest, sharp and ugly.

Garrett laughed, not noticing. "You should at least find out what she wants, man. If she's gonna keep showing up, might as well enjoy the view."

The words hit a nerve I didn't know was exposed. "Why the hell would I care what some clingy, desperate freak wants?" I snapped. "She's probably just another attention-starved girl with no life, following guys around because she's too pathetic to get one of her own."

Garrett blinked, startled by the venom in my voice. "Whoa. Okay. Didn't mean to set you off."

Before I could say anything else, a sound cut through the quiet . . . a soft, broken sob. It was faint, like someone had tried to swallow it before it escaped.

We both turned toward the noise.

At the far end of the hall, all we saw was a door swinging shut. The echo of it closing seemed to stretch, bouncing off the walls until it faded completely.

Garrett frowned. "You think someone heard us?"

I forced a shrug, my throat tight. "Doesn't matter."

But the hollow feeling in my gut said otherwise.

He nodded slowly but didn't say anything else. We walked into class in silence after that, my pulse still pounding in my ears.

The anger didn't fade; it just sat there, heavy and sour, until I couldn't tell if I was mad at my dad, at my stalker . . . or at myself.

My phone buzzed again, another text from my dad. This time it was a link to some expensive fishing gear he didn't need and wouldn't use.

Dad: Think you could grab this for me, champ?

The message sat beneath it like it was nothing, like he hadn't just asked me to send him thousands of dollars.

I stared at the screen until everything else—the professor's drone, Garrett, that faint sob—faded into the background.

The phone screen went dark, and for a second, it felt like I did, too.

CHAPTER 5

OPHELIA

His words hit before I could prepare for them.

"Why the hell would I care what some clingy, desperate freak wants? She's probably just another attention-starved girl with no life, following guys around because she's too pathetic to get one of her own."

For a second, I couldn't breathe. The sound of his voice, sharp, irritated, careless, echoed down the hall and straight through me. I didn't wait to hear anything else. My feet moved before my brain could, carrying me in the opposite direction, fast enough that the edges of my vision blurred.

By the time I reached the end of the corridor, my chest was burning. I pushed through the nearest door without looking, into an empty study room. The lights were dim, the air still, and the moment the door clicked shut behind me, the world tilted.

A sob tore out of my throat before I could stop it. Then another. I pressed my back against the wall and slid down until I hit the floor, my knees pulled tight to my chest. The words wouldn't stop replaying. *Clingy. Desperate. Pathetic.* Each one landed like a stone thrown straight into my ribs.

I wanted to unhear it, to pretend he hadn't said it, but the sound of his voice was everywhere—inside me, around me, filling the room until it felt like it was breaking me open from the inside out.

My hands were shaking so hard I pressed them to my mouth just to quiet the sound of my crying. The tears came faster anyway, hot and endless, dripping down my chin.

I'd known he didn't see me. It had happened a thousand times. But hearing him say it, hearing the disgust in his voice . . . it felt like being gutted.

And the worst part was . . .

I agreed with him.

I don't know how long I stayed there. Minutes. Hours. Long enough for my tears to dry and my body to ache from the way I'd curled into myself on the cold tile. My throat was raw, my face sticky, and I felt hollow—like someone had scooped out everything inside me and left only the echo of his voice behind.

Eventually, I forced myself to move. My limbs were heavy and uncooperative, like they didn't want to belong to me anymore. I pushed myself off the floor and stumbled toward the door, wiping at my face with trembling hands. The hallway outside was quiet now and mercifully empty. I kept my head down as I walked, one foot in front of the other, like maybe if I didn't look up, no one would see how broken I was.

By the time I reached my dorm, my legs felt like they were made of glass. The key slipped in my shaking hand as I unlocked the door. The quiet hit me like a slap.

I lived alone. I'd made sure that I wouldn't be assigned a roommate. I couldn't risk anyone walking in and seeing the wall—the one that had become my secret, my shame, my shrine.

Posters. Printouts. Photos I'd taken from my phone, from the university website, from news articles. Notes I'd written after every game, every quote I'd memorized that he'd said. It covered the whole wall, stretching from the floor to the ceiling like a living thing made entirely of him.

And pinned near the center was the thing I was most ashamed of—a baseball cap with the Tigers logo stitched across the front. I'd taken it months ago after one of his interviews, when he'd set it down on a bench outside the locker room. It wasn't planned. I'd just seen it sitting there, his name still Sharpied on the inside brim, and before I could think, it was in my bag. I'd told myself it didn't count as stealing if he didn't notice.

Now, as it stared back at me from the middle of the wall, the realization hit hard. The cap wasn't some token of connection. It was evidence. Proof that I was doing it again.

My breath hitched as the memory surfaced—Nico's hoodie, the one that had gotten me sent away to begin with, the one my mother had thrown away in a fit of rage. This was the same thing. The same sickness. The same need to hold on to something that didn't belong to me.

I backed away from the wall, shaking my head. "No," I whispered, the word barely audible. But the truth was already there, raw and undeniable.

I hadn't changed. I'd just found someone new to break myself over.

I stared at the pictures, my chest tightening until I couldn't breathe. His smile stared back at me from a dozen angles. His arms raised in victory. His eyes, always looking past me, never at me.

Something inside me cracked.

A sound tore from my throat, half sob, half scream, and I launched myself at the wall. My hands hit first, then my fists. I ripped at the photos, shredded them, tore the edges of the paper until my fingertips burned. I yanked down everything I could reach, the tape snapping, the glossy pages crumpling in my fists.

"Stop," I gasped out, though I didn't even know who I was talking to. Him. Myself. Both.

Pictures fluttered to the floor, scattering around me like broken glass. I sank to my knees in the middle of them, surrounded by pieces of him I couldn't seem to let go of, my chest heaving as I whispered his name again and again until it stopped sounding like a person at all.

My gaze landed on the journal half hidden beneath a pile of torn notes. I knew which one it was before I even reached for it—the one with the bent spine and the ink that had long since bled through the pages. I'd written in it for months. Letters to him. Fantasies. My name paired with his. *Mrs. Adler*. Over and over and over until the words had stopped looking strange and had started to feel like something that could be real.

I flipped through a few pages, my breath hitching as I read lines I didn't remember writing. *He smiled at me today. He doesn't know it yet, but we're meant to be.* The handwriting blurred through my tears. The sound that left me this time wasn't a scream . . . it was smaller, broken.

Then I tore it.

Page after page. Rip after rip. Until the air was full of shredded paper, and my hands were raw. The notebook fell apart in my lap, the pieces raining down around me like ashes.

I told myself I was done. That it was over. That I could let go.

But then I saw it, a picture lying face down near my foot. I picked it up with shaking fingers, and flipped it over. It was him, mid-game, helmet in hand, that grin splitting his face wide open. He looked so alive. Untouchable. The kind of person the world revolved around.

I gripped the photo at the edges, ready to tear it in two. My hands wouldn't move. They just shook harder, the glossy paper bending but not breaking. I tried again, but my fingers wouldn't obey.

And then I crumpled.

I fell forward, the picture clutched to my chest, sobs ripping through me until my whole body shook. I pressed my forehead to the floor, surrounded by the wreckage of everything I'd built, and I finally understood . . . this wasn't love. It was sickness. It had always been sickness.

And no matter how hard I tried, I didn't know how to make it stop.

The knock of my heartbeat filled my ears long after the crying stopped. I didn't remember crawling into bed, only the dull ache in my hands and the torn scraps of paper stuck to my skin. My pillow was damp, my throat raw. I stared at the ceiling until the world blurred and went soft around the edges, until exhaustion finally pulled me under.

When I woke again, the room was dark. My phone buzzed on the nightstand, dragging me up from sleep that felt more like sinking. I blinked at the screen until the name came into focus.

Mom.

I swallowed, my tongue heavy. "Hey," I croaked in a sandpaper-thin voice as I answered the call.

"Ophelia," she said, her tone sharp with irritation. "Do you have any idea what time it is? Dr. Whitaker's office called me. You missed your session this afternoon."

My gaze shifted to the clock. 6:37 p.m. For a second, I couldn't process the numbers. Then it hit all at once. Afternoon. Appointment. Hours gone. "What?"

"They said you didn't answer your phone. Are you trying to get yourself put on an observation report?"

My throat went tight. "No, I—I took a nap . . . and I must've overslept."

"You *overslept* an entire afternoon?" she snapped. "Do you understand how that looks? Dr. Whitaker has to keep progress documentation for your program. If the university thinks you're backsliding, they could pull your independent status. You'll have to come home, Ophelia. You know this."

Her words hit harder than I wanted them to, mostly because they weren't empty threats. After I got into Tennessee, my mother had tried to have my acceptance withdrawn. She'd called the university herself, told them I was unstable, that I'd been hospitalized, that I wasn't ready to live on my own. They hadn't revoked my offer, but the school had made it clear. I was allowed to stay under supervision, with mandatory therapy and progress reports filed through Dr. Whitaker every month. If those reports ever hinted that I was slipping, I'd lose my "independent status." Which meant my mother would get exactly what she wanted—me back under her roof, back where she could watch me.

The idea made my stomach twist. I couldn't go home.

Her words blurred in my head as the panic started to creep in. My eyes darted toward the window, where the sky was bruised orange with sunset, and that's when I realized what else I'd missed.

Practice.

Matty's practice.

The thought sliced through me like glass. I'd never missed one before. Not once. Every day I'd been there in that parking lot.

And today I'd missed it.

"Ophelia," my mom said sharply, dragging me back. "Are you listening to me?"

"Yeah," I whispered. My chest ached. "I'm listening."

"You need to take this seriously. You're lucky they even approved your enrollment after you lied. You can't afford to mess up."

Her voice kept going, a steady stream of warnings and frustration, but I barely heard any of it. My body felt too heavy, my head thick and slow. I pressed the phone tighter to my ear, tears sliding silently down my cheeks.

"I know," I said when she finally paused for breath. "I'll do better."

"You need to," she said flatly. "This is all up to you not to mess it up like you have everything else in your life. Do you understand me?"

"I understand."

The words scraped out of me, quiet and automatic, the way they always did when she spoke to me like that. Agree, appease, survive. My chest felt tight, but I didn't let her hear it in my voice. I just stared at the dark space where my shrine used to be, the torn tape still clinging to the paint like scars.

She hung up a second later, leaving nothing but silence. I sat there, phone still against my ear, her words echoing in my head. *Like you have everything else in your life.*

The room got dark, the silence pressing down on me until it felt like the air itself was heavy. I lowered my arm, and my phone screen dimmed and went black, leaving only my reflection staring back—puffy eyes, red nose, the faint imprint of my pillow still on my cheek.

I tried to push aside what my mother had said by reminding myself that missing practice was *good.* It meant I was breaking the pattern. I'd done the unthinkable—I'd missed him. For the first time since I'd set foot on this campus, I hadn't watched him walk out on that field. I hadn't memorized every movement, every smile, every pass.

Maybe that was progress.

Maybe it meant I could change.

I drew my knees to my chest, resting my chin on top. The room felt bigger now, emptier, like even the shadows were keeping their distance. I tried to focus on my breathing. In. Out. In. Out. I could do this.

I didn't need him to exist. I could stop.

Tomorrow, I'd get up early. I'd go to class. I'd answer Dr. Whitaker's call and tell her what she wanted to hear. I'd eat breakfast in the cafeteria instead of in my car. I'd sit in the quad with a book that I'd actually read.

I'd start living for myself.

The words felt fragile, almost laughable, but I held on to them anyway. Because I couldn't give my mother the satisfaction of being right. I wouldn't let her drag me home and lock me back behind those whitewashed walls that still smelled like lemon and pity.

I wouldn't give her a chance to make good on her threats.

I'd be better. I'd *get* better.

I whispered it to myself, over and over, until the words lost meaning and became something else—a vow, a prayer, a plea.

But when I finally closed my eyes, all I could see was the field.

And him.

CHAPTER 6

MATTY

Sweat slicked the back of my neck as I pushed through another sprint, lungs burning, legs on fire. Parker was jawing at the O-line, Jace was laughing at something no one else thought was funny, and Coach blew his whistle in frustration.

I should've been focused on the drills we were doing, but my head wouldn't shut up. Everything had felt off all day, like my body was here but the rest of me was still trapped somewhere between my dad's voice on the phone and the string of texts he'd been sending since. Each one was another link, another thing he wanted me to buy, even though the money I'd already sent was supposedly for his overdue bills.

Aka his gambling debts.

My stomach refused to unclench.

At least Jace was being his usual annoying self.

"So, remember Riley's old roommate?" he started, shaking his arms and lining up for the route we were practicing.

"How could we forget?" I muttered. My voice came out rougher than I meant, but I couldn't help it when he'd just brought up the world's most terrifying person.

He grinned like he could feel my irritation. "She texted Riley."

"What did Creepy McCreeper say?" Parker asked, his tone way too eager for someone who clearly didn't grasp the trauma I was still trying to recover from. He'd never actually met Emma. He hadn't seen the way she stared like she was cataloging your organs for later. All he knew were the stories Jace and I had told him about her fascination with femurs and her unsettling love of murderous clowns and iced milk. You really had to meet Emma in person to understand just how much therapy she could make a man consider.

"She said her new roommate isn't *nearly* as interesting to watch."

I froze mid-step. *Fuck.*

Just hearing her name out loud made me break into a cold sweat.

Emma was a walking nightmare of a person, a girl who made you question whether reality had short-circuited whenever she was around. She had big eyes and a bigger smile, and that smile didn't quite match the words coming from her mouth. When Riley had started dating Jace, he somehow convinced me to distract Emma so he could sneak into Riley's dorm room to "be near her." Which translated to *spy on her like a psychopath and sleep in her room without her knowing*.

So I did it. I sat through the most terrifying date of my life while Emma told me she was "fascinated by human anatomy," especially "the texture of femurs." I'd spent the whole night wondering if she'd stolen a bone or two from a grave, or if she was secretly plotting how to get *my* bones out of me.

And now she was texting again.

"She—*she's texting her*?" I asked, my voice coming out all weird and screechy.

Jace frowned. "Well, not anymore. Riley doesn't even know how she got her phone number. She never gave it to her."

She was probably hiding in Jace and Riley's closet; that was probably how she got the number. I made a mental note to check every closet in our house when I got home. You could never be too careful.

"Riley thinks it was Emma's attempt at being sweet . . . like in a definitely-should-have-ended-up-on-a-true-crime-podcast kinda way," Jace mused.

Parker snorted. "Yes, real heartwarming. I bet she's crying herself to sleep at night, clutching the hair she probably cut off Riley's head while she was sleeping . . . like it's an unrequited love story."

See. I definitely needed to check the closets. And under the beds. And anywhere else a human-sized *demon* could be hiding.

Jace scrunched his nose up at that. "There's no way she doesn't have a playlist dedicated to Matty—one of those dramatic, longing ones with 'I Will Always Love You,' 'Under My Skin,' maybe 'Every Breath You Take'—really good ones like that," he mused.

I threw my water bottle at him. It hit his shin, which only made him grin harder.

I lined back up for the next drill, but my chest still felt tight. Maybe it was the pressure of the upcoming game. Maybe it was my dad. Maybe it was just me.

Coach blew the whistle, and we ran it again—routes, cuts, sprints. Jace cracked another joke about investments that hardly anyone laughed at. Usually, I'd at least toss something back, but I couldn't find it in me.

My thoughts were everywhere, and as I was melting down into an existential crisis . . . I glanced out toward the parking lot.

The sight of her beat-up car had become part of the background noise of my life, like the smell of turf or the sound of helmets clashing. I didn't look for it on purpose, not really. It was just . . . there. Every practice.

Except now, it wasn't.

"Hey." Jace bumped my shoulder. "Why aren't you appropriately worshiping me right now?"

I didn't answer. My jaw locked, my gaze fixed on the empty space where that car usually sat.

"What's up with you?" Parker asked.

"She's not here," I said quietly, the words slipping out before I could stop them. A strange pressure built in my chest, heavy and restless, like something inside me had gone off-balance . . . like the world had shifted an inch to the left, and I was the only one who noticed.

"Who's not here?"

I didn't look at them. My throat felt dry. "Why isn't she here?" I stopped, shaking my head.

"Who?" Parker asked again, obviously not getting that I was having a moment right then. "Your stalker?" He huffed. "Isn't that a good thing?"

"Yeah, Matty-boy, maybe she just finally decided to trade up and stalk someone funnier," Jace added.

It didn't feel good that she wasn't there. It didn't feel like relief. It felt *wrong*, as a matter of fact.

Something in my gut twisted, the same way it had when I saw my dad on my caller ID this morning. That crawling, anxious feeling that something was about to fall apart.

"Something's wrong," I said, the words barely above a whisper.

Before either of them could respond, I was already moving—helmet half off, cleats pounding against the turf as I sprinted toward the edge of the field, the sound of Coach calling my name fading behind me.

I sprinted across the field, my breath coming hard and uneven, the world narrowing to that one stretch of asphalt just beyond the chain-link fence. The turf gave way to gravel under my cleats, small rocks crunching underfoot as I cut toward the parking lot.

Her car wasn't anywhere.

I slowed to a stop, chest heaving, eyes sweeping over the rows of vehicles like maybe I'd missed it—maybe she'd just parked somewhere else today. But there was no sign of that dented car, the one that always sat crooked between the lines like it didn't care about the rules any more than she did.

Nothing.

The silence hit harder than I expected. Just the faint hum of traffic in the distance, a cold breeze brushing sweat from my neck, the whistle of the team still running drills behind me.

What the hell was I doing?

She was a stranger. A stalker. Someone who had been sitting out here for months watching *me*.

And yet the emptiness where her car should've been made my stomach twist. It was ridiculous. I should've felt relieved. Grateful, even. Instead, I just felt . . . wrong. Like I'd lost something I hadn't realized I was holding on to.

I ran a hand over the back of my neck, trying to shake it off, but the unease clung to me. I turned in a slow circle, scanning every corner of the lot, half expecting her to pop out from behind a car. But there was nothing but sun glare and empty pavement staring back.

A shout echoed from the field. Coach.

I hesitated another second, then blew out a breath and jogged back, slower this time. My legs felt heavier than they had a minute ago. Each step toward the field pulled something tighter in my chest.

Coach's whistle pierced the air the second my cleats hit the turf. "What the fuck, Adler?" he barked, his voice carrying across the field. "You feel like taking a jog in the middle of my drill?"

"Sorry, Coach," I said, catching my breath. "Thought I saw a kid get hit by a car in the parking lot. False alarm."

He stared at me incredulously for a long second, jaw working, then muttered something that sounded like *Fucking hell, I'm surrounded by idiots* before blowing the whistle again. "Get your head back in it."

I nodded, falling back into formation. Jace shot me a slightly concerned look but didn't say anything, something he would no doubt rectify the second practice was over. Parker smirked, mumbling something nonsensical about me being "struck by the curse," but I barely heard him.

I grabbed my helmet, slipping it on, the world narrowing again to drills and whistles. But underneath it all was still the strange, restless ache I couldn't shake.

It felt like a part of me had gone missing somewhere in that parking lot.

And I couldn't stop wondering if she'd taken it with her.

"Thank fuck," Jace groaned, bending over to rest his hands on his knees. "One more drill, and my hamstrings were going to file a complaint."

"Your hamstrings don't work hard enough to complain," Parker shot back, smirking as he toweled off.

Jace grinned, eyes sparkling with mischief. "You know what, Parkie-poo? Just for that, I have one for you."

"No," I said immediately, still feeling decidedly grumpy and off-kilter after my stalker's no-show . . . even with Coach's attempt to kill us.

"I'm ready," Garrett countered at the same time.

I glared at him for encouraging Jace. Jace had enough encouragement inside his head. He didn't need anything externally.

Jace cleared his throat with mock solemnity. "What's the difference between jam and jelly?"

Parker snorted. "Oh no."

"I can't jelly my—"

I slapped my hand over his mouth before he could finish. "Don't. Just don't."

He laughed into my palm, then licked me like the feral bastard he was.

"Ugh—" I yanked my hand back so fast you'd think I'd touched a hot stove. "You're disgusting."

Jace doubled over cackling while Parker nearly dropped his water bottle from laughing so hard.

"I'm not disgusting," Jace said proudly. "I'm *gifted.* Also, my saliva is probably worth money at this point, so you're welcome. That spit on your hand is probably worth, like, five million dollars right now."

I gaped at him. "There's so much I could say about that," I muttered, shaking my hand out like it was contaminated. "But I'm choosing peace today because I'm tired."

"Very noble of you, Matthew." I winced at his use of my full name . . . since it reminded me of my dad calling earlier. Jace raised an eyebrow at me.

"Alright, that's it! Helmets off, hit the showers! If I see anyone dragging ass, you're running suicides tomorrow!" Coach's voice cracked like a whip across the turf.

Groans rippled through the guys, cleats scuffing as they started toward the athletic building. Tank ripped his helmet off like it had just insulted his whole family. Jace removed his and flipped his hair dramatically, muttering something about shampoo endorsements.

My gaze automatically flicked toward the parking lot for the umpteenth time since I'd discovered she was missing.

But her car still wasn't there.

I tore my eyes away only to catch Jace stiffen mid-step, his grin twisting into something that resembled . . . terror, actually. "The day just got interesting, boys. Or creepy." He jabbed me in the ribs. "Isn't that Emma?"

Jace was squinting at the bleachers as if his life depended on it, and I reluctantly followed his gaze.

And sure enough—Emma.

Limp brown hair draped over her shoulders, and her posture was as stiff as a corpse propped up for a family photo. She sat with her knees tucked in, a massive poster spread across them. Slowly, deliberately, she lifted it high.

MATTHEW ADLER, I SEE YOU WHEN YOU'RE SLEEPING.

My stomach hit the turf.

Parker gagged on his water, sputtering and coughing until he bent double. "Nope. Nope, nope, nope."

Jace threw his hands in the air. "Unbelievable. Are you kidding me right now? You've got *two* stalkers? I don't even have one! This is favoritism of the highest order."

"That's not—" I started, but he cut me off, glaring at me like this was somehow all my fault and I'd asked for it all.

"Unfair, Adler. Some of us have to work for love. You're out here collecting psychos like trading cards."

I pinched the bridge of my nose. "You literally stalked Riley until she gave in. Neither of you need psychos because you and Parker *are* psychos."

"Coerced," Jace corrected proudly, chest puffing up like he deserved a damn medal. "I coerced my Riley-girl into becoming the love of my life. There's a difference. Mine was strategic. Artful."

"Exactly," I shot back, deadpan. "You're stalker enough for the both of us."

Parker wheezed, barely upright, clutching his water bottle like it was holding him together. "Why aren't we more scared about the fact that she's here?"

Jace huffed, still glaring. "I want one. Equal rights. Equal creeps."

"Take Emma, then," I muttered. "She's clearly auditioning."

I was keeping an eye on her as Jace complained, obviously, but I still jumped when Emma stood up and started descending the bleacher steps, each one slow and measured, her hair swinging like a metronome with the rhythm of her walk. The sign stayed clutched against her chest, the black letters bold enough to burn into my retinas.

The rest of the team had already drifted away, leaving just the three of us frozen at the edge of the field. My pulse thudded hard enough to rattle my ribs.

"Why do I feel like I'm about to die?" I whispered, barely moving my lips.

"Because you might be," Jace murmured back, head tilted, expression equal parts amused and unsettled.

Parker muttered a curse under his breath, but I couldn't spare him a glance. My eyes were locked on Emma, pinned there like if I looked away for even a second she'd break into a sprint, knife flashing out of nowhere.

Every muscle in my body screamed to move, to backpedal, to run, but I stayed rooted. Watching. Waiting. Keeping my gaze fixed on her the way you keep your eyes on a wild animal—because the second you blink might be the second it lunges.

Emma tilted her head. Just a fraction. Then she raised her hand—two fingers up—and slowly dragged them across her own eyes, like she was recording me. Like she was marking me.

Parker sucked in a breath. "Nope. Noooope. She's doing the 'I'm watching you' thing. I hate it."

Jace looked delighted, like this was prime-time entertainment. "I feel like we should clap. Or at least tip her a dollar."

"Shut up," I hissed, my throat bone-dry.

Emma's lips curved. Not a normal smile. Her smile stretched too wide, like she was trying on the expression and hadn't practiced enough in the mirror. Then she mouthed something. Three distinct words.

Go to sleep.

I swear my blood iced over.

She didn't wait for a reaction. She just turned with that slow, floating walk of hers and disappeared around the bleachers, sign still clutched to her chest like a trophy.

Silence stretched among us.

Then Parker croaked, "Okay. I hated that. I'm gonna have nightmares."

Jace, unfazed, cocked his head and said, "She's probably going home to pour herself a tall glass of milk. With ice."

The three of us shivered at once.

"Serial-killer behavior," Parker muttered.

"Yeah," I said, still staring at the empty bleachers. "And somehow, I'm on her list."

We finally broke out of our frozen huddle, feet dragging across the turf toward the locker room. Jace kept muttering about how unfair it was that I'd collected two stalkers before he'd even gotten one, while Parker said prayers under his breath like he was warding off evil spirits.

I let them talk, my helmet hanging loose at my side, my legs carrying me on autopilot.

Halfway down the path back to our locker room, I glanced toward the lot. *Again.*

And again . . . the car wasn't there.

So many times over the past few months I had caught myself wondering—not with fear, not even with dread—just a quiet, gnawing curiosity. What was it about me that kept her coming back? What did she see that made her stay?

But now all I could think was . . . what had made her go?

The thought trailed behind me into the building, heavier than the pads on my shoulders.

"Fine," Jace said suddenly, breaking the silence with a dramatic sigh. "So, maybe I don't have stalkers. But I've still got that extra inch on you, so really, who's winning here?"

I turned, snarling before I could stop myself. "It's a quarter of an inch, asshole."

Parker choked on his water all over again, laughing so hard it echoed around us.

Their laughter carried down the hall, easy and careless, but it barely touched me. Because underneath it all, one thought kept looping through my head—if she was gone for good, why did it feel like I'd just lost something I never actually had?

CHAPTER 7

OPHELIA

I shivered as I stood on the sidewalk, the morning air slipping through my sweatshirt and sinking straight into my skin. It was freezing . . . though maybe that was just me. Maybe it was the kind of cold that came from the inside, that settled in your bones when you'd finally run out of feeling.

I stared at the glass doors of the communications building like they were guarding something dangerous, monsters waiting on the other side to tear me apart if I dared to walk through. My breath came out in white clouds, fogging in front of me before drifting away.

After the call with my mom yesterday, I'd collapsed back into bed, too drained to cry anymore. My body had felt heavy, my head aching from everything I'd held in. I'd told myself I'd just lie there for a minute, but sleep came fast and mean.

I dreamed of him.

Not the Matty I used to imagine, the one who smiled when he saw me, who would someday understand . . . but the real one. His voice, hard and cold, slicing through my head. *Clingy. Desperate. Pathetic.* Over and over, until I'd jolted awake with those words clawed into my chest.

I'd fumbled for my phone on the nightstand, the screen lighting up just long enough to show me I was late—only twenty minutes until class. There'd been no time for anything. No shower, no fixing my hair, no painting my face into something better than what it was. I'd yanked on a sweatshirt and jeans, grabbed my notebook and backpack, and ran.

A burst of wind swept across the sidewalk, catching the ends of my hair and sending another shiver down my spine. I hugged my arms tighter around my notebook, taking a deep breath for what lay ahead. This was a good thing. Not fixing myself up, not trying to be someone worth noticing. Because that had been part of the problem, too—every careful outfit, every dab of lip gloss, every way I'd tried to make him look at me.

This was better. Honest. Ugly, even. The real me. The one who needed to stop.

You're done, I told myself. *You're getting clean.*

No more circling him. No more watching. No more letting Matty Adler drag me under just by existing. I was finished.

But apparently, the universe liked to test me fast. Because my brand-new vow to get clean was already being tested first thing this morning—eight a.m. sharp, in Sports Media and Communication. The only class I'd managed to get into with him.

Back when I'd registered, it had felt like fate. Now, it just felt cruel.

My fingers tightened around my notebook, the edge cutting into my palm, and for a second, I almost believed I could do it, walk in, take notes, focus on anything but him. Then the door swung open, and I stepped inside . . . straight into the jaws of temptation.

The fluorescent lights hummed overhead as I walked in, the heat of the room a jarring contrast to the crisp cold outside. I hesitated in the doorway, my pulse loud in my ears. I knew this room too well, from the rows of desks to the smell of burnt coffee from the cart outside, to the hum of chatter that always died down the moment the professor entered.

Normally, I was here early. Early enough to claim my usual seat, two rows over and one back from his. Close enough to see the slope of his shoulders when he wrote, far enough away that no one would notice I was watching. I'd time it perfectly, arriving just before him and pretending to scroll through my phone, as if I didn't already know exactly when the door would open and exactly how he'd look walking through it.

Obviously, that hadn't happened today. Not after waking up late, not after running across campus with my hair still tangled from sleep and my heart racing for all the wrong reasons. But that was a good thing. It fit the new plan. The one where I stopped trying so hard, stopped showing up early just to breathe the same air as him. This was progress, I told myself. Messy, unplanned, barely held together, but still progress.

I took another hesitant step inside, the door clicking shut behind me, and instantly wished I hadn't.

The room was already full . . . completely full. Every desk occupied, every backpack slung over the backs of chairs, every laptop open and glowing. My gaze swept the rows in a panic, searching for a miracle, for some forgotten corner seat I could slip into unnoticed.

But there wasn't one.

My stomach dropped as I saw it.

Two empty seats. Both of them were beside him.

He was already there, leaned back in his chair like he owned the air around him. One arm draped lazily over the back of the seat next to his, hoodie sleeves shoved up to his forearms, the fabric stretching across his shoulders. He looked down at his phone, earbuds hanging loose, completely unaware of the chaos detonating inside me.

He was beautiful—unfairly beautiful.

I was frozen in place, gripping my notebook so tightly I could feel the cardboard bending. The sound of laughter and the clatter of someone dropping a pen blurred together into static. My mind went blank except for one truth I didn't want to admit.

The universe wasn't testing me.

It was laughing in my face.

For a long, paralyzed moment, I just stood there, pretending to scan the room like maybe another seat would magically appear if I wished hard enough. It didn't. Eventually, the professor glanced up, his eyes flicking toward me with a look that said *sit down or leave.*

So I moved.

Each step toward Matty felt like walking to my own execution. The soles of my shoes squeaked faintly against the tile, every sound too loud in the hush between bursts of conversation. I kept my eyes down, pretending to focus on the rows of desks ahead of me, but it didn't help. I could feel him there, the solid weight of his presence pulling at me like gravity.

I tried not to look. I really did. But the closer I got, the harder it became. A glance. Just one. And there he was, sunlight cutting across his profile, making him look like some sort of god. My stomach twisted, my pulse stuttering in my throat.

Another step. Another glance.

By the time I slid into the empty seat beside him, I was already failing every promise I'd made that morning.

He didn't even glance up when I sat down, didn't seem to notice the way my whole body went tense, every nerve screaming at me to keep still. His shoulders were hunched, muscles flexing beneath his hoodie as he leaned forward, the fabric pulling just enough to trace the lines of his back. His gorgeous jaw was set in concentration, a faint shadow of stubble catching the light as he rifled through his backpack, the sound of paper and crumpled wrappers filling the space between us. His hand paused, then dove back in, more impatient this time. He was looking for something.

My eyes flicked to his desk before I could stop myself. No pencil. No pen. Just a blank notebook and his phone.

Maybe he was looking for something to write with.

My heart thudded, traitorous and loud. I knew I shouldn't. If we actually interacted, if he looked at me or spoke to me, it would only make it harder to stop—harder to pretend I didn't orbit him. But my fingers were already moving, sliding open my pencil case like it was muscle memory, like they hadn't gotten the memo that I was trying to get clean.

I wrapped my hand around the spare pencil, gripping it so tightly my knuckles ached. I stared at it, whispering silently in my head. *Don't. Don't be that girl again. Let him find his own.*

But my hand didn't listen.

Because this was what I did. What I always did.

I hesitated for another heartbeat, telling myself it was nothing, that it was just polite, that anyone would do the same. Another lie. They came easy when it came to him.

I leaned the pencil toward him before I could stop myself. "Here," I said, my voice so soft it barely sounded like me.

It was the first word I'd actually said to him.

His head turned, and when his eyes landed on me, the air punched right out of my lungs. Up close, they weren't just blue; they were intense and startling, a color somewhere between turquoise and sea-glass green. Beautiful enough to make me want to fold in on myself.

For a heartbeat, he just stared. His mouth parted slightly, like he'd forgotten what he was about to say or like he hadn't expected to see me at all. His gaze flicked over me, slow and uncertain, taking me in as if he couldn't quite figure out where I'd come from. My cheeks burned under the weight of it, the heat crawling all the way to my ears.

Then he blinked hard, the moment snapping. He shook his head slightly, as if to clear it, and reached out for the pencil. His fingers brushed mine, and the touch was brief, nothing really, but it scorched anyway. The warmth of his hand lingered long after, and for one dizzy second I thought I might actually faint.

"Uh . . . thanks," he muttered, his voice deep and smooth, a sound that seemed to hum through the air and sink beneath my skin. It wasn't meant to be anything, just a polite acknowledgment, but to me it felt like more. Like a secret. Like the first word of something I'd been waiting my whole life to hear.

The professor started talking at the front of the room, his voice a distant hum I barely registered, even though I was pretty sure he'd just announced a pop quiz. I was too busy trying to breathe, too busy replaying that single word, *thanks*, on a loop in my head.

Matty shifted beside me, the faint scrape of his chair cutting through the professor's monotone. His arm brushed mine, a slow, accidental graze that sent another shock straight through me.

He leaned in, his voice sexy enough to make my pulse trip. "You saved my ass," he murmured, the hint of a grin curling at the edge of his words. "I forgot he gets off on surprise quizzes."

More heat rushed to my face, spreading down my neck until I could feel it everywhere. The words *gets off* replayed in my head, turning my thoughts bright and flustered until I was sure the whole room could see the blush burning through me.

I was such a freak.

His breath was brushing my skin, though, his arm still grazing mine, and every nerve felt alive and traitorous.

It was too much. Too close. Too good.

And the worst part was that I knew he was just being friendly. But to me, it felt like the universe was whispering that I'd never really escape him.

My eyes darted down to my desk. I couldn't look at him and survive it.

He's still waiting for me to respond, I realized after a second . . . when he still hadn't pulled away. My throat felt tight, though, and it was like my mind had gone blank. I finally managed a weak smile and a small nod, staring at the scratched surface of my desk instead of him.

His voice slipped in quietly, like he was sharing a secret meant only for me. "What's your name?"

For a heartbeat, my entire body lit up. I'd imagined this moment so many times, him asking, him wanting to know me. My lips parted, breath catching, ready to give him everything.

But then it hit me . . . yesterday. His voice. The words he'd said. *Clingy. Desperate. Pathetic.* I could still hear them, *feel* them, in fact, like they were a piece of me now.

If he knew it was me, the girl who'd been watching, following, memorizing every piece of him . . . he'd hate me. He already did.

The light inside me flickered and went out.

I swallowed, my throat tight, the words coming out barely louder than a breath. “It doesn’t matter.” They scraped their way out of me, rough and splintered, leaving something raw and bleeding behind.

But he didn’t look away. His head tilted slightly, a crease forming between his brows like he couldn’t quite believe what he’d heard. He leaned in a little closer, voice softer this time, almost disbelieving. “What did you just say?”

My hand trembled against the desk. I pressed it flat, forcing myself to stay still, to hold it together even as every part of me threatened to crack open right there in front of him.

“Mr. Adler.” The professor’s annoyed tone cut through, and the moment broke. Matty straightened, muttering an apology, and the class snickered. I wanted to disappear with so many eyes on me.

But his quiet didn’t last long. He started tapping the pencil I’d given him against the desk, the sound soft but relentless, like a pulse I couldn’t block out. Every few minutes, his voice found me again . . . low, teasing, impossible to ignore.

“Come on,” he murmured once, close enough that I could feel the warmth of his breath. “You don’t look like a Sarah.”

Another time, “You’re really not gonna tell me? Not even your first initial?”

Then, with a grin I could hear even without looking, “Guess I’ll just call you my hero for now.”

Each word tugged at something inside me, loosening the threads I’d spent the last twenty-four hours trying to tie down. I kept telling myself I wouldn’t answer. That I wouldn’t give him the part of me that still ached to belong to him.

Then he spoke again, softer, more thoughtful this time. “Didn’t know my hero was gonna be the most beautiful girl I’ve ever seen.”

The world tilted. My heart stopped, my breath right along with it. *Beautiful?* I hadn’t even brushed my hair. I’d thrown on a sweatshirt, dark circles under my eyes, the remnants of yesterday’s tears probably still smudged on my cheeks.

My mind scrambled to make sense of it. He couldn’t mean it. Not really. Maybe he *did* know who I was already. Maybe this was his revenge. A sick joke to get back at the stalker who’d been pathetic enough to follow him for months.

My stomach turned cold. I stared straight ahead, not daring to move, not daring to breathe, every part of me caught between wanting to disappear and wanting him to say it again.

By the time class ended, my nerves were shredded. Every second of that hour had been a slow, exquisite kind of torture . . . his arm brushing mine when he shifted, the scrape of his pencil against paper, the sound of his voice when he asked a question. It was too much stimulation, too much proximity, too much *him*.

I'd spent months watching him from a distance, building him up into something untouchable, and now he was right there, talking to me, looking at me, saying things that didn't make sense. Compliments that short-circuited my brain. Every rule I'd made for myself was unraveling, and I couldn't keep up with the pieces falling apart inside me.

I fumbled my things into my bag the second the professor dismissed us, my hands shaking so hard I dropped my notebook twice. I could barely breathe, let alone think. I just needed out, needed to get away from the weight of his attention that pressed down on me like it knew every one of my weaknesses.

But, of course, he followed, falling into step beside me like it was the most natural thing in the world.

"Hey," he said, softer this time. "Thanks again. For the pencil."

I froze again, my tongue glued to the roof of my mouth, every word I might have said dissolving before it could form. My brain scrambled for something, anything, that wouldn't sound like I was coming apart inside.

Finally, I managed to breathe, my voice barely steady. "You already said that."

"Doesn't mean I don't mean it." His grin curved easy, but there was something heavier underneath it. "It was the only thing keeping me from turning in a blank page. That deserves at least a name in return."

I bit my lip, the corner of my notebook digging into my fingers as I fought the urge to smile, to give in, to let him pull me back under.

"Matty!"

His teammate Garrett's voice cut through the hallway, casual, teasing, familiar. And just like that, the air shifted.

The name slammed into me like a punch, dragging yesterday back in brutal clarity—his voice in that hallway, so cruel. *Clingy, desperate freak.* Garrett standing next to him.

My stomach twisted. Whatever warmth had been in my chest turned to stone.

I forced a breath, straightened my shoulders, and stepped toward the sunlight spilling through the doors. The moment I pushed them open, the cold rushed in to meet me, biting at my cheeks and clawing down my throat.

It stole my breath, but maybe that was better. Maybe the shock of it could freeze everything burning inside me.

"Hey!" His voice followed me out into the cold, carrying too easily across the quad. "Can't wait to see you again, most beautiful girl in the world!"

My entire body locked. Heads turned. A few students laughed.

Mortification flooded through me, hot and stinging, and I ducked my head, hurrying faster. My pulse thudded in my ears as I turned the nearest corner, out of sight, out of reach, pressing my back against the brick wall like I needed something solid to hold me upright.

I squeezed my eyes shut, whispering the words over and over, a prayer and a punishment all at once. "I'm done. I'm done. I'm done." I wanted to believe it. I wanted to feel the clean break of something ending. But it didn't come.

Because I wasn't done.

The pull was still there, wanting and aching, dragging me toward him no matter how much I fought it. My body felt hijacked, every muscle keyed up and desperate to move closer. Before I even realized what I was doing, I was leaning forward, peeking around the corner like my body had stopped taking orders from me.

He was easy to spot. Because of course he was.

Matty was walking beside Garrett and Jace, moving through the crowd like they owned it. Garrett was laughing at something Jace said, and Jace, animated and loud as ever, was talking with his hands, grinning like even he was amused by what he was saying.

My hands were still shaking so badly I had to clasp them together, and my nails were biting into my palms. I told myself to stop, to turn away, to keep walking. Instead, I followed. One step, then another. Slow. Careful. Shame rising higher with every breath.

The crowd of students thickened, swallowing the trio for a moment. But I still tracked him, searching for the dark sweep of his hair, the easy rhythm of his stride, the way his shoulder brushed Jace's in that familiar way like they'd known each other their whole lives.

A girl appeared that I didn't recognize from the ones who usually tried to get his attention. She was pretty, confident, her smile one that had probably worked a thousand times before. She reached for his arm, leaning in, saying something that made her lips curve wider. My stomach dropped so fast I thought I might be sick.

I braced myself for the grin I knew so well.

But it didn't come.

His expression shifted, hardening, his reply short enough that she froze. The smile faltered on her face, and she slipped back into the current of students, disappearing with a few backward, longing glances.

Garrett and Jace both turned to look at him, the same puzzled expressions flickering across their faces. Garrett raised an eyebrow, and Jace's grin faltered for half a second, like they were both wondering what the hell that had been about. But Matty just kept walking, his jaw tight, his eyes fixed straight ahead.

My chest clenched. It wasn't relief that filled me . . . relief would have been mercy. It was something worse. Because even if he could look at her like that, dismissive and distant, it didn't matter. He would never look at me at all if he knew the truth. Even if this morning hadn't been just a cruel joke, nothing would still make it mean something.

The ache hollowed me out, leaving behind a silence that hurt to touch.

I stopped walking. My body felt heavy, like the air itself didn't want to let me move. I wrapped my arms around my middle, pressing hard, trying to keep from coming apart. Finally . . . I turned around.

Each step away felt like wading through wet sand—slow, impossible, suffocating. I could still hear Jace's laugh cutting through the noise of the crowd, though, and I walked faster, willing it to fade.

Because I had made a promise. And even if I kept breaking it every time he breathed, I had to keep trying.

CHAPTER 8

MATTY

The desk felt too small for my frame, my knees pressing up against the underside like it had been designed for middle schoolers, not Division I athletes. My shoulders still ached from practice, the ghost of my pads lingering even after a shower and a night's worth of sleep. I stared at my phone, scrolling through Instagram mindlessly, but the pictures blurred together, my brain still stuck somewhere between exhaustion and everything that had gone wrong yesterday.

A text from Jace popped up, and I tapped it open.

Jace: I just remembered that we completely forgot to mock you yesterday for sprinting off the field to find your stalker 😂

Jace: Frankly, I'm disappointed with myself.

I groaned silently, dragging a hand down my face. I'd honestly thought I'd gotten away with it. Discussing my deranged behavior yesterday was the last thing I wanted to talk about.

Then I frowned. And did he just use the word *frankly*? Since when did Jace talk like that? Or anybody, really.

Me: Are we going to talk about what you just said?

Jace: I literally texted you to talk about what I just said.

Parker: . . .

Jace: Don't . . . me, Davis. I know you think you got that from Walker, and that's completely unacceptable. You got that from me. And possibly my brother. Not from wildly overrated professional Dallas hockey players.

Jace: We are the No Drama Llamas.

Jace: We're not followers. We. Are. Trendsetters.

I grinned at that. Parker's brother, Walker, played in the NHL. He was the starting goalie for the Dallas Knights, and he had his own group of friends on his team that had their own brand of chaos. Jace could get a little competitive with them sometimes.

Me: I just wanted to know why you used the word *frankly*, but I guess I can also remind you that I never approved of that group name.

Parker: I, too, would like to know why you used the word *frankly*. It seems suspicious, frankly.

I texted back a . . . because it seemed fitting.

Parker: Also . . . I'll make sure to tell Lincoln Daniels that you think he's wildly overrated next time I talk to him. I'm sure that will go over well. You'll be a big hit at the next Christmas party.

Me: Good point, Parkie-poo.

Jace was probably pissing himself right now. Lincoln Daniels, the Dallas Knights star center, and Parker's brother's teammate, was actually terrifying . . . and definitely not overrated.

Jace: Obviously Parker's big brain isn't working right now. I obviously would never include Lincoln in that description. I would also like to bring us back to what we were talking about.

Jace: The fact that our boy Matty is in love with a stalker.

I huffed at that. It was laughable that Jace would ever tease me about having a stalker, considering that if you looked up the word in the dictionary, it actually wouldn't have a definition. It would just say *Parker Davis and Jace Thatcher*, and everyone would understand.

Me: Pot, meet kettle. Seems to me it wouldn't be much different than Riley and Casey being in love with the two of you, now would it?

Me: But also, I'm not in love. I had concern as a citizen of the world for the safety of . . . another citizen of the world. That was it.

Parker: What the hell is a citizen of the world?

Jace: That's why you're my bestilicious number one today, Parker. Using that big brain of yours to tell my bestilicious number two he's an idiot.

Me: I thought you said that wasn't a ranking "per se."

Jace: Maybe it is, maybe it isn't. But someone has to keep you on your toes.

I sighed and set the phone face down on the desk before they could come up with anything else. The screen buzzed once more anyway, vibrating against the cheap wood like it was laughing at me.

There was a rustle beside me, books shifting, a chair scraping, and I caught the faint scent of coffee and something floral. I didn't bother looking over. I didn't feel like talking to anyone.

A throat cleared at the front of the room. I looked up to see the professor leaning against the desk with a smirk that set off instant alarms. That look never meant anything good.

Pop quiz. It had to be a pop quiz.

Swearing under my breath, I glanced down at my desk. No pencil. No pen. Nothing but my useless phone and a sinking feeling in my gut.

I dug through my backpack, irritation bubbling up as I flipped through loose papers, crumpled receipts, and an empty protein bar wrapper. No pencil. No pen. Nothing.

Perfect.

"Where the hell is it," I muttered under my breath, shoving my hand deeper into the bag. I came up with lint, a bottle cap, and a sticky note with Jace's handwriting that just said *buy lube*. I crumpled that fast, my ears burning, and shoved it back inside.

"Here," a soft voice whispered.

I turned my head.

And froze.

Wow.

She sat one desk over, angled slightly toward me, a yellow No. 2 pencil held out in her delicate fingers like it might burn her if she held it too long.

Her hair caught the classroom light, blonde but not flat. Streaks of honey and gold ran through it like sunlight poured directly into the strands. And her eyes, fuck, her eyes were copper . . . warm and alive, like pennies just pulled from sunlight. They caught the light when she moved, shifting between amber and bronze, impossible to look away from once you noticed them.

Pennies just pulled from sunlight?

I was losing my fucking mind.

She blushed as I stared at her. Not just pink cheeks, either. Color flooded her neck, spreading down to the collar of her sweatshirt, blooming across her skin like I'd caught her doing something indecent just by existing near her.

Her lips parted slightly, like she'd been about to say something, then pressed together again. Her gaze flicked down, and she shoved the pencil toward me like she couldn't stand to hold it any longer.

Normally, I would've just taken it and moved on. But something in me paused, curious, reckless, and I let my fingers brush hers as I took it. The contact was small, barely anything, but the heat of her skin hit me like static.

"Uh," I said brilliantly, still holding the pencil like it was something fragile. "Thanks."

The wood was warm from her hand, and for a reason I couldn't name, I didn't set it down right away.

Instead, I kept staring.

Because there was something about her. Something that hooked sharp and fast under my skin and refused to let go.

The professor started talking, but his voice barely registered, words washing over me without sticking. I couldn't focus on any of it. My attention kept slipping back to her . . . the glint of light in her hair, the quick, careful way she turned a page, the tension in her shoulders like she was trying to disappear into herself.

I'd never seen anyone like her. Not just pretty—*arresting*. A beautiful that hit like a punch you didn't see coming, that knocked something loose inside you before you could brace for it. There was a softness to her face that didn't match the way she held herself, like she was half terrified of being noticed and half hoping someone finally would.

I couldn't look away. Every time I tried, my eyes found her again, like my brain had decided she was the only thing worth focusing on.

I shifted in my chair, and my arm brushed hers. Barely. But she tensed like I'd burned her.

"You saved my ass," I said before I could stop myself, leaning closer. I wanted to hear her voice again. "I forgot he gets off on surprise quizzes."

The words left my mouth, and I instantly regretted them. *Smooth, real smooth*. I'd played in front of packed stadiums, done press interviews, handled reporters . . . and somehow, a single girl with a pencil had me forgetting how to talk like a functioning human.

Her breath hitched, faint but audible. I bit back a grin. She was blushing again, somehow even deeper than before. The color rushed up her neck, staining her cheeks until she looked like she might combust right there. And despite how awkward my attempt at flirting had been, it still was affecting her.

She looked like she wanted to disappear under the desk, but she nodded anyway, eyes locked on the scratched surface in front of her. Her breathing came in small, uneven pulls, like she was trying to survive the moment by sheer force of will.

How the hell had I never seen her before? This wasn't a big class. I usually sat in the same spot, head down, avoiding eye contact so no one got the wrong idea and tried to talk to me. I usually remembered faces, even forgettable ones, but hers? There was definitely no way I'd forget *that*.

Had she just transferred? Been sitting somewhere else this whole time? Or had I really been that wrapped up in my own world not to notice her until now? The thought unsettled me in a way I didn't like.

I needed to know more. Anything. Something to go on.

I leaned in slightly, my voice low so only she could hear. "What's your name?"

Her head tilted the tiniest bit, like she was weighing whether to answer at all. For a second, I thought she wasn't going to speak. Then, so softly I almost missed it, she whispered, "It doesn't matter."

I blinked, sure I'd misheard her. My brow pulled tight before I could stop it. "What did you just say?"

She looked up for half a second, and it felt like taking a hit to the chest. Those copper-colored eyes caught the light, and for a moment I forgot what air was.

"Mr. Adler." The professor's voice cut through the moment, sharp enough to snap it clean.

I straightened immediately, muttering an apology while a few people snickered. My face felt hot, but not from embarrassment. More like frustration.

I tried to focus on the lecture, since I'm sure I'd just bombed the pop quiz . . . but it didn't last long. My hand started moving on its own, tapping the pencil she'd given me against the desk. The rhythm filled the silence between us.

"Come on," I murmured teasingly, leaning toward her. "You don't look like a Sarah."

Nothing. Not even a glance.

"You're really not gonna tell me? Not even your first initial?" I asked, aiming for the easy grin that usually got me what I wanted, softening my tone like I was teasing, not pushing.

Still nothing, though I saw the twitch of her hand on the desk like she was holding herself still.

I let my voice get a little growly, hoping maybe she would think it was hot. "Guess I'll just call you my hero for now."

That got a tiny reaction—her fingers tightening around her notebook. I couldn't explain it, but the need to see more, to get another response out of her, pressed deeper.

After a few minutes, I said it before I could think better of it. "Didn't know my hero was gonna be the most beautiful girl I've ever seen."

She froze. Completely. Her shoulders went rigid, her face pale even under the blush. I'd expected her to smile or laugh or at least look at me—but she didn't move. Not even to breathe.

Something about it twisted in my chest. I wasn't sure if it was guilt or something else entirely.

By the time class ended, I felt strung out, like I'd spent the entire hour trapped in a room with the air slowly thinning. Every second beside her had been too much—the faint scrape of her pencil, the shift of her hair when she moved, the way she never once looked at me even though I could feel her every heartbeat in the air between us.

I'd been watched before. People stared at me all the time, girls, fans, classmates who thought getting close might get them somewhere . . . but this wasn't that. This wasn't attention. This was distance that *hurt*. It crawled under my skin and made me itch for something I couldn't define.

The professor's voice faded in and out, a low buzz that couldn't hold me for more than a second. I should've been relieved when it ended, but I wasn't. I was restless. Wired. My knee bounced under the desk, my fingers tapping against the wood as she gathered her things, her hands shaking as she put her things away.

I wanted to say something, *anything*, to make her look at me again. To make her eyes meet mine so I could figure out what the hell was happening. Why she felt like gravity and benediction all at once. Why it felt like I was missing something that had been right in front of me the whole time.

I'd never felt it before. That pull. Not even close. It was ridiculous, really, how desperate it made me. One class, one conversation, and I was already searching for excuses to make her stay a few seconds longer.

When she stood, the spell of stillness shattered. My chair scraped back before my brain caught up, legs tangling with the desk. I nearly went down, catching myself on the edge just in time. She didn't even glance back, just kept walking toward the door, clutching her notebook like it was armor.

I scrambled after her anyway, heart thudding way too hard for something this stupid, falling into step beside her like my body had decided for me.

Up close, she was even smaller than I'd realized, swallowed up by a faded sweatshirt that looked soft enough to sink into. Her hair was loose and wild, catching the light like it had a mind of its own. No makeup that I could see, just clear skin, flushed from the cold . . . and me, her lips pink and bare.

Any other girl would probably have looked plain. Average. Every girl who threw themselves at me usually came with the full production—lashes, gloss, contour. But even those girls with all their practiced perfection couldn't hold a candle to her. She was effortlessly beautiful in a way that made my chest tighten, like she didn't have to try, like existing was enough to wreck me.

The thought came out of nowhere and hit hard . . . an image of just scooping her up, throwing her over my shoulder, and carrying her somewhere no one else could look at her. The possessive urge jolted me so hard I had to blink and take a literal step back, shaking my head like I could knock it loose.

"Hey," I said finally, my voice quieter than I meant. "Thanks again. For the pencil."

She froze again, her back going rigid. I saw her throat move as she swallowed, her fingers gripping her notebook like it was the only thing keeping her grounded.

"You already said that."

"Doesn't mean I don't mean it." I tried for easy charm, but something rougher slipped out beneath it. "It was the only thing keeping me from turning in a blank page. That deserves at least a name in return."

Her lips parted, just barely. For a second, I thought she might actually answer, and my pulse kicked hard enough that I forgot to breathe.

"Matty!"

Garrett's voice cut through the hallway noise, loud and teasing.

She flinched. A visible, full-body flinch.

My eyes flicked toward him for half a second, just enough to see his grin falter as he followed my line of sight to her. He was still staring when I looked back.

She was gone. Already halfway to the doors, walking fast, her head down like she couldn't get out of there quick enough.

Garrett's voice trailed off, confusion pulling at his features. He was still watching her, and something inside me went tight. I wanted to tell him to stop looking. To stop *seeing* her.

Whatever I was feeling was hot and violent. I wanted to hit him. Or shove him. Or just plant myself between him.

I wanted to tell him she wasn't *his*.

The thought blindsided me, reckless and possessive, and I had to clench my fists to keep from acting on it. I'd known her for less than an hour. I didn't even know her name. But the idea of anyone else looking at her like that made something wild spark in my chest.

"Hey!" The word tore out of me before I could think better of it. I stepped forward, my voice louder, rougher. "Can't wait to see you again, most beautiful girl in the world!"

It came out half teasing, half desperate . . . like if I said it right, she'd turn around. Like I could catch her eyes one more time and make sense of whatever the hell this was.

But she didn't.

Her back just went more rigid, the slightest pause in her step, and for a heartbeat I thought maybe she would. Then she kept walking. No glance over her shoulder, no smile. Just gone, swallowed by the sunlight outside.

And for reasons I couldn't explain, it felt like the air went with her.

"Holy shit."

I spun around, heat flooding my neck. Jace leaned against the wall like he'd been there forever, arms crossed, grinning like it was Christmas morning.

"You—" I started, too fast.

"I," he cut in smoothly, "just witnessed the great Matty Adler once again falling all over himself for a girl. What is this, the second time in twenty-four hours? Truly historic. ESPN's gonna want the rights to that clip." He fell to his knees. "'Can't wait to see you again, most beautiful girl in the world,'" he cried mockingly.

"I hate you," I muttered, dragging a hand down my face.

He got to his feet, eyes gleaming with way too much delight. "You know, Matty-kins, I've seen you bulldoze six-foot-five linebackers without breaking a sweat, but one tiny blonde and suddenly you're yelling about a writing utensil like it's a love sonnet? This could be the second-best day of my life."

"What's the first best day of your life?" Garrett asked, sounding intrigued.

Jace waggled his eyebrows. "I'll give you a hint. First word rhymes with *Piley*, second word rhymes with *magina*."

Garrett and I both just gaped at him, but at least I was distracted for half a second.

Yep, the half a second was over. I was thinking about her again.

"Was that . . . feral?" Jace cocked his head thoughtfully. "It felt feral. Like watching a caveman discover fire. But way hornier."

"Jace," I warned, but that only lit him up more.

He pressed his fist to his mouth like he was trying not to laugh, then failed miserably. "You kind of sounded like a Disney prince after three concussions. I'm surprised she didn't run faster than that."

"She didn't—" I started, then cut myself off because yeah, she sort of had run away.

"I swear I've seen her before," Garrett mused as we started walking down the sidewalk.

I growled softly at the fact that he was still thinking about her, and Jace heard it and smirked.

Asshole.

"Parker needs to hear about this update," he muttered, pulling out his phone.

I lunged for it, and he dodged, grinning like a jackal.

"Thatcher—"

"Ooh, you last-named me. Must be serious," he said as he pressed send on the text. He tucked the phone into his pocket, smirk still welded to his face. "But seriously, Matty-kins. Who is this girl? I'm ready to have another best friend."

Before I could lose my mind about the thought of him anywhere near her, my name rang out.

I glanced to the left, and saw Lindsey walking toward me. We'd hooked up a few times, and I was usually down to talk to her . . .

But that wasn't the case today.

She reached for my arm, her fingers brushing the sleeve of my hoodie. "I was hoping I could come over tonight," she said with a big smile, the insinuation clear in her voice.

Normally, I would've smiled. Been up for a hot fuck, or at least let her down gently if I wasn't in the mood. It wasn't hard to play nice.

The second her hand touched me, something in me went feral.

"I'm busy," I said, sharper than I meant to.

Her smile faltered, confusion flickering across her face before she mumbled, "Oh—okay. Wow. Sorry, I didn't mean to . . ." She gave a nervous laugh that sounded more like a hiccup. "Didn't realize you were *seeing someone*."

"Well, I am," I said automatically . . . not understanding why it didn't taste like a lie.

"Right," she muttered, cheeks flushing as she stepped back. "I'm sorry."

She tried to laugh it off again, but it fell flat. A moment later, she was gone, swallowed by the tide of students, leaving behind nothing but the faint smell of her perfume and the ghost of her hand still burning on my sleeve.

I resumed walking. Jaw locked. Eyes forward.

I could feel Jace's and Garrett's eyes glued to the sides of my head as we walked.

"Taken, huh . . . ?" Jace finally asked innocently.

"I'm really confused," Garrett muttered. "Who's your girlfriend?"

"Don't ask any more questions," Jace whispered loudly. "He's got a serial-killer face on, and I don't have any cookies to pay him off."

That finally got me to look at him incredulously.

"Just to let you know, if we are keeping count, you are my bestilicious friend number two today. So suck it," I growled.

"Bet I know who number one is," said Jace, doing that weird eyebrow thing again as he flipped his long blonde hair around dramatically. "And it ain't Parkie-poo, my lad."

I huffed, but I was too wrecked to get any more words out. All I could think about was *her*. Her copper eyes, her soft, nervous voice. The one who'd said *It doesn't matter* like it was a confession.

I could still feel her everywhere—the brush of her hand against mine, the tremor in her breath, the warmth of her skin. It lingered like something sacred and poisonous all at once.

I needed a bucket of ice. Or holy water. Maybe both.

Because I was starting to think she hadn't just gotten under my skin.

She'd cursed me.

CHAPTER 9

MATTY

Thursday night, and I was losing my mind.

I sat on the edge of my bed, elbows on my knees, phone clutched in my hand like it might magically buzz with her name. The house was quiet except for the faint hum of the AC, but my head wouldn't shut up.

I'd never been mad at a weekday before, but Thursday had officially joined the list. Because tomorrow meant no class. And Saturday meant a home game. Which meant it'd be *days* before I saw her again—if she even showed up after seeing me act like a lunatic.

I needed to know her name.

I'd already thought about asking the TA for the roster. It would've been easy enough; she liked me, always smiled too long when I turned in papers. But what was the point? I didn't even know where to start. I couldn't just scan a list of fifty names and magically know which one belonged to her.

I tilted my head. Maybe it could work? Maybe I'd just *feel* it. Like there'd be a glow around her name, something that tugged you straight to it.

I exhaled sharply, shaking my head. "Stop acting like an idiot, Matty," I muttered under my breath.

I still didn't know how I'd missed her before.

Every time I thought of it, I felt sick. Because there was no universe where I could've missed her before that day. Not her face. Not her eyes. Not that quiet, nervous energy that had felt like a trap I'd walked right into.

I tossed my phone onto the comforter, rubbed a hand over my jaw, and stared at the ceiling.

Jace could find her. Hell, Jace could find anyone. He was a hacker in all but name, and if I asked, he'd have her name, address, and social security number in under an hour.

Except Jace was out with Riley tonight, some fancy dinner before the team hotel lock-in tomorrow. Knowing Jace, he'd probably carry Riley into his room afterward, and they'd be at it all night, so I wouldn't get a chance to ask him for help. Which meant I was on my own.

And I was desperate.

So desperate it was starting to feel like a problem.

I leaned back, staring at the dark ceiling, the image of her burned behind my eyelids anyway. Copper eyes. Shy smile. The sound of her voice, quiet but sharp enough to stick under my skin.

I'd had girls throw themselves at me, chase me after games, flirt in every way imaginable. None of them had ever gotten this kind of hold on me.

My cock twitched, already hard just from the thought of her. That soft curve of her lips, the way her hair fell over one shoulder, the dark flush on her cheeks when she'd caught me staring. I shifted on the bed, trying to ignore it, but the ache was relentless, growing heavier, tighter, until it felt like my whole body was strung taut. I was harder than I'd ever been, and I hadn't even touched her. Just the memory of her was enough to make my pulse hammer, my blood roaring south.

I groaned, dragging a hand down my face, but it didn't help. The pressure in my jeans was unbearable now, my cock throbbing with a need I couldn't ignore. I tried to think of something else, game stats, tomorrow's practice, anything, but her face kept slipping back in, those eyes locking on to mine, that quiet voice pulling me deeper into her mystery.

"Fuck it," I muttered, popping the button on my jeans. My hand moved before I could stop it, shoving the denim down just enough to free myself. My cock sprang up, hot and heavy against my stomach, the small silver piercing at the tip glinting faintly in the dim light, a stupid dare from Jace last summer that I'd never gotten around to taking out. I'd kept it because it felt too damn good to remove, the way it heightened every sensation.

My dick was already leaking, the bead of precum catching on the metal, and I hissed at the intense, electric jolt as my fingers brushed it. I wrapped my hand around myself, the piercing making every touch hit deeper, pleasure and pain twisting together until it stole the air from my lungs.

I pictured her again, those copper eyes wide, her lips parted like she was surprised, maybe even curious. I imagined her watching me now, that shy smile turning wicked, her voice whispering my name, even though she wouldn't give me hers. My grip tightened, stroking slow at first, each drag of my hand tugging at the piercing, sending jolts of extreme ecstasy shooting through me. My hips bucked up, chasing the sensation, the image of her so vivid I could almost feel her there, her breath against my skin, her hands instead of mine.

I growled, my strokes getting faster, rougher. I could see her leaning closer, her hair brushing my chest, her lips hovering just out of reach, maybe even tracing the piercing with a curious finger. My cock ached so bad it hurt, every nerve screaming for release, the metal adding an edge to every movement. I wanted to know what she'd sound like, gasping, moaning, saying my name. I wanted to know how she'd feel, tight and warm, her body moving with mine.

My head tipped back, a moan ripping out of me as the pressure built, coiling tight at the base of my spine. I was close, too close, too fast, but I couldn't stop, I didn't want to. Her face was all I could see, her eyes burning into me, everything about her pulling me under. One last hard stroke, the piercing catching just right, and I came with a choked groan, hot and messy across my stomach, my whole body shaking with the force of it.

I lay there, panting, my heart hammering in my chest. The room was quiet again, but she was still there, lingering in my head, her shadow sharper than ever. I had to find her fucking name or I'd lose my damn mind.

A faint creak snapped my eyes open. My closet door swung open slowly, and a figure stepped out, swallowed by shadow.

"What the fuck," I breathed, half off the bed before my brain caught up. My heart slammed in my chest, every muscle locking tight as the figure straightened. It took me a second to process what I was seeing . . . the black Sphinx mask, sleek and feline, gleaming faintly in the dark.

He didn't speak at first, just stood there, the weight of him filling the room until I could barely breathe.

"This has been one of the more *interesting* deliveries of my life," he finally said, his voice edged with amusement as he tossed a crimson envelope onto the bed. It landed with a soft *thud* next to my phone. Before I could process it, he turned, striding out of the bedroom, the door clicking shut behind him.

I stared after him, my brain short-circuiting, body still buzzing from release. What the hell just happened? My pulse spiked again, shock slamming through me like a freight train. I scrambled up, wiping the cum off my stomach with my sheet before I yanked my jeans over my hips. The zipper got caught in my haste.

"Fuuuuuuck," I snarled, nearly blacking out. There was nothing worse than zipping up your motherfucking dick.

I stumbled to the door in a haze of pain, flung it open, and tore down the hallway, checking all the rooms, the front door, every corner of the house. Nothing. No trace of him. Like he'd vanished into thin air.

I stood there, chest heaving, the crimson envelope burning a hole in my mind. That mask, that envelope, it could only mean one thing. I'd finally gotten my first Sphinx trial.

Even if the guy had just seen my dick . . . all I could feel at that moment was *relief*. For months, I'd watched Jace and Parker breeze through their trials like they were nothing. Jace treated it like a joke. Parker barely mentioned his unless he was dragging us along to help him. None of it was a big deal to them.

For me, though . . . the Sphinx was everything.

I'd spent my whole college career terrified of losing what little I'd scraped together. No matter how many NIL checks came in, no matter how many fans wore my jersey, that fear stayed put. One wrong move, one bad play, and I'd be back where I started . . . just another broke kid from nowhere with a busted dream and a family hanging by a thread.

But the Sphinx . . . the Sphinx was my way out. My safety net. My ticket to a life where doors wouldn't slam in my face. Membership meant power that didn't depend on touchdowns or stats. It meant *control*.

I stumbled back to the bed, eyes locked on the crimson envelope like it might disappear if I blinked. My hands shook as I tore it open, the paper giving way with a rough rip. Inside was a single card, black ink scrawled in neat handwriting: *Membership Dossier. Rutherford College.*

I just stared at it, the words refusing to make sense. Rutherford College? The elite school with the kind of money that could buy a new building every time one needed fresh paint? The only thing I really knew about Rutherford, besides their reputation for breeding trust fund geniuses and that they also had a prep school called Rutherford Academy on their same campus, was that their football program was *elite*. Not as good as ours right now, obviously, but Jackson Parker had played there before going pro. Now he was lighting up the NFL, and I'd even gone to a few of his games, watching from the stands while pretending I didn't envy every damn second of his life.

And what the hell was a *membership dossier* anyway? Now was one of those times when Parker's big brain would've actually come in handy. He probably would've rattled off some theory about secret archives and power structures while I stood there trying to make sense of a damn envelope.

I frowned, trying to sift through the blur of memory. The night of our Sphinx initiation felt like something out of a half-remembered dream, so unreal I still wasn't sure it had actually happened. I remembered the bag yanked over my head, the rough hands dragging me down a flight of stairs, the air growing colder the deeper we went. Then the smell of wax and smoke. Candles everywhere, flickering off the stone walls. Dozens of people stood in front of us, their faces hidden behind those sleek black masks, their voices distorted and rhythmic.

I swallowed hard.

Was this membership dossier some kind of record of everyone who'd ever worn the mask? Every name, every generation, carved into something meant to last forever?

If so, this wasn't just a file. It was their holy grail.

What the hell was I supposed to do with it? *Steal it*?

The question burned in my mind, wild and impossible. If there was one thing I'd learned from helping Parker with his trial and hearing Jace's stories, though, it was that nothing the Sphinx did ever made sense until it was too late to back out.

Fuck. How was I going to steal something from Rutherford? Where would it even be?

I flipped open my laptop, the screen lighting up my dark room with a soft blue glow. My fingers hovered over the keyboard as I typed *Rutherford College Sphinx* into the search bar.

Nothing.

I tried again, this time just *Rutherford College secret society.* A few hits came up, rumors, conspiracy blogs, an article about some fraternity scandal, but nothing even close to what I was looking for.

That didn't make sense. We didn't even have a Sphinx chapter there. So why the hell would my trial be tied to that school?

I leaned back in my chair, rubbing a hand down my face. My mind spun through every name that might have answers, every connection that might make sense . . . until one stood out.

Jagger.

Jace's older brother.

The guy who somehow knew everything about everyone and was also impossibly rich. No one was really sure what he did for a living, but the general consensus was *something illegal.* Probably mafia-adjacent. Definitely sketchy.

I pulled out my phone and shot him a text.

Me: So . . . you know anything about Rutherford College?

It took a few minutes before the typing bubbles appeared.

Jagger: The fancy one? Why the hell are you asking me about that?

That was a fair question. I'd probably just interrupted him mid-weapons deal. He probably had a gun in one hand and his phone in the other.

Me: I just need some . . . info.

Jagger: That isn't vague at all, Matty-kins.

I scowled at that. The Thatcher genes were apparently strong. Jagger was just as obnoxious as his brother . . . although much scarier. So, I wasn't going to tell him that.

Jagger: I know their dean's a prick. His name's Alfred Harrington. Old money, thinks his shit doesn't stink.

I hesitated, thumb hovering over the keyboard. Everyone in our group knew Jagger was a Sphinx, and whatever power the society had, he'd kept his hooks in it. If anyone would know the truth, it'd be him.

Me: Is he part of the Sphinx, by chance?

The bubbles popped up, then disappeared. Then popped up again.

Jagger: Why would I tell you that?

I stared at the screen, waiting, pulse ticking faster.

Finally, another text came through.

Jagger: Yeah. He is.

Jagger: Any other questions, or can I get back to it?

I briefly wondered what *back to it* meant. Sometimes Jagger would answer Jace's calls in the middle of sex when he was bored. But *back to it* could also mean he was . . . killing someone.

I'd better not ask. Some things were above my pay grade, and body bags were one of them.

I typed out a hasty *thanks, I'm good*, and threw my phone down.

Tapping my fingers on my desk for a second, I frowned. If I was going to pull this off, I couldn't do it alone. It was time to cash in a few of the *unlimited* favors Jace and Parker owed me.

Not only did Darla now possess exclusive photos of me in my cowboy era, and Emma, Riley's old roommate, was possibly going to kill me and cover herself in my skin suit because of the dinner date Jace had forced on me . . . but Parker's Sphinx trial had ended with me getting chased through a damn cemetery at midnight after we dug up some dead lady's grave for a ring. *A ring*. I could still hear the shovel hitting the coffin as I felt my soul leave my body. Ghosts were basically my number one fear, and I'd risked eternal haunting for that idiot.

A full-body shiver ran through me just thinking about it. Yeah. Those two literally owed me everything.

I picked up my phone and texted Jace first. And then texted him again. And again, each new text containing escalating levels of menace.

Me: Romeo. Drop everything now and get home.

Me: I'm serious. I don't care if Riley's mid-forkful of pasta. This is life-and-death.

Me: Secret-society type of death just in case you were wondering.

Me: Stop making out and check your damn phone.

Me: If you don't, I'm giving Darla your phone number. Who knows what she will do with it.

Me: Probably hack into it somehow and see all the dick pics on there, I'm sure.

Me: Pick. Up. I WILL DO IT, JACE THATCHER.

A few seconds later, the bubbles appeared, then vanished, then came back.

Jace: I'm on a date, you psychopath.

Jace: This seems very drama llama of you, and not in a good way.

Jace: Also, how dare you threaten me with nudes. Do you want her to stalk me forever? What else would she do after seeing lil Jace?

Me: Weren't you just complaining about not having stalkers? On second thought, I would actually be doing yet another favor for you, so maybe I need to think of something else.

Jace: Well.

A minute passed.

Me: JACE THATCHER, THIS IS IMPORTANT.

Jace: Oh, sorry. Got distracted for a second. Riley-girl was eating spaghetti.

I didn't know what that meant. Also, I didn't want to know what that meant.

Jace: I've had some time to reflect.

Me: So kind of you to do that in my time of need.

Jace: I've decided I'm not sure I actually want stalkers. As you know, or as I need to remind you . . . I prefer to do the stalking.

Jace: Plus, I remembered that whole thing with the three-nippled woman with the tattoo of my face who was sending me pics for a while. So, I'm not sure it's as glamourous as you make it out to be. That was . . . a lot.

I gaped at the phone, wondering when I had ever given the impression of glamour at any point in my life. But he had a point . . . I'd had to delete the pics of the three-nippled woman from his phone because he'd been too traumatized to do it . . . and I'd also been traumatized in the process.

His texts also made me remember something else . . . I'd been so busy thinking about my mystery girl that I hadn't even looked at the parking lot once during practice to see if my stalker had returned.

Crazy.

I felt weirdly guilty about that, but also, my mystery girl obviously had magical powers of distraction, and I couldn't be blamed.

My mystery girl . . . What was I even thinking?

I shook my head. *Focus, Matty. Sphinx first. Girl second.*

I could do this.

Me: I have two words. Iced milk.

Me: Oh, and one more. Femur.

Me: You owe me, Jace Thatcher.

It took him a minute to answer, and I almost threw my phone across the room while I waited.

Jace: Calm down, motherclucker. I just paid the bill, and we're on our way. Of course I'm going to help you with your Sphinx thingy. I'm your bestilicious friend number one.

I got a little calmer after his text, although there was a lot to unpack in there, namely his use of the term *motherclucker* in the same sentence as *bestilicious*.

I'm glad he was Riley's problem now.

Meet you at Parker's house, I typed out, standing up from my desk to find some dark clothing. That was what you were supposed to wear for a heist, right?

Jace: I'll think of some code names on the drive.

I shook my head and got dressed, and then it was time for my next task. Dragging Parker Davis from Casey's side.

CHAPTER 10

MATTY

Crunch.

Crunch.

I flinched again, gripping the steering wheel like it was the only thing keeping me from losing my mind.

"Can you not?" I hissed, glancing in the rearview mirror.

Jace looked up mid-bite, an Oreo halfway to his mouth. "What?"

"That. The chewing. The crunching. The aggressive consumption of cookies while I'm trying to plan a possible felony."

He raised a brow, unfazed. "Stress-eating, Adler. You know it's a coping mechanism for me."

"Maybe your coping mechanism should be thinking of ways to steal a top-secret document from a highly secured college dean's office."

He stared at me like I was an idiot, then shrugged and took another slow, obnoxious bite.

Crunch.

"I'll pass on that, thank you," he said with a full mouth. "I'm the beauty of this operation. You've got Big Brains next to you."

"It's true," Parker commented sleepily. Not using his brain at all at the moment since he'd just woken up from a nap.

This was too much.

"Give me those," I hissed, reaching a hand out behind me.

"No, you'll throw them out!" Jace said indignantly, frantically stuffing the cookies into his mouth so that his cheeks were bulging. "I will not give in!"

Crumbs sprayed my face, and I growled as I turned back to the road and away from the chocolate projectiles.

The crunching continued, and then suddenly an Oreo was thrust in my face.

"Here," he said begrudgingly. "We all know how you feel about beauty sleep, and you're not you when you're hungry and tired. So eat a cookie."

"I think there's a commercial that talks about that," Parker mused as I snatched the cookie from Jace's hand.

I did, in fact, feel much better the second I had it in my mouth.

Not as good as if I had her *in my mouth, though.*

I'd lost it.

I stopped my car about half a mile from the gates, the engine humming as I shifted into park. The headlights cut through the fog just enough to show the looming iron archway ahead, RUTHERFORD COLLEGE spelled across the top in perfect lettering.

I stared out the windshield for a long moment, taking in the view beyond it, the sprawl of the campus, lit like a damn postcard. A massive green stretched out at its center, crisscrossed with pale concrete paths that glowed under the lamps. The buildings surrounding the lawn looked like someone had stolen them straight from Ancient Rome—white marble, perfect columns, gold accents gleaming even in the dark.

Jace let out a low whistle from the back seat, Oreo dust still on his shirt. "Fancy. Is this where the rich kids sacrifice people?"

"Feels about right," I muttered.

Parker stirred in the passenger seat, stretching like his nap had been the most restful hours of his life. His hair was a mess, his voice rough. "That was a quick drive," he commented.

Jace popped his head between the seats. "You're kidding, right? You slept the *entire* drive. I had to listen to Matty's murder playlist and contemplate death."

"I focus better rested," Parker said, deadpan, then leaned forward, squinting through the windshield. "Alright. Here's the plan."

Both of us turned to stare at him.

"'Plan'?" I repeated. "You've been unconscious for three hours. How the hell do you have a plan?"

He ignored me, pointing toward the marble buildings. "That central green? It's probably where the main administrative offices are. That will be where the dean's office is. If Dean Harrington's a Sphinx member, then the dossier's in there. No way a guy like that wouldn't keep it close. Power-hungry assholes love holding proof they're important."

"Why wouldn't he just keep it at his house?" I asked, feeling overwhelmed. I was a football player for fuck's sake, not a wannabe felon.

Parker didn't even blink. "Because his house can be easily broken into. His office? That's protected by university security and card readers . . . and the kind of ego that thinks no one's stupid enough to try."

Jace blinked. "Did you—did you just Sherlock that in ten seconds flat?"

Parker shrugged, already reaching for the duffel bag at his feet. "I pay attention. Plus, Rutherford's campus layout's online. I looked it up before we left."

I gaped. "Before we left? As in the five seconds *before you fell asleep*?"

He gave me that infuriatingly calm grin. "Preparation, Adler. Try it sometime."

Jace snorted. "I'm sorry, but you snored through a Whataburger run and two gas station stops. Don't act like you're some tactical genius."

Parker ignored him, checking his watch. "We've got about four hours before sunrise. We'll jog to campus, hop the east fence, cross the quad, and hit the admin building. Third floor, corner office."

I sighed. "Quick, quiet, no improvising."

Parker gave me a look and then nodded at Jace, who was crunching again. "You realize who you just said that to?"

"Yeah. I realized it was a mistake as soon as the words came out of my mouth."

Jace opened his door. "Improvisation is how legends are made."

"It's also how idiots get arrested," I grumbled.

"Tomato, tomahto."

I shoved my door open, the night air biting against my skin as I stepped out. Gravel crunched under my sneakers. Behind me, Jace pulled his hood over his head, tucking his blonde hair inside like he was going undercover.

"I'm too recognizable with these flowing locks," he announced to no one in particular.

"Yeah," I said, locking the car. "Every security camera's gonna stop dead when it sees Rapunzel breaking and entering."

Parker snorted as he slung the small duffel over his shoulder and started down the dirt shoulder toward the trees lining the road. "Let's move."

Jace fell into step beside me as we started jogging, the cold biting through the silence.

After a few minutes, he puffed out a breath. "So, I did come up with something helpful for this . . . fun little adventure."

Parker glanced back at him over his shoulder, somehow not tripping on the tree roots snaking out of the sidewalk. "And what would that be, Thatcher?"

"Code words," Jace announced proudly.

I groaned loud enough to startle a bird out of a nearby tree. "Oh, for fuck's sake."

He grinned, undeterred. "If things go south, say, 'Hurt.' That means run. If you need a distraction, say, 'Fix You.' And if we're totally screwed—like, cops, alarms, divine punishment—say, 'Creep.'"

Parker frowned. "Those are all names of depressing songs."

"Exactly," Jace said. "Inspired by Matty's 'I Hate My Life' playlist from the drive. You missed the show since you were drooling on yourself in the passenger seat."

I shot him a look. "You're not funny."

"Maybe not," he said, jogging backward with a grin. "But when this ends with us in handcuffs, my mugshot is definitely going to go viral."

Parker snorted like he'd never heard something more ridiculous, and Jace laughed, the sound echoing through the empty street. The marble columns of Rutherford glowed faintly in the distance. My lungs burned, my nerves buzzed, and somewhere in the back of my head, a tiny voice kept whispering that this was a terrible idea.

But when Jace threw me a wink over his shoulder, humming the *Mission: Impossible* theme while he ran, I couldn't help it. I picked up the pace.

Cold air slapped me in the face. The night smelled like damp grass. Somewhere far off, a train horn wailed, long and judgmental.

The wrought iron fence rose ahead, black and shiny under the moon. A camera perched above the gate blinked lazily, sweeping the area in slow arcs.

Parker crouched low, his eyes tracking the movement. "Fifteen-second rotation. We go on three."

I blinked. "You counted?"

He didn't look up. "Twice. The guard in the booth checks his phone between passes, too. He's scrolling Instagram."

Jace and I stared at him.

"How the hell do you *know* that?" Jace whispered.

Parker finally glanced over his shoulder, expression unreadable. "I pay attention."

Jace leaned toward me, muttering, "I'm starting to think he's not actually human."

"Yeah," I said quietly, still watching Parker. "Either that or he's got Google Maps implanted in his brain."

The camera turned. "Go!"

We climbed. The iron was slick with dew, freezing against my palms.

Halfway up, Jace grunted behind me, muttering a string of curses that could've peeled paint.

"Shit! I'm stuck!"

I looked down. His hoodie had caught on one of the top spikes, the fabric twisted tight like it had declared war on him. He tried yanking it free, but the motion only made it worse.

"Dude," I hissed. "Just take it off."

"In what world is stripping mid-felony a good idea?" he whisper-yelled, still flailing.

Parker sighed and then reached up, grabbed a handful of Jace's hoodie, and yanked. The fabric tore loose with a rip loud enough to make my stomach clench. Both of them tumbled over the top, hitting the ground on the other side in a graceless heap of limbs and swearing.

"Graceful," I muttered, dropping down beside them and landing in a crouch. My knees protested the impact.

"I'm built for highlight reels, not stealth," Jace snapped, standing up and brushing himself off.

"You're built for hospital bills," Parker said flatly, shoving the duffel back over his shoulder.

Jace scowled. "Love the support, guys."

"Shut up," Parker said. "We're exposed."

We crouched low. The quad stretched out like a movie set—manicured lawns, marble benches, a fountain so fancy it probably had an endowment.

"Even their grass smells rich," Jace whispered.

"That's called fertilizer," Parker said, his eyes scanning the walkways.

We crept forward, keeping to the shadows, our shoes sinking into damp grass. Halfway across, a motion light flared to life, flooding the space in harsh white.

We froze, every muscle locking tight.

"Don't move," Parker hissed.

Jace tilted his head slightly toward me. "It's a light, not a sniper," he whispered.

"Do you want to test that theory?" Parker shot back.

Silence stretched, the buzz of the lamp loud enough to make my skin crawl. Then—*click*—the light blinked off, plunging us back into darkness.

Jace grinned. "See? Easy."

I rolled my eyes. "You say that now. Wait until we're sprinting for our lives."

Parker didn't respond, already motioning for us to move. We darted across the remaining stretch, the marble looming larger with every step until we reached the admin building itself.

FAIRFAX ADMINISTRATION HALL was carved deep into the stone like a warning.

I stared up at them, chest tight. "Sounds friendly," I muttered.

"Yeah," Jace said, smirking. "Like welcome-to-your-impending-arrest friendly."

We crept along the back of the building, the marble slick beneath our shoes. A security camera blinked above a service door, its red light cutting through the dark like it was judging us.

"Seriously?" Jace whispered. "They just leave this out in the open?"

"Not for long," Parker murmured.

Jace pulled a strip of black tape from his pocket, probably left over from one of his "creative projects," and stretched up to slap it over the lens. The red light disappeared.

"Pretty sure that's not how security systems work," I said.

Parker crouched beside the door, peering through the narrow glass pane. "The feed's live, but I bet no one's actually watching it. Colleges always have, like, one guy covering thirty monitors, and he probably has YouTube open on another screen. We've got time."

He set the duffel down quietly and unzipped it, the soft *clink* of metal echoing in the silence. Then he looked up at Jace. "You're up."

Jace blinked. "Why exactly do you think I'm qualified for *breaking and entering*?"

Parker's mouth twitched. "Because Jagger's your brother."

Jace stared at him for a beat, then snorted. "Okay, fair point." He crouched by the lock, rolling his shoulders like a man about to compete in the Lockpicking Olympics, and started working the picks with unnerving precision.

The metal gave a soft *click*, and the door creaked open, the smell of polished wood and old money spilling out to meet us.

I stared at the open doorway, then back at Jace. "Great. Now I have even more questions."

He grinned, pocketing the picks. "Good. Means I'm keeping our relationship interesting. Wouldn't want you to get bored, Matty-kins."

We slipped inside. The temperature dropped immediately, the air still and heavy, like the building itself was holding its breath. The corridor stretched ahead, dim and spotless, every sound amplified in the silence. Somewhere deeper inside, a clock ticked steadily, marking the seconds we didn't have.

Portraits lined the walls, stone-faced men in dark suits, each with the smug look of someone who'd never been told *no*. Their painted eyes seemed to track us as we crept past.

"Creepy," Jace whispered. "I feel like they can smell public school on me."

"Keep moving," Parker muttered.

We took the stairs, the old wood creaking with every step, each groan loud enough to make my pulse jump.

Third floor.

The hallway stretched ahead, thick carpet muffling our footsteps. Trophy cases glinted faintly in the dim light, reflecting fragments of our shadows as we moved.

Parker froze suddenly and lifted a hand. "Security guard. End of the hall."

We ducked behind a massive bronze statue of some long-dead founder who looked like he'd have sued someone for breathing wrong. A flashlight beam sliced through the dark, creeping closer.

The guard's radio crackled. "All clear in the east wing."

Boots thudded closer. I held my breath as the light skimmed past, so close it brushed over my shoe, then turned away.

We didn't move until the sound of footsteps faded.

"Ten out of ten," Jace whispered. "Almost peed myself."

"Please don't," Parker hissed.

We started forward again, slower this time, every creak of the floor sounding like a siren.

At the end of the hall, a gold nameplate caught the faint light: DR. ALFRED HARRINGTON, DEAN. The letters gleamed like someone polished them every day.

"Showtime," Parker said under his breath as Jace crouched by the lock.

"Your two-minute Google search didn't happen to tell you if there was an alarm in his office, did it?" I asked sarcastically.

Parker shrugged without looking away from Jace. "I guess we're about to find out."

I exhaled. "Super reassuring."

A heartbeat later, there was a soft *click*. The latch gave way.

"I'm such an asset to this organization," Jace muttered arrogantly. "Riley's going to be so proud of me."

I patted him on the shoulder like the good boy he was, and we moved into the room.

Harrington's office was everything you'd expect of a man who collected power: a massive mahogany desk, two leather chairs that looked expensive enough to scold you, bookcases wall to wall, and a portrait of some mustached benefactor glaring down at us like he smelled trouble.

"Alright," Parker said in a low voice. "We're looking for the ledger. Probably old. Possibly framed or locked up."

"That's a lot to go off of," I said dryly.

Parker shot me an annoyed look.

Jace drifted to the bar cart, lifting a bottle and sniffing like he was auditioning for a liquor commercial. "The man's got bourbon older than us. This is the good stuff."

"Step away from it," I hissed.

"Fine." He put the bottle down with exaggerated care. "But if we die tonight, it would be better to come back as a drunk ghost than a sober one. I'm just saying."

I didn't bother responding to that one.

I started with the drawers. There was old correspondence, a fountain pen with a nib the width of a toothpick, receipts for donations that could buy a small country, and an absurdly large stash of peppermints.

Parker's hand skimmed along the spines on the shelves. "Nothing," he said tightly.

Jace bent toward a glass-fronted cabinet that stood between the bookcases. The cabinet was bolted to the wall, glass domed in front of a velvet-lined shelf. A small brass plaque read COLLECTION. He peered closer and whispered, "Maybe he keeps it with his . . ."

His elbow clipped a decorative globe sitting on a side table. The thing toppled, hit the floor with a heavy *thud*, and rolled once before stopping against the baseboard.

Everything went louder for a second. We all froze.

"Jace," Parker breathed.

"It was an accident!" Jace hissed, getting immediately defensive. "It—Look, it was top-heavy, okay? Physics!"

"You breathed near it," I snapped.

A faint *chirp* sounded from above us, almost like a clock trying to get our attention. Parker's face dropped.

"Oh no," he muttered.

The chirp escalated into a high, insistent tone. Red lights flared along the crown molding. The security system caught it.

"Run!" I barked before thinking.

But before chaos could fully take over, something caught my eye . . . a glint of gold behind the desk, barely visible through the shadows. I froze, squinting. There, half hidden behind a framed diploma and a row of dusty law books, sat a narrow glass cabinet recessed in the wall. A single light flickered weakly inside, illuminating the edge of a black, leather-bound ledger.

"I think this could be it!" I shouted.

"Grab it and go," Parker ordered.

I grabbed a crystal paperweight from the desk and swung it against the glass. The first blow scored a spiderweb crack that shimmered in the red light. The second hit splintered it. The third shattered the panel with a spray of glittering shards.

I shoved my arm through, a cut on my palm blooming hot, and hauled the book free. It was heavier than it looked, the leather cold and smelling faintly of dust and disinfectant. I tucked it under my arm and sprinted for the door as the alarm rose to a scream, and the ceiling lights strobed angry red.

From the hallway, someone shouted, "Security! Who's in there?"

I froze mid-step, one hand on the doorknob, heart slamming against my ribs.

"Window!" Parker barked.

He was already there, wrenching it open, the night air cutting through the blaring alarm. Jace climbed out first, muttering, "I was just kidding about the hot mugshot. I can't handle prison."

"Move!" I hissed.

The door burst open behind me. "Stop!" a voice yelled.

Yeah, that wasn't happening.

Parker dove through the window next. I was right behind him, one arm clamped around the leather ledger like it was a newborn. My sneakers hit the fire escape with a metallic *clang*. The ladder groaned under our weight.

Jace was already halfway down, his voice echoing up the metal frame. "Pretty sure my hoodie just ripped again!"

"Cry later!" I shouted, vaulting over the last rung.

We hit the ground running, alarms still wailing above. The night exploded into noise—flashing red security lights, radios squawking, the slap of our sneakers across wet grass.

"This way!" Parker yelled, cutting left across the green.

I followed, lungs burning, my heartbeat slamming against my ribs. Jace pounded along beside me, somehow grinning through it. "You know what's crazy?" He gasped. "We're technically stealing from a rival school. That's the definition of school spirit!"

I rolled my eyes.

A beam of light swept across the lawn behind us. A guard shouted something about "trespassers."

Jace whispered, "Do we qualify as trespassers if we're technically on a mission from a secret society?"

"Yes!" Parker snapped under his breath.

We ducked behind a row of hedges as the beam passed over. My chest heaved, sweat slick under my hoodie. Somewhere to the right, sprinklers kicked on, hissing like snakes.

"Who the hell waters grass at two a.m.?" Jace wheezed.

"Rich people," I muttered.

We crawled along the hedge line. Two more guards jogged toward us, radios blaring.

"Split up!" Parker whispered. "Meet at the fence!"

He veered right. Jace followed me left.

We sprinted past the fountain, feet pounding on the cobblestones. The marble statues of old benefactors watched, smug and useless.

"Why is it always cardio with this group?" Jace panted. "Couldn't the Sphinx test loyalty with, like, yoga?"

"Keep running!" I snapped.

Behind us, a flashlight beam clipped my shoulder. "Hey! Stop!"

Jace shouted over his shoulder, "Can't! Gluten allergy!"

"Not helpful!" I said through gritted teeth.

We cut between two dorm buildings. Voices echoed above and I glanced up and saw students leaning out of windows, their phones raised. Great. Exactly what we needed.

If this went viral, we were dead.

A siren wailed somewhere near the front gate.

"This way!" I hissed, grabbing Jace's arm and pulling him behind a building.

We slid into the shadow of a dumpster that smelled like old pizza. I pressed my back to the brick wall, gasping.

Jace bent over beside me. "Great workout plan, by the way. Break into an office, flee armed security, maybe puke behind a trash can. We should tell Coach about this one."

"Listen," I hissed.

Footsteps pounded past, fading as they headed toward where we'd just come from.

Silence.

I let out a long breath, my adrenaline crashing hard. My hands shook as I clutched the ledger to my chest.

Jace was grinning like he'd just stepped off a roller coaster instead of outrun campus security. "You realize we just pulled off something out of a heist movie, right? I'm, like, George Clooney in *Ocean's Eleven*—but hotter."

"I'm not even going to respond to that," I muttered.

"You two alive?" Parker whispered suddenly.

I nearly jumped out of my skin. He emerged from the shadows, his hoodie streaked with mud, breathing hard but grinning.

"I thought we were meeting by the fence?" I said, straightening up.

"I wasn't sure the two of you would make it," Parker responded, raising an eyebrow.

I nodded because . . . that was a possibility.

Jace threw an arm around him, and Parker almost fell over. "That's why you're my QB," he said proudly. "Also, would now be a good time to tell the two of you that I lost a shoe?"

We all looked down. One of his socks was soaked through.

Parker blinked. "How do you even manage that?"

"Artistry," Jace said. "You wouldn't understand."

I laughed despite myself, the sound rough and breathless. The tension cracked like ice breaking.

Parker grinned. "Alright, fun's over. Let's get out of here."

We slipped from behind the dumpster and cut through the narrow alley we'd found ourselves in. The smell of turpentine mixed with something floral—perfume? No, maybe I was smelling fertilizer again.

Parker led, crouching down, checking corners. I made another mental note to ask him how he was so good at this.

The criminal life was definitely not for me.

We were halfway across the grass when a spotlight flared behind us.

"Freeze!"

Spoiler alert, we didn't.

We ran.

My thighs screamed. Jace cursed every god he knew.

"That's the fence!" I gasped, spotting the glint of metal ahead.

We were almost there when the worst possible thing happened . . . Jace tripped.

Not a stumble. A full-body, limbs-everywhere wipeout.

He went down hard, face-first into the grass with a noise that sounded like a dying walrus.

"Go without me!" he groaned dramatically. "Save yourselves!"

"Get up!" I hissed, yanking his arm.

He popped up, grass in his hair, and sprinted again. "All part of the plan!"

We hit the fence. Parker was already halfway over. I shoved the ledger under my hoodie, climbed, and nearly slipped when my sweat-slick palms hit the cold metal.

A flashlight beam swept across us. "I said to stop!" a guard yelled.

"Not today!" Jace yelled, vaulting over.

We dropped down on the other side and hit the ground running again.

The asphalt chewed at my shoes, the cold air burning in my chest. Freedom wasn't clean, it turns out; it was sweaty and filled with a shaky kind of relief where you were proud you hadn't pissed yourself.

Behind us, the alarm still howled. Ahead, the dark stretch of road promised nothing but silence.

We didn't stop until we reached the car.

I collapsed against the hood, chest heaving. Parker bent over, hands braced on his knees, gasping. Jace sprawled flat on the pavement, arms and legs splayed like a crime-scene outline.

"Well," he said between ragged breaths, "that went perfectly."

"Perfectly?" Parker wheezed. "You tripped, lost a shoe, and almost got us caught."

Jace straightened, still gasping, and flashed a grin. "Yeah, but I stuck the landing—and that's what people will remember."

"I don't even know what that means," I said as I slid down next to him, clutching the ledger. My hands still shook, but a laugh broke out anyway—wild and breathless and uncontrollable. Within seconds, Parker cracked, too, shaking his head. Jace followed, the three of us laughing like lunatics in the dark. The kind of laughter that only came when you realized you'd somehow pulled off something impossible.

Finally, Parker wiped his face, still grinning. "We need to go. *Now.*"

We piled into the car, doors slamming in near unison. I jammed the keys into the ignition, tires squealing as we tore down the empty road. The glow of the campus faded in the rearview mirror, alarms still wailing somewhere behind us.

Silence settled heavy over the car, only the hum of the engine filling the space. My pulse was still hammering when I heard it—*crinkle.*

I frowned. "What was that?"

Another *crinkle.*

I glanced back. Jace sat there, seat belt crooked, hair a wreck, an Oreo halfway to his mouth.

He froze mid-chew, his eyes meeting mine. "What?" he mumbled around the cookie. "Along with stress-eating, I also believe in recovery snacks."

Parker groaned. "You're unbelievable."

Jace grinned, unbothered. "Maybe. But I'm calm, and you two look like you just aged ten years, so who's really winning?"

I snorted and shook my head, glancing down at the ledger in my lap.

One trial down. One step closer to Sphinx membership and all it would mean for me.

But as the road unspooled in front of us, my mind drifted back to the other thing clawing at me . . . another puzzle I hadn't solved.

My mystery girl.

I pressed my foot down on the gas, a faint smile tugging at my mouth.

Time to figure out her name.

CHAPTER 11

OPHELIA

The phone buzzed like it was trying to tell me a secret I didn't want to hear. I let it sit in my palm and vibrate for a beat, which felt like resistance, and then I answered because my mother's name didn't allow for dramatic pauses.

"Hi, Mom," I said in the voice I'd practiced with Dr. Whitaker for situations where honesty would be a liability.

"Ophelia." No hello, no niceties. My mother always started like she was reading a report that needed auditing. "How are you right now?"

I looked at the tiger head next to me, painted eyes, ridiculous smile, and wished it could warn her off. "Fine. I'm about to go out on the field."

There was a pause, but she didn't ask about my game-day duties. She never did. My mom had never been to a game, never even pretended to care about football or school spirit.

Not that that was why I was doing it . . .

"You sound tired." Her tone wasn't gentle; it was clipped, controlled, the kind she used when she was assessing, not asking. "Did you reschedule with Dr. Whitaker yet?"

I hesitated. "I got busy."

"That's not an excuse," she said, her voice going colder. "You'll call tomorrow to reschedule. Do you understand?"

My grip tightened on the tiger head beside me. "I will."

"Good." Another pause. "And you've been keeping up with your grounding exercises?"

The word made something in me tighten. "Yeah," I said after a beat. "I've been doing them."

"You're sure?" she pressed, that familiar edge of suspicion creeping in.

"I'm sure."

There was a stretch of silence, then the sound of her measured inhale. I didn't have time . . . but she went through the checklist anyway—Dr. Whitaker, breathe, name five things, call someone—the routine she'd drilled into me until I could recite it in my sleep.

"Text me after the game," she said finally. "Just a quick 'I'm fine.' Don't make me remind you."

"I'll text," I said.

It was easier than arguing.

"Good." And then the line went dead.

I slipped my phone into my pocket and pulled the tiger head on, the foam pressing in around my face until the world shrank to a narrow tunnel of fabric and mesh. The inside smelled like Febreze . . . not a crisp kind of clean, but the desperate kind, two quick sprays trying to cover a season's worth of sweat.

The foam head scratched against my forehead every time I moved, the neckline rubbed the skin under my jaw until it burned, and my exhales came back at me hot and sour.

The crowd roared somewhere beyond the tunnel, the band already playing. I took a steadying breath and stepped out into the light.

Instantly, the noise hit . . . drums, whistles, a thousand voices melting into one. The world outside reduced itself to two grainy ovals of mesh, a tunnel of color and motion that made everything feel far away.

And honestly? I was glad for it. The narrowness. The heat. The way no one could see my face.

Underneath the fur and foam, nobody could tell how empty I looked. How much effort it took just to stand here, pretending to cheer when all I wanted was to disappear. The anonymity was the only thing that made it bearable, the only reason I could still show up without crumbling.

I hadn't started out looking like this.

When I'd tried out, it was for *him*. Because if I couldn't sit beside him, couldn't touch him, couldn't *have* him, at least I could stand twenty yards away instead of two hundred. Close enough to breathe the same air and pretend that was enough.

Now, it felt like punishment.

He was still here, out there on the field, helmet glinting under the lights . . . but every second, I had to remind myself I was done with him. I had to force my eyes to stay off number twenty-three, to cheer for the team without looking for him. And the worst part was, I'd be stuck in this suffocating suit for the rest of the season, waving and dancing and pretending like I wasn't cheering with a broken heart.

I guess at least I was good at it. Once, tumbling had been mine. Saturday cheer gyms, chalk dust in the air, roundoffs and back handsprings until my wrists ached. Competitions where the mats smelled like rubber and sweat, and the sound of the crowd was enough to make me feel like I mattered.

The years away from a mat had rusted it all. So the week I saw that flyer and I'd gotten the idea to be the tiger, it had felt like starting over.

I'd practiced everywhere I could.

The rec center in the weird hour between intramurals and the janitor making his rounds. My dorm room with a pad that was basically a yoga mat pretending to be a spring floor. I pulled and stretched until my hamstrings cried, I rocked into bridges until my shoulders loosened, I did roundoffs into wobbly back handsprings until the fear shut up. The first time I didn't fall, I lay on the floor and laughed until I was crying because I was so shocked that I'd managed to do it.

I auditioned. I got the phone call. I picked up the suit the same day they handed me the laminated schedule that said when I'd be on the field, when I'd learn dances with the team . . . when I'd be a cartoon with a permanent grin.

And since that moment, every eight-count had been for him.

Now, I didn't know who it was for.

The speakers thumped, and the crowd swelled like a tide. The first horn stab of Beyoncé's "Crazy in Love" punched across the stadium, and the student section lost their collective minds. To my left, the dance team snapped into motion, ponytails arcing like metronomes, sequins strobing in the lights. Their smiles were a language; I didn't speak it, so the suit did it for me. I raised my foam paws, tilted the tiger head on the beat, hit the arm sweeps big enough to read in the upper decks.

It was loud enough to make my bones hum. Bass rumbled through the turf. The drum line under the bleachers added a heartbeat to the song. The counts clicked in my head the way they always did now—five, six, seven, eight, hit-hit, travel, hold—and my body moved, grateful for the instruction manual. Grateful I was just the tiger . . . a joke everyone could love.

Instead of the joke I really was.

I clapped and popped my knees and threw in the back handspring on the diagonal I'd practiced three hundred times in the rec center when no one was looking. The head wobbled and then settled; I landed with my feet exactly on my taped marks. The crowd roared like I'd done something miraculous. The dancers next to me grinned toward the first row. My breath scraped my throat and came back to me damp. For a handful of beats, moving swallowed everything else.

My gaze finally slipped before I could stop it, though, drawn by something I couldn't seem to fight. It tunneled through the mesh, cutting past the dancers, the band, the cheer arc, the roaring crowd . . . past everything until it landed exactly where it always did.

Matty Adler stood at the sideline, his helmet tucked under one arm. His black hair was curled damp at the ends; the tape on his right wrist flashed white, then dull, then white again as he flexed his fingers. Parker said something, his mouth wide with a laugh, and Jace, because he was apparently incapable of not being a cartoon even when there was already a cartoon on the field, did a ridiculous shimmy the exact second the horns hit again.

Matty wasn't paying attention to me. He just stood there. Calm. At ease. The sort of confidence that drew every eye without even trying.

And even though he wasn't looking . . . I still danced harder.

The final beat crashed. The dancers froze in glittering lines, and I struck my pose in the middle, foam paws raised high. The whistle blew, the crowd erupted, and the field began to clear.

I tugged at the Velcro under my chin, my lungs begging for air. Sweat was sliding down my spine, soaking my sports bra, and my hair was plastered against my temples. I wanted to rip the tiger head off right there.

But I couldn't.

Not yet. Not while the team was still shifting onto the field.

The kickoff thundered, and the ball sliced through the air before vanishing into a blur of helmets and motion. The crowd roared, a single, pulsing wall of sound as players collided and the band blasted to life. The dance team peeled toward the benches, laughing and fanning themselves, their glitter catching the lights like scattered sparks.

"Take five!" one of the spirit coordinators called, waving me off toward the tunnel.

Grateful for the break, I grabbed a water bottle and jogged off the sideline, the tiger head bobbling with every step. My gaze wanted to stray toward the field to look at him, but I kept it straight ahead this time.

Progress.

Inside the tunnel, the noise faded to a hum as the crowd, band, and announcer blurred into the background.

I tugged the head off and let out a heavy breath. Cool air hit my skin, washing over my sweaty hair and flushed face. It felt incredible after the stifling heat inside the suit, the kind of relief that made my shoulders drop and my pulse slow. I took another deep breath, the air tasting clean and alive compared to the recycled heat I'd been breathing for the last quarter.

A whistle blew out on the field, high and urgent, the sound echoing down the tunnel. It was followed by a rush of noise that wasn't cheering. The crowd's roar shifted, rough and angry, and then I heard booing.

I froze mid-sip, the water bottle paused halfway to my mouth.

The announcer's voice crackled faintly through the speakers, too muffled to make out over the commotion. Another whistle. Shouts. The restless wave of thousands of voices rising at once.

My fingers tightened around the bottle. I stepped closer to the tunnel entrance, light spilling over my shoes. I couldn't see the field, only the edge of it, where shadows flickered in and out of the glare.

Then two figures came into view. A trainer, and beside him, Matty.

He was limping, one arm slung around the trainer's shoulders for balance. His helmet hung from his hand, his other arm held tight against his ribs. Sweat stuck his hair to his forehead, and his face was set in a hard, unflinching line. He didn't look at the stands, didn't acknowledge the noise, just kept walking.

Each step looked like it cost him.

I stood there frozen, the tiger head heavy in my hands, my heart pounding so hard it made me lightheaded. My stomach sank like a stone.

He was coming straight toward me.

I fumbled for the tiger head, trying to lift it, but before I could get it over my face, he looked up. Our eyes met across the stretch of tunnel, and for a second, the rest of the world disappeared.

Shock flickered across his face, halting him mid-step. The trainer glanced at him in confusion, murmuring something I couldn't hear. Then, slowly, his expression changed. The tension in his jaw eased, and a small, crooked smile tugged at his mouth . . . the kind that had wrecked me a hundred times before when I'd watched him direct it to someone else.

The trainer said something again, tugging lightly on his arm, but Matty didn't move. His gaze stayed locked on me. That smile deepened, lazy and warm, and even from where I stood, I could see the faint dimple crease his cheek.

"Well," he said slyly, "I didn't realize the tiger was actually the most beautiful girl on campus."

My face went up in flames. I could feel it, even through the heat still clinging to my skin. His grin widened like he knew exactly what he was doing.

"You're blushing again," he said softly, amused, like it was a secret only we shared.

My throat tightened. I swallowed hard and managed to find my voice. "Are you . . . are you okay?" The words slipped out before I could stop them, my worry too obvious for a person who was supposed to be a stranger.

He tilted his head, considering me. For a heartbeat, the smile faded, replaced by something gentler, almost tender. "I'm okay, baby."

The word *baby* hit me physically. My knees went weak. I had to grip the edge of the tiger head just to stay upright, hoping he couldn't see how my hands trembled.

He chuckled quietly, the charm sliding back into place. "So," he said, the corner of his mouth curving again, "you gonna tell me your name yet? Feels like since we're both so into school spirit, I deserve to know who's behind the stripes."

I couldn't speak. Couldn't even breathe. I just shook my head.

And when he laughed, I realized . . . he didn't think it was weird. He didn't see it as anything more than a coincidence that I was the tiger.

The relief that flooded through me was dizzying. He didn't know. He had no idea.

He smiled wider, his eyes glinting. "Alright, then, Tiger. Keep your secrets."

"Adler," the trainer said exasperatedly, pulling on his arm again. "Let's get that ankle looked at."

Matty exhaled through his nose, still watching me like he wasn't ready to move. "Yeah, yeah, I'm coming," he muttered, his grin lingering as he continued past me.

He'd barely taken three steps when a voice echoed from the far end of the tunnel . . . the spirit coordinator appeared, her tone clipped and impatient.

"Five minutes are up, Ophelia!"

Her voice cracked through the air like a gunshot. My whole body went still.

Matty stopped. The trainers did, too, glancing at each other. Slowly, he turned his head back toward me.

"Ophelia?" he repeated, his voice soft, almost curious. The name rolled off his tongue like he was testing it, tasting it . . . savoring it. "That's your name?"

For a heartbeat, his grin flickered, half amusement, half disbelief. Then it shifted, tightening at the edges, something darker creeping in beneath the charm.

My stomach twisted.

He didn't say anything else, just looked at me for a long moment before the trainer tugged him forward again. But that look, sharp and knowing, followed me long after he disappeared down the tunnel.

By the time the fourth quarter rolled around, the ache in my chest hadn't faded. The crowd pulsed with a wild kind of energy, the bleachers shaking under the weight of stomping feet and shouting voices. It felt like the whole stadium was breathing in unison—loud, fevered, unstoppable.

But all I could feel was that last look he'd given me . . . etched behind my eyelids, sitting heavy under my skin. I'd replayed it a hundred times between cheers and tumbles, between the fake energy and the forced exuberance. Every time, my stomach flipped the same way it had when he said my name.

"Alright!" the spirit coordinator shouted, clapping her hands as the scoreboard flashed 21–17, South Carolina on top. Losing Matty had been a big blow, even with all the offensive weapons on the team. "Last push! Big finish!"

Groans rippled through the sideline, but the girls still forced bright smiles, shaking out their pom-poms as the band kicked up another fight song that sounded a little too hopeful for how the game was going.

I nodded, though the world outside the mesh was a blur of lights and sound, a haze of orange and white. My legs ached. My throat was dry. And every so often, when the noise died down between plays, I thought I could still hear his voice.

I forced my arms to move, my head to nod in rhythm, but my thoughts were nowhere near the field. They were on him. The tunnel. His voice when he'd said *baby*.

The crowd suddenly erupted again, a surge so fierce it vibrated through the turf and up my legs.

I scanned the field until I spotted him . . . Matty, jogging back onto the field, his stride uneven with the faintest limp.

He jogged to his spot on the line, shaking out his hands as the offense reset. Parker shouted something to him, and Matty turned his head, nodded once, and settled into position.

My breath caught. He shouldn't have been out there, not after limping off like that, pain etched into every move. But there he was, determined as ever, his jaw tight . . . eyes locked downfield like he could will the game to bend his way.

The line shifted. The center snapped the ball, and the roar of the crowd fell into a strange, suspended hush . . . like the whole stadium was holding its breath.

Helmets cracked, bodies slammed, and through the chaos, I caught a flash of him. Matty. Breaking free. His stride uneven but relentless, driving forward as if pain didn't exist. Parker launched the ball, a perfect spiral slicing through the sky.

And Matty caught it.

He dodged the first defender with a quick side step that shouldn't have been possible on that ankle, the second with a twist that left the guy grabbing at air. Two more came for him, closing fast, and Matty cut left, slipping through the gap like he'd rehearsed it a thousand times.

The field opened up ahead of him. Forty yards. Thirty.

The crowd's noise climbed, a rolling thunder that shook through the turf and into my chest. He shouldn't have been that fast. Not when he'd limped off barely an hour ago.

A defender dove, fingertips grazing his jersey . . . but Matty didn't break stride. He drove forward, the ball locked tight against his side, every step defying reason.

And then he crossed the line into the end zone. Touchdown. The scoreboard flashed. The Tigers won.

Momentum carried him a few more feet before he dropped to one knee, his head bowed, clutching the ball to his chest like he could feel the heartbeat of the win inside it.

The crowd had gone feral. Students vaulted over barriers. The band screamed out the fight song like it was a war cry. Gold-and-white confetti cannons exploded somewhere to my left, dusting the field in a storm of color and light.

But Matty wasn't looking at the crowd as he stood up, he wasn't taking in the way they were worshiping him.

His gaze cut through the noise, searching . . . and then locking. On me?

My feet stuttered to a stop, the heavy tiger head bobbling slightly as heat prickled down my spine. He was still twenty yards away, his teammates slapping his back, shouting, celebrating . . . but he still didn't take his eyes off me.

A nervous laugh caught in my throat as I glanced over my shoulder, half expecting to see someone else behind me. A cheerleader, a reporter, anyone who actually belonged in his world. But there was no one in particular I could see. Just me.

My lungs forgot how to work.

He started walking. Then jogging . . . slow, uneven steps at first, the limp still there. The helmet came off with one easy motion, his dark hair curling at the edges, sweat glinting along his neck. The lights hit his face, and that grin, completely devastating, spread across his mouth.

Cameras might've been everywhere, the whole stadium watching—but it still felt like he was moving through the noise just for me.

My breath caught behind the mesh as he closed the distance between us, stopping right in front of me. His gaze traveled over the ridiculous suit like he could see straight through it.

Then he smiled. The slow, dangerous kind that usually meant trouble. I'd learned that after all my months of watching him.

"I have to say," he murmured, leaning closer, "finding out you've been here on the sidelines with me all season? It feels like fate."

The words sent a rush through me, hot and dizzying. I took a small step back, the tail of the suit brushing the turf.

He didn't let me retreat.

Matty reached out, his gloved hand catching the side of the tiger's head, holding it steady. His thumb traced the painted cheek, and the world tilted on its axis. The crowd, the band, the deafening roar . . . all of it blurred into silence.

Then he leaned in.

His mouth pressed against the mesh, not my skin, but close enough that it didn't matter. The faint scratch of fabric, the heat of his breath, the pressure—it stole every thought I had. The kiss wasn't soft or careful. It was fierce, unapologetic, the kind meant to leave a mark even through layers of foam and fur.

Some part of me knew he was kissing the *tiger's* grin . . . that our lips weren't actually touching. But my heart didn't seem to care. It felt like the whole world had just shifted around that single impossible moment.

So impossible, it felt like I would wake up any second now and find out I'd been dreaming this entire time.

I was vaguely aware of the stadium getting even louder . . . of students screaming, and the band losing their rhythm entirely. Somewhere close by, I think someone shrieked Matty's name.

All of it was background noise, though. Nothing compared to the fact that his arms were wrapped around me and he'd pulled me against him even though everything about my tiger costume was awkwardly shaped.

He pulled back with that grin that could end civilizations. "Guess I'll have to do that again when you're not wearing twenty pounds of fur," he said, his voice low enough that it was meant only for me. "Gotta let everyone know who my lucky tiger really is."

The words had barely left his mouth when a sideline reporter rushed in, shoving a microphone toward him as her camera crew swarmed closer. "Matty, how's the ankle? What was going through your head on that play? Was that kiss planned?" she fired off.

Matty didn't even blink.

He snatched the mic right out of her hand.

"Ophelia," he said into it, his voice amplified just enough to carry over the nearest cameras and sideline noise. That grin curved slow and certain, the kind that said he knew *exactly* what he was doing . . . and that he wanted everyone close enough to hear it. "You can run if you want, but everyone here just saw it. I'll find you. Tunnel, dorms, hell, even the moon, if I have to."

The crowd detonated. The reporter gaped. Cameras flashed like lightning.

I froze, my heart slamming so hard I thought I'd pass out right there in the suit.

Then instinct kicked in.

I turned and ran, sprinting for the tunnel, the tiger head wobbling, foam paws thudding against the turf. The roar of the crowd followed . . . screams, laughter, the echo of his voice chasing me down the field like a fire I couldn't put out.

The kiss still burned through the mask, seared into my skin, into my pulse.

And beneath it, one thought pounded hard and undeniable in my head.

I don't think Matty Adler is ignoring me anymore.

CHAPTER 12

MATTY

I can feel you staring at me," I said without looking up.

The tape around my wrist was slick with sweat. I pulled at it slowly, the edges catching on my skin.

Jace didn't even try to deny it. "Hard not to when you just made out with the mascot on live TV, Matty-kins."

The locker room erupted. Towels smacked against benches, someone whistled, and Parker's laugh rolled above the noise.

"You're one of us now," Parker said, his voice full of smug satisfaction. "Welcome to the club of men who've lost their minds over a girl."

I dragged a towel over my face, not bothering to respond.

Garrett snorted from across the aisle. "Difference is, your girls didn't have fur."

Jace grinned. "He's breaking new ground. I'm proud."

I shot him a glare, but he just grinned wider, that pretty-boy, golden-hair-falling-in-his-eyes grin that made Riley forgive him for saying shit like that.

"Her name's Ophelia," I said reverently.

I hadn't stopped saying it in my head since I heard it shouted down the tunnel during the game.

It rolled around my brain on constant replay. Every syllable had its own pull. Soft, dangerous. Beautiful. Just like her.

Ophelia.

It was ridiculous how much power a single word could have. How her name alone could make me feel something claw its way up my chest like it belonged there.

Jace whistled delightedly. "Is that the same girl you met in class a few days ago? The one I witnessed you screaming after like a lunatic as she was walking away?"

Parker laughed under his breath. "Wait, that was her?"

I didn't answer, which was answer enough.

Jace shook his head with a grin. "Her name and a public make-out in one week? Impressive, *Matthew*. I wouldn't have thought you had it in you."

I scowled at him. "Need I remind you I have multiple stalkers? Obviously, I have game when it comes to women."

"Then why does she keep running away from you?" Garrett mused.

"And why has your parking lot stalker been a no-show as of late?" Jace pointed out.

My scowl deepened at that reminder. Although, it had been hard to remember anything about that with Ophelia taking up so much room in my mind.

Parker tossed me a bottle of water, and I caught it without looking. I twisted the cap and took a drink, preparing myself for whatever mockery I was going to get next.

Jace leaned forward, elbows braced on his knees, that grin turning wicked. "So, what's the plan, Adler? You gonna lurk outside the tunnel until she shows up? Steal her mascot head and keep it as a trophy? Sleep with it under your pillow?"

I tilted my head, letting my voice go quiet and thoughtful. "Hmm. Should I sleep under her bed instead? Maybe put a tracker in her neck? Or get her kicked out of her dorm room so she has to move in with me?"

The group went silent for half a beat.

Jace froze mid-smirk. "You—"

Garrett's gaze flicked between us. "That sounds . . . oddly specific."

Parker didn't even try to hide his grin. "It does, doesn't it?"

I smirked at him. "Should I make another list for you?"

That earned a low laugh from Parker, the kind that said he was both amused and absolutely unbothered. "Go ahead. I could use a refresher."

I groaned, dragging a hand over my face. "I need to remind myself not to take romantic advice from the two of you."

Parker's grin widened. "You say that now, but give it a week, and you'll be calling us for tips."

Jace nodded. "You can't deny that we're experts in getting the girl."

I snorted. "I guess that's one way to describe felony-level courtship."

Parker didn't even flinch. "I prefer to call it *effective-level* courtship."

"Y'all are hilarious," I muttered.

I was giving them a hard time, but I couldn't deny my mind was going to some crazy places.

Not the pillow thing. I wasn't that far gone.

But other things . . .

Like how I wanted to know the exact brand of perfume she wore, what time she went to bed, what she looked like sleeping.

I wanted her routine mapped out in my head like a playbook—every move, every breath, every fucking heartbeat.

I wanted to know what her face would look like if I slipped a note under her door that said *I miss you*, even though she didn't know she was mine to miss yet.

I wanted to steal a strand of her hair, twist it around my finger like a ring until it was part of me.

I wanted to hack into her phone's location data, watch that little dot pulse across campus, knowing I could be there in seconds if she strayed too far.

I wanted to leave my jersey in her dorm closet, folded neat with a drop of my blood on the collar from a fresh cut, just to mark the space as mine.

I wanted to carve our initials into the goalpost at the stadium, deep enough that they'd have to tear the whole thing down to erase it.

Holy shit.

Why did none of those things actually feel crazy . . . ? Why did they instead feel . . . inevitable?

Maybe not the hacking her location thing . . . I'd probably never be able to figure out how to do *that*.

But the rest . . . They all didn't seem like things completely out of the realm of possibility.

Shit.

"You're thinking about her right now, aren't you? I can practically hear the obsessive narration forming in your head," teased Jace.

"Go to hell," I said mildly.

He laughed. "You're already there with me, man. You just don't know it yet. And spoiler alert . . . it is sweet."

Parker leaned back, a towel slung around his neck. "He's got that look we all had. The one where you're pretending it's just curiosity. I'll just save you the suspense—it never is."

The guys' laughter filled the room again, but I barely heard it.

Because they weren't wrong.

Even if I wanted to fight it . . . I was starting to wonder if it was already too late.

I could still feel her against me, the way her body trembled.

Ophelia.

I twisted the cap back onto the water bottle and leaned forward, elbows on my knees.

I wasn't sure what the next step was . . . I just knew it involved me finding her.

And keeping her.

Not because I was supposed to, but because I *needed* to.

Fuck.

The hallway outside the locker room was mostly empty now, the sound of the crowd long gone. There was nothing but the echo of my sneakers against the concrete and the faint hum of lights burning overhead.

My hair was still damp from the shower, my hands jammed in my pockets, the collar of my hoodie brushing my jaw. I should've felt calm by now—the interviews were done, the press had gotten their sound bites, the trainers had cleared my ankle.

But calm wasn't happening.

My pulse was still running the game like it hadn't ended. Every time I blinked, I saw her . . . the flash of her eyes in the tunnel, the way she'd whispered when she spoke like she didn't know if she was allowed to talk to me or not.

I didn't think I could go the whole night without seeing her again.

Jace had somehow hacked into the school records system earlier—on his phone, of all things—and pulled up the dorm list like it was nothing. He'd texted me her room number during the postgame press conference with a winking emoji and the words *Don't do anything I wouldn't do*.

Which, considering who it came from, covered exactly nothing.

I hadn't even opened the message yet, afraid that once I saw it, I'd use it.

But standing in that hallway, the temptation was about to kill me.

I could picture it, me standing outside her window, watching her lie in bed, her hair spilling across a pillow.

My fingers itched toward my phone.

Just to look. Just to *see*.

One glance.

I was still trying to decide which version of crazy would make me feel less pathetic when I turned the corner—and stopped short.

"Matty!"

Lizzie came tearing down the hallway, her pigtails bouncing, the sleeves of her orange hoodie flapping past her hands. She was half flying, half tripping, and I barely had time to catch her before she collided with me.

"Whoa there," I said, laughing as my little sister wrapped her arms around my waist. "You trying to take me out before next week's game?"

"You won!" she said, muffled against my chest. "You said you'd score for me!"

I glanced down at her and smiled. "And I did, didn't I?"

She nodded enthusiastically, her ponytails hitting my chin.

I smoothed a hand over her hair, still smiling—and then I looked up.

The smile dropped before I could stop it.

Dad was walking toward us, his steps measured, that half smile fixed in place . . . the one that he used when he was trying to impress someone. Usually he wore a jersey to my games, but tonight he was dressed up. Dark jeans, a crisp button-down, his watch polished and cuff links gleaming.

Strange.

Beside him was a man I didn't recognize, dressed in a tailored suit with a clipboard under one arm and slicked-back hair. He looked like a contract given human form.

I peered behind them, expecting my mom and brothers to be somewhere. They always came. Even if it meant five hours in the car, even if it meant getting home at two a.m., they showed up—every single game. Mom with her orange scarf and hoarse voice. The boys in face paint, yelling my number like lunatics.

I didn't see them, though.

"Nice finish," Dad said as he reached us, his voice smooth . . . and weird. "That last touchdown—you made it look effortless."

"Thanks," I said, keeping my tone neutral.

He motioned to the man beside him. "This is Kenton Hale. He's been helping me with a few things."

Kenton stepped forward, offering a hand. "Good to meet you, Matthew. How's the ankle holding up?"

I blinked, caught off guard. "Fine."

He smiled, polite and unreadable. "You looked solid out there. Strong close."

"Appreciate it."

Dad's hand landed on Lizzie's shoulder. "We were just about to grab dinner. Thought you'd want to join us."

Before I could answer, Lizzie gasped like he'd told her a secret. "Please, Matty? Daddy said we're going somewhere *really* nice! They have chocolate cake with sprinkles."

I looked down at her. She was practically bouncing, tugging at my arm with both hands, her face glowing with that mix of hope and sugar-fueled joy that made her impossible to resist.

"Please?" she begged again, her grin wide. "You have to come with us!"

I couldn't help the small grin that tugged at my mouth. "When do I not, princess?"

She squealed, wrapping her arms tight around my waist. "I knew you'd say yes!"

"I'm predictable," I said, smoothing a hand over her hair again.

Dad's smile returned, faint but satisfied. "Car's waiting out front."

Lizzie skipped ahead toward the exit, humming. Kenton followed at a polite distance, clipboard still under his arm, every inch the polished stranger.

I lingered for a second, my gaze drifting back to Dad.

He did look good . . . sharper than I'd seen him in months. The kind of detail work he only bothered with when there was something to gain.

The sight made something tight twist in my chest.

I always went to these dinners. Every home game. They were never about celebration—just long, uncomfortable nights at overpriced restaurants where he ordered the steak, the wine, the dessert, and I paid the check without argument.

It was routine by now. A quiet transaction disguised as family time.

Speaking of family time . . . I cleared my throat. "So where's Mom? And the boys?"

He didn't miss a beat. "They stayed home this time. Long drive."

My stomach sank. "Mom never misses a home game."

"She needed a break. She's been taking on more shifts," he said easily, already turning toward the doors. "Let's go. Your sister's starving."

I followed him out, any more words sticking in my throat.

Except when we stepped into the night air, it wasn't his old beat-up pickup waiting by the curb.

A black sedan idled under the stadium lights, sleek and glossy with tinted windows and a uniformed driver standing at the door.

Lizzie was already bouncing beside it, wide-eyed. "Whoa. It's like a movie car!"

I slowed. "What's with the driver?"

Dad's tone was casual. "It's Kenton's. He offered."

Of course he did.

My jaw flexed as I stared at the car. Men like Kenton didn't *offer* anything unless there was something in it for them. And my dad didn't say yes unless he'd already figured out how to make that favor work to his advantage.

The whole thing reeked of performance—his cleaned-up look, the too-nice car, the timing. Like he'd staged the evening before I even stepped out of the locker room.

I shoved my hands in my pockets. "I can just meet you there. Need to grab something from my car anyway."

Dad glanced at me with a tight, annoyed smile. "Don't be ridiculous."

Before I could reply, his hand landed between my shoulder blades, the kind of gentle shove that wasn't really gentle at all. "Get in, Matthew."

It wasn't a request.

So, I did what I'd been doing my whole life—I followed his orders.

The driver opened the door, and Lizzie climbed in first, still marveling at the leather seats. I ducked in after her, sliding to the far side, and Dad took the spot beside Kenton, who looked perfectly at home.

The door shut with a quiet *thud* that sounded . . . ominous.

Cologne and the smell of old money lingered in the car, and the hum of the engine filled the silence until Dad started talking, loud and confident, like he was pitching a deal instead of sitting in the back seat with his kids.

"You should've seen his last drive against Alabama," he told Kenton in a voice full of rehearsed pride. "Fourteen yards out, double coverage, still found the opening. He's always been good under pressure."

Kenton made an approving sound. "Impressive."

Lizzie tried to jump in. "And he promised—"

"Best completion percentage on the team," Dad cut her off, not even glancing her way. "And his yards after catch are ridiculous this season."

She slumped against me, quiet now, tracing little circles on the back of my hand with her finger.

I stared out the window, watching the city lights smear against the glass as we sped through downtown.

He kept going. Stats, rankings, scouting reports.

Kenton nodded along, polite, smiling when appropriate.

Lizzie didn't try again.

And I didn't bother stopping him.

Because I already knew this wasn't about football.

It was about whatever deal was waiting for us at the end of the drive . . . and the part of me my dad was trying to sell.

The restaurant was even fancier than the usual places my dad found for me to pay for. Low lights pooled over linen, servers moved like rehearsed ghosts, and the menu read like a challenge. I'd eaten in plenty of nice places since coming to college, but this one didn't feel like a restaurant.

It felt like a negotiation waiting to happen.

We were led to a corner table that was tucked away from the rest of the dining room. The leather banquette was soft enough that Lizzie flopped back into it and squealed. "Look at the lights!" she breathed with huge eyes, staring up at the giant chandelier above us. "Can I get the cake *and* the ice cream for dessert?"

Dad chuckled, sliding the menu toward her. "Of course, sweetheart. Anything you want."

The way he said it made something sour rise in my throat. Both he and Kenton seemed to be trying very hard to pretend like this was all normal.

And for a while, it all *was* normal.

Lizzie chattered about the mascot, asking why I had kissed it, and I let myself briefly smile at the thought of Ophelia.

Dad chuckled. "That was one hell of a touchdown celebration, son. The crowd loved it. Stuff like that sticks. It's great for your brand."

I didn't bother correcting him. Let him think it was about publicity instead of the girl I couldn't stop thinking about.

It was easier that way.

Kenton made pleasant noises while Lizzie continued to chatter throughout dinner, nodding at all the right places. He asked, offhand, about her teacher and whether she liked school. There was something too smooth about it, like he'd practiced being kind just enough to make people trust him. I didn't buy it, but Lizzie beamed at the attention, and I let her have it.

We ate. The food arrived like small sculptures . . . seafood that tasted like the ocean had been edited for flavor, steak sliced thin and served like an afterthought to the sauce. Dad made more small talk by asking me about our championship chances, while Kenton complimented me on my "marketability," and all the attention I was getting.

When the waiter finally walked away after dropping off our desserts, Kenton turned his glass in his hand, the reflection of the candlelight glinting off his watch. "You've built quite a reputation for yourself, Matthew," he began. "It's impressive. The kind of thing people notice."

Dad smiled like he was being complimented, too. "He's worked for it. Always has."

"Discipline like that," Kenton said. "It's rare. And valuable."

There it was.

I kept my tone flat. "I'm sure it is."

He smiled like he'd been waiting for the cue. My eyes flicked to my father, who was sitting there, his face eager, practically leaning forward in anticipation.

"Which brings us to why I wanted to take you to dinner tonight."

Lizzie's spoon clinked against her bowl. I felt her eyes flick toward us but she stayed quiet, distracted by the tiny dish of ice cream the waiter had just brought to go with her cake.

Kenton leaned forward slightly, elbows on the table, voice lowering. "You've got something most people don't—access from *inside* the team. You see things before anyone else does. A guy limping in practice, a tweak he's hiding, who's not running full speed, who's taking extra treatment. Little details, nothing major. But information like that . . ." He paused, smiling faintly. "It's worth a lot. To the right people."

My grip tightened around the fork.

Dad spoke next, clearly trying to tamp down his excitement and pretend like this was no big deal. "He's not talking about anything dangerous, Matty. Just . . . strategic insights. You could help us all out."

I stared at him. "You want me to feed you information about the team?"

"Not just us," Kenton corrected, still calm. "We're a network. Think of it as . . . risk assessment. A way for investors to make informed decisions. No harm, no foul."

"That's betting," I said flatly.

Kenton smiled like I'd said something quaint. "That's *business*. And in business, information is currency."

He let the words hang there.

My pulse thudded in my ears. "You're asking me to sell out my teammates."

Dad frowned, like I was being dramatic. "Don't say it like that. You wouldn't be hurting anyone. Just letting us know when something might affect a game. If someone's ankle's bothering them, if Parker's shoulder's tight before kickoff, if a starter's not at a hundred percent. The coaches already know—this would just—broaden awareness."

Broaden awareness. Fucking hell.

Kenton folded his hands neatly, looking every inch the businessman instead of the criminal he was. "All you'd do is send a text. Quiet. Anonymous. You'd be paid well for it. And you'd be helping people place smarter bets, which keeps the market stable. It's all aboveboard in its own way."

I almost laughed. "'In its own way'?"

He ignored that. "You'd be surprised how many athletes are already part of it. We don't ask anyone to throw games, Matthew. You'd never compromise play integrity. We just need information. Early information."

Dad nodded, like this was all perfectly reasonable. "You could make a lot of money, son. More than most players see in their first five years in the NFL."

I dropped my fork, the sound loud in the quiet room. "You're out of your damn mind."

Kenton didn't flinch. "You don't have to decide tonight. But I'd think carefully before saying no. It's not illegal to talk. And people appreciate loyalty."

The word *loyalty* landed like a threat wrapped in velvet.

Dad leaned closer, his voice soft, persuasive. "Think about your future, Matty. All it takes is one injury, and the NFL's gone. This? This could set you up for life. You've got to be smart."

I stared at him. "Smart isn't selling information to a bookie."

Kenton's mouth twitched. "That's a very narrow way of looking at it."

My blood was roaring now. I could feel it under my skin, that familiar storm I only got on the field. "You're talking about gambling rings. You're talking about manipulating lines and insider trading on people's injuries. You want me to spy for you."

Dad's expression hardened. "Lower your voice."

"No." I stood abruptly, the chair scraping across the floor. Lizzie jumped, spoon clattering against porcelain. "You brought my little sister here to make this look like a family dinner. You dressed up. You waited until dessert to pitch me like I'm a fucking mark. I'm not doing it."

"Matty—"

"I said no."

Kenton's tone stayed infuriatingly calm. "You'll want to be careful about closing doors too quickly. The people I work with value cooperation."

I looked him dead in the eye. "So do I. Which is why I'm not getting into business with an asshole like you."

Lizzie's lower lip trembled. "Matty, don't go," she whispered.

I crouched next to her, brushing her hair back from her face. "I'm sorry, princess," I murmured, pressing a kiss to her cheek. "Finish your cake, okay? You deserve it for being my number one fan."

"Don't leave mad," she said, tears spilling down her cheeks.

I smiled, even though it hurt. "I'm not mad at you."

Dad was gaping at me in shock. Kenton just watched with cold eyes.

I turned and strode out before either of them could say another word. The air outside hit hard, cutting through the heat still crawling up my neck. My pulse was still hammering when I heard it behind me.

"Matthew!"

My father's voice filled the air, sharp and authoritative . . . like I was still fifteen and supposed to come running.

I didn't slow down.

"Don't walk away from me, young man!"

The sound of my name was swallowed by the wind, and I started to jog, knowing he wouldn't be able to catch up with me.

A second later, my phone buzzed in my pocket with a call from him.

Of course.

It started ringing again the second after I sent it to voicemail. Then again. And again.

I clenched my jaw, hit ignore, and kept going until the lights from the restaurant were a smear behind me. I didn't even know where the hell I was headed. I just knew I needed distance, asphalt, and air that didn't smell like him.

When the screen lit up for the fifth time, I thumbed to Jace's contact and hit it.

He picked up on the second ring. "What's up Matty-kins?"

"I'm walking," I said.

"Walking where?"

"Along the road. Somewhere between downtown and losing my mind."

That got his attention. "Everything okay?"

"No." My laugh came out hollow. "Not even close."

There was a pause, then his voice shifted, serious now. "You want me to come get you?"

"Yeah," I said quietly. "And bring alcohol."

"Bad night?"

"Worse," I muttered, staring at the long stretch of highway ahead. "I need to get drunk before I start breaking things."

Jace exhaled softly through the line. "Alright. Stay where you are, bubs. I'm on my way."

The call clicked off.

A second later, my phone buzzed again—Dad.

The name lit up the screen like a warning I didn't need.

I let it ring until it stopped, shoving the phone deep into my pocket as the night stretched out in front of me.

Shit. What the fuck had just happened?

CHAPTER 13

OPHELIA

"Oh my gosh. I can't stop watching!"

The phone was inches from my nose, the video looping for what had to be the tenth time.

"Too bad you can't see your face." One of the girls giggled, leaning over her friend's shoulder. "If he'd known who you were, it would've been even better."

Another laughed, tossing her hair. "Yeah, can you imagine? Matty Adler making out with you *on purpose*? That would've been the coolest thing ever."

Their words hit harder than they meant them to. Because he didn't know who I was . . . not in the way that mattered.

The others crowded closer, squealing as they watched Matty's hands grip my mascot-clad head and kiss me like the world had stopped spinning.

"That's so hot," one of them shrieked over the music. "If that were me, I'd have never taken that costume off."

"Do you even realize how viral this is?" another added, waving her drink for emphasis. "You've hit, like, a million views. Everyone's talking about it!"

I tried to laugh, but it came out thin. The sound of it got swallowed by the bass thudding through the floor.

Some of the cheerleaders had invited me out after I'd run into the locker room, insisting I *had* to come out with them. They'd never invited me before, and I knew it was only because of what Matty had done . . . but the thought of sitting in my dorm room alone, obsessing over him, had been an unbearable thought.

So I came.

And it was a mistake.

I was surrounded by cheerleaders who smelled like vanilla body spray, half of them drunk, and all of them living for the gossip.

Music pounded through the walls, bass rattling the cheap cup in my hand. Someone's playlist battled against the noise, a blur of drunk laughter, off-key singing, and a heated argument about fantasy football. The air was thick with perfume, beer, and the faint burn of weed drifting from the kitchen.

"I can do this," I whispered to myself. It was *good* to be doing this.

Normal girls went to parties. Normal girls laughed, danced, flirted.

Normal girls also didn't keep glancing at the door every thirty seconds, though, waiting for the man they were obsessed with to walk through it.

"Hey," a voice said beside me.

I turned.

The guy had been hovering around for the past fifteen minutes. He stepped closer now, smiling a little too wide.

"You're in my class, right?" he asked, leaning closer so I could hear him over the music. "Intro to Psych?"

I nodded, trying to place him. I hadn't been very good at noticing other people existed besides Matty. "Yeah, I think so."

"Ryan," he said, offering a hand. "Or maybe you already knew that."

He had sandy hair, a clean jawline, and the kind of easy grin that probably worked on most girls. His T-shirt stretched just enough across his shoulders to say he played some kind of intramural sport, but not enough to make him dangerous.

The kind of boy Dr. Whitaker might even call *safe* for me because my brain wouldn't attach to him.

"So," Ryan said, still smiling. "You come to parties like this a lot?"

I laughed softly. "Not really."

"Guess tonight's a good night to start." His gaze flicked toward the group of cheerleaders still showing the viral video to anyone willing to look. "You're kind of the main event."

I forced a smile, the back of my neck prickling. "Lucky me."

His fingers brushed my wrist, casual, testing. My pulse didn't quicken; it just existed, steady and dull. I tried to focus on his voice instead of the echo of Matty's voice in my head.

You're sick, I reminded myself. *You ruin everything you touch. You need to find someone like this . . . someone normal.*

Ryan's hand lingered just long enough to make it clear he'd noticed I hadn't pulled away. "It's pretty loud in here," he said, raising his voice over the music. "You wanna go outside? There's a firepit out back. Way easier to talk."

I hesitated, my gaze flicking toward the door again . . . the same door I'd been watching all night. No sign of Matty. Just smoke, laughter, and the faint glow of string lights through the kitchen windows.

"Sure," I heard myself say. "Outside sounds good."

He smiled, looking relieved. "Cool. Bring your drink."

I did. And as he led the way through the crowd, I told myself this was progress.

Normal girls went outside with normal boys.

And I was *trying* so hard to be normal.

We stepped onto the porch, the night cool and damp. Laughter spilled from inside, but out here it was quieter. The firepit flickered in the backyard, flames bending in the breeze, the light catching on empty bottles and the edges of someone's abandoned hoodie. I wrapped my arms around myself and stared at the fire until my eyes blurred.

He moved closer, resting his hand on the railing beside mine. "You're kind of hard to read, you know that?"

I shrugged, my eyes still on the flames. "Maybe you're not reading the right language."

He laughed, and it was easy and harmless, doing absolutely nothing to my insides. "Guess I'll have to learn it."

His face dipped toward mine.

I froze.

Every instinct screamed at me to move, to lean away, but I couldn't, not fast enough. Before his lips could touch mine, a burst of cheers erupted from inside the house, the sound spilling through the open windows and rolling across the yard.

I turned toward the noise on reflex, and his kiss brushed my cheek instead.

Ryan blinked, confused, as the voices grew louder, spilling into the night, chanting *Thatcher* and *Davis* and *Adler* like they meant something holy.

And just like that, my pulse finally remembered how to move.

My breath hitched.

He was here.

The sound of his name wrapped around me, and for a second all I could think about was how badly I wanted to see him . . . and how dangerous that was.

You have to stay away. He would think you were disgusting if he knew who you really were . . . what you've been doing.

But he also called you baby, another inside voice said.

It didn't matter.

I swallowed hard and turned back to Ryan, forcing a smile I didn't feel. "It's freezing out here," I said, my voice barely steady. "Want to sit by the fire?"

He smiled, oblivious. "Yeah, sure."

We walked across the yard, weaving through groups of people huddled together under string lights. The firepit crackled at the center, orange light flickering across faces and half-empty cans. I sank onto one of the benches, the warmth licking at my knees, the smoke stinging my eyes.

Ryan sat beside me, close but not too close, talking about something—his friends, a class project, maybe a game coming up. I tried to listen. I nodded, laughed at the right times, told myself to focus.

Normal. Just be *normal.*

But the sounds around us started to change. Conversations cut off mid-sentence. Someone's laughter trailed into silence.

I felt it before I saw it—the sudden shift in the air, the weight pressing against the back of my neck.

I looked up.

And there he was.

Matty stood at the edge of the firelight, the glow catching on the chiseled line of his jaw. The flames turned his skin gold, and his dark hair gleamed like it had been spun from the same heat that fed the fire. He looked unreal . . . like some kind of god who'd stepped straight out of the flames just to find me.

He wasn't smiling. He was just staring . . . straight at me.

The cup in my hand trembled and for one long heartbeat, I forgot how to breathe.

"Ophelia." Ryan's fingers brushed my arm. "You okay?"

"I'm fine," I lied.

Matty's gaze cut to where Ryan touched me. His jaw flexed once before his eyes lifted back to mine.

"Come here," Matty said, his voice sliding through the air, making every nerve in my body react before my brain could catch up.

Ryan blinked, glancing between us. "Wait—you *know* him?" He gave a confused laugh. "I thought you didn't."

My throat felt tight. "I don't," I said quickly, turning back to Ryan like that made it true. "We've just . . . seen each other around campus."

He didn't look convinced. His gaze kept flicking toward Matty, uneasy. "He's staring at you."

"No, he's not," I murmured, forcing a shaky laugh. "Ignore him. Tell me more about that business class you mentioned."

Ryan tried, talking about the group project again, but the words barely landed. His eyes kept darting toward the fire's edge—toward Matty, who hadn't moved, who just stood there watching me like he was waiting for me to admit something.

Then Matty said my name. "Ophelia."

The way he spoke it was nothing like when Ryan had.

Ryan's version had been soft, uncertain, testing whether I'd look at him.

Matty's was a command disguised as my name, rough around the edges, strong enough to crawl under my skin and take root.

Heat shot through me so fast I forgot how to breathe. Every part of me went still, caught between the fire's warmth and the dizzy rush of hearing him say my name again.

I forced a smile that felt like it might crack my face. "Hey, um," I said to Ryan, already standing, gripping my cup too tightly. "Do you want to dance?"

He blinked in surprise, but nodded, letting me tug him back through the door and into the noise.

I didn't look back, but I could feel Matty's gaze on me, crawling over my skin . . . impossible to shake.

The living room was packed, lights flashing red and blue from a cheap LED strip across the ceiling. Bodies swayed and collided, laughter spilling into shouts. I pulled Ryan toward the middle of the crowd, letting the crush of people swallow us whole.

He grinned, his hands settling tentatively on my hips like he was waiting for me to flinch. I didn't. I nodded once, and we started to move.

It should have felt freeing, the bass thudding through the floor and noise drowning out thought. But the harder I tried to lose myself in it, the more I could feel *him*.

Matty.

Somewhere behind me. Maybe by the wall. Maybe closer. My heartbeat stuttered to match the rhythm of the bass, uneven and frantic.

Ryan leaned close, shouting over the music, "Relax!"

Relax.

As if that were possible.

I forced a nod, rolling my hips just enough to sell it. The crowd whooped, clapping to the beat, a blur of lights and sound and heat. One of the cheerleaders shoved another drink into my hand. I took a sip and barely tasted it.

Every nerve in my body told me he was still watching.

I tried not to look, but my eyes found him anyway.

Across the room, near the doorway, Matty stood with his arms crossed, shadows from the pulsing lights cutting across his face. He wasn't smiling.

Jace and Parker were beside him, their girlfriends laughing at something I couldn't hear, but Matty didn't join in. He didn't even pretend to be part of the conversation. People stopped to talk, clapping him on the back, trying to draw him in, but he barely looked their way.

His attention was fixed on me.

I told myself I was imagining it, that the lights were playing tricks, but for a split second, I could have sworn there was hunger in his eyes.

Ryan followed my gaze and stiffened. "Is he still staring at you?"

"Nope," I said too quickly.

"Sure looks like it."

I laughed weakly.

He spun me gently, trying to keep it playful, and when I turned back, Matty was gone. The air in the room felt thinner without him in it, which made no sense and too much sense all at once.

Ryan leaned close, his lips near my ear. "You wanna get out of here?"

My stomach twisted at his connotation. "Just—one sec," I said, trying not to sound as panicked as I felt. "I need to use the bathroom."

He nodded, looking excited. "Yeah, sure. It's right down the hallway behind the kitchen. I'll wait for you here."

I slipped from his hands and wove through the crowd. The hallway beyond the kitchen was dim, quieter except for the muffled bass thudding through the walls.

Halfway down the hall, I stopped and pressed my palm to the wall, breathing hard.

You're fine. He's gone. You're fine.

The bathroom door stood slightly ajar. I pushed it open, flicked on the light, and closed it behind me.

Cool white light hummed overhead. The mirror showed a girl I barely recognized, her cheeks flushed, hair mussed from dancing . . . eyes too bright. I turned on the tap and let the water run, focusing on the steady stream instead of the reflection staring back at me.

The door suddenly eased open, and he filled the doorway like he'd been carved to fit it . . . Matty.

He didn't speak right away. Just looked at me, water dripping from my fingertips into the sink. Then he stepped inside and quietly shut the door, sealing out the music and laughter until it was just us and the sound of running water.

"I told your date you wouldn't be coming back," he said quietly.

I gaped at him. "Why would you tell him that?"

His mouth curved. "I just figured it'd save him the disappointment," he said innocently. "His night was never going to end with you."

For a second, the room tilted. I couldn't breathe or think. Because what he'd said, what it seemed like he *meant*, was everything I'd ever wanted to hear. Every fantasy I'd built around him when I was alone in my room, staring at his face glowing on a screen. Every dream that had felt too pathetic to ever believe it could come true.

But hearing it now, in his voice, with that look in his eyes . . . it didn't make sense.

My fingers tightened around the edge of the sink until they ached. I jerked my head away from him, staring hard at the trickle of water circling the drain.

Click.

The sharp flick of him locking the door filled the room, loud in the sudden stillness.

Slow footsteps followed, the sound echoing against the tile, each one drawing closer.

Closer.

Until the heat of him pressed against my spine and a shiver raced through me so hard my fingers rattled against the sink.

I slowly looked up.

In the mirror, he loomed behind me, his broad shoulders swallowing the frame. I looked small and breakable next to him, his eyes locked on mine with an intensity that pinned me in place.

He reached around me, arm brushing mine as he twisted the faucet shut. The *click* cut the room to silence, leaving only the uneven hitch of our breaths hanging between us.

The girl in the mirror *still* didn't look like me. Her pupils were blown wide, her lips parted, a blush spread across her chest. She looked caught somewhere between fear and something she didn't want to name . . . like she'd fallen straight down a rabbit hole and woken up in a strange new land that had everything she'd ever wanted.

"I'm confused," I whispered, the words shaking as they left me. "I don't understand what's happening."

He tilted his head slightly, studying me through the mirror. "You don't?" His voice was quiet, almost thoughtful. "You really don't feel it?"

Before I could ask what he meant, his hand lifted.

I watched in the mirror, wide-eyed, as his fingers reached for me and traced a slow path along my shoulder. The touch was soft, almost reverent, like he was testing the reality of me.

My breath stuttered and vanished, caught somewhere between my chest and throat as the world narrowed to the heat of his hand on my skin.

The touch was barely there, just the edge of his fingers skimming down my arm, but it might as well have set me on fire.

A small sound escaped me, half gasp, half plea. My eyes stung. I'd imagined this—*him*—so many times that it felt like a cruel trick for it to finally be real. All those nights I'd pictured what it would be like for him to reach for me, to touch me like this, and now he was.

How could this be happening?

He leaned in, close enough that I could feel his breath ghosting across my neck. "Tell me you don't feel it, too, pretty baby," he murmured.

My hands trembled on the sink. "I . . ." The word barely made it out. My pulse thundered against my ribs.

"Why do you keep running?" he asked softly.

"I'm not—"

"You are," he murmured. "Every time I get close, you disappear, Ophelia."

My name rolled off his tongue like a prayer and a threat all at once. It hit me low in the belly, filthy and sweet. My knees buckled a fraction, and the tiniest whimper slipped past my lips before I could trap it.

His grin was smug and victorious. "Do you like when I say your name, sweet girl?"

Before I could answer, his hands clamped onto my hips and spun me to face him. The mirror vanished, and there was just Matty, inches away, eyes blazing.

Up close, he was brutal in his beauty.

His hair was a dark, careless mess, the kind that begged to be touched, and his jaw was tense enough that a muscle jumped when he looked at me. But it was his eyes that undid me—bright and alive with something I couldn't name. Looking into them hurt, like staring straight into sunlight and realizing too late you couldn't look away.

"You don't know me," I breathed, the protest thin as paper.

Not like I know you, the voice in my brain whispered. *Not like I've memorized the way you chew your mouth guard on third down, how you crack your neck before a lecture starts, the brand of cologne you slap on in the morning.*

His thumbs dug in, pinning me to the sink. "You're right. I don't know you. But I want to know *everything,*" he said soothingly. "Every flavor of lip balm you keep in your backpack. Every song you play on repeat when no one's listening. The way your breath catches right before you come." His gaze dropped to my mouth, lingered, and then dragged back up. "I want it all."

I want to know everything.

The words landed like a fist to the chest. I panicked.

He'd find out, somehow. About all of it.

That I hadn't come to this school for a degree, but for *him.*

That I'd watched every practice from the parking lot, hoping for a glimpse of him.

That I knew his schedule, his stats, his favorite drink before a game.

That I'd waited outside his classes just to see him walk by me once.

He'd put it together piece by piece, and when he did, he'd see me for what I really was . . . obsessed, broken, *wrong.*

He'd see the freak I'd been trying so hard not to be.

I tried to twist away, but his grip only tightened, grounding me. "Hey," he murmured, his voice dropping into something softer . . . coaxing. "Look at me."

I couldn't. My eyes stayed locked on the hollow of his throat, the way his pulse beat steady under the skin. He ducked his head, chasing my gaze until I had no choice.

"Ophelia." Another slow, deliberate roll of my name. My spine arched without permission. "I'm not asking for a résumé. I'm just asking for . . . you."

His thumb brushed the waistband of my jeans, a touch so light it felt like a question, and his mouth found the curve of my ear, his breath warm against my skin.

"I want the parts you're scared to show anyone," he said, softer now, like it was a promise instead of a threat. "The ones you hide. I want *all* of it."

The words sank into me, molten and dangerous, and for a heartbeat I couldn't tell if he was saving me or destroying me.

My lungs burned. *Just once*, the thought whispered, wild and traitorous. *One night*. One taste. Then I'll let him go. I'll bleed him out of my system and pretend I'm clean again.

His hand slid beneath my shirt, his palm flat against my stomach, heat spreading fast until it hurt to stand still. "Tell me no," he whispered in a frayed voice. "Say it, and I'll stop."

But I couldn't. The word tangled in my throat and died there.

His eyes fluttered shut, like he'd been bracing himself . . . for me to end it. But when they opened again, they were dark, undone, and sure of exactly what was about to happen.

He leaned in, closing the space inch by inch until his breath mingled with mine. The air between us thickened, humming with something that felt dangerously close to inevitability.

His lips brushed against mine.

It was barely a touch, soft enough to be a mistake, but the world tilted anyway, everything in me tipping toward him. A whimper broke from my throat, quiet and raw, the kind of sound that belonged to someone losing control.

For a dizzy second everything rewired—and my head filled with the ridiculous, crystalline thought: *So this is what it's like.*

My first real kiss.

And it was with him.

A tear slid down my cheek before I even realized I was crying.

Matty drew back, just enough to see me, his eyes flicking over my face like he couldn't quite believe what he was looking at.

He reached up, his thumb tracing the path of the tear, catching it before it fell. For a moment, he just stared at the wet shine on his skin, then back at me . . . like the sight of it had knocked him off course.

"Please," I whispered.

Something in him shifted . . . his softness snapping into hunger. His jaw tightened, pupils blown wide, and then his mouth crashed against mine.

It was fierce and unrestrained, stealing whatever air I had left. The world blurred around the edges, lost to everything but him. I followed his lead instinctively, clumsy at first, then desperate, matching the rhythm he set like I'd been made to find it.

He tasted like something dangerously close to *home*. Our mouths fit in a way that shouldn't have been possible, like all the space I'd been saving inside myself had been carved for this, for *him*.

The kiss was all teeth and heat and need, like he'd been starving for it just as much as I had. I kissed him back, chasing the taste of him, my hands sliding under his shirt before I could think better of it.

My fingers met warm, solid skin, his muscles shifting beneath my touch, and for a breathless moment I just *felt*. The strength. The reality. I'd imagined this for so long that the truth of it stunned me . . . the impossible weight of him, alive and here, his heartbeat drumming against my palms like proof that this wasn't a dream. It was too much.

A moan ripped from his throat, almost pained, like my touch hurt.

His kiss was a brand, his lips demanding, sucking my bottom lip, his teeth grazing just enough to make me gasp. My body arched, pressing against him, feeling the hard length of his cock through his jeans, already straining for me.

"Matty," I panted, breaking the kiss, but he didn't stop.

His mouth moved everywhere, frantic, like he was trying to map every inch of me with his lips. He kissed the corner of my mouth, my cheek, the wet trail of another tear. Then lower . . . across my jaw, down the column of my throat, open-mouthed and greedy. He sucked at the pulse beneath my ear, teeth scraping, tongue soothing, marking me with every breath.

"Mine," he growled against my skin in a ragged voice. "Every fucking part of you is mine."

Something fluttered and twisted deep inside me, like my body already belonged to the words he'd just spoken.

He kissed my collarbone, the hollow of my throat, the slope where my neck met my shoulder. He gripped my hips, and I gasped as he lifted me onto the counter in one smooth motion. The edge bit into the backs of my thighs as he stepped in, fitting between my legs like he'd been there a thousand times before. His lips never stopped, tracing heat across my skin, marking me in ways I'd never come back from . . . like he couldn't get close enough, couldn't taste enough, like every breath between us belonged to him.

He broke the kiss just long enough to growl against my mouth, "I have to taste you."

The words didn't register at first . . . until he sank to his knees, the quiet *thud* of them hitting tile snapping everything into focus.

Oh.

He meant *that* kind of taste.

The realization slammed into me, and my stomach flipped, my thighs clenching on instinct, but he was already moving.

His hands were shaking as he fumbled at my waistband. Not the steady, practiced grip of someone in control. No. This was a frantic need. His fingers slipped on the button once, twice, a low, frustrated growl rumbling from his chest as he yanked harder. The denim caught on my hips, resisting, and he *tore* it down with a desperate jerk that scraped my skin and sent the button skittering across the floor.

My panties snagged with them, sliding halfway down my thighs before he hooked a thumb under the lace and pulled them the rest of the way. The fabric tore with a loud rip, but he didn't even flinch.

Cool air hit me, and I gasped, legs trembling, exposed and bare beneath the weight of his stare.

The sight of me like that—naked, open, *his*—seemed to slam the brakes on him. His hands froze midair, chest heaving like he'd just run a sprint. For one suspended heartbeat, he just *looked*, eyes wide and dark, drinking me in like he was trying to burn the image into his soul.

Then he exhaled, shaky and reverent, and leaned back on his heels, his eyes fixed between my thighs like I was a fucking masterpiece. His fingers traced the inside of my thigh first, slow and teasing, inching higher until they brushed my folds. I whimpered, my hips twitching forward without my permission.

"Fuck," he breathed, parting me gently with his thumbs, dragging them through the slick heat there. I was dripping, swollen, every nerve screaming for more. He circled my clit lightly, just enough to make my breath hitch, then dipped lower, coating his fingers in me. "Such a pretty baby," he murmured, sounding awestruck, like he couldn't believe what he was seeing. "Look at you, all pink and wet for me. Perfect little pussy, just begging."

My hands gripped the sink harder, knuckles white, as heat flooded my face and core. His praise wrapped around me like a vise, making me throb.

Matty's gaze lifted to mine, holding me captive as he pressed one finger against my entrance. "That's it, sweet girl," he whispered, pushing in slow, so slow I felt every inch stretch me. "You're so tight . . . and taking me so good already." The fullness made me clench, a soft moan spilling out. He added a second finger, curling them just right, stroking a spot inside that lit me up like fireworks. "Yeah, just like that. You're doing so fucking good, Ophelia. Feel how you're gripping me? You were made for this."

I was panting now, hips rocking into his hand as he pumped deeper, his thumb rubbing firm circles over my clit. The wet sounds filled the room, lewd and hot, every thrust of his fingers building that coil tighter. "Fuck, you're beautiful," he groaned, watching my face, my body, like he couldn't get enough. "You're going to come so hard, baby. You deserve every second of it. Look at you . . . all mine."

His words were as good as his fingers. That was all I wanted . . . to be his.

The pressure built fast, and I fell over the edge, shattering with a cry, clenching around him, waves crashing through me until I was shaking, boneless against the sink.

He didn't stop until I was spent, and then he eased his fingers out slowly, the tips of them slick . . . with me. Matty licked them clean with a satisfied grin. "Good girl," he murmured. "I knew you'd taste good."

Heat flooded my face, a fierce blush burning from my chest to my ears. I couldn't look away from him. My heart was hammering like it wanted out of my ribs.

His eyes flicked up, catching the flush, and that grin widened—slow, wicked, *knowing*.

"Fuck, look at you," he rasped. "Blushing like that after coming all over my fingers? You're killing me, Ophelia."

His hands slid up my thighs, and he spread me wider. His thumbs brushed the sensitive skin just inside my hips, and I jerked again, oversensitive, another whimper slipping free. He held me down with one hand splayed across my lower belly, the other keeping me open.

"Stay still, baby," he whispered. "Let me take care of you."

His first lick was slow, dragging from my entrance to my clit in one long, delicious stroke. My back arched off the counter, a broken sound tearing from my throat. He groaned against me, the vibration shooting straight through my core.

"Fuck, yes," he growled into my skin.

He licked again, slower, savoring, tongue swirling around my clit before sucking it gently between his lips. My hands flew to his hair and I tangled my fingers in the dark strands, pulling hard. He didn't flinch . . . just hummed in approval, the sound rumbling through me.

"Matty—"

"That's it," he praised in a muffled voice. "Say my name. Let me hear how good I make you feel."

He flattened his tongue, lapping at me like he couldn't get enough, like my taste was a drug. Every stroke sent sparks up my spine, my thighs shaking, trying to close around his head. He pushed them wider, pinning me open, completely at his mercy.

"So sweet," he murmured, pulling back just enough to blow cool air over my clit. I cried out. "I love how you drip for me. I love how you clench when I do this—"

He sucked hard, teeth grazing just enough to make me see stars and forget for a second that he'd just said *love*. My vision blurred, and my breath came out in desperate gasps. He slid one finger back inside me, curling it, stroking that spot that made my toes curl. Then another. He pumped slow and deep, matching the rhythm of his tongue.

"You're so tight," he groaned, pulling back to watch his fingers disappear into me. "So fucking perfect. Look at you . . . taking me so well. You were definitely made for this, pretty baby. Made for *me*."

I couldn't speak or think. All I could do was feel . . . his mouth, his fingers, his voice wrapping around me like chains I never wanted to be rid of. He curled his fingers harder, tongue flicking faster, and the pressure built again, faster this time, coiling tight and hot in my belly.

But then he *moved*.

His tongue dragged lower, past where I expected, tracing a hot, wet path down to my ass. The shock of it hit like lightning—intimate, forbidden, *wrong* in the best way. I squirmed hard, thighs clamping, a startled cry ripping from my throat.

"Oh—"

"Shh," he soothed, his voice dark and intimate. "Relax, baby. Let me have all of you."

He licked again, circling the tight ring of muscle, teasing, tasting. My hips jerked, half panic, half pleasure so intense it hurt. His hand on my belly pressed harder, holding me still.

"Fuck, you taste good everywhere," he groaned, tongue pressing firmer, breaching just enough to make me gasp. "So responsive. Look at you—squirming for me. You love this, don't you?"

I still couldn't answer. The sensation was overwhelming . . . dirty, perfect, *his*. I wanted him to do anything he wanted to me.

I wanted him to have *everything*.

He licked back up to my clit, sucking hard, fingers thrusting deep, and the contrast sent me spiraling.

"Matty—please—"

"Come for me," he demanded. "Come on my tongue. I want to taste it when you fall apart."

He sucked my clit hard, fingers continuing to thrust, his tongue gliding back down to tease my ass one last time.

I shattered.

The orgasm ripped through me, violent and blinding. I screamed his name, back bowing, thighs clamping around his head as wave after wave crashed over me. He didn't stop, he just kept licking, kept stroking, kept drawing it out until I was a sobbing, oversensitive, begging *mess*.

Only then did he slow, easing his fingers out, licking them clean again with a low, satisfied moan. He pressed soft kisses to my inner thighs, my hips, my trembling stomach, working his way back up.

When he finally stood, he pulled me into his arms, holding me tight as I shook. His lips brushed my temple, my cheek, my tear-streaked face.

"My perfect girl," he murmured, almost worshipfully. He pulled me into him, lips colliding with mine again, his tongue sliding deep, letting me taste myself on him.

It was strange, shockingly intimate. Salty-sweet, warm, a little tangy, like skin and want and something I'd like to think was uniquely me. Not just a flavor, but proof. Proof that he'd had his mouth on me, inside me, and now carried a piece of me inside him. The thought hit hard, a dark thrill curling in my stomach.

He'd swallowed me. My essence was on his tongue, had slid down his throat . . . become part of him. I moaned into the kiss, greedy for more, licking deeper, chasing every trace like I could keep him there forever.

"You okay?" he asked as he pulled away, his voice soft and sweet.

I nodded, nuzzling against his chest, my whole body *reeling*.

He smiled against my skin. "Good. Because I'm nowhere near done with you."

Knock-knock-knock.

"Yo, open up! I gotta piss!" a slurred voice yelled through the door, rattling the handle.

I jerked hard, heart lurching into my throat, thighs clamping shut on reflex. Matty didn't flinch, though. He just smiled, lazily, like the guy on the other side didn't exist.

"Occupied," he finally called back calmly, his thumb tracing idle circles on my hip.

The banging stopped, and I listened as footsteps shuffled away.

I stared up at him. *Does he do this all the time?* The thought slithered in, cold and cruel, leaving a sting that spread through my chest. *Hook up in bathrooms . . . make girls scream on a stranger's counter?*

It was actually something I wouldn't know about, because I'd never followed him to a party before, too scared to go.

A terrible, twisted part of me didn't care.

This time it's me.

I knew it was unhealthy, toxic, *wrong*, but I was still burning, still coming down from the high he'd given me, and logic felt a million miles away. All I could feel was the ache between my legs, the taste of him on my tongue . . . the way he was looking at me right now like I was the only girl in the world.

And right now, that was enough.

CHAPTER 14

MATTY

My cock was still throbbing, soaked inside my jeans, the wet spot warm and sticky against my thigh. I'd come in my fucking *pants* like a teenager, just from tasting her, from feeling her clench around my fingers and screaming my name. One lick of her sweet, dripping pussy, and I'd lost it, no warning, no control, just a crazy, blinding rush that hit me so hard I'd nearly blacked out.

And I was already hard again.

Fucking hell.

Ophelia was trembling in my arms, her skin flushed and glowing, those perfect lips of hers swollen from my mouth. Those copper eyes that had haunted me since the first time I saw her were glassy and dazed . . . *mine.* I'd done that. I'd put that look on her face. I'd made her come so hard she'd cried.

I wanted to fall to my knees and thank whatever god let this happen. I couldn't believe that I'd ever been in a bad mood tonight. My dinner with my dad seemed like it had happened a thousand years before.

The knock on the door barely registered. Nothing mattered but her. I called out "occupied" without looking away, my thumb still stroking her hip like I could brand the feel of her into my skin.

I searched her gorgeous face, my eyes tracing every flicker . . . her parted lips, the flush riding high on her cheeks, the way her lashes fluttered like she was still catching her breath.

What is she thinking? I wondered. *Was that as life-changing for her as it was for me?*

The taste of her still coated my tongue, sweet and addictive, like honey laced with something that made me feral . . . and I couldn't stop myself. I slammed my lips against hers again, kissing her deeply, like I could crawl inside her mouth and live there. My hips rolled on instinct, pressing the hard, aching length of me against her bare thigh.

She gasped suddenly, her hands clutching my shoulders.

Ah, she must have felt it . . . the wet patch seeping through my jeans.

Her eyes snapped open, and she broke the kiss. She looked down and brushed her fingers against the soaked denim and barely held in a groan. Her gaze flew back to my face, shock widening those copper eyes. "What—" She gasped.

I grinned shamelessly. "Yeah. You did that, pretty baby."

Her lips parted, another stunned little sound escaping.

"I came in my pants the second I tasted you," I rasped, leaning in to nip at her bottom lip. "One lick, and I fucking lost it. And I'm already ready to go again . . ."

Her blush flared, but pride flickered in her eyes. I kissed her again, harder, making sure it was engraved in her head how attracted I was to her.

I wanted her to feel good about herself when it came to me.

She *owned* me.

I broke the kiss, only to drag my mouth down her throat and scrape my teeth against her pulse, sucking a mark that would bloom purple by morning and hopefully show anyone who looked that she also belonged to someone.

Me, obviously.

My hands shook as they slid under her thighs, lifting her higher on the counter so I could grind against her more, the soaked denim chafing my cock in the best way. Every roll of my hips pulled a whimper from her, and I swallowed it like oxygen.

Take her home. Chain her to the bed. Never let her leave.

The thought hit savagely, a growl rumbling in my chest. I pictured her wrists in cuffs, ankles spread, my sheets twisted around her naked body while I fucked her over and over for days. Weeks. Forever.

Except . . . when I'd pushed my fingers inside her, there'd been resistance . . . She'd gasped like it hurt and *didn't* at the same time.

I was pretty sure she was a virgin. And if not a virgin—although I wanted to kill someone thinking of another guy touching her—then at least very inexperienced.

When I had sex with her, it couldn't be on some random bathroom counter with some drunk pounding on the door. It would be in my bed with candles, clean sheets . . . her name carved into the headboard. Perfect. *Mine*.

I pulled back just enough to rest my forehead against hers, breath ragged, heart pounding like I'd just run sprints. Her scent, sweat, sex, *her*, filled my lungs, and I wanted to drown in it.

She shifted on the counter, thighs spreading wider, and a wince flashed across her face. A soft, pained sound slipped out before she could stop it.

I froze, worry spiking through the haze. "Are you sore, sweetheart?"

Her cheeks flushed deeper, eyes dropping. "Yeah . . . a little, but it's a *good* sore," she blurted, almost tripping over the words like she was scared I'd take it the wrong way.

Pride hit me hard, a dark, possessive thrill curling in my gut. *I did that*. Made it so she would feel me hours from now.

Marked her in a way no one else ever would again.

Underneath the rush, though, I made a mental note to watch her . . . She liked to be my good girl, to please, even when it hurt. I never wanted to let that sweetness be something that hurt her.

I cupped her face, my thumb brushing her lip as I grinned. "Fuck, I love that."

Ophelia bit her lip, then glanced toward the door. "I guess we should go back out there," she said in a small, disappointed voice.

She looked worried suddenly, her fingers twisting in my shirt, tugging like she didn't want to let go.

I didn't want to, either.

The idea of stepping back into that noise, of having anyone else look at her . . . it felt wrong.

But I couldn't keep her in a dirty bathroom forever.

"I guess we should," I murmured, even though every part of me rebelled against it.

I slid my hands to her waist and lifted her off the counter, setting her gently on her feet. She wobbled, and my grip tightened automatically. I didn't miss the tiny wince, or the way she tried to hide it behind a shy smile.

"Easy," I said softly, letting my thumb trace the edge of her hip again because I couldn't *not* touch her.

I glanced around, huffing out a quiet laugh when I saw the torn scrap of lace on the floor. I grabbed the ruined panties, holding them up by one finger. The lace hung in shreds—my best handiwork, if I did say so myself.

"These aren't making a comeback, sweet girl."

Her blush flared, but a giggle escaped, and I savored the sound.

I brought the scrap to my nose, inhaling her scent. It was sweet and musky . . . my new favorite aroma.

My cock pulsed, another hot spurt leaking into my already soaked jeans. I squeezed my eyes shut, forcing myself to picture Emma and iced milk, anything to keep from coming again right there.

That actually worked quite well.

"I'm keeping these," I rasped, hoping the roughness in my voice didn't spook her.

I opened my eyes to find her nodding eagerly, eyes bright, like the thought of me keeping her panties lit her up inside. *Fuck, she's cute.*

I slipped the torn lace into my back pocket with a wink.

She continued to stand there, wobbly and trusting, letting me kneel to tug her jeans up. I realized I'd popped the button clean off . . . and another low chuckle rumbled out of me. "Guess I owe you new jeans, too," I murmured, fastening the denim as best I could with the zipper alone.

It hit me again . . . how perfect she was. Ophelia seemed perfectly content to let me take care of her. No protest, no fuss, just soft eyes and that little smile, handing me the reins like it was the most natural thing in the world. My chest tightened, a fierce, warm ache spreading through me.

I *loved* it.

Loved her letting me handle every detail, loved that she was already trusting me to take care of her.

I caught her hand and turned toward the door, but she stiffened, the smallest tremor running through her fingers.

"Hey," I murmured, glancing back at her. She looked nervous. Was she worried about what people would think if they saw us?

I leaned close. "It's okay, sweetheart. Anyone who sees us is just going to be thinking that I'm the luckiest bastard alive."

Her breath caught, the corners of her mouth trembling into the shyest smile I'd ever seen. Then it faded, her voice small and uncertain. "I just . . . I don't want it to be over," she whispered. "I don't want you to not see me again."

For a second, the words didn't quite register—like she was speaking a language my brain hadn't caught up to yet.

"Not see you again?" I repeated, frowning a little.

She nodded, her eyes suddenly glassy, like she was about to cry. "After this. You'll go back out there, and I'll just be . . ." She trailed off, swallowing hard. "I don't want that."

A low ache punched through my chest. I tightened my hold on her hand, forcing her to look up at me.

"Ophelia," I said quietly, "that would be impossible."

Her brow furrowed, lips parting.

"You're all I see."

For a heartbeat, she just stared at my face. Then her whole face lit up . . . like sunrise breaking open right in front of me. She literally beamed, and I swear the air around us changed. It was all I could do not to put her back on the counter and start everything all over again.

I let out a breath I hadn't realized I was holding and brushed my thumb over her knuckles. "You ready now, sweetheart?"

She nodded, squeezing my hand tight. "Yeah," she whispered.

"Good girl," I murmured, and pushed the bathroom door open.

We'd barely taken two steps into the hallway when a familiar voice practically shouted my name.

"Matty! Thank *fuck*!"

Garrett appeared out of nowhere, hair mussed, shirt untucked, eyes wide like he'd just survived a war zone.

"You have to save me," he begged, grabbing my shoulder. "Parker and Jace ditched me! They left with Casey and Riley, and now some girl's trying to—" He broke off, glancing over his shoulder. "Oh fuck. There she is."

I followed his gaze just in time to see a tipsy brunette waving what looked like a Sharpie.

Garrett groaned. "She wants me to sign her *baby*. Not her shirt. Not her arm. Her actual *baby*. I obviously didn't know she was a mom when I hooked up with her! She's acting like her baby is stashed somewhere around here. I'm terrified!"

Ophelia snorted beside me, and I couldn't help the grin that spread across my face.

"Sounds like you're famous now. I've autographed footballs, but never babies. Good for you," I said dryly.

He glared. "Famous? She just asked if my autograph would help with child support, Matthew. Help!"

Ophelia laughed then, soft at first, then a full, bubbling laugh that made my chest tighten all over again.

Garrett's head snapped toward her mid-groan. The second he saw her, his expression shifted—brows lifting, mouth parting like he'd just put something together he wasn't supposed to.

Ophelia's laughter faltered instantly. I felt her hand tense in mine, her fingers slipping until she was barely holding on.

"Hey," I started, frowning, but she was already shaking her head, eyes darting between Garrett and me.

"I have to go," she said suddenly in a thin, panicked voice.

"Go?" I repeated, completely thrown. "What—"

But before I could finish, the Sharpie girl finally made it to us, waving the marker like a weapon.

"You can run, but you can't hide!" she squealed. "You *have* to sign my baby!"

Garrett recoiled like she'd pulled a knife instead of a marker, and in the chaos, Ophelia slipped free.

I caught the flash of her hair as she darted into the crowd, gone before I could even call her name.

Something snapped inside me.

Before I knew it, my fist was buried in Garrett's gut.

He doubled over with a strangled wheeze, nearly dropping the Sharpie the baby-lady had handed him. "Son of a bitch— What the hell, Adler?"

"What did you do to her?" I snarled, catching his shoulder as he straightened. "Why were you looking at her like that?"

He blinked, eyes watering. "I wasn't— What are you—" He sucked in a breath, clutching his stomach. "I just— She looks familiar, okay? That's it! I swear to— Matty, I wasn't trying to— Holy shit, you hit hard."

I stared at him, trying to read if he was lying, but Garrett just groaned and waved a hand weakly toward the crowd. "Seriously, man, I can't place it. I just know I've seen her before."

That didn't help. At all.

My pulse hammered as I looked past him, scanning the crush of people spilling through the hallway. Music and laughter swelled from the main room, flashes of orange light from the TVs playing the game replay. But no Ophelia.

"Damn it," I muttered, already moving.

"Matty!" Garrett called after me, still half bent and nursing his stomach. "If you find her, tell her I'm sorry for existing!"

I ignored him, pushing through the crowd, heart racing like I was still on the field. I shoved past a group of guys in team jackets, ignored the slap on my shoulder from one of the linemen, and pushed through the back door into the night.

Cool air hit my face, sharp enough to burn in my lungs.

I scanned the street, empty except for a few stragglers smoking by their cars, headlights flashing as people backed out. No Ophelia.

"Fuck."

I ran a hand over my face, chest tight, and that's when I remembered Jace's text.

With her dorm room number.

I didn't think twice. I took off down the sidewalk. Every streetlight I passed felt too bright, every shadow too long. My legs moved on instinct, just like they did on the field . . . driven, focused, refusing to stop.

I didn't slow until I saw a brick building ahead. Her dorm.

I jogged up the steps two at a time and yanked open the front doors. The warm air inside hit like a wall after the cold outside.

The RA at the front desk froze mid-sip of her soda, her eyes going wide. "Uh—aren't you—"

But I was already moving.

I jogged straight past her, the slap of my shoes echoing down the hallway. I barely registered the cheap dorm carpeting, the smell of popcorn and floor cleaner, the half-closed doors leaking music and laughter. My chest heaved, not from the run, but from the mess of adrenaline still coiled under my skin.

I didn't stop until I was outside her door.

My hand lifted automatically, ready to knock . . . and then I froze.

What the hell was I doing?

It hit me like a helmet to the gut. I knew her room number. I shouldn't know that.

Any normal girl would think it was creepy as hell if some guy showed up outside her dorm when she'd never told him where she lived.

Fuck.

I lowered my hand slowly, the wood of the door inches from my knuckles.

"Think, Adler," I muttered under my breath, but the words came out rough, useless. I didn't have a good excuse, no explanation that didn't make me sound insane.

I leaned in, pressing my ear to the door. There was noise—movement, maybe—but not crying. Thank fuck.

Still, the tension in my shoulders refused to ease.

"You can't scare her off," I whispered to myself.

Because then I'd have to do something crazy to keep her with me . . . and our house didn't have a basement like Parker's.

My fingers flexed against the doorframe, reluctant to let go. Finally, I dragged myself back a step, then another, until the door blurred into the rest of the hallway.

Tomorrow.

Tomorrow I'd fix this.

I'd "run into her" outside her dorm, play it casual, make her smile again.

And this time, she wasn't running from me.

Not ever again.

Ophelia

The door clicked shut behind me, and I just stood there for a second, forehead pressed to the cool wood, lungs fighting to keep up. The quiet of my room hit like an aftershock—too still, too soft after everything that had just happened.

My heart wouldn't slow down. It thudded against my ribs, wild and uneven, like it didn't know how to stop chasing him.

"You're an idiot," I muttered, shoving both hands into my hair.

I'd run. Again.

He'd said the sweetest thing anyone had ever said to me, and I'd bolted like the building was on fire.

But the second Garrett had looked at me like that—like he'd just solved a puzzle—I'd panicked.

Because I was pretty sure he'd *seen* me before.

Not just anywhere. That last time I'd parked near the field during practice, watching Matty run drills like I always did, Garrett had walked right by my car. He hadn't looked in—at least I didn't think he had—but the window had been cracked, and every time I saw him since, a little jolt of terror hit.

What if he remembered? What if he told Matty?

The thought made my stomach twist. Matty would think I was insane.

He couldn't find out.

I pressed a shaking hand to my mouth, trying to breathe past the panic clawing at my throat.

"You're an idiot," I whispered again, this time softer, almost like a prayer.

Because all I'd ever wanted was for him to see me. And now that he finally did . . . I was the one who couldn't face it.

I let my forehead rest against the door a second longer, then pushed off, a tiny, secret smile tugging at my mouth. My legs felt like jelly, thighs brushing together with every step, and the soreness hit sweet and insistent between them. I stopped mid-room, breath catching.

I may have run . . . but it didn't change that . . .

It had happened.

He'd kissed me. His fingers, his tongue . . . they'd been inside my body. He'd growled my name like it belonged to him. I shifted again, wincing at the tender ache, and the smile widened. Proof. Real, undeniable proof etched into my body.

My hand drifted to my lips, still swollen, still tasting him. I could feel the ghost of his teeth, the heat of his breath, the way he'd looked at me like I was the only thing in the universe. My knees buckled a little; I sank onto the edge of the bed, pressing my thighs together to chase the throb.

He gave me orgasms. Plural. Loud, shaking, *his*. And he'd come in his jeans just from tasting me. I bit my lip hard enough to sting, a giddy laugh bubbling up.

I dropped onto the bed, eyes fixed on the ceiling, then closing as my heart thrashed in my chest, refusing to calm. I was back in that bathroom again, hearing his wrecked voice, touching the wet spot, savoring the grin he'd given me, like I'd handed him the world. My fingers curled into the sheets, and I let myself feel it all: the soreness, the ache, *him* still clinging to my skin.

I'd spent so long imagining this moment—what it would feel like if he looked at me, really looked—and now that he had, the room seemed to sway under the weight of it.

My eyes fluttered open, catching on the floor. My shoes I'd kicked off yesterday after class were there, one of them lying on its side. The sight of something so ordinary after a night like this felt unreal, like the world should look different now, because I did.

Then I saw the mess.

The torn pages, ripped photographs, scraps of tape curled like wilted petals. The pieces of everything I'd sworn I was done with.

Sliding off the bed, I crouched down, my fingertips grazing the pile. Bits of glossy paper stuck to my skin. There he was—half a smile, a flash of dark hair, his number scrawled on a jersey sleeve. My throat tightened.

I'd destroyed it all when I'd promised myself I'd stop. I'd told myself I wasn't that girl anymore—the one who waited outside practice, who memorized the shape of his shadow against the field lights.

But tonight had changed everything. Hadn't it?

The thought was soft, coaxing. I smoothed a torn corner of his face, tracing the outline of his grin. It didn't feel like madness now. It felt like hope.

I gathered the fragments carefully, laying them on the desk in a trembling mosaic. My fingers moved before I could think. Strip after strip, I pressed the pieces together, fitting them like a puzzle until his image began to reappear.

Each *click* of the tape made my heart jump.

His smile returned first, that lopsided curve that had wrecked me the moment I saw it on the computer screen. Then his eyes, that impossible blue that never looked the same in pictures. I kept going—his hands, the edge of his uniform, the faint smudge of dirt across his jaw.

By the time I finished, the wall looked almost whole again. Imperfect, patched, some tear stains visible in the right light . . . but he was back where he belonged. Watching me.

I stepped back after I hung up the ball cap I'd taken from him, my breath trembling out of me. "You're mine," I whispered before I could stop myself. Not loud, not certain, just a tiny promise that seemed to fill the room anyway.

My desk chair bumped against my knees. I sank into it, heart still racing, and pulled the new journal from the drawer. I'd bought it yesterday to replace the one I'd torn apart. The cover still smelled like fresh paper and glue, the corners crisp, unbent by restless hands. Opening it to the first blank page, I picked up a pen and hovered it over for a second before my hand started moving.

Mrs. Adler.

The ink bled slightly where I pressed too hard.

Mrs. Ophelia Adler.

The name looked beautiful—too beautiful to be real. I wrote it again, slower this time, tracing each letter like a prayer. The words blurred as my eyes stung, but I didn't stop. The page filled with the shape of his name next to mine, the curl of the *M* looping into my *O*, over and over until it felt like breathing.

My pulse steadied as I wrote. The chaos in my head quieted, every thought narrowing to the rhythm of the pen.

When I finally lifted my hand, the page was full. Dozens of tiny futures stared back at me.

I turned to the next page.

Our wedding, I wrote at the top of the page.

The words wouldn't stop coming, the blue ink curling across the page faster than I could think.

White lights strung through the trees.

The smell of honeysuckle and roses in the air.

He's waiting for me at the end of the aisle, hands in his pockets, that half smile that makes my heart stumble.

His hands find my waist.

He looks at me the way he did tonight—but softer. Certain.

He says my name, not rough or hurried, but steady. Forever.

My breath hitched into something that almost sounded like a laugh.

It wasn't crazy to dream about this. Not anymore, right?

He'd kissed me. He'd wanted me.

He'd never know the real me, the girl who'd waited and watched and loved him long before he ever saw her, but that was okay.

He'd still love a version of me, which is all I'd ever wanted.

I pressed my palm to the journal page, smudging a few of the words, and closed my eyes. I could almost hear his voice again, saying my name like he was treasuring it.

For the first time in years, the ache in my chest eased.

The world outside my window was silent, the campus asleep, but inside my tiny dorm room everything glowed—my wall, my words, my perfect dream.

And sitting there, ink on my fingers, surrounded by his face and his name, I let myself believe it.

Just for tonight.

CHAPTER 15

MATTY

By the time I finally gave up, the sun was already high, the campus dead quiet.

In my brilliant plan from the night before, I'd somehow forgotten one minor detail—it was Sunday today.

And apparently Ophelia, like most students on campus, didn't leave her room on Sundays.

Which meant I'd spent five straight hours camped outside her dorm, half hidden behind a damn oak tree like some idiot stalker, waiting for her to come out.

She never did.

Not once.

At one point, I actually thought about dressing up like a pizza delivery guy—stealing a Domino's hat, showing up at her door, and pretending there'd been a mix-up so I could "accidentally" deliver her lunch.

Just so I could see her face.

The plan even sounded reasonable for about five seconds.

Then I realized she could probably figure out pretty easily that I did not, in fact, work for Domino's, and that obviously made that plan too risky.

So, I settled for the next best thing.

I ordered a pizza, waited until it showed up, and set the box right outside her door. Then I knocked once, hard, and sprinted down the hall like a fugitive before she could open it.

Real smooth, Adler.

Maybe it wasn't flowers or a grand romantic gesture . . . but at least she had something to eat.

Although, I guess I could have allowed the pizza guy to deliver it to her door himself instead of risking her seeing me.

But the thought of some stranger standing there, looking at my girl, even for a second . . . Yeah, no. I couldn't stomach that.

Regardless, I was now sitting on my couch at home—running on no sleep, half a protein bar, refusing to shower because I couldn't stand the thought of washing her off me, and packing enough frustration to start a small riot.

It also didn't help that my dad had been texting all day, demanding we "talk" about last night. Every buzz of my phone made my jaw clench tighter, stacking another layer onto the foul mood already brewing. His tactic today was to try to convince me that I'd "misunderstood" Kenton and that I should let him explain.

I stared at the latest message.

Dad: You're overreacting, son. Kenton didn't mean anything by it. He was just joking around. Don't make this into a bigger deal than it is.

My thumb hovered over the screen, heat crawling up my neck.

Yeah, sure. Because threatening me because I didn't want to get involved in a gambling ring and jeopardize my whole life was *hilarious*.

I tossed the phone onto the cushion beside me, his text echoing in my head long after it hit the couch. The man had a real gift for pretending his bullshit didn't stink.

"Fucking catch the ball!" Jace screamed as he lofted a throw pillow at the TV like the receiver's hands were a personal affront.

I glanced glumly at the replay—the receiver had dropped an easy pass from Jackson Parker, right in the end zone. The ball bounced off his chest and hit the turf, the crowd erupting in boos loud enough to shake the speakers.

Jace slammed his palm on the coffee table and leapt up so fast his beer wobbled on the coaster. "I would never drop that," he said, pacing like he was practicing a postgame interview. "When I get to the pros? Never. That was amateur hour. Unacceptable. You hear me, future opponents? I. Do. Not. Drop."

Parker snorted and didn't bother looking up from his phone. "Keep the pep talk to the mirror, Thatcher," he said.

I glanced over, expecting to see him scrolling through game stats or maybe the team group chat.

Nope.

I saw . . . pink.

For a second, my brain short-circuited trying to process what I was looking at. I could see rows of pastel bottles, someone's hand under a UV light, and a blow dryer was faintly humming.

Was that . . . a nail salon?

I blinked and leaned closer. Yep. Parker was sitting there glued to a live stream of the *inside of a nail salon.*

It took me a solid three seconds to realize what I was seeing. Or rather, *who* I was seeing as Casey's friend Natalie appeared on the screen.

"Wait . . . is that—"

He didn't even look up. "Casey, Riley, and Natalie," he said flatly.

My eyebrows shot up.

"You're watching them get their nails done?"

"I'm watching *Casey* get her nails done," he corrected, giving me a faint shrug, his eyes still locked on his phone.

I leaned closer, doing my best to sound casual even as my brain immediately started plotting. "So . . . hypothetically speaking, how does one, uh . . . do that?"

Parker's gaze finally flicked to me, suspicious. "Do *what*, Adler?"

"Nothing," I said quickly, straightening like a guy who definitely wasn't considering installing hidden cameras on a girl so he could track her everywhere.

Parker stared a beat longer, then went back to his phone.

Out of nowhere, Jace huffed a laugh. "She's so cute."

I glanced up and blinked.

Jace was holding up his own phone, grinning like he'd just cracked the code to life. On his screen was the *same* salon, same pink walls, same terrible background music—just a different pair of hands in frame.

Longer nails this time. Glitter polish. Definitely Riley.

"It's always so cute how they talk about us," Jace mused, leaning back on the couch like he was watching a rom-com instead of a manicure.

Parker didn't even glance up. "She's probably telling them about how you tried to make Pop-Tarts in the toaster *with the foil still on*."

"I like a challenge," Jace said defensively. "Keeps my reflexes sharp."

"If you could challenge yourself somewhere I don't sleep, that would be great." I scowled, realizing now why the house had smelled like it had almost burned down when I'd walked in.

"Shh," Jace said, raising a finger. "She's saying something about me."

Two seconds later, the receiver on the TV dropped another pass, and Jace exploded.

"CATCH THE DAMN BALL!" he roared, chucking the nearest throw pillow at the screen, nearly spilling his beer in the process.

My phone buzzed again, the vibration enough to grate on my last nerve. I didn't even have to look to know that it was my dad again.

I scrubbed a hand down my face and sank deeper into the couch . . . definitely sulking.

Jace's eyes kept flicking between the TV and his phone, a sappy, lovestruck grin tugging at his mouth every time Riley's voice came through the speaker. He'd shout at the TV one second and then melt into a goofy smile the next.

Parker wasn't even pretending to watch the game. He hadn't looked up once, completely absorbed in whatever Casey was saying on the other end. His mouth curved into that quiet, content smirk that only showed up when it involved her.

I sat there, surrounded by two fully grown men acting like they'd been shot by five billion of Cupid's arrows, and tried not to lose my mind.

That's what I want, I realized.

And right now, the girl who made me feel like I finally had something worth wanting was somewhere I couldn't reach.

I clenched my fists against my knees.

Yeah, I was definitely losing it, and I definitely needed a distraction. Or in about ten seconds I was going to rush out of here and pound on Ophelia's door, ruining everything just as it was getting started.

I glanced around the living room, trying to find something, *anything*, since obviously football wasn't cutting it today. My eyes snagged on a brown box by the front door—an Amazon sticker half peeled back because Jace had obviously tried to open it before being distracted by Riley's ass . . . That exact scenario happening at least ten times a week.

Something clicked. I'd placed the order weeks ago on a stupid impulse and then forgotten about it when life got loud. My tattoo kit.

I sat up so fast the cushion squeaked. Perfect.

I shoved off the couch, grabbed the box, and tore it open, spilling everything across the coffee table. Metal pieces clinked against the wood. Needles, tiny ink bottles, cords that looked way too complicated for someone who hadn't slept, and an instruction booklet the size of a novella.

That got their attention.

Jace stopped mid-rant and leaned over the back of the couch. "Um . . . tell me that's not what I think it is."

Parker finally looked up from his phone, his eyes widening. "No," he said immediately.

I frowned. "I didn't even say anything yet."

Jace pointed at the spread like it might bite him. "Because I already know that look. That's your I'm-about-to-ask-you-to-do-something-stupid face."

"I'm pretty sure you're the only one with that kind of face," I drawled, raising an eyebrow.

Jace grinned unrepentantly.

Parker dropped his phone onto the cushion beside him, scrubbing a hand over his jaw. "Matty, you can't just . . . tattoo things."

"Not things," I corrected, grinning as I picked up the machine and examined it like I actually knew what I was doing. "People."

Jace barked out a laugh. "Is now a good time to tell you I like my skin without tetanus?"

"Come on," I said, sitting forward and plugging a cord into the power pack. "You two always say I never try new hobbies. Look at me—personal growth."

"I literally have *never* said you need to try new hobbies," Parker exclaimed.

I grinned and reached for the thick instruction pamphlet, flipping it open just long enough to see a wall of diagrams and safety warnings. The thing read like a legal contract mixed with medical jargon.

I stared at it for maybe two seconds before tossing it back onto the table. "Yeah, I think that YouTube video I watched is gonna be more helpful," I mused, grabbing the tattoo gun like I had a license for this sort of thing.

Parker's eyes widened. "Please tell me you mean a *certified training* video."

"Eh," I said, shrugging. "It had upbeat music and a guy named InkDaddy69 in the title. Close enough."

Jace choked on his beer. "InkDaddy *what*?"

"Focus," I said, testing the pedal until the machine whirred to life. "You two are gonna help me."

Parker blinked. "Help you *what*—bury your mistakes?"

"Help me *not* do something insane," I corrected, pointing the needle vaguely in their direction. "Because right now, thanks to you two and your nauseatingly happy relationships, I've been infected with whatever disease makes a man go completely feral over a girl. And if you don't distract me, there's a solid chance I'll end up on Ophelia's doorstep with a marriage proposal and a matching set of handcuffs."

Jace grinned, leaning back like this was the best entertainment he'd had all week. "So the solution is . . . letting you stab us?"

"Temporary insanity requires extreme measures," I said seriously, lining up the ink bottles like I was preparing for surgery. "One tiny tattoo each. Team solidarity. Bleeding for a brother. Take your pick of inspirational slogans."

Parker groaned, dragging a hand down his face. "You're out of your damn mind."

"Exactly," I said. "Which is why we need to start *immediately*."

Jace looked from me to Parker, then down at the buzzing needle. "You know," he said, grinning, "I've done dumber things for friendship."

"That's true." I nodded as I tested the pedal. The motor buzzed to life with a whine that was equal parts thrilling and terrifying.

Parker held up both hands like I was wielding a chainsaw instead of a needle. "Shouldn't you, I don't know . . . practice on a banana first or something?"

I squinted at him. "How's stabbing a piece of fruit gonna help me tattoo a human?"

He opened his mouth, then closed it again. "I don't know. I just read that somewhere." There was an edge of panic in my QB's voice.

Before I could reply, Jace plopped down right in front of me, rolling up his sleeve with the kind of enthusiasm that only comes when you're about to make a bad decision.

"Don't worry," he said, grinning like a man with nothing left to lose. "I'll be your banana, Matty."

I ignored the clear innuendo in that statement as I set up the supplies like I'd been doing this for years: wipes in a neat row, gloves ready, paper towels fluffed, alcohol on hand.

"I would just like to state for the record that this qualifies me for bestilicious friend number one today," he announced confidently.

I glanced up at him and then over at Parker. "Last I checked, Parker didn't make me go on a date with someone who wanted to use my bones to flavor her soup. It might take a while for you to slip back into that number one role, buddy."

Jace scowled, looking offended. "It's just a *per se* ranking anyway," he muttered. "And that seems like a compliment by the way, that she would want *your* bones in *her* soup. I bet not everyone would qualify for that. So, I still don't know what the big deal is anyway."

I shivered just thinking about my dinner with Emma, ignoring the weird thought I'd just had that I'd be okay with Ophelia saying something like that to me.

I pressed the pedal again to distract myself from whatever weirdness had taken over my brain.

"Ready?" I asked.

"Born ready," Jace said, which is Jace-speak for *I will do this and then pretend it hurt a lot on purpose*. It's exactly the kind of bravado that makes him lovable and mildly terrifying.

I stared at the little sheet of stencils that came with the kit. "Too bad there's not a llama," I mused.

"Um, you know what? It might be better to start off with something simpler. Although, I do appreciate you finally acknowledging our group name," Jace commented, rifling through the paper.

"But also, if you think I'm letting you do a face or anything larger than a quarter, you are out of your mind," Parker said, sounding very serious.

"Relax," I said, continuing to pick through the stencils. "I'm not about to etch your senior portrait on your arm, Parker. I'm thinking something classy. Timeless. Like . . . a lightning bolt. Or a tiny football. Or, ooh—" I grinned. "A heart with my initials."

Jace cackled at that one. "Hell yes, brand me, Daddy."

My smirk fell. "Never say that again."

There was only one person who was allowed to call me *Daddy* . . . and she was unavailable right now.

Jace just waggled his eyebrows like he was going to think it even if he couldn't say it.

Parker sank farther into the couch. "What about a dot . . . or an invisible line?"

Jace snorted as he rummaged through the stencil pile. "A minimalist piece. Very avant-garde. We can call it *The Absence of Pain*."

I rolled my eyes. "I'm not even going to ask where you learned the word *avant-garde*."

"It's probably some weird sex thing," Parker muttered, glancing at his live stream again like he was thinking of a weird sex thing right then as he stared at Casey.

Ugh. *Don't think about sex.*

"I've got it!" Jace suddenly announced, his eyes lighting up like he'd just solved world peace. "NDL."

Parker blinked. "What's an NDL?"

Jace shot him a look. "The *No Drama Llamas*, of course . . . Where's that big brain of yours, Parkie-poo?" he asked sarcastically.

I shook my head. "We still have never agreed on that name," I reminded him.

Jace waved me off like that was a minor technicality. "Yeah, well, I'm the leader of the group, so my vote counts more. It's catchy, it's ours, and it's gonna look badass in all caps."

Parker and I both snorted at the same time.

He glared between us. "What?"

Parker lifted a brow. "Leader of what, exactly?"

"The group!" Jace said, gesturing around like it was obvious. "The vibe. The brotherhood. The brand."

I leaned back, smirking. "Pretty sure the last time we let you lead, we ended up banned from an Applebee's."

"That was a *misunderstanding*," he shot back. "And everyone gets banned from Applebee's at some point. It's just something that happens."

Parker's head whipped toward him. "I've literally never heard that."

He pointed at me triumphantly. "See? I'm the leader because I hear things. This group would be nothing without me."

"We definitely wouldn't be the No Drama Llamas," I agreed.

Jace grinned, clearly taking that as a win instead of the insult it was. "Exactly. You're welcome. Now let's make it official."

Before Parker or I could say anything else, Jace held up his arm like it was about to get knighted. "Alright, Adler. Let's do this before I lose my nerve."

Then he started . . . breathing. Weird, exaggerated, *labor-breathing*—in through the nose, out through the mouth, shoulders rising and falling.

Parker stared. "You're not about to give birth, you know."

Jace glared up at him mid-inhale. "It's called pain management, Parker. Maybe look it up before you start judging."

Parker blinked. "Pretty sure you stole that from a prenatal yoga video."

Jace ignored him, switching to short, loud exhales that sounded like he was trying to blow out birthday candles on a deadline. "Women obviously know what they're doing, so of course I'm going to try their techniques," he explained between puffs.

I grabbed a wipe and cleaned the spot on his arm. "That actually makes sense," I mused.

"This isn't the first time that I've said this," he said, eyes squeezed shut like he was summoning inner peace—or a demon, "but I'm not sure why you always seem so shocked when I say smart things."

Parker and I exchanged another look.

Jace cracked one eye open and caught us. "I see that look," he said, his voice muffled through his steady breathing. "And I'm choosing to ignore it because that's what leaders do."

I tried to keep a straight face as I snapped on my gloves and Jace's shoulders tensed immediately.

"Okay," he said, his voice rising slightly, "maybe just count me down so I know when it's happening."

"Sure," I said. "Three—"

The needle hadn't even touched him yet before he sucked in a huge, dramatic breath, his whole body locking up like he was bracing for impact.

"Two," I continued, fighting a laugh.

"Wait, wait, wait, I wasn't ready—"

I pressed the pedal. The needle hit skin with a sharp *buzz*.

Jace yelped. "OH MY GOSH, WHY DID YOU *LIE*?!"

Parker leaned forward, elbows on his knees. "If he passes out, I'm calling Riley."

"Shut up," Jace muttered, glaring at him.

Jace was *covered* in tattoos already. I suddenly felt bad for every artist who'd had to deal with this level of chaos while holding a needle.

He gritted his teeth, breathing like a man in labor again. "Okay, okay—this is fine. Totally fine. Pain is weakness leaving the body."

"That's what they say," Parker agreed.

"Don't distract the artist," Jace hissed, though his voice came out about an octave higher than normal.

I smirked, focusing on the line. "Almost done."

"Don't say 'almost done'!" he yelped. "That's code for 'something worse is coming'!"

I bit back a laugh, keeping my wrist steady. The tattoo gun buzzed steadily while Jace alternated between whimpering and pep-talking himself like he was running a marathon through a haunted house.

"Breathe," I said calmly. "In through the nose, out through the mouth. Just like your pregnancy classes taught you."

"I AM BREATHING!" he practically screamed with wild eyes. "I AM THE WOMAN!"

That was it. I lost it. My shoulders shook as I tried not to laugh directly into his arm.

"NDL for life, baby," he groaned, sweat beading at his temple. "No drama . . . only llamas . . ."

"Done," I said, finally lifting the needle and wiping the fresh ink clean.

He blinked, chest still heaving. "That's it?"

I nodded. "That's it."

A slow grin crept across his face. "I didn't even cry."

"Are you sure about that?" Parker asked, pushing his sleeve up as he sat down next to me.

Jace ignored him, twisting his arm to admire the crooked, slightly uneven *NDL* scrawled in black. "That's beautiful," he breathed reverently.

I set the machine down. "You're welcome," I said, feeling oddly proud.

Parker sighed as he offered me his arm.

Jace grinned, already leaning forward like an overexcited coach. "That's my boy."

"Less commentary, more disinfectant," Parker muttered, though he didn't pull away.

I grinned, snapping on a new pair of gloves. "At least one of you knows how to commit without screaming."

Jace crossed his arms. "I was *expressing emotion*, Adler. It's called range."

"Of course," I said, cleaning the spot on Parker's arm. The machine buzzed to life again. Parker didn't even flinch. His jaw stayed locked, eyes fixed ahead, calm and steady while I worked.

It took less than two minutes. When I lifted the needle and wiped the skin clean, the fresh *NDL* sat there . . . smooth, straight, and way too perfect compared to Jace's.

Jace immediately leaned in. "Why is his straight?"

"Because he didn't twitch like a toddler on Nerds Gummies," I said, glancing down at my arm and wondering how I was going to do myself.

Jace was still scowling. "This is favoritism. Pure and simple. I demand a do-over."

"No do-overs," I said firmly, capping the ink bottle. "That's not how tattoos work. Or life."

Parker flexed his arm once, examining the mark with a nod. "It's fine. Small. Subtle. And if anyone asks, I'll say it's a reminder not to let idiots with impulse-buys near my skin."

"Fair," I murmured, grabbing a fresh wipe. "My turn."

Jace's eyes widened. "Wait, you're gonna tattoo yourself?"

I shrugged, trying to play it cool even as my pulse kicked up. "How hard can it be? It's just three letters."

Parker leaned back, crossing his arms with a skeptical look. "Famous last words. You sure you don't want one of us to—"

"Nah," I cut him off, snapping on new gloves. "I've got this. Besides, if I screw it up, it's on me. Literally."

Jace hopped up and circled around like a hype man at a boxing match. "Okay, but if you pass out or start bleeding everywhere, I'm here for you."

"Thanks, Thatcher," I muttered, opening the bottle again, and dipping the needle into the ink. I pressed the pedal, testing the buzz against the air one last time. My hand hovered over my skin, steady . . . ish.

Deep breath. In through the nose, out through the mouth. Jace's pregnancy breathing might've been onto something.

The needle touched down on my forearm, and—holy shit—that sting was sharper than I expected. Like a cat scratching with fire claws. I gritted my teeth, forcing my wrist to move in a straight line. *N . . . D . . . L.*

It wasn't pretty. The lines wobbled a bit, like Jace's had, and the *L* came out a little thicker than planned. But there it was: *NDL* etched into my skin forever.

I lifted the machine, wiping away the excess ink. "Done."

Jace whistled, leaning in close. "Not bad, Adler. Kinda crooked, but in a charming I-did-this-while-lovesick way."

Parker nodded approvingly. "Solid effort. Now, wrap it up before we all get infections."

I glanced down at my own tattoo, hoping it wasn't already too late for that. The skin was red around the edges, and the crooked *NDL* looked like it had been done by a sleep-deprived caveman. Which, to be fair, wasn't far off.

"Are you thinking about the fact that we're blood brothers now since we just shared a needle?" Jace asked, far too casually for someone who should've been panicking.

I looked up slowly. "I *wasn't* thinking about that, actually."

Parker looked a little green as he tipped his head back against the couch. "Fantastic. Can't wait to explain to the trainer why we are showing up with matching infections and a team name that sounds like a preschool craft circle."

Jace just grinned, admiring his arm like it was a masterpiece. "No Drama Llamas, baby. We suffer together."

I smiled weakly at that thought. I felt like I was suffering already.

The adrenaline was wearing off fast, leaving behind the itchiness that I'd had the second Ophelia had run away last night. I guess for at least a few minutes the noise in my head had gone still.

But as the buzz of the machine faded, the ache crept back in. The wanting. The restlessness.

Now, all I had to do was survive the night and pray she wouldn't think it was weird if she saw me "accidentally" lingering outside her dorm at six a.m.

Because honestly? I wasn't sure I could make it that long.

I glanced at Jace. "Want to let me do another one?"

CHAPTER 16

OPHELIA

I wasn't supposed to be here.

I'd reminded myself that at least twenty times since leaving my dorm, but my feet clearly didn't care about logic or dignity . . . or the hundred other promises I'd made to stop doing this.

The street was quiet, an early morning stillness that made every sound feel amplified: the *crunch* of gravel under my shoes, the whisper of wind brushing past the mailboxes, the occasional car door slamming somewhere blocks away.

And there I was, standing across from *his* house.

Matty's, of course.

The porch was dark, only the faint spill of light from one window breaking through the shadows. It wasn't hard to spot which one was his; it was the third from the left, blinds half drawn, a narrow band of warm light cutting across the glass.

I shouldn't know that. I shouldn't know what time his car usually pulled in after practice, or that he always turned off the porch light a little after midnight, or that when that single window still glowed against the dark, it meant he was awake, probably sitting on the couch with his legs sprawled, watching film or replay highlights until his eyes went heavy.

But I did.

Because I'd been watching him long before he ever saw me.

And now that he *had*, now that he'd looked at me like I wasn't invisible, I couldn't stop.

I shivered, the early morning chill cutting through my sweatshirt. I wrapped my arms tighter around myself, wishing I could shake off the hollow, jittery feeling that came with being here.

Yesterday, I'd done so well. I'd stayed in my room. Stayed safe. Stayed sane. I even thought maybe I could handle it, handle *him*, like a normal person.

Even when the pizza showed up.

Someone had knocked, and I hadn't even gone to the door at first. I'd assumed it was a mistake . . . because no one ever knocked on my door.

But after a minute, curiosity won. I'd cracked the door open, and there it was.

A pizza box sat right at my feet, still warm, grease staining the cardboard. No sign of a note or name.

I'd stood there staring at it, debating what to do.

Eventually, hunger had won over paranoia, and I'd carried it inside, telling myself it was just some weird mix-up.

I knew it wasn't from him. *Of course* it wasn't.

But the second I took a bite, my mind betrayed me anyway—picturing Matty in the hallway, that crooked grin on his face as he set the box down.

Like he knew I hadn't eaten. Like he was thinking about me too.

It was ridiculous. Impossible.

And I still couldn't stop replaying it.

After that, the quiet had turned into noise, and the noise had turned into ache, and by midnight I'd cracked wide open with the urge to see him.

Now, I was standing under the faint streetlight across from his driveway, trying to convince myself that this wasn't what it looked like.

I wasn't stalking him.

I just . . . couldn't stay away.

I just needed proof he was real, that the way he'd touched me and looked at me and said those things in that bathroom wasn't something I'd dreamed up.

The wind picked up, tugging at my hair and the hem of my hoodie. I took a step closer to the curb, my pulse pounding so loud it echoed in my ears.

A shadow moved behind the blinds, and my breath hitched.

He was there. Awake. Moving.

I knew I should walk away before he saw me, before this crossed into something even worse than it already was.

But my feet wouldn't move. They felt rooted to the pavement, like the sight of him had pinned me in place.

All I could do was stand there, staring at that sliver of light, pretending I wasn't hoping he'd come to the window.

My throat burned as I tried to swallow past the mix of nerves and want twisting inside me.

A part of me almost called his name, just to see what would happen. Just to know if he'd come outside.

But the saner part, the one still clinging to pride and fear, kept me still.

Because if he saw me like this, standing in the dark and staring up at his window like the unhinged, lovesick mess I was, his expression would change.

I could see it already . . . his mouth curving in disgust, his eyes going cold.

He'd never look at me the same way again.

The front door opened.

The sound was so sudden and unexpected that my whole body jolted. My breath caught mid-chest, nerves snapping tight. For a second, I thought I'd imagined it . . . that my brain had finally turned on me completely.

But then light spilled across the porch as the door was opened wider, cutting through the dark.

Matty stepped outside. Sneakers on, keys in hand, hair messy like he'd been pacing instead of sleeping. A worn gray Henley clung to his chest, and for a second he just stood there, scanning the street.

His brow furrowed, like he was turning something over in his head. *You're being stupid*, I thought I heard him whisper.

Panic surged through me, cutting through the haze of shock. Every part of me screamed to move, to run, to do something, but my feet were still refusing to obey, heavy and unresponsive, as if fear itself had pinned me to the ground.

His gaze swept the street until it locked on me, and in an instant, everything inside me went quiet.

He froze, just for a second, like he couldn't quite believe what he was seeing.

I braced myself, waiting for the dread and disgust to twist his face, waiting for him to finally see me the way every other man eventually did when they realized what I was.

Except . . . it didn't come.

His eyes widened, and his whole face lit up, raw and real and achingly bright.

"Thank *fuck*," he called in a voice rough with . . . relief?

Was that what I'd really just heard?

Before I could even think, he *ran*—across the walkway, down the steps, straight toward me.

I stumbled back a step, too stunned to do anything but stand there as he reached me, his hands catching my waist, pulling me into him like he'd been waiting his whole life to find me.

He buried his face in my neck, his breath shuddering, inhaling deep like he was gulping me in.

"I was losing my fucking mind," he muttered unsteadily against my skin, the words vibrating against my throat. His arms locked tighter around me, like if he let go even for a second, I'd vanish.

I was still frozen, every nerve ending on fire. I didn't know what to do with my hands or my heart or the thousand wild thoughts clawing through my head. I'd spent so long imagining this—him seeing me, wanting me—and now that it was happening, now that it didn't seem to be a onetime fluke . . . I couldn't breathe.

He pulled back just enough to look at me, his eyes sweeping over my face like he needed to soak in every inch, to prove I was real. The porch light behind him haloed his silhouette, and when he lifted his head, his eyes were a fierce, impossible blue.

"I was beginning to think I'd made you up," he said quietly, like he didn't even mean to say it out loud. "Like you were just . . . in my head."

My lips parted, but no sound came out.

"I couldn't stop thinking about you," he continued, a small, disbelieving laugh slipping through. "Every time I closed my eyes, you were there. And when I couldn't find you anywhere, I started thinking maybe I'd dreamed the whole thing."

He broke off, shaking his head as his thumb brushed my jaw, soft and trembling. "I thought maybe you didn't want to see me again."

The words hit somewhere deep. The thought of him *searching* for me was too much, almost unbearable. My chest felt like it might crack open from the pressure building inside.

"You . . . searched for me?" The question came out in a gasp before I could stop it, the sound shaky, like I was afraid of the answer.

Something flickered in his eyes . . . something that wasn't just relief. It glimmered there for an instant, a flash of knowing that made my stomach twist. His thumb stilled against my cheek, his voice low but certain.

"I need your number," he said, like it wasn't a question. "Your dorm room. All of it."

My breath caught. "Why?"

His gaze softened, but there was a thread of something else beneath it—possession, maybe. Or at least that's what I was dreaming I was seeing. "Because I don't ever want to lose you again."

That single sentence stole what little air I had left.

I wanted to tell him I'd been here the whole time . . . just not where he could see me. That I'd wanted to go to him but couldn't, because I was too scared he'd realize what I was.

"I—" The word barely scraped out, more breath than sound.

He didn't let me try again.

Matty's hand slid to the back of my neck, and then his mouth was on mine. Warm, assured . . . a little desperate. The world tilted. My fingers tangled in his shirt, clinging like I'd fall apart if I let go. His other hand cupped my cheek, holding me steady as he kissed me again and again, like he was trying to relearn the taste of me.

It felt like stepping into sunlight after living too long in the dark. Blinding, overwhelming, and so warm it almost hurt.

He finally drew back, resting his forehead against mine while his uneven breaths brushed my lips. His voice was soft, almost a whisper. "Why are you crying, Ophelia?"

I hadn't even realized I was until he said it. My face was wet, my chest tight.

"It hurts," I whispered. It was all I could manage, all I could think to say. Because it did hurt—feeling this much, wanting this much, finally being seen after hiding for so long.

His arms tightened, gathering me closer until there was no space left between us. He kissed me again, slower this time, his lips barely moving against mine.

"I know," he murmured against my mouth. His voice cracked just a little. "It hurts for me too, pretty baby."

I let out a broken sound, half sob, half laugh, and sank into him completely. His heartbeat pressed against mine, fast and real, grounding me in the only truth that mattered.

For the first time, the ache didn't feel like it was swallowing me whole.

It felt like it was being *shared.*

CHAPTER 17

OPHELIA

For a long moment, neither of us moved. I could feel his heartbeat thudding hard against my chest, his breath still coming fast where it brushed my temple.

And then he shifted. One arm slid under my knees, the other around my back, and before I could process what was happening, I was lifted clean off the ground.

"Matty—" My voice came out startled . . . dazed. "What are you doing?"

His grip only tightened as he started walking toward the house. The morning air rushed past, cool against my face, and the sound of his keys jingled faintly where they still hung from his hand.

He didn't look down at me when he answered. "Taking you to my bed," he said simply. "Where I've been picturing you since the moment I saw you."

My pulse stuttered so hard it almost hurt. "You . . . what?"

He glanced down then, his mouth curving into something between a smirk and a confession. "Every time I closed my eyes," he repeated again.

The front door came into view, still half open from when he'd run out to me. The sight of it sent a shiver through me, a mix of panic and want so strong I was worried I was going to pass out.

This was it.

The place I'd been desperate to see since the day I first stepped on campus.

I was about to go inside his house. With him.

My fingers curled tighter in his shirt as he carried me over the threshold, every step sending my pulse into overdrive. I could smell him now—soap, skin, and something sensual that made my head spin.

He carried me down the short hallway, the lights dim, his shoulder brushing the wall like even he couldn't walk straight while holding this much need.

We passed a couch I'd imagined him sprawled on so many nights, the faint smell of coffee and cedar clinging to the air. I wanted to look at everything, to memorize every inch of the space that belonged to him, but my focus kept pulling back to him . . . to the warmth of his arms, the sound of his breathing, the steady rhythm of his steps.

When he reached his bedroom, he nudged the door open with his foot and crossed to the bed. The sheets were messy, half pulled back, like he'd been tossing and turning instead of sleeping.

He set me down gently on the edge of the mattress, his hands lingering at my waist before sliding up my sides. My heart felt too big for my chest, my skin buzzing where his fingers trailed.

"Matty," I breathed.

He looked down at me, eyes dark, pupils blown out, every inch of him strung tight like he was barely holding himself together. His thumb brushed beneath my chin, tipping my face up toward his.

"You look even more perfect on my bed than I imagined," he said quietly, the words sinking deep and spreading through me like heat under my skin.

They didn't scare me. They filled something hollow inside me that had always been empty before. Every syllable felt like a thread stitching together all the pieces I'd lost—the ones that already belonged to him, even before he'd known it.

He leaned in, his forehead nearly brushing mine, his voice a rough whisper. "Now I don't have to imagine anymore."

The kiss that followed wasn't soft . . . it was hungry, consuming, like he'd been starving for me. His mouth claimed mine, stealing my breath only to give it back, over and over, until the world narrowed to the press of his lips and the heat between us. I stopped knowing where I ended and he began.

He cupped my face, then let his hands drift down the curve of my neck and along my sides. I was trembling again . . . or maybe I had never stopped.

I'd never get used to this.

Never.

My fingers tangled in his shirt, clutching the fabric like it was the only thing keeping me upright.

When he finally pulled back, his mouth hovered just above mine, his voice unsteady, almost wrecked. "Tell me if you want me to stop."

I shook my head fast, probably looking half crazed with how desperate I felt. "I don't," I said instantly. That was the last thing I wanted. I wanted more, more, more.

There was no end to how much I wanted him.

Something flickered in his eyes, relief again, maybe, or the same kind of madness that had been living in me for months. He let out a ragged breath and kissed me again, slower this time, like he wanted to memorize every heartbeat between us.

"That's good . . . because I don't think I could even if you begged me to," he murmured against my mouth, the words thick with want. "Every time I touch you, it's worse."

It was like that for me too, worse in the way obsessions always are once they're fed. Like something inside me had tasted what it wanted and refused to go hungry again. Every time he touched me, it felt like my body learned a new way to crave him. The ache didn't fade when he pulled away; it multiplied, spreading through me until even breathing without him hurt. I'd told myself for so long that I could manage it, that wanting him in secret was safer. But now that I'd felt his hands, his mouth, his voice breaking against my skin . . . I knew I'd never survive pretending again.

Matty's eyes darkened, that relief turning into something hotter, more primal. He groaned low in his throat, the sound vibrating against my lips as he kissed me again, deeper this time, his tongue sliding against mine in a way that made my toes curl. His hands roamed, slipping under the hem of my sweatshirt, his fingers splaying across my bare stomach.

The touch was incendiary, a live current that burned through me until I arched into him without thinking.

His palms were warm, calloused from football, and every inch they explored left a trail of fire. I could feel the weight of him through the thin fabric, the solid strength of his body pressing closer, like he couldn't stand even an inch of distance between us.

"Ophelia," he murmured against my mouth, each syllable seeming to drip with the same longing I was feeling.

His fingers traced higher, brushing the underside of my bra, and I gasped, the sensation shooting straight to my core, pooling low and hot. He pulled back just enough to look at me, his blue eyes burning, making my heart stutter in my chest. “You’re so beautiful. Look at you . . . already coming apart for me. My pretty baby.”

The words hit me like a wave, praise wrapped in filth, and I melted under them. *Pretty baby*. How many times had I replayed those words yesterday, his voice deep and claiming in my head, echoing through me like a song I couldn’t stop humming? I’d dreamed of this moment so many nights, alone in my bed, fingers tracing paths on my own skin while picturing his, his broad hands, his full mouth, and the way he’d look at me like I was everything.

And now it was real . . . his hands on me, his breath mingling with mine, his body pressing me back against the mattress, the sheets cool beneath my shoulders.

He tugged at my sweatshirt, lifting it over my head in one smooth motion, exposing my skin to the cool air of his room. The early morning darkness cloaked the window, the faint glow from a streetlight outside casting soft shadows across his bed, across his face, highlighting the gorgeous line of his jaw, the curve of his lips.

I shivered, not from the chill, but from the way his gaze raked over me, hungry and reverent, like he was seeing something sacred.

“Fuck, look at these gorgeous tits,” he groaned in a voice thick with awe, cupping one breast through my bra, his thumb circling my nipple in slow strokes until it stiffened under his touch, straining against the lace. “So fucking perfect. I need them in my mouth.”

He dipped his head, his lips sealing over the damp fabric, sucking with just enough pressure to make me gasp, the wet heat of his mouth bleeding through, teasing the sensitive peak beneath.

I moaned, back arching off the bed, pushing myself harder into him, desperate for more.

“Matty . . .” My voice was breathy, needy, and I tangled my fingers in his hair, holding him there, feeling the soft strands slip between my knuckles.

He switched to the other side, teeth grazing just enough to make me squirm. A sweet ache pulsed between my legs, the soreness from Saturday flaring with every tug of his mouth, a delicious reminder of his fingers buried deep, his tongue lapping at me until I shattered.

He unclasped my bra with a flick of his fingers, tossing it aside carelessly. His mouth was on my bare skin in an instant, tongue swirling around my nipple while his hand kneaded the other, rolling it between thumb and forefinger.

"You taste so good," he muttered in a muffled voice, the vibration of his words against my skin sending shivers down my spine. "Every inch of you is perfect. My good girl, letting me have you like this."

His words were sweet poison, seeping into my veins, making me ache for more. He lavished attention on my breasts, sucking one nipple hard while pinching the other gently, rolling it until I was writhing, my hips grinding against the air in search of friction, my core throbbing with need. He took his time, alternating between soft licks and sharp nips, his free hand sliding down my side, tracing the curve of my waist, the dip of my hip, mapping me like he wanted to remember every contour.

I'd been obsessed with him for so long. I'd built entire worlds around him in my head, nights spent replaying glimpses of him, fantasizing about his touch, his voice. And now, he was here, real and solid, his mouth marking me, his hands claiming me.

I wanted to absorb every detail: the way his dark hair fell over his forehead, damp with a hint of sweat; the flex of his shoulders as he moved, muscles bunching under skin; the tattoos inking his arms—an intricate sleeve of symbols and patterns that told stories I wanted to learn with my fingertips, my tongue. I wanted to trace them all, lick along the lines, taste the salt of his skin, feel the raised edges of ink under my lips, commit every swirl and shadow to memory.

"Matty," I whispered, my hands roaming over his back, feeling the muscles shift under my palms, the heat radiating from him like a furnace. My nails scraped lightly down his spine, and he shuddered, a low growl escaping him. "I need to see you. All of you."

He lifted his head, and his eyes met mine. They were glazed and heavy with lust, his pupils wide enough to swallow the blue. "Anything you want, pretty baby."

He sat back on his heels, pulling his shirt over his head in one fluid motion, the fabric catching briefly on his shoulders before falling away. His body was a masterpiece, powerful and sculpted, tapering from a strong chest to a narrow waist, defined abs etched from years of training, that deep V-line disappearing into his jeans like an arrow pointing to sin.

I'd seen him shirtless before—out on the field, when he went running and I'd followed him, in those moments when he'd seemed untouchable, a living, breathing fantasy I had no right to want. But this . . . this was different. There wasn't a crowd or a camera or distance between us. He was here, right in front of me, skin within reach, real in a way that made my throat ache.

A new bandage clung to his arm, but I barely registered it; I was too caught up in everything else. Another tattoo, a band of geometric patterns, wrapped around his bicep, intersecting with a quote inked in fine script that read *Rise. Always Rise.*

My breath caught.

He was going to see mine.

The same words curved along my ribs in French. They did mean something to me, every word of them . . . but I'd gotten them from him. From the day I saw that tattoo on his arm during practice, the sun hitting his skin just right, the words burning into my brain and never leaving.

I'd needed them after that.

Emotion tangled with desire, tightening my chest. I reached up slowly, almost reverently, my fingers trembling as I touched him. I traced the lines of ink over his pec, following them to the steady rhythm beneath, the pulse that matched mine, wild and human and his.

"You're so beautiful," I breathed, the words slipping out before I could stop them. My voice was small, shy, the kind of confession that made my cheeks burn. "I can't believe I'm touching you."

For a split second, mortification fluttered in my chest.

But if he noticed, he didn't show it.

His gaze didn't waver, didn't mock. Instead, something softer flickered there, something that made my stomach twist in a way that had nothing to do with lust and everything to do with how he looked at me . . . like my words had just undone him.

My fingers followed the ink, dipping into the valleys of his abs, circling a small scar just above his hip, a pale mark from some old injury. I leaned in, pressing a kiss to one tattoo, then another, my tongue darting out to taste him. I licked along the edge of a pattern on his ribs, feeling him tense, his breath hitching. Another kiss to his collarbone, my teeth grazing the skin, and he groaned, his hand coming up to cup the back of my head.

His breath hitched again, and he groaned deeper, his hand covering mine, pressing it harder against his chest.

"You're killing me, Ophelia. Touch me all you want. I'm yours."

The words sank into me like a brand, carving their way straight into my heart. I wanted them to be true. Wanted *I'm yours* to mean *you're mine . . .* not just for tonight, but always. The sound of his voice saying it made every fragile, impossible thing inside me ache to believe it.

He leaned down, capturing my mouth in another kiss, his body pressing me back into the mattress, the weight of him delicious, grounding. His hands worked at my jeans, fingers fumbling with the button in his haste, then sliding the zipper down slowly, teasingly, the sound loud in the quiet room. He peeled the denim down my legs, taking my panties with them, the fabric catching briefly on my hips before giving way. I was completely bare beneath him now, the cool air kissing my skin, but his gaze was fire, warming me from the inside out, making me feel exposed and cherished all at once.

He paused, sitting back to look at me, his eyes roaming over my body like he was committing it to memory—every curve, every flush, every tremble.

"Fuck, look at you. Spread out for me, so wet and ready. My pretty baby, all mine."

His fingers traced lightly over my inner thighs, parting them wider, the touch feather-soft at first, then firmer, spreading me open. I whimpered, the anticipation building, my core clenching at nothing.

He dipped his head, pressing open-mouthed kisses to my stomach, my hips, the sensitive skin just above where I ached most, his stubble scraping deliciously.

"I haven't stopped tasting you since Saturday," he rasped. "That bathroom— Fuck, I've come five times just replaying how you flooded my tongue, how you drenched my fingers, how fucking sweet you were. Best thing I've ever had in my mouth. I'm getting it again, baby. Tell me you want my face buried in this pussy as bad as I do. Say it."

His words made me blush, heat flooding my face and core, but they also made me bolder, the praise igniting something confident inside me.

I'd dreamed of this, too . . . of pleasing him, of making him lose control the way he did to me, of tasting him and watching him unravel. "Yes," I said huskily, my voice thick with want. "But I want to taste you, too."

His eyes widened, a pleased grin spreading across his face. "Yeah? You want my cock in that pretty mouth?"

"Please," I begged.

He shifted, undoing his jeans with quick, eager movements, shoving them down along with his briefs, the fabric pooling at his knees before he kicked them off.

His erection sprang free, huge and thick, the tip glistening with precum, the small silver piercing at the head catching the dim light, a glint of metal that made my pulse race.

I stared, my mouth watering, my obsession flaring at the sight of him—bigger than I'd imagined in my dreams, veined and hard, curving slightly upward, the piercing a promise of something new, something intense.

"Yes," I breathed, the word slipping out before I could stop it, raw and desperate. "Yes. I need it."

A rough groan tore from his throat, the sound vibrating against my skin like it came from somewhere deep and uncontrollable. "Fuck, baby, that's it. Show me how bad you need it."

I leaned forward, my tongue darting out to lick the tip, tasting the salty precum beading there. It was addictive—musky, slightly bitter, but uniquely him, a flavor that sank into me like a drug, flooding every sense, making my head spin and my core clench. I wanted to drown in it, to bottle it, to live with it on my tongue for the rest of my life.

I whimpered, the sound surprising even me, shameless and desperate, and took him deeper into my mouth, my lips stretching around his girth, the piercing cool against my tongue.

He was too big.

I couldn't take all of him . . . my jaw already burned from the stretch. But I sank down as far as I could, lips sealed tight, tongue swirling the piercing in slow circles.

My hand twisted at the base, slick with spit and precum, matching the rhythm of my mouth. It was my first time, but I was desperate to get it right, to feel him lose control because of me.

A thrill shot through me as I watched his face contort in pleasure, his head falling back, a low moan escaping his lips, his tattoos shifting with the strain in his neck.

"Ophelia— Shit," he hissed, his hand tangling in my hair, not pushing, just holding, grounding himself as his hips twitched. "Your mouth's fucking unreal. Hot, wet, fucking perfect. My good girl, sucking me so good. Look at those pretty lips wrapped around my cock, begging for more."

His praise spurred me on, and I bobbed my head, hollowing my cheeks, swirling my tongue around the piercing, feeling it bump against the roof of my mouth, the metal warming quickly.

I experimented, flicking my tongue against it, tracing the slit, earning a sharp gasp from him, his thighs tensing under my free hand. He groaned louder, hips bucking slightly, his free hand fisting the sheets until his knuckles whitened. "That's it, baby. Take what you can. You're doing so well—making me feel so good. Fuck, your tongue— Keep doing that. Suck harder, yes, just like that."

I hummed in happiness around him, the vibration making him curse under his breath, a string of filth spilling out. "Fuck, yes, baby. It's so good."

His thighs tensed further, the muscles in his abs clenching, the tattoos rippling with every breath.

Precum spilled in a steady stream, coating my tongue in a salty rush. I chased every drop, swirling, sucking, greedy for more, the flavor exploding across my senses. It was better than any dream, and the fact that I was the one drawing it out of him, that I held this power over the man I'd worshiped from the shadows, made my head spin. I'd replayed this moment a thousand times in the dark, but it was nothing compared to the way his taste flooded my mouth, to the way it made me feel invincible.

My hand twisted faster at the base, slick with spit and him, while my lips sealed around the head, sucking hard, then easing into soft, teasing flicks across the slit. My other hand traced the ink on his abdomen, fingers mapping every line and shadow, then dipped lower to cradle his balls, rolling them gently, feeling them tighten under my touch. He shuddered, a broken string of praise tumbling out, voice cracking with every breath.

"You're a fucking miracle, baby. Look at you, swallowing me down, pulling every drop out of me. My perfect girl, worshiping this cock like it's yours. It is yours, isn't it? You fucking love it."

His voice was strained, his abs clenching harder, the tattoos rippling like waves.

I whimpered in agreement, the sound muffled around him. I did love it. I wanted to worship it, to drain every last pulse from him and keep it inside me. I wanted him to spill down my throat, hot and thick, and I'd swallow it all happily, letting it settle deep in my stomach like a secret I'd carry forever.

I wanted him to feed it to me every day, to mark me from the inside out, to let me taste his release on my tongue at breakfast, lunch, and in the dark hours when the world was quiet and it was just us.

"Fuck," he growled, yanking out of my mouth with a slick, filthy *pop*. A thin strand of spit clung between us for a heartbeat before snapping. He clamped two fingers around the base of his cock, knuckles white, chest heaving as he dragged in ragged breaths.

"I'm not coming until I'm inside you, Ophelia. That's nonnegotiable."

A shiver raced through me, heat flooding my cheeks and pooling low. I nodded, breathless, the words barely a whisper. "Yes. I want that. *Please*."

He eased me back onto the mattress, palms sliding down my arms until my shoulders hit the sheets. His gaze never left mine as he settled over me. "My turn," he murmured.

My body thrummed with need, my lips tingling from the stretch, my jaw sore in the best way. He positioned himself between my legs, his cock pressing against my entrance, the piercing cool against my heat, a teasing promise. "Matty," I whispered, my hands on his shoulders, fingers digging into the inked skin, tracing the patterns there. "You . . . you'll be my first."

The words slipped out before I could take them back, hanging in the air between us.

A sudden wave of fear tightened my chest . . . fear that he'd hesitate, that the weight of being my first would spook him, send him retreating.

I just wanted him to know.

That I'd saved myself for him.

That it was him.

That it had always been him.

He froze. But he didn't seem startled. Instead it was like a switch had flipped for him, locking everything into perfect, inevitable focus.

His fingers dug into my hips, a fierce, claiming pressure that made my breath hitch. A shaky exhale left him, and his blue eyes swept my face as he drank in every flicker of vulnerability like he was etching it into memory.

"Fuck," he rasped reverently. "I knew it." His thumb grazed my cheek, softer now, but the heat in his stare only flared brighter. "No one else has ever touched you. I'm so lucky, sweetheart."

He brushed a kiss against my lips, then spoke against them, his words slipping out in a low murmur that I felt more than heard. "And no one else ever will."

CHAPTER 18

MATTY

No one else.

The words hit me like impact and oxygen all at once . . . stealing my breath even as they filled something inside me. My heart hammered against her, wild and unrestrained, every beat screaming *mine*.

I'd obviously suspected it after the other night, but hearing her say it out loud?

Knowing for sure?

It unlocked something savage in me, a possession that had been simmering since the day I'd seen her, now boiling over.

I gripped her hips harder, fingers digging into her soft skin, needing to anchor this moment, this truth. My eyes raked her face, flushed, wide-eyed, lips swollen from my cock . . . and I committed it to memory.

My little virgin. Completely untouched. Mine to ruin. Mine to keep.

"Fuck," I rasped, the word torn from my throat. "I knew it." My thumb swept her cheek, softer than the storm raging inside me, but my stare burned. "No one else has ever touched you. I'm so lucky, sweetheart."

The thought alone made my cock throb against her thigh, leaking more precum onto her skin.

I was shaking with it—the need to claim, to mark, to erase any possibility of anyone else. She was *mine*. Had always been meant for me, even if I'd only just found her.

I brushed a kiss against her lips, trying to control myself, a growl trapped behind my teeth. "And no one else ever will," I promised.

I crushed my lips to hers, kissing her like a lock snapping shut—teeth scraping, tongue invading, sealing the promise that she'd never know another man's hands, another man's mouth, another man's cock. She was claimed now, whether she knew it or not.

I lined up at her entrance, bare, the piercing brushing her slick heat.

A beat of hesitation hit me . . . I'd never had sex without a condom.

Not once.

Me and the guys even used to lace our condoms with hot sauce after hookups, paranoid some cleat-chaser would try to fish it out of the trash and play baby-trap . . . Jace's idea, of course.

But with her?

Fuck that. I wanted every drop inside her, wanted her to carry me, wanted her pussy painted white with proof she was mine.

"Tell me if it hurts," I whispered, pressing soft kisses to her forehead, her nose, her lips, every inch I could reach while my hands traced her ribs, her hips, committing the body that belonged to me now to memory. "You're doing perfect, Ophelia. My brave girl."

I pushed in slow, inch by inch, and fucking hell . . . the heat of her, the raw, untouched grip, it was fucking unreal. Her walls clamped around me like a fist, slick and scorching, fluttering in panic and welcome all at once. Without latex it was just her, pure and perfect, stretching around every vein, every ridge, the piercing catching on her tightness and dragging a broken gasp from her throat.

My vision blurred.

I'd never felt anything this good, this right. I paused, forehead to hers, struggling to breathe, fighting the animal urge to bury myself to the hilt and never leave. "That's it, pretty baby. Open for me. So fucking tight, so wet. Mine. I could live inside this pussy, never pull out, never let another person see you again."

A soft whimper slipped from her throat, and I felt a fresh rush of slick heat coating me, her walls fluttering harder.

Fuck.

She seemed to love when I praised her . . . loved when I claimed her out loud. I filed it away: My girl got wetter when I told her she belonged to me.

She relaxed, taking a few more inches of me inside her, and I groaned as my control frayed. The way she stretched around me, the slick drag, the heat . . . It was heaven, better than any fantasy. I wanted to stay inside her forever, feel her pulse around me, mark her from the inside out. "Tell me how it feels," I demanded. "Tell me you love it."

"I love it," she panted, her nails digging deeper into my shoulders. Her eyes lifted to mine, copper in the dim light, blown wide and wild. "I want more."

The words punched the air from my lungs. *More*. My virgin girl, still stretched around me, begging for deeper, harder, *mine*. A growl ripped out of me, and my hips snapped forward on instinct burying myself to the hilt, and her back bowed off the bed with a broken cry.

"Fuck, yes," I groaned, the sound torn straight from my chest. "You said you wanted more? I'll give you everything. Every inch, every drop, until you're dripping with me."

"Yes," she breathed, the word a sultry purr that slid down my spine. "Give me that."

Her hands roamed up my back, palms gliding over sweat-slick skin, tracing every ridge of muscle, every line of ink like she was mapping territory she'd already claimed. A small, wicked smile curved her lips, soft at the edges, filthy in the middle, and it lit a fuse inside me.

I started moving. Slow, controlled strokes. Pulling out until just the piercing teased her entrance, then driving back in, deep and punishing, letting her feel every vein, every throb, the metal dragging against that spot that made her eyes roll.

"I love how you take me," I rasped as my mouth sealed over her nipple, sucking hard, teeth grazing as I slammed in again. "So fucking beautiful. So *mine*. This pussy . . . it's strangling me, begging me to stay. I don't ever want out. I want to live right here, buried in you, feeling you pulse around me every second of every day."

Her legs locked around me, hips meeting mine, and I lost it, snapping faster, the bed creaking, headboard slamming.

Mine. Mine. Mine.

The obsession consumed me. Her taste was still on my tongue from Saturday, her virginity was now on my cock . . . her future was in my hands. The way she clenched, the wet sounds filling the room, the way her body arched into mine . . . It was everything. I wanted to drown in her, to stay buried deep, to never pull out.

"Come for me," I growled, thumb on her clit, rubbing tight circles. "Milk me, baby. Scream my name. I want to feel you fall apart around me."

She shattered, walls clamping down, pulsing around me in hot, greedy waves. Her cries rang off the ceiling brokenly, and the way she squeezed me, tight, wet, *mine*, nearly snapped my spine. I couldn't stay inside, not if I wanted to paint her the way I needed to. I yanked out at the last second, fisting myself hard, and came with a roar, thick ropes of cum striping her stomach, her tits, her throat, marking every inch of skin I could reach.

I dropped over her, palms gliding through the mess, rubbing it into her like sacred oil, coating her breasts, her ribs, her belly, sinking it deep into her skin until she glistened with me. She arched into every stroke, eyes glazed, lips parted on a silent moan, like she was drunk on being claimed.

I scooped a thick ribbon from between her thighs, and brought it to her mouth. She didn't hesitate. Her tongue darted out, and she eagerly lapped it up, sucking my fingers clean with a low, erotic moan that vibrated straight to my cock.

Her eyes fluttered shut, lashes dark against flushed cheeks, and she *savored* it, tongue curling, throat working, another moan spilling out as she swallowed. "More," she whispered in a wrecked, greedy voice.

The sound alone almost had me hard again.

I pushed two cum-slick fingers back inside her, curling deep, feeding her what was left. "Take it," I rasped. "Every drop. You're keeping me inside you. Always."

She whimpered, thighs trembling, and I kept going, pushing my cum deeper, watching her pussy clench around my fingers, greedy for more. Her hips rolled up to meet every thrust, a soft, broken moan spilling from her lips as she took it, took *me*. I leaned down, licked a stripe up her neck, tasting myself on her skin. "All mine," I whispered against her pulse.

She shivered, a full-body tremor, and her hands flew to my hair, gripping tight. "Yes," she breathed, keeping her eyes locked on mine. "Yours. Keep me full of you . . . please." Her walls fluttered around my fingers again, another wave of slick heat coating my hand, and she arched her neck into my tongue, chasing the taste of us together.

I rolled us, pulling her on top, arms caging her close as I pushed back inside her.

"You're perfect, baby. I'm so proud of you, taking me, coming for me. My pretty baby." I brushed damp hair from her face. "Rest for a minute. We're nowhere near done."

She melted against me, and I stayed buried inside her. The feel of her stirred me fast, though. My cock thickened . . . stretching her open again.

Her eyes widened, a soft gasp escaping as she felt me swell, filling her completely once more. I flexed deliberately, and she tightened around me.

"Look at what you did," I murmured, brushing my lips against her ear. "I'm already hard for you again. I may never let you out of my bed."

Her lashes fluttered, then she locked eyes with me . . . dark and wicked, *mine*. "I'll never say no to that," she whispered huskily, and before I could process it, she pushed up on my chest.

Her tits bounced with the motion, heavy and flushed, nipples still wet from my mouth. She planted her knees on either side of my hips and *rode* me, slow at first, grinding down until my piercing dragged, then lifting until just the tip kissed her entrance before slamming back down.

"Fuck—" I choked, hands flying to her hips, fingers digging into soft flesh. She was soaked, cum and slick coating my shaft, dripping down my balls with every obscene roll of her hips. Her pussy swallowed me whole, greedy, clenching like it was trying to keep me locked inside forever.

I watched her tits continue to bounce, watched her head fall back, lips parted on broken moans as she fucked herself on my cock, taking what she wanted, *owning* me.

I thrust up to meet her, hard, relentless, the wet slap of skin on skin filling the room. "That's it, pretty baby," I ground out. "Ride me. Take every inch. You're gonna drain me dry, aren't you?"

She whimpered, nodding, hips snapping faster, and I felt her walls flutter, already close again. I sat up, mouth latching onto a nipple, sucking hard, teeth grazing, and she shattered around me, pussy spasming, gripping me with every pulse. I followed with a roar, spilling deep inside her, flooding her until it leaked out around us.

She collapsed onto my chest, trembling, and I held her tight, my cock still twitching inside her.

Fuck. I really may never leave this bed.

Ophelia

The world had gone quiet.

It was a silence that only came after something life altering. It was a soft, aching quiet that hummed under my skin and made even breathing feel like a sacred act. The air in Matty's room was heavy with warmth, the scent of *us* clinging to the sheets, the way the sunlight still lingered across the bed from where afternoon had spilled in through the blinds.

We hadn't left. Not once.

The hours had blurred, melting together into something slow and endless, a rhythm that felt like breathing him in and exhaling everything I'd ever been afraid to want. Somewhere in the middle of it all, he'd mumbled something about practice, reaching for his phone and typing out a text.

"I'm sick," he'd said, fake coughing as he sent the excuse to someone.

He'd grinned after sending it, that crooked, dangerous smile that made my heart squeeze.

And then he'd turned off his phone and tossed it on the nightstand like the rest of the world could wait.

I hadn't thought Matty Adler was capable of skipping practice for anything. But he had. For me.

The realization sat deep in my chest, glowing and terrifying all at once.

Now, hours later, the sun had long since started to fade, and the soft golden light filtering through his blinds had shifted into dusk. I still held him inside me—I couldn't bear to let him slip out, thighs locked, walls fluttering every time he shifted, like the thought of emptiness was unbearable. A pale white film glazed my skin, his cum dried in soft streaks across my breasts, my stomach, my throat, shimmering faintly whenever I breathed. His arm lay heavy across my waist, our legs tangled beneath the sheets, his heartbeat pulsing underneath me steadily. The sound of it soothed me in a way I didn't know how to explain.

I'd never felt anything like this before, this strange, dizzy mix of peace and fear and wonder. Like I'd spent years running and, for the first time, someone had caught me without trying to trap me.

Matty had his face buried against my neck, his breath soft and even, his hand drawing idle circles against my stomach. The weight of his palm was an anchor. Every time he shifted, I could feel the muscles in his arm flex, the scratch of stubble against my skin. I'd thought I'd be shy afterward, maybe embarrassed or unsure what to do with myself.

But I wasn't.

I felt . . . safe.

His voice came quiet, a low rumble against my ear. "Are you hungry?"

I smiled, eyes still closed. "Not yet."

"You sure?"

"Mm-hmm. You've been feeding me all day."

I'd swallowed him down every time he'd let me, first from my mouth, then from my skin, then from his fingers pushed deep inside me. I was obsessed with it, the thick, salty heat of him coating my throat, filling me up, marking me from the inside. He'd scoop it off my stomach, my breasts, my thighs, and I'd open for him like it was the only thing I ever wanted to drink. All day. Every drop. I could still feel it, warm and heavy inside me, and I still was craving more.

He laughed under his breath, the sound vibrating through me, and I struggled not to moan when his piercing hit me just right. "I meant real food," he murmured. "I think we burned through a week's worth of calories."

Heat rose to my cheeks, even though the words weren't teasing, not exactly. There was something soft in the way he said it. Like he was still in awe that I was really there.

A pause stretched between us, not uncomfortable, just full. I could feel him thinking.

"What's your favorite movie?" he asked suddenly, his voice drowsy, the kind of tone that came from hours of lazy, half sleep. He'd been doing that all day . . . asking things. Between the kisses and the laughter and the slow, endless tangling of limbs, he'd kept slipping in questions like he was trying to map me from the inside out. Like knowing me was something he couldn't get enough of, either.

I blinked, trying to think. "Um . . . I don't know. I used to like *Pretty Woman*. My mom had it on DVD."

"Good choice," he said, pressing a small kiss to my shoulder. "Classic."

His fingers kept tracing slow patterns against my skin, gentle and aimless. "What about favorite food?"

I didn't answer out loud. I just thought it, dreamy and shameless. *You. Your cum. It's my new favorite food, salty and warm and all mine.*

He huffed, like he'd heard every word in my head. "Besides my cum, dirty girl."

I winked at him, and he pulled me closer. "Anything sweet," I murmured.

He hummed, his breath warm against my ear. "I would've guessed that. You're so sweet."

It was corny, but I loved it anyway. My lips curved before I could stop them, a quiet, helpless smile I buried against his arm. No one had ever said things like that to me and meant them, not like he seemed to, soft and certain, like sweetness was something good to be.

He kept asking things. My favorite color. Where I wanted to travel. If I believed in luck.

And every question made me ache a little more.

Because I realized I hadn't asked *him* a single thing.

It wasn't that I didn't want to. It was that I already *knew*.

I knew his favorite number—the one on his jersey, the one he'd worn since he was twelve. I knew what he ate before every game. I knew what kind of music he played when he drove home from practice, what brand of body wash he used, how he hated being late and was a creature of habit.

Which made him skipping practice today a really big deal.

I knew the names of his siblings, the way he laughed when he was trying not to, the exact spot on his cheek where his dimple appeared if you caught him off guard.

I knew too much.

And suddenly that knowledge, all those stolen details, felt too heavy to hold.

He shifted behind me, his arm tightening slightly, pulling me closer until my back was flush with his chest.

"You're quiet," he murmured, his lips brushing my shoulder.

"Just thinking," I whispered.

"About what?"

"You."

He laughed softly, a breath against my skin. "Good answer."

When I didn't say anything else, he nudged my side gently. "Ask me something."

I blinked, caught off guard.

"What?"

He smiled against my neck. "You've let me ask you everything. I want you to ask me something. Anything. Whatever you want to know."

I froze.

My mind scrambled for questions, any question, but it was like trying to find something new in a story I'd already memorized. Everything I could think of, I already knew.

He was waiting, though, so I searched for something. Anything.

"Have you . . ." My throat felt tight. "Have you ever been in love?"

The question slipped out smaller than I meant, fragile and stupid. *Idiot.* I could've asked about his favorite color, favorite song . . . anything safe. Instead, I'd cracked myself open.

Matty went still behind me. His fingers froze on my hip. The room turned thick, the quiet pressing in.

I couldn't stand it. Heat flooded my face, the shame terrible and sudden. I shifted, pulling away fast. His cock slid out of me with a wet *pop* that made me want to disappear. I curled onto my side, knees to chest, hiding my face in the pillow.

He didn't move for a beat. Then the mattress dipped. His hand settled warm on my shoulder, not pulling, just resting.

When I finally turned my head to look at him, he was already watching me.

His eyes caught the dim light, unreadable. But it didn't seem like he was avoiding the question. Or that he was about to run screaming from the room. It seemed like he was just *feeling* it. Turning it over in his mind before letting it go.

"Yes," he finally said.

The single word cut through me. My chest went tight, my stomach hollowing out.

I didn't even know why it hurt so much. Of course, someone like him had been in love before. Of course there had been other girls.

Still, I felt it. The sting. The twist. The foolish, impossible jealousy that burned hot and fast.

I looked away before I could stop myself, my breath catching. "Oh."

For a heartbeat, he didn't say anything.

Then, softly, so soft I almost didn't hear it, he said, "With you."

My head jerked back toward him. "What?"

His eyes didn't waver. "You asked if I've ever been in love," he said simply. "Yeah. With you. From the second I saw you."

The words sank deep, spreading through me in a rush that felt both shattering and whole. Like he'd just spoken something my heart had been waiting its entire life to hear.

He said it like it was fact. No hesitation. No teasing smirk. Just truth.

And it was too much.

Tears blurred my vision before I felt them fall. My chest tightened, my throat aching as the first one slid down my cheek.

He saw it immediately. "Hey," he murmured, sitting up slightly. His hand caught my face, thumb brushing under my eye. "Hey, look at me."

I did. Barely. My vision swam.

"You're crying," he said softly, his brows drawing together. "Why are you crying, pretty baby?"

I tried to smile, but it trembled. "Because . . . you mean it."

His jaw flexed, and for a second I thought he might say something, but instead he just kissed me. Slow and deep . . . nothing like the frantic kind of kisses we'd shared earlier. This one was careful, almost worshipful.

When he pulled back, he rested his forehead against mine. "Of course I mean it."

I couldn't stop crying. It wasn't the ugly, hiccuping kind of crying. It was quieter than that, the kind that comes when you've been holding too much inside for too long and suddenly someone gives you permission to let it go.

Matty brushed the tears away one by one, his fingers tracing down to my jaw. "I'm surprised you couldn't feel it," he whispered.

I swallowed hard. "Something like that feels more like a hope than a reality."

His mouth curved into a small, disbelieving smile. "You make it sound impossible."

"It felt impossible," I admitted. "Before you."

He searched my face, obviously not understanding what I meant. But then he kissed me again, softer this time, like a promise.

We lay there in silence, his hand running slow lines down my spine, my fingers tangled in the sheets. Every once in a while, his thumb would drift over the back of my neck, a quiet reminder that he was still aware of me.

I couldn't stop staring at him . . . the faint stubble along his jaw, the way his lashes cast small shadows across his cheeks, the tiny scar above his brow I'd noticed from the first photo I'd ever seen of him.

He caught me staring and smiled. "What?"

I shook my head. "Nothing."

He tilted his head. "You're thinking something."

I hesitated, then said quietly, "Just that I never thought I'd end up here."

His smile softened. "With me?"

"With *you*," I said, my voice small. "And you saying things like that."

Matty's expression shifted; something tender flickered behind his eyes. "Get used to it," he said, "because I'm not planning on stopping."

I laughed softly, the sound half choked by tears. "You always know exactly what to say."

He leaned in until his lips brushed my ear. "Only with you."

I closed my eyes, the warmth of his voice sinking into me, wrapping around all the broken, jagged places that had been empty for so long.

I didn't tell him that I'd spent years dreaming of someone saying those words. That I'd built entire fantasies around the idea of his love.

The last of the daylight faded, leaving us in the hush of his room. The hum of the ceiling fan. The steady rhythm of his breathing.

He shifted once, his arm tightening around me, and then his breaths evened out, deep and slow . . . sleep taking him easily, like it always must for people who didn't live inside their own heads.

Another tear slipped free before I could stop it, sliding down my temple onto his pillow. The thought came quiet but sharp, cutting through the softness of the moment.

He never asked.

He hadn't asked why I was standing in front of his house this morning, trembling and half crazed. He didn't wonder how I knew where he lived, or why I'd been there at all.

Because he didn't really know me.

He couldn't love me, not the real me, because he hadn't seen her yet.

I closed my eyes, letting the dark press in. His heartbeat pulsed against my back, warm and steady, and still . . .

Somewhere deep inside, I knew it couldn't last.

Love built on secrets never does.

But that didn't stop me from wanting to keep it, to clutch it with both hands, even as the edges cut into me, even as I felt it slipping through my fingers.

I would try to hold on to it for as long as I could.

CHAPTER 19

OPHELIA

The campus sidewalk stretched out in front of me, cracked concrete dusted with brittle leaves under the pale afternoon light. My earbuds were in, but no music was playing—I hadn't pressed play. I just wanted the illusion of being busy, of functioning like a normal person.

But I wasn't thinking about class. Or the people passing by. Or anything real.

I was thinking about Matty.

About waking up tangled in his sheets, his arm draped heavy across my waist, his skin still warm against mine. About the faint smell of him, soap and sweat and something that already felt like home. About how, when we finally dragged ourselves out of bed, he'd caught my wrist at the door, pulled me back in, and said it, soft, almost shy, but certain.

I love you.

The words had followed me out of his house, trailed me all the way across campus, looping through my head like a song I couldn't stop replaying.

Now, everything felt dim in comparison. The sound of traffic. The chatter of other students. None of it mattered.

All I could see was him. The way he'd looked at me when he said it . . . like he already belonged to me.

I could still feel it, too, that dangerous flutter under my skin. It made me imagine things that would terrify him. White fabric. Soft lights. His eyes when he turned and saw me walking toward him.

It felt inevitable right now, though. Now that I'd had him, I would do anything it took not to let him go.

It was why I hadn't said *I love you* back yet.

Not because I didn't feel it. But because it didn't feel *big enough*.

What I felt for him went so far beyond those words that it scared me. It wasn't just love . . . it was everything. All-consuming. Boundless. Like he'd been stitched into my veins, like my heart had rewritten itself around his name.

That was why I'd stayed quiet. Because if I tried to say it out loud, it wouldn't come out soft or simple. It would be too much.

And I wasn't ready for him to see *that* part of me yet.

"There she is!"

The words came from somewhere behind me, close enough to make the hairs on my neck lift.

I spun around so fast my earbuds nearly flew out. Nothing. Just the cracked sidewalk, the half-empty quad, a few students trudging past with backpacks and coffee cups, none of them looking at me.

Then I caught movement at the edge of my vision—a flash of blonde hair catching the light before disappearing behind the brick column of the library.

I froze mid-step, squinting like maybe if I narrowed my eyes enough, I'd X-ray the wall and catch whoever it was.

No one.

"Okay . . ." I muttered, turning back around, forcing my legs to keep moving, even though my skin prickled with that creepy feeling of being watched.

Half a block later, it happened again.

A shuffle of sneakers against pavement. A whisper too low to make out.

I stopped dead, spinning in a full circle.

This time, I caught it clear as day. A blonde ponytail vanishing behind the student center.

I opened my mouth to say something, but before I could, another voice hissed—clear, urgent, and definitely not meant for me. "Crap. She heard us."

My eyebrows shot up. *Us?*

Oh, fantastic. I hadn't just acquired one creeper. I had multiple. Like Pokémon, but worse.

I wasn't exactly in a position to judge anyone for lurking, but still . . . being the one on the *other* side of it felt wrong. Especially when the only person I'd ever want watching me was Matty.

The wind shifted, carrying what sounded like a hushed argument from behind the building. A sharp *shh*. Then the unmistakable slap of a hand hitting a forehead.

I groaned under my breath. "This would be a really inconvenient time to be murdered."

The whispers started again, fast and panicked, like middle schoolers caught playing ding-dong ditch.

"She's looking this way—"

"I told you to stay lower—"

"Well, you're the one who—"

Another frantic shush.

I stood there, bag slipping off one shoulder, staring at the corner where the voices had tangled themselves up.

Whoever these mystery women were, they weren't exactly criminal masterminds.

All I could hope was that if I pretended hard enough not to care, maybe they'd get bored and slide back into whatever hole they'd crawled out of.

I tugged my bag higher on my shoulder, took a deep breath, and started walking again.

Behind me, someone hissed, "Go, go, go!" followed by the sound of running feet.

Yeah. Totally normal.

I stopped in my tracks, spun on my heel, and shouted, louder than I meant to, "Why exactly are you following me?"

The whispers went quiet for half a beat, and then . . . chaos.

More frantic whispering. "Shh!"

Another voice groaning, "Told you she'd catch us!"

I folded my arms, trying to look annoyed instead of anxious, my foot tapping against the concrete in quick, uneven bursts I couldn't quite control.

Finally, three heads peeked out from behind the corner of the building.

Not the shady creeps I'd imagined. Not at all.

And I knew exactly who they were . . . even if I wasn't supposed to.

Casey, Parker's girl, stood in the middle, her glossy raven hair catching the light, tall and striking in that quietly intimidating way she had. Beside her was Riley, Jace's girl, all golden hair and long legs, the kind of pretty that made people stop mid-sentence. The third one, the shortest of the group and equally as gorgeous, had a bright blonde ponytail and an expression halfway between excitement and panic. Natalie. Their best friend.

They exchanged quick looks, like deciding who was about to be sacrificed.

Natalie sighed dramatically and stepped out, marching toward me with her hands raised in mock surrender.

"Thank goodness," she announced in a voice cheerful enough to carry across the entire quad. "The spy life is exhausting." She fluttered her hands like she'd just dropped invisible binoculars. "But if you need me to look up anyone on the internet, I can definitely do that. My FBI-agent-level stalking skills are unmatched."

My eyebrows climbed so high they were practically in my hairline. "What?"

"Don't worry," she chirped, stopping right in front of me, all smiles and dimples. "We're harmless. Promise. Just . . . dedicated. In an admirably nosy way."

Behind her, Casey groaned, dragging a hand down her face, while Riley mouthed something that looked a lot like *oh my gosh.*

Natalie just beamed at me like we were already best friends.

She tilted her head, eyes sparkling like I'd just been adopted into some secret sorority. "Can I call you FiFi? You look like a FiFi."

I blinked. "Do I . . . know you?"

I mean, I *did* know them.

I'd watched them from afar every time they'd been near Matty . . . but obviously we'd never met in real life.

From behind her, Casey pinched the bridge of her nose and sighed like she'd aged ten years in ten seconds. "Don't mind her," she said dryly. "I'm Casey." She gestured vaguely at herself, then nodded toward Riley, who gave a little wave.

"Riley," Riley added warmly, like she was trying to balance out Casey's deadpan.

"And Natalie!" Natalie chimed, beaming and practically bouncing on her toes. She jabbed her thumb toward her chest like I'd missed that she was introducing herself.

"You're . . . dating Matty's friends," I blurted, my voice pitching awkwardly high.

The words tumbled out before I could reel them back, and the second they landed, I wished the ground would just split open and swallow me whole.

I'd said that too fast.

Normal people wouldn't just *know* that. I could practically feel the panic creeping up my throat as I scrambled to think of something, *anything*, that would make it sound less like I'd been watching them for months.

I was so screwed.

All three of them exchanged glances.

"Aw, Adler does love us! He talked about us!" Natalie squealed, clapping her hands together before looping her arm through mine.

Relief crashed through me so hard my knees nearly gave out. They thought *he'd told me about them*. Not that I already knew . . . every name, every face, every photo I'd memorized like it was gospel.

Warm, bubbly, and impossible to resist, Natalie started steering me across the quad before I could even form a protest.

"It's so nice to meet you!" she said, dragging her words out like they had been centuries in the making. "We've been begging him all morning to let us meet you! Any girl who can keep Adler in his room for twenty-four hours and convince him to skip practice . . . You have powers, woman. But nooo, he's been all growly and possessive. 'Stay away from her, don't scare her off, she's mine, grumble grumble.' So we took matters into our own hands."

My brain short-circuited halfway through that sentence.

"I— Wait— What?"

"Growly," Natalie repeated cheerfully. "You know, all protective and territorial, like some giant caveman. It's kind of hot, honestly. Very *mate-for-life* energy. Which, obviously, you're into."

I opened my mouth, closed it again, and managed a strangled, "I . . ."

Casey muttered something under her breath that sounded like *you're going to scare her away*, while Riley smiled kindly, the same way you would at a skittish animal you don't want to spook.

Meanwhile, Natalie squeezed my arm tighter, grinning like she'd just declared us blood sisters. "Don't worry, FiFi. We're totally normal."

My mouth opened, but no words came out. Nothing. Just a faint, useless squeak like I'd swallowed a kazoo.

I wasn't used to this. Girls. Normal—or maybe not-so-normal—girls wanting me around. High school had been a battlefield I'd lost before I even stepped onto it. After everything with Nico, the sideways stares, the whispers in the hall, the rumors that followed me like shadows . . . well, I hadn't exactly walked out of there with a thriving girl gang and collection of friendship bracelets.

Standing here with three beautiful, confident women like them made something deep inside me ache. *Yearn*, even. I wanted to belong. I wanted them to like me so freaking much.

And yet, the yearning tangled with panic, squeezing tight. They didn't know. They couldn't know. If they ever saw how broken I really was, they'd bolt like everyone else.

I was so far in my own head that I almost missed it.

"No Drama Llamas," Natalie declared brightly.

My head jerked up. "Wait. What did you just say?"

I'd heard Jace mention it a few times while joking with Matty after practice, his voice carrying across the field while I hid in my car, desperately listening out my windows to catch anything I could.

I was pretty sure it was supposed to be the name of their friend group. But I wasn't positive. And I hadn't wanted to ask Matty and tip him off that I'd heard of it to begin with.

Maybe I could find out now.

"Nothing," Casey cut in quickly, her tone flat but her cheeks pink. "It's not an official name. You don't have to go along with it."

Natalie gasped like Casey had just committed treason. "Excuse me? That's blasphemy." She leaned in, stage-whispering dramatically, though half the quad could probably hear her. "Don't listen to her. She's just unsure of our branding potential. Obviously, it's the group name. It's destiny."

Riley groaned, tipping her head back to glare at the sky like it might rescue her. "Don't say anything to encourage her . . . or Jace."

A giggle escaped my lips, and Casey gave me a look that said *welcome to the asylum* before tugging her phone out like she wanted plausible deniability for the entire interaction.

Natalie suddenly gasped, spinning toward me with the kind of dramatic flair usually only reserved for stage musicals. "Oh! Phone. Good call, Case."

She whipped hers out of her back pocket, pink glitter case sparkling in the sun, and shoved it into my hand like it was a baton in some relay race I hadn't signed up for. "Type in those digits, FiFi."

I stared at it, utterly bewildered. "Why?"

Her face fell into a frown so exaggerated it almost looked cartoonish. "What do you mean, 'why'? So we can hang out, of course."

I blinked at her, throat tightening around words I wasn't sure I wanted to say. "You . . . want to hang out with me?"

Before Natalie could unleash another gasp, Riley slipped to my other side and threaded her arm through mine, her smile softer than Natalie's but just as sure. "Of course we do."

That was it. The wobble in my chest went from tremor to earthquake. I swallowed hard, trying to act normal, like this wasn't the first time ever that anyone had wanted me around just because.

Okay, maybe it wasn't just because. They'd wanted to meet me because of Matty.

But that could change to wanting to hang out with me because they liked me. Right?

"Okay," I said, keeping my voice light, casual. Normal. Totally normal. I typed my number in, handed the phone back, and hoped no one noticed how shaky my fingers were.

"Perfect," Natalie chirped, firing off a text. My phone buzzed with a message I assumed was from her. "We're going to get our nails done, obviously. And coffee. And you're going to sit with us at the games because the three of us together are already iconic, but with you? Absolute chaos. The fun kind."

My stomach dropped. "Oh. Actually . . ."

Natalie's head snapped up, eyes narrowing in mock suspicion like she was expecting me to try to run and planning how she was going to tackle me before I could do it. "Actually what?"

I braced myself. "I'm . . . uh. The team mascot."

There was a beat of silence.

Then Natalie shrieked, "NO WAY." She bounced on her toes, clapping like she'd just won the lottery. "You're kidding. You're literally the tiger?"

"Um." Heat rushed up my neck. "Yeah."

"This is fate. You are my hero," Natalie declared, eyes sparkling. "I'm the biggest Tigers fan on the planet, so obviously this is another sign we're supposed to be best friends." She grabbed my hands and shook them like we were sealing some kind of deal. "Do you understand? You're my new favorite person."

"And she usually only reserves that for baristas when they remember her complicated latte order," Casey said, sounding impressed.

Natalie scoffed. "This is so much bigger than good coffee, Casey. She's the freaking tiger! That might even beat out Nerds Gummies!"

Riley and Casey both gasped like that was the boldest thing she'd ever said.

I stared at them. I was sure there was a goofy smile on my face as I did it.

And I kept thinking . . . *they don't ever need to know.*

They didn't need to know that I hadn't become the mascot because I loved the Tigers. Or because I wanted to dance. Or even because I wanted to be part of something bigger.

They didn't need to know that the only reason I put on that sweaty tiger head in the first place was because it got me within twenty yards of Matty Adler.

"Lunch," Natalie announced, snapping me out of my thoughts. She pointed at me with all the force of a drill sergeant assigning orders. "Today. You, me, Casey, Riley. No excuses."

Casey's mouth curved, a quick grin breaking through before she nodded. Riley followed instantly, her hair shining in the light as she nodded along, too, eyes bright. It was like they'd just collectively decided this was the best idea in the world, and somehow, I was part of it.

"Today," I echoed, my voice small but hopeful.

Natalie beamed like I'd just agreed to a blood pact. "Good. It's settled." She tugged Riley forward, already launching into a ramble about where they should eat, and Casey trailed after them, shaking her head but not objecting.

I stayed there for a second, watching them go.

And then—

A smile stretched across my face, wide and real, the kind I couldn't remember the last time I'd felt. My chest felt light, almost giddy, like I'd been carrying a boulder around my whole life and Matty had finally shown me what it felt like to set it down—like he'd given me a world where I didn't have to keep holding my breath.

Friends.

I had lunch plans.

As we parted ways, the echo of Natalie's laughter still hanging in the air, I hugged the feeling close like it was the most fragile, precious thing in the world.

Maybe this was what normal felt like.

And maybe, just maybe, I could hold on to it.

They don't need to know . . .

The professor's voice droned on at the front of the room, words blurring into background noise as I stared blankly at my notebook. I hadn't written anything in twenty minutes. My pen just hovered uselessly over the page while my stomach tied itself into tighter and tighter knots.

Lunch.

With them.

I'd started off thrilled, obviously. But the closer it got, the more my excitement started to unravel into panic. Because what if once they got to know me, really know me, they didn't like me?

And if they didn't like me . . . what if they told Matty?

The thought made my pulse flutter. Maybe I should text Natalie and cancel. Say I wasn't feeling well. That would be true enough—my nerves were practically making me nauseated.

I slipped my phone out from under the desk, thumb hovering over her contact.

And then the door opened.

Every head in the room turned as someone stepped into the doorway.

Matty.

He leaned one shoulder against the frame, his black Henley stretched tight across his chest, orange sweatpants hanging low on his hips, and those perfect blue eyes finding me instantly. It felt like the whole room disappeared for a second.

The professor stopped mid-sentence. "Can I help you?"

Matty's voice was smooth but steady when he answered. "Yeah, sorry to interrupt, but I need to borrow Ophelia."

My name hit the air like a fire alarm. My head snapped up, heat flooding my face as everyone turned to stare.

The professor frowned. "Class is almost over. Can it wait?"

"No, ma'am," he said easily, flashing a smile that made my insides twist. "It's important."

There was a beat of silence, the kind that stretches just long enough to make your pulse go wild. Then she sighed, defeated. "Fine."

Matty grinned, boyish and unapologetic, and I watched as my hardened professor literally swooned.

I didn't blame her . . . I was swooning, too.

I scrambled to shove my notebook and pen into my bag, my hands shaking as I stood. A few whispers rippled behind me, someone giggled . . . someone else muttered *holy shit.*

I didn't look back.

Matty stepped aside to let me pass, but the second the door closed behind us, he caught my wrist and pulled me down the short stretch of hallway, out of sight of the windowed door.

"Matty—what are you—"

He didn't let me finish.

Before I could take another breath, his mouth was on mine.

Everything stopped. My notebook slipped from my hands, hitting the floor with a dull *thud.* He pressed my back against the wall, his hands framing my face, his kiss deep and consuming and dizzying. It wasn't gentle. It was the kind of kiss that said he'd been waiting all morning to taste me again.

My head spun. Every thought, every worry about lunch with the girls, or being good enough dissolved under the weight of him. His tongue brushed mine, and the noise that left my throat didn't even sound human.

He rested his forehead against mine, his breathing still uneven and hot between us.

"I couldn't wait a second longer," he murmured hoarsely, pressing himself against me so I could feel how hard he was. "I left class early and sprinted here, watching from the window and trying to hold myself back."

He grinned unrepentantly. "As you can see, I lost that battle."

A thrill ran through me. The image of him, restless and wanting, watching from the window, fighting the same pull that had wrecked me for months . . . I loved it.

I loved knowing he couldn't stay away. That whatever this was, it wasn't just in my head. My hands slid up his chest, feeling the steady hammer of his heart beneath my palms, and I couldn't stop smiling, couldn't stop touching him.

"You looked far away in there," he teased. "What were you thinking about?"

I took a deep breath, summoning the courage to answer honestly. But he'd just revealed how much he missed me, right? So was it alright for me to do it, too? He wouldn't get scared? "I was thinking about you," I finally admitted shyly.

A slow grin curved his mouth, the kind that always made my knees go weak. His thumb brushed my jaw. "Good," he said softly. "Because I can't stop thinking about you for even a second. At this rate, I'm not even going to graduate unless I figure out a way to focus in class."

He kissed me again, slower this time, and for a second, everything outside that hallway vanished.

Lunch. Classes. Whispers. None of it mattered.

It was just him. Always him.

I was vaguely aware of doors opening and people coming out into the hallway, but I couldn't spare them a look. When he was near, it was like no one else existed.

"Let me take you to lunch," he urged as he pulled back just enough to get the words out.

My heart leapt, my lips parted . . . ready to say yes, to say anything he wanted . . .

"Matthew *Clay* Adler," Natalie's voice rang out like a trumpet, cutting through the air. "Step away from our new best friend."

Matty didn't move. He actually growled against my lips. A low, frustrated rumble that vibrated down my spine.

"First . . . how do you know my middle name? And second . . . she's *my* best friend," he shot back, eyes still locked on mine like he was daring me to contradict him.

I *also* knew his middle name. But I wasn't ever going to admit that.

"Also, how do you even know her?" he added after a second, a cute, confused frown spreading across his lips.

"That was three things, Adler," Natalie snapped.

There was a chorus of laughter and soft gasps from somewhere over Matty's shoulder. I finally moved my head enough to see them—Natalie standing like she'd just declared war, Casey with one arched brow and a smirk, and Riley biting back a smile like this was the best entertainment she'd had all week.

"Oh, this is good," Natalie whispered loudly, practically vibrating with glee.

Out of nowhere, Jace appeared, radiating the same energy as a fire drill during finals week. "Who's your best friend, Riley-girl?" he demanded dramatically before scooping Riley clean off her feet. She shrieked, laughing as he spun her around in the middle of the hallway, her hair flying and her arms flailing.

"I'm your best friend!" Jace crowed, spinning faster. "Your bestest friend!"

"Put me down, you psycho!" Riley smacked his shoulder, even as she laughed harder, clearly not meaning it.

Finally, Jace set her on her feet—well, kind of. He didn't actually let her go. Instead, he wrapped both arms around her waist and snuggled his head against her shoulder like a giant golden retriever who thought he was a lapdog.

Riley rolled her eyes but didn't push him off, her cheeks flushed with affection.

Casey beamed, her whole face lighting up as she watched them. It was the kind of look that made me ache a little, even though I couldn't quite place why.

"Don't look at him anymore," Matty muttered under his breath, almost sounding jealous as he tugged me closer like he was blocking my view of the entire Riley-and-Jace spectacle.

"Excuse you," Jace said, dramatically affronted. "How can you *not* look at this?" He made a Vanna White motion to himself, nuzzling Riley's hair for good measure. "I'm giving you award-winning content for free."

"You're giving me heartburn," Matty shot back in a voice as dry as sandpaper.

"Heartburn?" Jace gasped. "That's just love trying to crawl out of your chest."

Natalie clapped her hands together like she was at the theater. "Casey, see. I told you that was a thing!"

Casey elbowed her, but she was smiling, too.

Matty ignored them all, turning his gaze back to me—serious now, like he'd remembered something important. "Remember Ari Lancaster's radius idea, Jace?"

Jace perked up. "The one with the circles?"

Matty nodded. "Yeah. We need to implement that."

"Wait," Natalie cut in, brows knitting. "Is this a football thing or . . . like, a sex thing?"

"Neither, Bennett. It's a girlfriend rule, obviously," Matty said with a smirk, steadying me with a hand on my waist when I nearly stumbled at the word. "Ten feet minimum around my girl. Twenty, if the guy looks like he lifts." He glanced over at Jace. "So obviously, you would just need to abide by the ten-foot one. I'd like to inform you, though, you are violating my radiuses right now."

Jace's eyes widened in outrage. "How am I supposed to make new best friends with Ophelia if I've got to stay twenty feet away? I'm a hands-on kind of guy!"

"It's only ten," Matty deadpanned.

"Details," Jace said breezily, waving his hand like it didn't matter. "Ophelia, back me up here. Wouldn't you prefer a Jace Thatcher bear hug over a Matty Adler sulk in the corner?"

I opened my mouth, but no sound came out. There was so much going on right now, and I was pretty sure Matty had just referred to me as his girlfriend in front of almost his entire friend group.

A girl could only handle so much at one time.

Matty grinned. "She's obviously following the rules already, like the good girl she is. You can't talk to her unless you're ten feet away."

"Fucking hell. He just called you *good girl*, Ophelia. Gird your loins, sister. You might be pregnant," Natalie said, grabbing onto Casey like she was in danger of falling to the floor.

My head was spinning.

"Nice to meet you, future bestie," Jace said as he threw out his hand.

Everyone laughed except for me.

Because I was suddenly feeling guilty.

I knew Jace Thatcher. Just like I knew them all.

Not personally, obviously. But in the same way I'd memorized Matty. By watching. By listening. By piecing things together from practice fields and glimpses in the student union.

I knew Jace was loud, ridiculous, always the first to crack a joke. I knew he had an ego the size of the stadium but a loyalty that matched it. I knew Riley had been his from the second he laid eyes on her, and he wore that devotion like armor.

I already knew more about him than he could guess.

I was such a freak.

Matty pressed my hands against my side with zero subtlety. "Tell the bad man," he murmured, eyes locked on mine, "to stay a radius away from you."

The seriousness in his tone, paired with the ridiculous wording, knocked the angst right out of me, and a startled giggle burst out before I could stop it.

Jace grinned like a cat about to cause trouble. He lowered his hand and then immediately picked up Riley, swinging her around again until I was sure she was about to throw up. "See? She laughs at me. It's fate. She wants me within the twenty-foot radius."

"Lunch," Natalie declared, pointing dramatically toward the exit like she was leading a parade. "All of us. Right now."

Matty groaned, dragging a hand down his face. "*I* was going to take her to lunch."

"Sorry, Adler," Natalie singsonged, already looping arms with Casey and Riley. "We asked her first. You're lucky we're even letting you tag along."

He muttered something under his breath that sounded a lot like *I hate llamas*, but he still reached for me. His fingers slid between mine, warm and certain, like it was the most natural thing in the world.

"Fine," he said, giving my hand a light squeeze as we started walking. "But only because I think she likes you."

My pulse skipped, the air catching somewhere in my throat.

"Do you . . . want to go?" he asked softly, his voice lower now, meant only for me.

I nodded, shy but sure. "Yeah."

We fell into step beside the others, his thumb tracing lazy circles over my knuckles, and I tried to focus on anything other than the dizzy, floating feeling in my chest.

After a moment, I couldn't hold it in. I glanced up at him, praying this wouldn't end in embarrassment. "Did you mean it?" I asked quietly.

He looked down at me, brows pulling together. "Mean what?"

"That I'm . . . your girlfriend."

For a second, he just stared at me. Then that slow, devastating smile spread across his face, the one that made everything else disappear.

"Yeah, pretty baby," he said, leaning close enough for his breath to brush my temple. "You are."

The words sank into me like honey . . . slow, golden, and so sweet it almost made my teeth ache.

And as we walked across campus, his hand still wrapped around mine, that feeling hit me again, like I wasn't just watching a dream from far away.

I was in it.

CHAPTER 20

OPHELIA

The diner Matty steered me into smelled like frying oil, pancake syrup, and coffee so strong it could probably polish a floor. Neon signs buzzed above a row of cracked vinyl booths, and the floor tiles were the kind of yellow-white that promised decades of stories under their scuffs.

If I'd been alone, I would've turned around and walked out. Noise pressed against me from every angle . . . forks scraping plates, ice rattling in glasses, laughter pinging off chrome-edged counters. I could feel my lungs tightening, my brain already negotiating exit strategies.

But then Matty's hand tightened around mine, and all the anxiety flapping around inside me . . . it settled. "C'mon, pretty baby," he murmured, tugging me toward the corner booth.

Calling it a booth was generous. It was more like a small, padded amphitheater, somehow big enough to fit the seven of us. Natalie slid in first, waving her phone around and talking so fast it took me a second to realize she was mid-rant about pancakes.

Casey followed, sliding in beside her, while Parker, who had met up with us on the walk over, squeezed in next to her. Jace and Riley took the opposite side, Riley's head resting against his shoulder as he waved a fork through the air, animatedly reenacting how he'd gotten himself banned from Applebee's.

Matty slid in beside me, taking up way too much space and still managing to make me feel like there was nowhere safer in the world to be. His thigh brushed mine under the table, warm and solid, and I could smell soap and skin and the faint scent of salt on his neck when he leaned close.

He pressed a quick kiss to my temple before anyone noticed. "You okay?"

I nodded, though I wasn't sure if that was true. My heart was already racing, but not from panic this time. From *them*. From *this*. From the realization that I was sitting at the same table as the people who filled Matty's world.

"FiFi!" Natalie announced suddenly, pointing at me with her fork like she'd just spotted a celebrity. "You have to tell me more about being the tiger!"

Every head turned.

Matty blinked. "What did you just call her?"

Natalie looked positively delighted. "FiFi. Obviously."

"Obviously," Jace echoed with a grin, stealing Natalie's syrup packet.

Natalie pointed her fork at him in warning before turning back to Matty. "Don't give me that look. She's part of the No Drama Llamas now. You can't sit at this table without a nickname. It's, like, the first commandment."

Matty stared, his expression somewhere between disbelief and resignation. "The first what?"

"The first *commandment*, Adler," Natalie said with a straight face. "Commandment one: Thou shalt have a nickname. Commandment two: Thou shalt eat a pancake. She's fulfilling the prophecy."

"I don't think everyone in the group has a nickname," said Parker, disengaging himself from staring at Casey long enough to join the conversation.

"Sorry, but you're wrong, Davis," Natalie said. "We all do."

"It's true," said Jace. "And Riley has, like, twenty."

"I have twenty?" Riley asked, raising an eyebrow.

Jace hooked an arm along the back of the booth behind her and leaned in, his eyes bright with mischief. "Riley-girl," he said instantly, as if no one had asked a question so easy since *what's two plus two*. "Riley-bean. Ri-baby. Ri-ri. Riles. Rye Bread. Rye Whiskey. Ri-licious. Ri-nator. Riley-from-the-Block. Riley-won't-admit-she-snores—"

"I don't snore," Riley said, shoving an elbow into his ribs.

"She doesn't," he agreed without missing a beat, then added in a stage whisper, "She sings quietly through her nose. It's adorable."

Riley flattened her palm against her face. "I regret asking."

"Want me to keep going?" Jace offered, delighted. "Because I've got at least ten more locked and loaded. Ri-gasm. Ri-pocalypse. Ri—"

"Stop," she hissed, turning so red I thought steam might whistle out of her ears.

"Yeah, Jace, quit before you get hit with a *Ri-straining order*," Parker drawled.

I stiffened at that word, but no one noticed. They were too busy gaping at Parker.

"Did he just make a joke?" Jace asked, sounding dumbfounded.

"I take it back," Parker groaned, looking embarrassed.

Jace grinned. "Nope. I'm not forgetting this. I feel like a proud dad. I'm just so happy right now."

Parker scoffed, but there was a slight blush to his cheeks. He pressed a kiss to the side of Casey's head, and she looked up at him like he hung the moon. I didn't blame her for that. With his dark brown hair, eyes an impossible shade of blue, and that easy, confident grin, he looked like he could talk the sun into rising early.

A waitress with a pen tucked behind her ear walked up to the table, her gray hair pulled into a no-nonsense bun and laugh lines framing her eyes.

"You guys again," she said, shaking her head with a smile. "Didn't I just see you in here the other night? And the night before that . . ."

Jace grinned up at her, all charm and dimples. "What can I say, Mildred? Your cheese fries are my love language."

She snorted, trying, and failing, to hide the blush that crept into her cheeks. "Flattery again, huh? You used that line last week."

"Only because it worked," Jace said, leaning back with a cocky smirk.

Her mouth twitched despite herself. "Flattery gets you refills, sweetheart, not free food."

"Noted," he said, winking. "But I'm still gonna try."

She rolled her eyes, smiling now. "Alright, what's everyone having?"

"Five orders of cheese fries," Jace announced, and Riley's eyes widened. "And a glass of milk. Oh! And a corn dog!"

Matty turned toward him, his expression horrified. "You're disgusting."

"I'm a growing boy," Jace said, unfazed. "And I didn't ask for milk with ice; nothing to be afraid of, Matty-kins."

Milk with ice? Only serial killers did that. I glanced up at Matty, thinking I'd found another inside joke I didn't know about, and my skin itched to find out more.

"I'll have a burger," Riley said before glancing at Jace. "And I want some of those cheese fries."

"You're lucky you're so pretty and perfect and wonderful, Ri-licious. Sharing cheese fries is a big deal."

Natalie pretended like she was choking.

Matty leaned over. "You're pretty and perfect and wonderful, too," he whispered to me.

I almost melted into the seat.

"Chicken wrap," Casey told the server politely.

Parker grinned. "And cheese fries. You need more sustenance than that."

"Big word, Davis. Another thing I'm proud of you about," Jace announced.

"I'll have a burger and cheese fries," Parker said, ignoring Jace.

"Strawberry lemonade and pancakes," Natalie said. "But hold the strawberry and add extra lemons."

Mildred blinked at her. "So . . . a regular lemonade?"

"Don't stifle her art," Jace whispered solemnly.

I ordered chicken fingers, and Matty glanced up when it was his turn. "Double bacon burger with—"

"Extra bacon and fry sauce," I finished without thinking.

He looked at me curiously, like he was trying to figure out how I knew that. Heat crawled up my neck.

Natalie leaned forward before I could try to explain myself, clapping her hands once as Mildred walked away. "Okay! Now that we've all confessed our deep emotional truths through food orders, tell us everything."

It took a second to process her words because I was still freaking out about what I'd just done. Matty's gaze was digging into the side of my head, and I could only imagine what he was thinking. "Everything?"

"*Everything*, everything," she confirmed. "Favorite color. Least favorite condiment. Hobbies. Aspirations. Your mysterious aura. Why you look like a FiFi. What you like to do when—"

"Don't forget she's mine," Matty interrupted, a serious look on his face. "You're going to find out how perfect she is with all these questions. And I don't want you to forget that."

"Possessive much?" Natalie murmured, though the corners of her mouth tilted up.

"It's a No Drama Llama thing," Jace commented helpfully, tapping on the bandaged tattoo on his arm that Matty had told me about.

The banter skittered across my skin like champagne bubbles, but it was hard to concentrate. Matty was going to kill me if he kept saying all these sweet things.

But maybe that meant he'd forgotten about my bacon and fry sauce mistake.

Jace drummed his fingers on the table, eyes gleaming with the kind of warning that meant nothing good. "Serious question," he announced. "Do you guys know the difference between ooh and ahh?"

Riley groaned. "No."

Parker pinched the bridge of his nose like he felt a migraine approaching. "Please don't."

Jace's grin sharpened. "About three inches."

Everyone groaned almost in unison.

"Or in Matty's case, about two inches," Jace added as an afterthought.

Matty's snarl was immediate, his cheeks going red as he cut a glare across the table and then glanced down at me, a little panic in his gaze. "That wasn't a scientific experiment. The results weren't accurate. And it was only a quarter of an inch."

"I'm not sure I know what you're talking about," I said, amused. "But if we're talking about dicks, I think yours is perfect."

The table went dead silent.

Even Jace blinked.

"Oh my gosh," I whispered, wanting to crawl under the table.

And then—chaos. Natalie folded over her forearms, wheezing with laughter. Riley coughed and made a choking sound. Parker's shoulders were shaking. Even Jace lost it, laughing so hard he knocked into the ketchup bottle.

Matty just stared for a second, then his mouth curved into the brightest smile I'd ever seen. His beam that followed could've powered the whole diner.

I'd embarrass myself every day if it made him look like that.

Mildred returned with drinks. Natalie took an extravagant slurp of her very regular lemonade and declared it life-changing. Jace tried to steal my water, and Matty slapped his hand away without looking.

"Mildred, darling. Why did Cinderella get kicked off the football team?"

"No—" Riley started, too late.

"Because she kept running away from the ball," Jace finished, looking insufferably pleased with himself.

Mildred chuckled, shaking her head as she walked away, and Parker glared at Jace as if he could banish him from the planet by thought alone.

"I have one more," Jace said, undeterred. "It's a new one. What's the difference between a tire and three hundred and sixty-five used condoms?"

"Jace," Matty warned, fighting a grin.

"One's a Goodyear." Jace beamed. "The other's a *great* year."

Everyone was still laughing as the plates hit the table—a greasy, glorious parade of burgers, fries, pancakes, and things that probably violated a few FDA guidelines. Natalie kept peppering me with questions between bites, and I was finally starting to relax.

A shadow fell across the table, and Natalie stopped mid-sentence.

I looked up, expecting Mildred back with refills . . . and I immediately understood why everyone had gone still.

A girl stood at the end of the booth.

She was pale, almost translucent under the diner's fluorescent lights, with stringy brown hair that hung flat around her face and wide-set, haunting eyes. She stared at us silently, and I realized . . . she wasn't blinking.

"Emma," Riley greeted, visibly forcing a polite smile. "Hi."

Emma's head tilted a fraction. "My roommate moved out," she said in a voice too calm to be casual. "If you ever want to move back in, Riley. She didn't like me watching her sleep."

The entire table froze.

Jace's arm clamped tighter around Riley, pulling her flush against him. He slid her over his lap until she was seated on his other side, farther away from Emma. "Yeah," he said. "That's a really nice offer. But she's going to have to pass."

Emma didn't acknowledge him. Her gaze drifted to Matty . . . and somehow she still hadn't blinked.

I had the urge to throw myself in front of him so she couldn't stare at his face. He was *mine*.

"I had a beautiful dream about us, Matthew," she said sweetly.

Matty's throat bobbed as he swallowed. "Oh . . . um, that's nice?" he said nervously.

Her lips curved in a delicate smile. "We were getting married."

I resisted the urge to launch myself at her.

"Oh," he said weakly.

"In our graves," she added.

The silence was absolute. Even the buzz of the diner seemed to pause.

Natalie blinked first, sitting up straighter with a too-bright grin. "Cool! Love a theme wedding. Can't wait to see the invitations."

Jace coughed into his napkin to cover a snort. Parker buried his face in his hands.

Emma just smiled again . . . still not blinking. "Sweet dreams."

When she finally turned and walked out, the whole table seemed to exhale at once.

Jace leaned back, eyes wide. "Well," he said. "That's one way to kill a vibe."

I blinked at him, still trying to process what had just happened. "Who . . . who was that?"

Riley groaned, rubbing a hand over her face. "My old roommate."

"And one of Matty's stalkers," Jace added helpfully, picking up his fry again like we hadn't just witnessed something out of a horror movie. "He's got a whole collection for some reason—though, if we're being honest, I'm obviously more stalk-worthy."

Matty didn't miss a beat. "You want me to remind you about Ms. Three Nipple?"

Jace froze mid-bite, color draining from his face. "Point taken."

The others laughed, the tension easing back into something familiar and warm, but I couldn't join in. My throat felt tight, my hands suddenly cold against my lap.

Stalker.

The word echoed in my head like a bell tolling too loud.

Because it didn't take much—one slip, one overheard comment—for everything I'd tried to bury to surface. For them to look at me and see *her*.

I stared down at the half-eaten fries in front of me, then lifted my gaze just enough to see them, Natalie still grinning, Jace shoving Riley's shoulder playfully, Parker trying not to smile, Matty watching me with quiet curiosity.

I didn't want to lose this. Any of it.

So I smiled, too, pretending my heart wasn't pounding like it wanted to escape.

CHAPTER 21

MATTY

Coach had been on our asses all afternoon.

Coverage drills. Sprint ladders. Tackling form. Again and again and again.

He'd been brutal all season, but now, with the NCAA Football Playoffs about to start, he looked like he might start personally tackling people just to prove a point. Nobody was safe. Not even Parker.

By the time he finally blew the last whistle, my legs felt like sandbags and my brain was just static. The guys were still in the locker room arguing about dinner plans and ice baths, but I'd slipped out early.

There was only one thing I needed to do.

And that was to see Ophelia. At my place. Where she'd said she would meet me.

I was halfway across the parking lot when I noticed him.

A man stood near the gate, the late afternoon sun glinting off the metal clasp of his notebook. Windbreaker, slacks, pen tucked behind his ear. He didn't look like a fan.

"Matthew Adler?" he called out, his voice practiced and friendly in a way that put me on edge.

I slowed. "Yeah?"

He stepped forward, flipping open his notepad. "Ben Carrow, *Knoxville Daily Record.* Sorry to bother you, but I just had a quick question or two."

"Sorry, I don't have time," I said automatically, already angling to pass.

"Won't take long." He smiled that reporter smile that didn't reach his eyes. "There've been rumors—talk that someone on the Tennessee roster might be connected to a gambling ring. Point shaving. Insider bets. You wouldn't happen to know anything about that, would you?"

For half a second, I couldn't breathe.

Because I knew *exactly* what he was talking about.

Flashbacks of the dinner slammed through my head—the fancy restaurant, Kenton's watch catching the light as he said *information is currency*. The way my dad's eyes had gleamed as Kenton explained the new "business opportunity."

I'd think carefully before saying no.

Fuck.

I forced a short laugh that sounded wrong in my own ears. "A gambling ring? That's ridiculous. Nobody on this team's doing anything like that."

Carrow's eyes narrowed slightly. "So you haven't heard anything? No one's approached you? You're sure?"

"Positive." I shoved my hands in my hoodie pocket, tried to keep my face still even as heat crept up my neck. "You're wasting your time."

"Hmm," he said mildly. "I've heard your father's name come up a few times. He's been around the team a lot this season, hasn't he?"

My jaw locked. "He's a proud dad. Comes to games. He's not around any more than other parents."

"Right," Carrow said, still writing. "Just making sure."

My pulse was thundering so hard it drowned out everything else. "Look, I've gotta go. Practice ran late."

He raised his brows, unbothered. "Sure thing. Just thought I'd ask."

"Yeah," I muttered, already walking away.

I could feel his stare between my shoulder blades all the way across the lot. I didn't look back. My hands were clenched so tight in my pockets my knuckles ached.

By the time I reached my car, my pulse hadn't slowed. I climbed in, slammed the door, and just sat there for a minute, breathing through my teeth.

What the fuck was I going to do?

I pulled out my phone; my thumb hovered over Dad's contact in dread for half a second before I hit call.

He answered on the second ring. "Well, look who it is," he said sarcastically.

"Cut the crap," I snapped. "A reporter just cornered me outside practice. Said there are rumors someone on the team's tied to a gambling ring." My voice dropped to a hiss. "You wouldn't know anything about that, would you, Dad?"

There was silence. Just long enough to confirm what I already knew.

He finally sighed, all patronizing patience. "Matthew, we need to talk about Kenton's offer—"

My grip tightened. "Are you serious right now?"

"You need to think rationally," he interrupted, his tone edging into that smooth, reasonable cadence that always made me want to punch something. "You're sitting on an opportunity most players would kill for. Kenton's connected; he could set you up for life. And the information he's asking for isn't compromising anything. It's smart business—"

I hung up.

The call ended mid-word, his voice slicing off clean.

For a second, I just stared at the screen, my reflection flickering in the dark glass—jaw tight, eyes wild.

I scrubbed a hand over my face, taking deep breaths as I tried to calm down.

But calm wasn't coming.

If this grew, if that reporter started digging, if the NCAA got wind of it, if Kenton decided to push this . . . it could destroy everything.

I'd told the guys about that dinner the night it happened. After Jace picked me up, he and Parker had sat with me in silence while I tried to figure out how to breathe again. They'd promised it would be fine. That I'd done the right thing.

Later that night, I'd gone to that house party just to get drunk enough to forget. I'd wanted noise—music, people, anything to drown out the sound of my dad's voice and erase the image of Kenton's smug smile.

And then I'd seen Ophelia . . . and I'd basically forgotten all about it.

I was definitely thinking about it now, though.

It felt like a lit fuse, hissing closer by the second.

I couldn't let it reach Jace or Parker . . . or anyone else on the team.

And I definitely didn't want it touching *her*.

Ophelia.

The thought of her steadied me for half a second. The girl who caused everything to make sense. She didn't seem to like me for what I might be someday. She looked at me like I was already it.

For the first time, my future wasn't just about me . . . it was about *us*.

Which meant I couldn't afford to let it fall apart.

I shook my head, started the engine, and pulled out of the lot. My phone buzzed against the console. I stared at it for a long second before calling my agent instead.

He answered on the second ring. "Matty? What's up?"

"Hey," I said, trying to sound like I didn't care either way. "Any new offers come in?"

A pause. "Not since the last one. You thinking about leaving early?"

The question hit harder than I expected.

That had never been the plan.

From the start, it had always been me, Parker, and Jace, four years, side by side, before the draft would pull us in different directions. We'd promised ourselves that. Finish what we started. Go out together.

But now, I didn't know.

The ground beneath everything felt unsteady, and for the first time, I wasn't sure if keeping that promise was smart—or suicidal.

If that story grew legs, if reporters kept sniffing around, if the NCAA started investigating . . . it wouldn't matter that I'd said no. The whole team could go down with it. And my dad? He'd sell his soul before taking the blame.

Leaving early might be the only way to get clear before the fallout hits. To get somewhere new, sign a contract, and stockpile enough money to protect the people I cared about.

Safer.

Cowardly maybe, but safer.

"I don't know," I said finally, my voice rough. "Just . . . keep an eye out, okay? Let me know if anything comes up. Anything."

"Sure thing," he said carefully. "Everything okay?"

"Yeah," I lied.

I hung up before he could ask more.

I didn't know what I was doing . . . just that I needed options. Money. Security. A plan.

Something to hold on to if everything else went to hell.

I had so much to lose.

And I wasn't letting anyone take it.

CHAPTER 22

OPHELIA

I lay in Matty's bed, the sheets cool and silky against my bare skin, every nerve humming with anticipation. He'd told me about the spare key—tucked under a fake rock by the back door—and I'd found it easily, my fingers trembling as I slipped it into the lock.

I was glad I hadn't known where it was before. If I had, I wouldn't have been able to stop myself from sneaking in months ago, from crawling into his space, his life, long before he'd ever noticed me. The thought sent a shiver through me, equal parts shame and thrill.

Once inside, I'd lost myself in him.

I'd gone through his drawers, his closet, his bathroom . . . touching everything, inhaling the faint trace of his cologne, his soap, *him*.

His clothes hung neatly in a row, that faint mix of detergent and him still clinging to the fabric. I pressed a shirt to my face, breathing him in until my knees went weak.

I'd found a half-empty bottle of his body wash in the shower and opened it, letting the scent flood my senses, my thighs pressing together at the memory of his hands on me.

Before I left the bathroom, I'd stolen one of his black T-shirts that he'd thrown on the floor after wearing it, and I'd stuffed it into my backpack.

Just in case he didn't want me to stay over one night.

I'd sleep in it, wrapped in his scent, pretending his arms were around me.

Now, naked in his bed, I sank into the mattress, the sheets sliding over my breasts, my stomach, my thighs like a lover's touch. The room was dim, the late afternoon light filtering through the blinds in golden slats, painting stripes across my skin. I was alone, but he was everywhere. His scent lingered on the pillow, his cleats were scattered by the door, and an empty coffee cup sat forgotten on the nightstand.

A low ache pulsed between my legs, hot and insistent, and I couldn't help it.

My hands moved on their own, one sliding up to cup my breast, thumb circling my nipple until it peaked, hard and aching. The other drifted lower, over the curve of my hip, fingers slipping between my thighs.

I was already soaked, slick from the moment I'd climbed into his bed, from the thought of him walking through the door and finding me here. I spread my legs wider, the cool air kissing my heat, and sank two fingers inside myself, gasping at how easily they slid in, how needy I was.

I pictured Matty . . . his inked arms flexing as he pinned me down, his blue eyes dark with want, that piercing glinting as he pushed into me. My fingers moved faster, curling, stroking that spot that made my hips buck. I pinched my nipple harder, imagining his teeth, his tongue, the way he'd praised me, called me his pretty baby, his good girl.

"Matty," I whimpered, eyes squeezing shut, my world narrowing to the slick heat between my legs, the ache building. My thumb found my clit, circling in tight, desperate strokes, and I was close—so close—my breath hitching, thighs trembling, every muscle coiling. I could almost hear him, feel him, his cock stretching me, his cum painting my skin, filling me up. My fingers thrust deeper, wet sounds filling the quiet room, and I was right there, teetering on the edge, chasing that release that was all him, only him—

"Now *this* is a sight to come home to."

His voice was laced with hunger . . . and it hit me like a spark to gasoline.

My eyes flew open, but I didn't stop, couldn't stop.

Matty stood in the doorway, shoulder leaning against the frame, his gaze raking over me possessively. The sight of him, sweat-damp hair, sweatshirt clinging to his chest, tattoos peeking from his sleeves . . . it sent me over. I came with a broken cry, my pussy clenching around my fingers, waves of pleasure crashing through me as my hips jerked off the bed. My thighs shook, slick dripping down my hand, and I moaned his name shamelessly as the orgasm ripped me apart.

He pushed off the doorframe, kicking the door shut behind him with a sharp *slam* that echoed through the room. His eyes never left me as he stalked forward, peeling his hoodie over his head in one fluid motion.

The fabric hit the floor, revealing the hard planes of his chest, the dark ink swirling over his skin, his abs flexing with every step, the deep V of his hips disappearing into his sweats.

"Look at you," he rasped.

"Fingers buried in that pretty pussy, coming all over my sheets without me. You couldn't wait, could you, baby? Had to fuck yourself thinking about my cock stretching you open, filling you up, ruining you for anyone else. Bet you were imagining me pinning you down, making you scream."

I moaned, the sound needy, my fingers still thrusting slowly inside me, slick and trembling from my orgasm.

His words lit me up again, heat flooding my core, and my hips rolled instinctively, chasing the friction as my pussy throbbed.

He stopped at the edge of the bed, towering over me. The thin fabric of his sweatpants did nothing to hide the hard line straining against them—a promise of what was coming.

"Keep going," he ordered with blazing eyes. "Show me how wet you got for me. Show me what's mine. Spread those legs wider, baby—let me see that pussy dripping for me."

Another moan spilled out, louder, as I obeyed, fingers curling deeper, thumb still circling my clit in tight, desperate strokes.

My pussy was soaked, dripping onto the sheets, the wet sounds unapologetic in the quiet room, my thighs slick with my release that glistened in the dim light.

I spread my legs wider, wanting to give him a full view as I fucked myself harder, my other hand sliding up to pinch my nipple as I stared up at him.

The pleasure was overwhelming, and I was trembling as I teetered on the edge of another climax, the burning weight of his gaze making me wetter, needier.

He dropped to his knees on the mattress, the bed dipping under his weight, and grabbed my wrist, pulling my fingers free with a wet *pop*. I whimpered when he pulled away, my hips jerking forward on instinct, need tightening low in my stomach as my pussy clenched around nothing.

Matty brought my fingers to his mouth, sucking them clean, tongue swirling around each digit as he tasted me with a groan that vibrated through me.

"Fuck, you taste like heaven," he muttered, his eyes locked on mine as his tongue flicked between my fingers like he was starving, savoring every drop. "Sweetest pussy I've ever had. No one's ever gonna touch this but me. You're mine—every inch, every moan, every fucking drop."

He shoved his pants down, kicking them off with his briefs. His cock sprang free—huge, pierced, the tip glistening with precum, veins pulsing with need, the silver glint of his piercing catching the light and making my mouth water.

He didn't wait, just grabbed my thighs and spread me wide. His fingers dug into my flesh as he thrust into me in one brutal stroke.

I screamed, the stretch burning so good as his piercing dragged against my walls. He filled me completely, bottoming out until I felt him in my throat, and my core was stretched to its limit around him.

"That's it," he hissed, hips snapping. "Take every inch. This pussy was made for me. Feel that piercing, baby? It's carving my name inside you, hitting that spot that rips the screams from your throat, that turns you into my begging little mess."

He fucked me relentlessly, the bed creaking under us, his hands pinning my hips as he pounded deeper. The headboard slammed against the wall in a steady rhythm that matched the wet slap of his balls against me.

I clawed at his back, my nails raking his tattoos and leaving red trails across the ink as I moaned with every thrust. The pleasure was building fast and fierce as my body arched into him.

His cock stretched me open, the piercing bumping that spot inside that made my vision blur, my toes curl . . . my breath catch in my throat.

"Matty—fuck, you're so deep." I gasped as my walls fluttered around him. I wrapped my legs around his waist, pulling him closer, deeper.

He leaned down, sucking my nipple into his mouth. His teeth grazed my skin as his tongue flicked just right, and then he bit down just hard enough to make me cry out. The dual sensation sent sparks through me, and I clenched harder around him.

"Love how you take me," he rumbled, his mouth hot against my skin as he switched to my other breast, lavishing it with the same attention, his hips never slowing as he drove into me.

"So fucking beautiful. So mine. This pussy—gripping me like it never wants to let go. I don't want it to. I want to live inside you, feel you wrapped around me every second, every day."

His hips snapped harder, the rhythm brutal, possessive as his cock dragged against every sensitive inch of me. The piercing continued to catch on my walls, sending jolts of pleasure through me with every thrust.

I was drowning in him, in the way he filled me, the way his muscles flexed under my hands, the way his eyes burned into mine, claiming me with every look, every stroke. My fingers dug into his shoulders as I shook, slick dripping down my thighs and pooling beneath us.

The sheets were soaked through, and I was oddly proud of that fact. I didn't want him to wash them. I wanted him to lie in this bed and smell me everywhere.

I pushed back against him, meeting every thrust, chasing every spark of pleasure as my moans grew more desperate.

"Matty— Fuck, I'm close." I panted as my insides tightened, the pleasure so intense it almost hurt. My clit throbbed with every grind against his pelvis.

He grinned wickedly and shifted his angle, one hand pressing down on my lower belly, the other gripping my thigh to keep me spread wide. His cock hit that spot over and over, dragging against my walls with every stroke, and pressure was building inside me.

Different, overwhelming . . . like a dam about to break.

I was trembling as I hovered on the edge of something new, something more intense than anything I'd done with him before.

"You're gonna give me more," he taunted in a thick voice, his eyes glinting with challenge. "I know you've got it in you, Ophelia. Let it go. I want to feel you soak my cock, want to see you lose it completely . . . I want to *drown* in you."

He pressed harder on my belly, thrusting deeper, his pace unforgiving, and I shattered—squirting hard, a gush of slick bursting out of me, soaking his cock, his thighs, the sheets in a hot, relentless flood.

"Fuck, yes," he growled as he pulled out fast, grabbing the coffee mug from his nightstand and holding it under me to catch every spurt. I stared, dumbfounded, as the clear liquid dripped into the cup.

My thighs were shaking uncontrollably as I went limp, every nerve in my body buzzing.

Shock froze me as he lifted the mug to his lips and tipped it back, drinking me down in slow swallows. His throat worked as he stared at me, a low moan escaping him as he savored it.

"You taste even better like this," he rasped as he licked his lips before setting the mug aside with a *clink*.

"Fuck, baby, you're gonna do that again for me. I'm not done tasting you."

He flipped me onto my stomach with a rough tug, yanking my hips up until I was on my knees, my face pressed into the pillow, my ass in the air.

I was still shaking . . . dripping, slick running down my thighs.

Matty didn't give me a moment to catch my breath, though.

He spread my cheeks wide, exposing me completely, and I gasped as his tongue dragged up my slit, lapping at the mess I'd made like he was starving for it.

"Every fucking drop," he muttered against me in a muffled voice, his breath hot on my sensitive skin.

He licked deeper, and his tongue thrust inside me, scooping out every bit of my release.

I moaned, my hips jerking back, pushing against his face, the sensation overwhelming as my clit throbbed from the attention.

His tongue didn't stop there.

He moved higher, circling my ass and teasing the tight ring of muscle with soft, wet flicks that made me whimper and my body tense before I melted under his touch.

"Matty—" I gasped in a breaking voice. He just growled, though, one hand gripping my hip to hold me still while the other spread me wider. His tongue pressed harder, breaching me, licking into my ass as he tasted . . . *claimed* every inch.

The pleasure was intense and perfect as he continued to devour me, sucking and licking until I was screaming into the pillow.

"Fuck, you taste so good everywhere," he groaned, pulling back just enough to speak as his lips brushed my skin. He slid his fingers inside me, curling deep to scoop out more of my slick so he could feed it back into his mouth.

He went back to my ass, licking harder, his fingers thrusting in and out of my core. The sensations were making me sob with pleasure as I pushed my hips against his face, desperate for more.

He ate me out like he was possessed, tongue and fingers working together, cleaning every drop, and leaving my body a mess of need and overstimulation.

"Gonna fill that mouth now," he grunted, finally pulling away. His face was shiny with my cum as he slammed his dick back inside me, the new angle making me scream.

I fisted the sheets as his hands gripped my ass, spreading me open again as he pounded into me. The piercing dragged against my walls and somehow hit new spots.

The bed shook violently, my breasts bouncing against the sheets, my moans muffled into the pillow as his balls slapped against my clit with every stroke and sent me spiraling toward another edge.

I desperately met every thrust, taking him as deep as I could.

"Matty—please," I begged brokenly. It was like I was on fire as another orgasm built fast.

He reached around and found my clit, rubbing in tight, ruthless circles as his other hand tangled in my hair, pulling my head back so I arched for him.

"Come again," he ordered. "I want you soaking me one more time before I feed you my cum."

His fingers pressed harder, his cock relentless, and I was gone again, my walls clamping down, another wave of slick gushing out that soaked us both.

The edges of my vision went hazy . . . but he didn't stop, fucking me through it, his growls mixing with my cries.

His pace only faltered as he neared his edge.

"I'm coming in that pretty mouth," he snarled as he pulled out at the last second and flipped me onto my back with a rough tug.

"Open," he ordered as he fisted his cock.

I did, opening wide with my tongue out, desperate for him. I reached for his thighs so I could pull him closer.

He came with a roar . . . thick ropes shooting straight onto my tongue, my lips, dripping down my chin, some hitting my cheeks, my neck, my breasts.

I swallowed greedily, the taste of him flooding me, salty and thick. My obsession flared as I licked every drop I could reach, my fingers scooping what landed on my face and sucking them clean with a moan as my eyes locked on his.

I wanted him to know how much I needed it. How much I craved him.

He collapsed beside me and pulled me into his arms. Our bodies were a mess of sweat and cum and my release.

"You're fucking perfect," he murmured, kissing my hair and my neck, his hands roaming my skin as he traced the mess he'd made. He smeared it across my breasts and my stomach like he was marking me all over again.

I curled into him, my body spent but buzzing.

His taste was on my tongue.

His cum was drying on my skin, inside me . . . *everywhere*.

The scent of us filled the room.

I was his, completely and utterly, and the thought sent a fresh wave of heat through me as I nestled closer, inhaling him . . . knowing I'd never want anything else.

I lay tangled against him, my cheek pressed to his chest, the rhythm of his heartbeat steady under my skin. The room was quiet except for that sound in my ear . . . living proof that this was real.

But I couldn't get something out of my head.

"I keep thinking I'm going to wake up," I finally whispered when the thought threatened to choke me. "That this—us—is some perfect dream I don't deserve."

Matty's arm tightened around me, his lips brushing my hair. "You're not dreaming, baby."

I smiled faintly. "That's exactly what someone in a dream would say."

He huffed a quiet laugh, and for a while, we just breathed together. My body should've been at peace, but my mind was already running back to places I didn't want to go.

"Do you know who Ophelia was in literature?" I asked finally.

He went still beneath me, thinking. "Was she a Shakespeare character?"

I nodded. "In *Hamlet*. She loved him so much that when he broke her heart, she lost her mind. She wandered into the river in her gown, singing songs until the current pulled her under."

Matty's fingers traced up my spine. "That's dark," he murmured. "Why would your mom name you that?"

I laughed, but it sounded more like a sigh. "That's what I asked her when I came home from school after we'd read the play in class." I traced the edge of his ribs with my fingertips, trying to keep my tone steady. "She told me she thought it was beautiful. That Ophelia was gentle and loyal, and she loved harder than anyone. She said the world broke her, but at least she never stopped feeling."

I paused, staring at the wall in the dim light. "But when I was fourteen, she told me the truth. She said she named me that because she almost died giving birth to me. She said she remembered lying there, hooked up to all the machines . . . realizing that what you love most can be the thing that kills you."

My throat tightened. "She wanted me to remember that. That love isn't soft—it's sharp. It demands something back."

The words still hurt, all these years later.

I didn't tell Matty the rest—that right after that conversation, when she'd found my notebooks and the names I'd scribbled inside them, she'd said it again. *You're living up to your name, Ophelia. The love you think you have for those boys is going to drown you one day.*

Maybe she'd been right. Maybe I'd always been standing at the edge, waiting for the river to take me.

Matty's hand slid up to cradle the back of my head, his thumb tracing slow circles against my neck. "Then she never saw this," he said softly. "Because what we have—it isn't the kind of love that kills you. It's the kind that keeps you alive."

My chest ached so hard I could barely breathe.

I wanted to tell him he was wrong, that he didn't know what my mother had seen in me. But his eyes were steady, sure in a way mine had never been.

"And if this is a dream . . ." He leaned closer until our foreheads touched, his voice a low promise. "Then neither of us is ever waking up."

I smiled against him, my eyes stinging.

Maybe the river inside me hadn't been waiting to take me after all.

Maybe it had just been waiting for him.

CHAPTER 23

MATTY

Creak.

The sound that woke me wasn't loud . . . just the soft *click* of the door to my room opening.

But it sliced straight through sleep.

My eyes snapped open.

Moonlight spilled across the room, catching the edge of the dresser and the mess of clothes on the floor. Ophelia was curled against me, her face tucked into my shoulder, her breaths puffing softly against my skin.

For half a second, I thought I'd imagined it—until I saw him.

A figure stood in the doorway. Black hoodie. Gloves.

The Sphinx mask glinting in the dark.

My pulse skyrocketed.

He didn't move at first . . . just stared at me. Then, with a flick of his wrist, he tossed something onto the bed—a crimson envelope that slid across the sheet and stopped against my thigh.

"Who needs porn," he murmured, voice muffled and mocking behind the mask, "when I'm assigned to Matthew Adler?"

I was on my feet before I could think, muscles tight and ready to break something.

But he was already gone.

The door hung open, the hallway empty.

For a long moment, the only sound was the faint hum of the air vent and Ophelia's quiet breathing.

I looked down at the envelope.

Same crimson wax. Same seal. Same sick feeling in my gut.

It had to be the same bastard who'd been in my closet the other night. Asshole. He was just lucky Ophelia had been covered up, or he would have been dead.

My jaw clenched.

We needed a security system. Cameras. Motion sensors. Something. Because clearly, door locks didn't mean shit around here.

I picked up the envelope, the paper thick and smooth under my fingers. I didn't have to open it to know what it was.

My next Sphinx trial.

I tore it open carefully, the seal snapping with a *crack*. A single sheet slid out, crisp white, the message printed in clean block letters that made my stomach tighten.

VOL NAVY DOCKS. ONE HOUR. COME ALONE.

Of course.

The docks on the Tennessee River weren't just some random meeting spot. Everyone on campus knew them. The Vol Navy had been a Tennessee tradition since the sixties—hundreds of boats docking near Neyland Stadium on game days, the river choked with orange and white, beer, and noise.

But right now, it was the middle of the night. The boats would be gone. The docks empty. Quiet.

The perfect place for the Sphinx.

I exhaled slowly, glancing toward the bed. Ophelia hadn't moved, still tangled in the sheets, the faint rise and fall of her chest catching in the moonlight.

She made a small sound, half sigh, half whimper, and her face scrunched like she was fighting something in her sleep. A second later, her hand reached out, searching blindly across the empty space where I'd been.

My chest tightened.

Even asleep, she noticed when I wasn't there.

She might not have said the words yet, but she didn't need to.

She totally loved me.

And I'd get the words out of her someday.

I found my sweatpants on the floor and slid them on.

Hoodie. Shoes. Phone. Wallet. Keys. The motions felt automatic, muscle memory taking over while I went over potential things the Sphinx could do to me.

Just as long as it doesn't involve dead bodies, I thought, once again thinking of Parker's trial. I could probably handle anything but that.

By the time I stepped into the hallway, my pulse had leveled into almost a game-day calm.

I pulled out my phone and typed out a text to Parker and Jace.

Me: Got a Sphinx trial. If I'm not back in two hours, try to find me.

Me: I forgot to take my bracelet off, so I'm making it easy.

Me: Parker, if you see this text first and can't figure out how to track me, ask Darla.

I hit send, hoping one of them would see my texts.

The friendship bracelets had started as a joke freshman year, Jace's idea, naturally. He'd handed them out with some dramatic speech about "binding our brotherhood in unbreakable thread" or some crap like that.

It wasn't until Parker's trials that we'd figured out the truth: Jace had built tiny trackers into them. Because apparently, in his mind, best friends didn't just check in—they ran covert GPS surveillance on one another.

I'd been meaning to take the damn thing off ever since.

But after years of wearing it, I barely noticed it anymore.

And maybe tonight, that was a good thing.

I tightened my hoodie strings, locked the door behind me, and started toward the car.

The drive down to the river didn't take long. Campus was mostly asleep, the streets washed in that eerie blue of late-night halogen and frost. My headlights caught the slow curl of mist rising off the Tennessee River as I pulled into the lot overlooking the docks.

The moment I stepped out of the car, the cold punched me.

Wind knifed across the water, biting enough to sting my eyes, and the air smelled like metal and wet wood.

The docks stretched out below, long wooden fingers reaching into black water. Everything was silent except the slap of waves against the pilings.

I scanned the docks, breath fogging in the cold, trying to figure out what the hell I was supposed to do next. Then something caught my eye near the end of the middle dock.

I squinted.

Was that . . . a package?

Of course it was.

I huffed out a laugh that turned to steam. *How original. A secret society and a mysterious package. Never would have thought of that.*

I was obviously being sarcastic.

Jamming my hands into my hoodie pocket, I started toward it, shoes thudding softly against the boards. Each step creaked.

When I reached the end, I crouched, frowning as I picked up the box. It wasn't heavy, just wrapped in plain brown paper, no markings.

"This better not be some kind of—"

A sound behind me—soft, quick.

I started to turn.

A bag dropped over my head, blinding me.

"Hey!"

Hands grabbed me—rough, fast, everywhere at once. I twisted, slammed my shoulder into someone, but there were too many of them.

Cold air hit my chest, and I realized, too late, what they were doing. Fingers tore at my hoodie . . . my sweatpants. Fabric ripped, scraped down my legs, until the night air hit bare skin, and my stomach lurched.

"Seriously?" I snarled, fighting to break free. "What the—"

Someone yanked at my ankles. My socks went first, then my shoes, ripped clean off as I tried to kick them away.

Rough hands caught my wrists, jerking them behind my back. Rope bit deep, pulling tight until the burn shot up my arms.

The world tilted sideways, the dock slick under my bare feet.

Before I could catch myself, a brutal shove hit between my shoulders and sent me flying.

The breath left my lungs in a grunt, and before I could even swear, I was airborne—then crashing down, the river swallowing me whole.

Cold exploded across every nerve as I hit the water, the shock punching the air straight out of my lungs.

Not water—ice. That's what it felt like.

It slammed into me, stole everything . . . air, thought, sound. My lungs seized, burning, while the current dragged me under.

The bag clung to my face, slick and suffocating.

Don't panic.

Easier said than done when your brain's screaming *up, up, up*, and you don't even know which way that is.

My arms were useless, bound tight behind me. I tried to kick, but the rope cut into my wrists, throwing off my rhythm, dragging me down faster with every frantic movement. The water roared in my ears, pressure crushing.

Think, Matty.

I twisted, rolling my shoulders, trying to feel for slack in the rope. Nothing. The knot bit deeper. I kicked again, harder this time, feeling the drag shift, the faint pull of bubbles rising somewhere above me. *That way.*

I followed the pain in my lungs, the instinct that screamed for air, angling my body toward where I thought the surface might be. My foot struck something solid . . . the riverbed.

Wrong direction.

I bent my knees and shoved off with everything I had left, forcing myself up, the bag rasping against my face, each second stretching longer than the last. The cold was eating me alive, turning muscle to stone, thought to static.

Keep moving.

My chest convulsed as a trickle of river forced its way in, burning down my throat. I jerked my head, shaking the bag loose, rubbing it against my shoulder until the fabric finally shifted just enough to pull away from my mouth.

Light flashed behind my eyelids . . . and then I broke the surface.

I gasped against the soaked bag, coughing and choking, dragging in oxygen like it might vanish again.

The bag still clung to my head, heavy and waterlogged, every breath a fight. My arms were bound, but I kicked hard enough to keep myself barely afloat.

Don't stop.

The current was pulling me downstream now, away from everything. My limbs were heavy, numb, shaking from cold and adrenaline.

Somewhere behind me, a voice called out, distant and distorted. Someone laughed.

Motherfuckers.

I didn't try to turn toward them. I just kept kicking, lungs shredding, every thought reduced to one brutal command: *Live.*

By the time my chest scraped the riverbank, I could barely feel anything.

I shoved myself up the muddy slope, kicking and rolling, using my shoulders for leverage. The ground was rough and frozen in patches, raking against bare skin as I dragged myself forward. Every muscle screamed, my lungs heaving like I'd swallowed knives. The cold had gone past sharp. It was bone-deep now, a heavy, crushing numbness that made it hard to tell if I was even moving at all.

When I finally collapsed onto solid ground, I just lay there for a second. My body convulsed in shivers. I couldn't stop. My fingers wouldn't close.

Move.

The word echoed, slow and far away, like my brain was shouting from another room.

If I stayed on the ground, I'd freeze.

I rolled onto my side and fought to sit up, my breath coming in ragged bursts. The bag still clung to my face, plastered against my skin. I dug my shoulder into the dirt and rubbed hard, twisting until the fabric snagged on a rock and tore. One final jerk, and it came free, ripping off with a gasp of air.

The air hit like fire.

I sucked in a lungful, coughed hard enough to see stars, then spat river water and bile into the grass. My wrists were still bound tight behind me, circulation long gone.

"Son of a bitch," I rasped. My teeth chattered so hard it hurt.

The only thought that made it through the fog was that I had to get warm. Fast.

I forced myself upright, swaying as the world tilted and steadied again. The river had carried me past the docks, but they weren't far—just a dark line down the shoreline.

My feet protested with every step, skin splitting against gravel and frozen mud. The air bit at every inch of my exposed body, the wind slicing through me like I didn't have skin at all.

Maybe my stuff's still there. The thought barely registered as hope, more instinct than belief.

By the time I reached the boards, my body felt foreign, heavy and shaking. My bare feet slapped against the wet wood, pain flaring up my legs with every step. My breath came in ragged white bursts as I made it to the spot where I'd been attacked.

Nothing.

No hoodie. No sweatpants. No wallet or phone.

Just empty boards and the black river below.

My pulse hammered in my ears. The cold wasn't an ache anymore—it was an invasion.

The bastards had taken everything.

Of course they had. The Sphinx didn't do anything halfway.

I just didn't know what the hell this one was supposed to test—other than *how not to die*.

I stared out at the water, teeth chattering so hard my jaw ached, reminding myself why I was doing this. Why I needed in. Connections. Protection. Power. Things I couldn't afford not to have . . . especially with what my dad and Kenton had started.

But if one of those masked freaks showed up right then, I was pretty sure I'd try to kill them. Naked and freezing or not.

I stood there for another minute, shivering so hard my vision blurred, waiting for someone to jump out and yell *surprise* or *congratulations, you survived.*

Nothing.

Just the wind, the river, and the sound of my teeth clacking like castanets.

A bitter laugh scraped out of my throat.

Guess that was it. Trial complete.

I looked down at myself—covered in mud, rope still cutting into my wrists, every inch of me frozen solid. My dignity had packed up and drowned somewhere upstream.

With a sigh that came out more like a groan, I started walking.

Because apparently, the only thing left to do was make the long, humiliating trek home.

Naked. Bound.

Frozen dick and all.

The walk back was pure hell.

Every step sent spikes of pain up my bare feet, the rope still biting into my wrists. The wind knifed against my skin, my body shaking so violently I half expected to shatter on the pavement.

Somewhere in the distance, music started pounding through the night, loud, ridiculous, and way too dramatic for two in the morning.

Bonnie Tyler. "Holding Out for a Hero."

Odd choice of song.

Headlights appeared a second later, bright and blinding, cutting through the dark. I squinted, wondering if I needed to throw myself into the ditch because it was another masked madman coming back for round two.

And also wondering if I was even capable of doing something like that.

But the vehicle wasn't slowing down.

It roared closer, the song getting louder, until I could make out the shape of a Jeep.

A familiar Jeep.

I blinked once. And then blinked again.

Was I hallucinating?

Because through the windshield, I could see a familiar-looking guy in a baseball cap drumming on the steering wheel, singing at the top of his lungs—completely oblivious to the naked, half-frozen idiot standing in the road.

The Jeep continued to approach, and the driver finally locked eyes with me.

Jace.

His jaw dropped, eyes bugging out, disbelief written all over his face. The Jeep shot past, tires screeching as he slammed the brakes a few yards too late.

For a second, I just stood there, blinking at the taillights, too tired and frozen to move.

Then the tires squealed again as he threw it into reverse, "Holding Out for a Hero" still blasting at full volume. The Jeep fishtailed, spun halfway, then roared back toward me.

I didn't even bother walking to meet it. I just waited.

Because if I'd made it this far naked, bound, and half dead, the least my best friend could do was come the last ten feet.

The Jeep skidded to a stop in front of where I was standing, tires squealing one last time before the engine idled. Bonnie Tyler was still belting her heart out about needing a hero, the lyrics echoing through the empty road like the soundtrack to my humiliation.

The driver's door flew open, and Jace jumped out, slamming it closed behind him.

"Matty?" His voice was pitched halfway between disbelief and panic as he raced toward me . . . before freezing mid-step, eyes darting down and then immediately away like he'd seen something medically concerning.

"Yes. I know I'm naked, caked in mud, my hands are tied behind my back, and I probably look like the before picture in a very illegal experiment. But please, take me home," I growled.

"What the hell did the Sphinx do to you?" he demanded, his voice cracking. "Was this, like, a *rebirth* thing? Should I start chanting?"

I just stared at him, shivering so hard my vision blurred. "They tried to drown me, actually."

Jace pressed a hand to his heart. "And to think, I was going to complain about how slow the seat warmers were in my Jeep. You win, buddy."

I was too tired to try to punch him.

His smirk faltered at my silence, replaced by something that looked a lot like alarm. "Oh shit. You're not just being dramatic. You actually almost died."

I sighed and nodded, and his gaze swept over me again, like he was trying to decide whether to offer me a blanket or an exorcism. "Okay, okay, hang on. I've got you."

He walked toward me and bent his knees, arms open, grimacing like this was the hardest thing he'd ever done.

I frowned. "What the fuck are you doing?"

"I'm gonna carry you to the car," he said, dead serious. "Just . . . maybe point that animal between your legs somewhere else. Even without that missing inch, it looks foreboding."

I gaped at him. "Please don't," I managed to choke out, my teeth clacking around the words.

He froze mid-squat, shoulders sagging in relief. "Oh, thank fuck. I might never have recovered from that. But I want you to make a mental note in your best friendship hierarchy that I was prepared to do it."

"Noted," I grunted.

I stumbled forward a few steps before realizing I was still trussed up like a Thanksgiving turkey. "Wait," I called hoarsely. "Untie me first."

Jace stopped, blinking like he'd only just noticed my wrists bound behind me. "Oh. Right. Good thing I've got all that survival training."

I gave him a flat look. "One day watching *Naked and Afraid* doesn't count, genius."

"Excuse you," he said, rummaging in his pocket for his keys. "I also watched the episode where the guy made fire with his shoelaces. I'm practically an expert. You're lucky to have me."

He crouched behind me, grumbling under his breath as he worked the knot. The rope had dried stiff against my skin, biting deeper every time he tugged.

"Fuck," he muttered. "They really went full *Fifty Shades* on you, huh?"

"Just untie it."

"Yeah, yeah, hold still— There." The final pull burned like fire, and then the tension released. I dragged my arms forward, groaning as the muscles screamed, pins and needles flooding up to my shoulders.

Jace straightened, surveying me with a look somewhere between impressed and horrified. "You, my friend, look like every cautionary tale the university uses to warn athletes about extracurricular activities."

I winced as I rotated my arms, trying to get the blood flowing again. "And you look like the guy who's about to drive me home before I freeze to death."

"On it."

Jace jogged ahead to the Jeep, fumbling with his keys and muttering something about hazard pay. The dome light flicked on as he yanked the passenger door open, gesturing grandly like a chauffeur greeting royalty.

"Your chariot awaits, Ice Man."

"Shut up," I muttered, climbing in. The leather seat was blissfully warm, but the second I sat down, every frozen nerve in my body screamed in protest.

Jace cranked the heat, and warm air blasted from the vents like he was trying to dry me out before mildew set in.

"Okay, first of all, you're paying to clean my Jeep because I like to have sex in here, and you currently smell like swamp rot and bad decisions. Second, are you sure you aren't dying, because I take hauntings seriously and want to be prepared."

"If I do die, tell people it was heroic. Not . . . whatever this is," I muttered, teeth chattering.

"I'll consider your request," Jace said magnanimously.

I looked around the cab, desperate for anything resembling fabric. "You don't have a sweatshirt or something?"

He scoffed. "Please. I keep my baby spotless. For said sex, obviously."

I stared at him. "You're unbelievable. And I know way too much about your and Riley's sex life."

He grinned. "I'm actually aspirational. And after the last few days, I'm pretty sure I know more about your sex life than you do about mine. I want that coffee cup sanitized, by the way, multiple times. Because it's my favorite one, and now you've ruined it."

I didn't have enough blood flow to blush as I thought about what I'd used his coffee cup for, but I also made yet another commitment to get better locks on my door.

He threw the Jeep into drive, the tires screeching as we pulled away. "I wonder how I would explain this to a cop?" he mused.

I shut my eyes. "Tell him we lost a bet."

"Oh sure. 'Sorry, Officer, my best friend almost drowned in the Tennessee River this morning. He's fine, though, look—his dick's still threatening traffic.'"

"Fucking hell."

The heater kicked harder, blowing enough warmth that the shivering finally dulled into a tremor. I leaned my head back, watching streetlights flicker through the windshield.

Jace's phone buzzed in the cup holder. He glanced down, then barked out a laugh. "It's Parker."

He held the screen up so I could see.

> Parker: Did you find him? He's not answering me, and I refuse to ask Darla for help with his tracker.

Parker: Which is still weird that we have by the way. We've never talked about just how often you use it.

A second later.

Parker: Also, why is there a "naked man on Neyland Drive" trending online? And why does it look like Matty in all the pictures?

"You're famous," Jace said delightedly. "I've always wanted to be friends with a star."

"He's all good," Jace read aloud as he typed out an answer to Parker. "He's alive. Mostly hypothermic. Probably sterile."

"I'm not sterile," I snarled. Although, honestly, I couldn't be sure about that. *I don't even think Ophelia's mouth could make my dick come alive again right now.*

It twitched in response, and I surreptitiously covered it so I didn't give Jace something else to mock me for.

"Parker would have probably had a sweatshirt in his truck," I told him.

"I can drop you off and tell him to come get you?" Jace said helpfully. "Because you don't sound very grateful right now. Your balls are literally sitting on my leather. I'm not sure Parker would have allowed that."

I thought about that for a second. He could be right. "I'm sorry," I finally huffed.

"Tell me I'm your bestilicious number one," Jace prodded.

"You're my—" I began.

Blue and red lights exploded in the mirrors, cutting off my words.

Jace's grin died as he pulled the Jeep over to the side of the road. "Great. I rescue one naked best friend from a cult initiation, and now I'm going to end up on some registry."

The flashlight hit the side window a minute later, slicing through the dark. I tried to hunch lower and cover my junk, but it just made me look guiltier and somehow *more* naked, I was pretty sure.

The officer rapped twice on the glass. Jace rolled it down, smiling like a man whose last three brain cells were performing CPR on one another.

"Evening, Officer," he said brightly. "Beautiful night for a drive, huh?"

The cop's gaze swung from Jace to me. His brows climbed higher with every inch of bare skin he clocked. "Son," he said slowly, "why is there a naked man in your passenger seat?"

Jace didn't even blink. "Science project."

The cop blinked in response. "What kind of science project?"

"The . . . uh . . . effects of extreme temperature on, uh, body recovery."

I groaned. "I fell in the river."

Jace nodded like that helped. "Totally part of the experiment."

The cop's flashlight lingered on me for a long, uncomfortable moment. "And you're telling me this experiment doesn't violate about twelve state laws?"

"Depends on the state," Jace said helpfully.

"Fucking hell," I muttered again, wanting to bury my face in my hands but knowing the last thing the officer needed was an eyeful of my dick.

It could be intimidating to some people . . . even in its frozen state.

The officer exhaled, clearly regretting every career choice that brought him to this moment. "You two smell like a frat party mated with a sewer." He leaned closer, squinting at Jace through the open window. "Wait a second . . . Aren't you two boys on the football team?"

My stomach dropped.

Jace froze, then flashed the kind of grin that usually preceded disaster. "No, sir. We, uh, just get mistaken for them a lot. It's the jawlines."

The cop gave him a long, flat look. "Right. And what's your name, son?"

"Uh . . . John. John Soto."

I turned my head so fast my neck cracked. *John Soto?*

The name alone made my brain short-circuit. John Soto was a hockey player on the LA Cobras, one of Parker's brother's old teammates. Walker had spent an entire summer calling him "the human mole rat" because he hated him so much.

Jace reached into the glove box, pulled out a wallet, and handed over an ID like this was completely normal. The officer took it, shined his flashlight on it, and frowned.

I watched in terror as he examined it—tilting it toward the light, flipping it over, running his thumb across the corner like he was personally trying to ruin our lives. My pulse thudded in my ears, the silence stretching so long I started calculating escape routes, all of which ended with me sprinting naked down Neyland Drive.

After what felt like an eternity, the cop looked back up at Jace, then at me—dripping, shivering, and praying. "You sure this isn't some frat hazing thing?"

"Not in a frat," Jace said cheerfully. "We're not frat material."

The cop sighed, rubbing a hand down his face. "Fine. Get him home before one of you catches hypothermia . . . or worse, ends up on . . . what's it called . . . TockTock again."

"Yes, sir," Jace said, dead serious. "We'll stay off all clock apps."

The cop blinked once, clearly too tired to care. He handed back the ID and trudged off toward his cruiser, muttering something about *kids and their internet dances*.

The lights faded, and silence filled the Jeep.

I turned to him slowly. "You gave him a fake ID?"

He shrugged. "Worked, didn't it?"

"Where the hell did you even get that?"

"Jagger," he said casually, putting the Jeep in gear. "And if you're questioning authenticity, I'll have you know that man's fake IDs could get into heaven."

I blinked at him. "You're unbelievable."

He grinned. "And yet . . . undefeated."

The Jeep rumbled back onto the road, tires humming against wet asphalt.

Neither of us said anything for a solid minute. My brain was still catching up to the fact that we hadn't been arrested—or exorcised.

Jace broke the silence first. "So, if you ever decide to die again, could you at least keep your pants on? I'm running out of excuses for naked men in my passenger seat."

"Noted," I muttered.

He glanced over, a smirk tugging at his mouth. "Also, I think after tonight I'm going to be Parker's number one bestilicious, too."

I laughed, half delirious from exhaustion. "And why's that?"

"Because I got a photo of your face when the flashlight hit your dick. You looked like a deer that'd just realized it was being photographed for *National Geographic*."

I jerked upright so fast I nearly hit my head on the roof. "You *took a picture*?"

Jace waggled his eyebrows at me. "Of course; it's going to be my new screen saver."

"Delete it."

"Can't. It's my friendship tax for tonight."

"Jace."

He grinned wider, eyes still on the road. "Relax, I cropped it. Mostly."

I groaned and then flopped back into the seat. I'd have to get it off his phone when I had more energy.

The rest of the drive passed in the hum of the engine and the steady roar of the heater. The world outside was still soaked in darkness, the streetlights bleeding into the wet grass.

"Hey," I said finally in a rough voice. "Thanks. For coming."

Jace glanced over, his grin softening. "Yeah, well. Somebody had to make sure your obituary didn't start with 'Local athlete found pantsless in river.'"

I huffed a weak laugh. "Still—thanks."

He shrugged like it wasn't a big deal. "What are best friends for if not for ride-or-die extractions?"

When we finally pulled up to the house, Jace idled in the driveway for a second. "I've got one for you."

"Really?" I said dramatically. "I'm literally sitting here naked."

He snorted. "I know, that's why your new nickname's Juggler."

"What?"

"Because somehow there are always balls involved when it comes to you."

I stared at him for a second in disgust, then shook my head as I opened the door, the cold hitting me like a slap all over again. I was halfway up the porch steps when I froze.

My stuff—hoodie, sweatpants, shoes—was sitting in a neat little folded pile on the welcome mat.

My jaw tightened, a low sound escaping before I could stop it. "Unbelievable," I snarled as I gathered them up and went inside, Jace following behind me.

The house was quiet, dimly lit from the kitchen nightlight. Ophelia was still asleep in my bed, tangled in the sheets, her face soft and peaceful in the half-light.

Something in me eased.

I quietly headed to the bathroom. The second the hot water hit, I groaned, the heat biting at my frozen skin until it burned.

Steam rose, swallowing the chill.

For the first time all night, I let myself breathe.

And I didn't stop until the water ran cold.

CHAPTER 24

MATTY

Breath steamed in the air, mixing with the tang of turf spray and the metallic sting of cold wind. The crowd's roar crashed and rolled through the stadium, thunder trapped inside a steel drum.

And I couldn't focus to save my life.

Because Ophelia was out there, dressed head to toe in orange fur and way too much school spirit, standing near the cheer squad with a flag balanced against her shoulder.

I'd never been attracted to the tiger before finding out it was her . . . or really thought anything about it . . . but now it was all I *could* think about.

"Adler!" Parker barked. "You plan on joining us or just freezing in place while you stare at your girlfriend in a fur suit?"

"Shut it," I muttered, adjusting my gloves.

"Translation," Jace said, jogging into position. "He's thinking about the tail again."

I rolled my eyes. "At least mine wags when she sees me."

He groaned. "Fuck. We're playing a football game, not starring in *Animal Planet: The Love Edition*."

The whistle blew. First snap.

The ball hit Parker's hand, and I took off downfield, the cold biting through my pads, lungs burning in the frigid air. The rhythm should've been automatic—run, cut, turn, catch.

Except I couldn't stop looking for her.

She was by the sideline now, waving the UT flag.

Watching me.

Always watching.

Our eyes met, or maybe I just felt it, and she raised a paw, forming a giant heart over her chest.

My cleat snagged the turf.

I stumbled once, then face-planted so hard my helmet bounced.

The crowd gasped . . . then groaned.

"And down goes Romeo!" Jace yelled, jogging over. "What was that—graceful falling practice?"

"I slipped," I muttered, spitting out turf.

"Sure," he said. "Slipped on her *love*."

I pushed to my feet, ignoring the ache in my jaw. When I looked over, she was still standing there, paws on her hips, and I could just picture her trying not to laugh.

My pulse kicked.

Yeah, she was definitely laughing.

The next few plays didn't go much better. I caught one, dropped another, and nearly ran into Jace when she started dancing with the cheer squad. Every move she made felt like it was meant for me.

"She's your girlfriend," Jace said during a time-out, shaking his head. "Not the North Star. You can blink."

"I'll just remind you that you sprinted off the field and chased Riley up the stands in front of everyone."

Jace smirked. "Yeah, but I scored *before* that. It's the key to the whole thing; you're supposed to score *before* the public humiliation."

"Working on it," I muttered, tugging my helmet back on.

We hit a time-out with two minutes left in the quarter. The offense jogged to the sideline, huddling near the heaters while Coach barked at the line. My lungs burned, steam curling from my mouth in the cold.

Movement caught my eye across the field—bright orange fur and confidence she only displayed when she was in the tiger suit.

Ophelia jogged out to midfield, tail swaying behind her, flag tucked under one arm. She slid into place at the edge of the cheer formation, the white and orange of her costume gleaming under the floodlights as the drum line thundered to life.

She started to dance.

Not the usual mascot flailing, either—this was sharp, confident, choreographed.

Step back. Hip pop. Spin.

Flag sweep that shimmered under the lights.

A quick twirl, then a drop to her knees, finishing with a playful flick of her tail that sent the crowd into a frenzy.

Cheers thundered from the stands, the band echoing the beat as she popped back up and bowed dramatically.

Parker groaned beside me, pulling off his helmet. "You're drooling, Adler. That's not what I want to see right now."

I wiped my mouth with the back of my glove. "Shut up and throw me the ball," I muttered, eyes still locked on her.

I actually knew that dance. She'd shown me the routine in my bedroom this week, and I'd been so turned on I'd pushed her against the wall and fucked her.

I grinned under my face mask. That was a good day. But they all had been good days since I met her.

The next drive started at our own thirty.

"Alright, loverboy. Time to focus. You want redemption or ESPN bloopers?" Parker quipped.

"Just get me the ball, QB," I said. "Let's go."

He laughed. "There's my guy."

The snap came. I ran my route like my life depended on it. Cut. Pivot. Acceleration biting against the turf. The defender stuck to me for five yards, then I broke clean. The ball spiraled through the cold night air, perfect rotation, perfect arc and . . . I caught it on the run, tucked it tight, and burst forward down the field.

When I crossed into the end zone, the crowd went wild . . . as they should, obviously. Teammates slammed into me, helmets clanging, shouting my name, but I barely heard them. Because all I could see was her—standing at the sideline, paws covering her mouth like she couldn't believe it.

I took a step back, dropped my shoulders, and grinned.

Then I started to move.

Step back. Hip pop. Spin.

Flag sweep—well, imaginary flag.

Drop to my knees, flick my imaginary tail, and finish with my hands on my hips.

The stadium lost its mind.

The cheer squad screamed, players were cracking up on the sidelines, and Jace was doubled over near the twenty-yard line, howling.

But I wasn't doing it for them, obviously. I pointed straight at her.

The tiger froze for a second, then slowly lifted both paws and did the same sequence back—ending with the tail flick and a salute.

My chest went tight.

Yeah, she was laughing again.

And I was so gone for her.

By the time I jogged off the field, Coach's face was red and his jaw was tense. "What the fuck was that, Adler? First Davis, then Thatcher, and now my tight end's out here auditioning for *Dancing with the Stars*?"

"Just having a little fun, Coach," I said, still half breathless.

He stared like he was two seconds from throwing his clipboard. "All my stars have lost their damn minds."

Grinning, Garrett called out from down the bench, "Not me, Coach. Still got mine."

Coach's glare snapped to him. "With my luck this season, I'm not betting on it, son."

Garrett's grin dropped, and he shivered like what Coach had proposed was horrifying.

I shoved his shoulder, but I couldn't stop smiling.

I had lost my damn mind.

And it was so worth it.

Ophelia

Matty hadn't stopped moving since the second we got in his car.

His knee bounced against the console like he hadn't just played a football game and he actually had a bunch of energy to spare. He tapped the wheel and adjusted the rearview mirror twice, even though nothing had changed. He ran his tongue over his teeth like he was about to go into a huddle, and for a guy who could stiff-arm men the size of refrigerators, he looked ridiculously nervous.

"I think you're more nervous than me," I joked, sliding my hand over his knee to still it. "And I feel like I'm walking into an ambush since you didn't tell me until after the game that I was meeting your family."

I smiled so he'd know I wasn't mad.

But inside, my stomach twisted.

They were his family. *His*. What if they took one look at me and saw everything I tried so hard to hide? What if they saw that something was wrong with me . . . that I wasn't normal, that I was trying too hard, smiling too much, saying the wrong thing?

Matty's friends had liked me, though. At least, they'd *seemed* to. They'd laughed at my jokes, treated me like I belonged. So maybe I could fake it again. Maybe if I smiled enough and said all the right words, his family would believe I was someone worth loving, too.

His aqua eyes flicked to me, quick, guilty, as if I'd caught him off guard. "You don't need to be nervous." His voice was low, but the words came too fast, like he was trying to convince himself as much as me. "My mom? She's great. And my siblings? They're going to love you. No question."

"Then why do you look like you're driving to your own execution?"

That earned me a huffed laugh, the corners of his mouth twitching, though his jaw stayed tight. "Because my dad . . ." He trailed off, then shook his head. "We didn't actually end last week on the best terms." He squeezed my hand, threading our fingers tight. "And I'm dreading you having to meet him."

The pause after *best terms* said more than the words did.

"Do you want to cancel?" I asked.

That softened him immediately. His shoulders lowered a fraction, his mouth easing. "You're so fucking sweet. But no, I want you to meet the rest of my family. I'm hoping he will behave better in front of you."

His eyes darted toward me again, serious this time. "Don't let him get in your head, okay? If he says anything stupid, I'll shut him down."

Warmth pooled in my chest, even while my nerves twisted tighter. He wasn't just nervous about me meeting them—he was nervous about *me seeing him with them.*

Like he had just as much to lose in this thing between us as I did.

"They're going to love you," he said again, firmer, protective. "How could they not?"

I could think of a million reasons why they wouldn't, actually.

I bit my lip, though, fighting the urge to say the words clawing at my throat: that even if they didn't, I'd do anything to keep him, to convince him he shouldn't let me go.

The Regency House was intimidating before we even stepped inside.

The brick façade glowed under iron lanterns, valets in long coats hurrying to take keys from cars that gleamed like spaceships. Matty's car was nice, but it looked almost hilariously out of place compared to the cars that were pulling in around us.

"Do you usually eat this fancy after games?" I asked with a frown, hating that I didn't know the answer to this already. I was usually finishing up mascot duties and couldn't follow him. From researching him, though, I knew that Matty didn't come from a wealthy family, so I was surprised we were eating here.

His jaw flexed. "Only when my dad's involved."

"Oh," I said softly, watching as he handed over the keys.

He gave a tight smile that didn't reach his eyes. "When I'm paying for it, he expects the best."

The words landed heavy, something brittle threaded through the calm way he said them. I frowned, wanting to ask more but stopping myself when the valet opened the door for us.

Matty got out of the truck and walked around to help me out. He slipped his hand to the small of my back and guided me forward like he could block the sting of whatever his last words had meant.

Inside, chandeliers spilled golden light onto white linen tables and crystal glasses. The smell of grilled steak and expensive wine hung in the air. I tugged at the hem of my navy wrap dress, suddenly wishing I'd had something nicer to wear.

"You look perfect," Matty muttered in my ear.

The hostess glanced up, blinked twice, and pasted on a smile polished enough to belong in a magazine. "Can I help you?"

"Adler party. They should be seated already," Matty told her, his arm tightening around me as she nodded and began leading us through the restaurant.

"Here we go," he muttered as we approached a round booth near the back that was filled with people.

Before I could brace myself, a high-pitched squeal broke through the low hum of conversation.

"Matty!"

A blur of pigtails and glitter sneakers launched out of the booth. His little sister barreled straight toward him, shouting his name far too loud for a place with a dress code. Matty laughed, catching her mid-run and scooping her up like she weighed nothing.

"Hey, Lizzie-bug," he said, spinning her once before setting her on his hip.

My heart melted at the sight—this big, six-foot-four college football player completely undone by a little girl in orange leggings.

Lizzie finally noticed me over his shoulder. Her eyes went wide. "Wow," she stage-whispered. "You have a *pretty* girlfriend."

Heat rushed to my cheeks. "Hi, Lizzie," I said, smiling. "I'm Ophelia."

She gasped, like the name itself was magic. "That's *so* fancy."

Matty chuckled, kissing the top of her head before setting her down. "Go easy on her, kiddo."

We made it the rest of the way to the booth where his family was waiting—two younger boys around middle-school age who immediately started whispering to each other, and his parents across from them.

I already knew what they looked like, of course. I'd seen their faces a hundred times before—in Facebook posts, holiday photos, and the occasional tagged picture from a booster event. But seeing them in real life felt different. His mom's smile was warm and a little tired. His dad's wasn't a smile at all.

Matty slid an arm around my waist as we reached the table, his touch steadying even as my pulse hammered.

"Everyone, this is Ophelia," he said, his voice carrying that easy confidence he always had on the field. "Ophelia, this is my family."

He nodded toward each of them in turn. "You've already met Lizzie . . . human glitter bomb and professional scene stealer."

Lizzie grinned, unbothered.

Matty smirked, then motioned to the two boys still half hiding behind their menus. "That's Barrett, and the one pretending not to make faces at you is Keller."

Both boys muttered awkward hellos, their cheeks pink.

Finally, his gaze lifted to the couple across the booth. "And these are my parents—my mom, Alice, and my dad, Ronnie."

His mom gave me a kind smile, her eyes soft and assessing all at once. "I'm so glad you're here, sweetheart," she said, her voice gentle, almost apologetic under the din of the dining room. "We're so thrilled to meet you."

Warmth flooded my chest so fast it almost hurt. I'd braced for politeness, or distance, or the kind of thin smile that meant *you're not what I pictured for my son.*

But this—this felt like real kindness.

I managed a small, careful smile. "Thank you for having me," I said, hoping my voice didn't shake.

His dad didn't stand. He just leaned back, arms crossed, offering a nod that felt more like an evaluation than a greeting. "So, you're the reason my son's been so distracted lately," he said, his voice smooth but edged.

My throat went dry. "I— Um."

"Dad," Matty muttered, his voice low with warning.

"What? At least she's pretty enough for a star like you."

His mom literally shrank in her seat, her cheeks flushed with embarrassment.

Matty's hand tightened at my waist, signaling a silent *ignore him*. "Let's sit down," he said, guiding me into the booth beside him.

Lizzie squeezed in next to me, still beaming. "I like you already," she whispered loudly enough for half the restaurant to hear.

I smiled, trying to breathe again. "Thanks, Lizzie. I like you, too."

The waitress appeared, a young woman in a crisp black vest with a notepad tucked against her hip. Her smile was bright, polished, almost eager.

"Good evening. Can I start you with something to drink?"

Before anyone else spoke, Matty's dad leaned forward like a general giving orders. "Bring us a bottle of Château Margaux. The 2009. Don't skimp."

The woman's smile widened. "Excellent choice, sir. A lovely vintage." She scribbled quickly.

His mom's pale blue eyes widened as she stared at her menu. "That's nine hundred dollars a bottle, Ronnie," she murmured under her breath, barely loud enough for me to hear. Then, more hopefully, "Maybe just a Diet Coke, dear?"

Her husband waved her off with a booming laugh. "Nonsense! The Tigers won. And that means we drink like champions."

The waitress nodded briskly. "I'll bring the wine right out, sir."

As she walked away, Matty's hand clenched around mine under the table, his thumb pressing hard into my palm. His jaw was stone, his aqua eyes locked on the tablecloth like he could burn a hole through it.

I wanted to lean into him, whisper something that would help . . . but I couldn't think of anything that would be enough.

I knew firsthand that when you had a difficult parent, sometimes words were *never* enough.

Which reminded me . . . I'd missed a call from my mother this morning. I needed to call her back. I frowned at the thought.

"So," Alice said, tipping her head toward me with a gentle smile. "Tell us about yourself. What are you majoring in at school?"

I shifted in my seat, tucking a strand of hair behind my ear while my brain scrambled for the right answer. "I'm majoring in psychology," I said finally, forcing a light laugh. "So . . . there's a lot of reading. Even more papers."

Ronnie smirked. "Psychology. Why would you major in that?"

I hesitated, the real answer clawing up my throat. *Because after being locked away and labeled with half the DSM, I wanted to understand what was wrong with me. I wanted to fix it.*

Instead, I smiled, picking at the edge of my napkin. "I've just always been curious about people, I guess. Why they do what they do."

"Sounds dangerous," he said dryly, leaning back.

Matty's hand brushed against mine under the table soothingly.

"Don't worry," I said softly, keeping my tone light, even though a trickle of sweat was falling down my back from how nervous I was. "I only psychoanalyze on Thursdays."

Alice chuckled, but Ronnie just grunted and took a bite of bread.

The waitress returned, balancing the dark green bottle in her hand like treasure. She presented the label with a flourish. "Château Margaux, 2009."

Matty's dad beamed like a king. "Perfect. Pour it."

She filled his glass first, then Alice's, but Matty waved her off when she reached for his.

"Just a Coke for me," he said.

"Same," I quickly added.

"Pour her some wine," Matty said, before turning to me. "If I'm paying nine hundred dollars for that bottle, my girlfriend's enjoying it."

The waitress blinked, then smiled wider. "Of course. And I'll bring your Coke right out."

After Matty had gotten his drink, Ronnie lifted his glass high, the ruby liquid catching the chandelier's light. "To Matthew," he announced grandly, "who's never forgotten his family!"

Everyone laughed like it was a joke, but Matty didn't move. His shoulders went rigid, his hand tightening around his glass. A grimace flickered across his face before he smoothed it over with a practiced smile.

We all clinked glasses. I pretended to sip my wine, but my eyes kept straying to Matty. He didn't drink. Just stared at the glass in his hand, his fingers flexing like he wanted to crush it.

By the time the waitress came back, her smile was brighter than ever. "Are we ready to order some appetizers?"

"Damn right we are," Ronnie said before anyone else could talk, slapping the menu shut. "We'll start with calamari. Spinach artichoke dip. Crab cakes. The ahi tuna. And the Wagyu meatballs—get two orders of those."

Matty's jaw tightened as his dad rattled off the list, each order louder and more self-satisfied than the last. The muscle in Matty's cheek ticked. He didn't say anything, though, just stared down at the table, fingers drumming once against the condensation on his glass before going still.

"Certainly, sir," the waitress said smoothly, practically glowing with delight at the growing price of the bill.

His mom ducked her head, her fingers knotting in her napkin. "That's too much food," she whispered.

"There's nothing wrong with trying what they have to offer," Ronnie said, unconcerned.

The waitress smiled at him like she agreed, then glanced around the table. "Will that be all, or should I pace them out?"

"Bring it all at once. And then we'll order our entrées."

The waitress nodded, jotting it down, but his dad wasn't finished. He leaned back in his chair, satisfied. "After all, my superstar football-playing son's footing the bill. Might as well enjoy ourselves, right?"

Matty's jaw flexed. He didn't look up. Just reached for his Coke and took his first long, slow sip like it was the only thing keeping him from saying what he really wanted to.

The waitress scribbled the last note, tucking the pad against her chest. "Wonderful. I'll get these started." She gave Matty a smile like he should be proud. Then she hurried off, practically glowing.

Matty didn't smile back. His shoulders had gone rigid, eyes fixed on the table like he could burn a hole through the linen. His hand that wasn't clenching his glass was still clamped around mine, fingers digging in just enough to sting.

I squeezed back, hard. Fury bloomed hot and protective in my chest, pulsing in time with my heartbeat.

I understood now why Matty had been dreading dinner.

The next course came and went in an awkward blur of silverware and forced conversation. Ronnie had, of course, ordered the most expensive thing on the menu—a tomahawk steak that could've fed a small village—and dug into it like he was making a point.

Alice tried to smooth the jagged edges of the table. She smiled, too bright, and reached for a story. "You know," she began, "when Matty was little, he used to run around the backyard with a football that was bigger than his head. He'd trip over his own feet, but he'd never let go of that ball. Not once."

Matty chuckled, rubbing the back of his neck. "Guess I had my priorities early."

"Uh-huh," Barrett piped up around a mouthful of mashed potatoes. "And you also used to practice tackling the mailman."

"Barrett," Matty groaned, dropping his face into his hands.

Alice laughed, her eyes twinkling. "Oh, it's true. And sometimes he'd do it without a diaper on."

"Mom," Matty said, dragging the word out in horror.

Lizzie dissolved into giggles. "You peed on the mailman!"

"I was *two*!" Matty protested, voice cracking. "And you weren't even alive yet. So how would you know?"

"Mommy told me," Lizzie retorted.

For a brief, flickering second, the whole table was smiling. The kind of laughter that felt almost normal . . . until the sound of a fork clinking against porcelain cut through it.

Ronnie's smile didn't quite reach his eyes. "So," he said, leaning back against the booth, "have you thought any more about the offer?"

The warmth drained from Matty's face in an instant.

I glanced between them. *Offer?*

Matty's jaw flexed. "Can we not?" he said tightly. "My answer was already no."

Ronnie raised a brow, unconcerned. "It's a big opportunity, son. Things like this don't come around twice."

"Yeah, you've said that a few times now," Matty snapped, his voice loud enough to draw a few curious glances from nearby tables. "And I said no the first time and the second time and the third time for a reason."

Alice's hand landed on her husband's wrist, gentle but firm. "Ronnie," she murmured, "not here."

His dad leaned in, eyes bright. "Gatorade hasn't called yet, have they? Neither has Puma. Or Yeti. Hell, not even Taco Bell has called. They're throwing money at kids half your size. I read Parker Davis pulled in over a million last spring just off endorsements."

Matty's jaw ticked.

"And Jace?" his dad went on, as if he couldn't see what he was doing to his son. "He's a wide receiver, not even the face of the team, and he's pulling in NIL deals left and right. Brand partnerships, commercials, interviews—hell, he's on a damn billboard downtown. This deal could be bigger than all of those."

Alice shifted uncomfortably, her smile brittle. "Ronnie—"

But he steamrolled right over her. "You're an idiot if you turn this down. A fucking idiot, son. One bad hit, and it's all gone, Matthew. You can't waste the moment. Parker knows it. Jace knows it. Do you?"

"Enough," Matty growled. "Weren't you so excited about my last NIL deal just a week ago . . . when it meant I could send you money to fix your . . . what was that again . . . your water heater? Or was it your car?"

The mockery in his voice was unmistakable—controlled, deliberate, meant to sting. And it did. His father's smile faltered, just for a second, before settling back into something colder.

His siblings were staring at the two of them with wide eyes, and Alice tried desperately to change the subject. "Ophelia, what's your favorite book?"

Ronnie wasn't finished, though. "Pretty girls like Ophelia don't look twice at athletes unless there's something in it for them. You going to risk losing her when you lose everything else?"

The insult cracked something inside me.

I remembered Matty's warning again. *Don't let him get in your head.*

But I wasn't offended for myself. I was offended for *him*.

The ugly words hung in the air.

Matty shifted violently beside me. "I said that's enough!" he snarled.

"You need to think about that," Ronnie insisted.

I snapped.

"He's second in receptions this season in a team full of superstars," I bit out before I could soften my tone.

They all turned toward me.

"Eighty-seven yards per game on average. Eight touchdowns. Three two-point conversions. Highest catch rate in the conference." The words tumbled out before I could stop them, my heart pounding faster with each one. "Against Alabama? A hundred and twelve yards on their top corner. Against Florida? The game-winning two-point conversion. He's already broken the school record for tight end receptions in a season—and it's not even over yet."

But the numbers weren't enough. Not for what I was trying to say.

"He volunteers at the youth center every week," I went on, my voice shaking now. "He tutors freshman players. He visits the children's hospital after practice. His GPA's nearly perfect, and somehow he still makes time for everyone who needs him."

I glanced at Matty, my throat tightening. "He's not just a good player . . . he's a good person. The best one I've ever known. I don't think you understand how lucky people are just to know him."

My chest ached, but I couldn't stop. "And me . . ." I drew in a shaky breath. "I'm lucky just to be with him. Even if he lost it all tomorrow—football, school, everything—he'd still be the most wonderful person I've ever met. And I love him. With all my heart."

My chest was heaving when I finished, and my fork was trembling slightly in my hand. The table had gone completely silent.

I swallowed hard, heat crawling up my neck. *Too much. You said too much. You shouldn't know almost any of that. You told him you loved him, you idiot.*

I'd just peeled back the curtain on how deeply I watched him, how obsessively I memorized everything about him.

I'd ruined everything.

I couldn't look at Matty's face. Couldn't bear to see whatever expression my words had left there. My pulse thundered in my ears, the silence stretching so long it became a living thing between us.

Then, suddenly, the booth shifted. Matty shoved back from the table, sliding out so fast his knee knocked against the edge.

"Well," he said tightly, his voice strained in that way that meant he was seconds from snapping. "On that note, we're gonna head out."

"Matty—" his mom started, but he was already reaching into his pocket. He tossed a bunch of cash onto the table, the motion clipped and final. "For dinner," he said. "Enjoy it."

Before anyone could answer, his hand closed around mine, warm, solid, trembling just a little . . . and he tugged me after him.

I scrambled to follow as he pulled me out of the booth, nearly tripping over my heels. "Nice to meet you!" I called weakly over my shoulder, my voice cracking as we hurried past the startled hostess at the front."

He didn't stop until the restaurant doors slammed behind us, the cold air biting against my skin.

"Matty—" I began, my voice shaking. "I didn't mean to—"

"We'll talk later," he said, the words controlled and even. Too controlled.

He didn't look at me as we crossed the cobblestone walkway toward the valet stand, his hand still gripping mine but his knuckles white, his shoulders rigid beneath his jacket. Every line of him screamed tension.

The valet scrambled to bring the car around, clearly picking up on the storm in his expression.

I stood there uselessly beside him, hugging my arms to my chest, the night air biting through my dress. My throat ached, every heartbeat pounding against the memory of my voice inside that booth.

The things I'd said. The way everyone had stared.

He knew now—knew I was too much, too intense, too strange. That I didn't know how to love someone without coming apart in the process.

When the car finally pulled up, Matty thanked the valet, handed him a bill, and opened my door without meeting my eyes.

I slid in silently, my pulse still thudding with shame.

By the time he got behind the wheel, the quiet between us felt unbearable. But he didn't say a word.

And I sat there, staring at my hands, certain I'd just destroyed the best thing that had ever happened to me.

CHAPTER 25

OPHELIA

The door to his room had barely opened before I was moving . . . fast, frantic, desperate to get out before he could tell me to.

The ride home had been silent. Not the comfortable kind of quiet, but the kind that hums with everything unsaid, pressing against your chest until it hurts to breathe.

Now, in the dim light of his room, I moved around like a ghost, grabbing my jacket from the chair, my phone from the nightstand, the small bag I'd left by the dresser. My hands shook too much to zip it, the sound of the teeth catching louder than it should've.

What had I been thinking, bringing this much to his room after just a week?

I was such a fucking freak.

Don't cry, Ophelia. Not here. Not in front of him.

My throat burned anyway. I blinked hard, vision blurring as I shoved the rest of my things inside.

"Ophelia."

He'd said my name quietly, but it was so unexpected that I jumped.

The strap of my bag slipped off my shoulder and hit the floor with a heavy *thud*. Books and pens scattered across the floor, spinning out in every direction. My journal slid last, flipping open right at his feet.

I froze, my breath catching as the pages fluttered.

He stepped closer, crouching down, his gaze falling to the open book.

"Don't," I whispered, my throat tight. "Please don't read that." I lunged forward, trying to snatch it out of his hands before he could open it.

Matty caught me easily around the waist, and he held me still with one arm as he picked up the book.

"Give it back!" I gasped, reaching, but he leaned away, holding the journal high in his other hand. "Matty, please—" I twisted in his grip, but he just tightened his hold around my waist, completely unbothered, like restraining me was effortless.

I didn't have to look to know what he saw . . . my handwriting crowding the page, his name scrawled again and again, words I'd written when missing him had felt unbearable.

Mrs. Adler. Scrawled in loops, in block letters, in frantic slanted script that dug too deep into the paper. Some words were circled in hearts, some were framed by doodled stars. His number was written beside my name, over and over, as if the act of pairing them might make it true.

My handwriting bled across the page, feverish, uneven, *aching*. There was no mistaking it, no hiding what it meant.

Heat rushed up my neck, flooding my face. I squeezed my eyes shut, humiliation breaking over me in violent, merciless waves.

It was like I was fourteen all over again.

"I found her notebook," my mom said, and I could hear the sound of paper being shoved across a table. "Pages and pages of their names together. 'Ophelia plus Nico. Mrs. Nico Alvarez.' His schedule, his mom's phone number, even his little sister's birthday."

The memory knifed through me, biting as ever. The shame of it. My parents' disappointed stares. The laughter in the cafeteria when my classmates had heard I had stolen Nico's hoodie. Nico's horrified face.

And now Matty was staring at the same kind of pages, only worse . . . because it was him. How I felt for him was so much more than anything I'd ever felt before.

"Please don't—" I croaked. I shoved at his shoulder, tears streaming down my face, desperate to wrench the journal away, to erase the pages before he could read all that was there.

Matty continued to hold me firm. His thumb brushed slow circles against my hip, the touch gentle enough to unravel me. With his other hand, he closed the journal in one swift motion and tossed it onto the bed.

He tipped my chin up, fingers warm against my skin as he forced me to meet his eyes.

My sobs only got worse, and apologies tumbled out like a broken thing. "I'm sorry, I didn't mean for you to see. I tried to stop. I shouldn't have written—" The words choked out of me, faster than any control I thought I had.

"Stop," he cut in firmly. His hand slid under my jaw, tilting my face until I met his gaze. The pressure was intimate, steady. "Stop. Look at me. Why do you think this is a big deal?"

My breathing hitched. He didn't look angry. Or disgusted. Just calm . . . and confused. Like he couldn't understand why I was falling apart.

I opened my mouth to blurt another apology, but he shook his head, cutting me off. His face had folded into something that was almost *fierce*.

"You don't ever apologize for wanting me." His thumb brushed over my cheek again, softer this time, tracing the damp trail of tears on my skin. "Not when I want you just as bad."

I shook my head, trembling. "Why aren't you mad? You *should* be mad. You should think it's weird," I insisted.

His jaw flexed, and suddenly he was pulling me tighter against his chest, like he was afraid I'd slip through his arms if he didn't hold on. His scent wrapped around me, and I breathed him in with desperate gulps.

"Listen to me, Ophelia." He kept a solid grip on my chin so I still couldn't look away. "I'm not saying it to make you feel better. I'm saying it because it's the truth. You writing my name doesn't make you crazy. It makes you . . . mine."

Heat coursed through me, disbelief warring with a sharp, needy thrill.

"You think I don't notice how careful you are around me?" His lips ghosted over my temple, the brush of them making my whole body shiver. "How you shrink back like you're not allowed to want what you want? Pretty baby, I want that. I want all of it. Every thought, every page, every little piece of you you've been hiding."

My throat closed. "But it's—too much."

It *was* too much.

And there was so much more than a journal. There was so much that I couldn't tell him.

"Not for me." He pressed a kiss to my cheek, lingering there, then trailed lower to the edge of my jaw. Each touch was a reassurance, a seal over the cracks inside me. "Never for me. You could fill every notebook in your room with 'Mrs. Adler,' and I'd still want more. Because that's not too much—it's exactly what I want. You giving me all of you. No shame. No apologies."

I whimpered, my hands clenching in his shirt like I'd drown if I let go.

"That's my good girl," he whispered, brushing his lips back up to the corner of my mouth. His breath was hot against my skin, each word trailing goose bumps in its wake. "Always trying so hard to do everything right.

Always tearing yourself apart because you think it's wrong to love me this much."

His hand splayed across my back, pulling me closer until I could feel the rough pounding of his heart against my chest. "You sat there tonight, defending me like it was as easy as breathing. You were incredible."

His voice roughened, like the memory had scraped something raw. "I couldn't even look at you in the restaurant . . . or in the car after, because I didn't trust myself not to pull over and strip you bare. I didn't trust myself not to lose it completely."

He lowered his head, his mouth brushing the shell of my ear. "It's not wrong, Ophelia. It's perfect. *You're* perfect."

My chest ached, but my knees had gone soft, heat pooling inside me insistently.

He felt the shiver ripple through me, and his grin curved into something wicked . . . and dangerous. "That's what you like, isn't it? Me telling you how good you are. My good girl. *Mrs. Adler*."

I nodded helplessly, a sob catching in my throat. "I shouldn't—"

"Shh." He kissed me then, gentle but sure, cutting the protest off before it could take hold. His tongue brushed mine, coaxing, not demanding, until I melted against him. When he pulled back, his hand framed my face again, his thumb stroking slow circles that made me tremble.

"You don't need to be smaller for me," he said firmly. "You don't need to hide. I want it all, Ophelia. The journals, the daydreams, the obsession . . . every bit of it. Because it means I'm yours the same way you're mine."

I couldn't breathe. The words, the praise, the touch—they surged through me, drowning out every trace of shame and leaving a hungry ache in their wake.

"I'd never thought anyone like you could exist," he admitted, softer now, his forehead leaning against mine. "And now that I've met you, you're the only thing that makes sense."

Tears blurred my vision, but this time they weren't from shame.

They were from fucking *relief*.

"Good girl," Matty murmured, kissing the corner of my mouth again. "Such a good girl for me. Say it back."

"I'm your good girl," I whispered.

"That's right." His smile was fierce and proud, the sort of look you give someone who's just won a championship. "And I'm proud of you for saying it."

The praise landed harder than anything I'd ever heard. My limbs went slack against him, breath stuttering, heart hammering so loud it erased every other noise.

He didn't rush me. He steadied me. His hands moved with purpose, one palm splayed low on my back, anchoring—the other cupping my cheek while his thumb made slow, patient semicircles like a metronome. He smoothed a hand down my spine and pressed me closer until the heat of him was a blanket I could breathe into.

"Breathe with me," he said softly, counting on his fingers. "In—two—three, out—two—three."

His chest rose against mine, and his rhythm was calm and solid and, impossibly, contagious. My inhales stuttered, then lengthened to match his until the room stopped tilting and my pulse found a steadier line.

His palm moved from my back up to my shoulder and stroked the slope in slow, steady pulls, fingers splayed like he was erasing the tremor from my skin. When my hands balled in his shirt, he threaded my fingers through his and held them there as if to say I couldn't get away even if I wanted. The pressure wasn't tight enough to hurt . . . it was the right kind of insistence that said you're safe to fall apart here.

"Look at me," he murmured, his voice brushing against my ear. I blinked up. The intensity in his eyes was strange. It wasn't hungry or amused . . . but reverent, like he was cataloguing something precious. "Say my name," he ordered.

"Matty," I breathed obediently, my voice shaking with the weight of my longing.

He smiled, a devastating curve, and tilted my chin with a calloused finger. "Again."

"Matty." I said it stronger now, my voice thick with the need to belong to him.

"Say what I call you," he urged, his tone soft but commanding, coaxing me to claim the truth he saw.

"Your . . . good girl," I whispered, the words blooming in my chest, no longer heavy with shame but light with possibility. They felt like a confession, a surrender to the part of me that craved his approval.

"Louder." His hand cupped the back of my head. "Say it like you mean it, Ophelia."

"I'm your good girl," I said louder, the phrase settling in my heart like a piece of me slotting into place. His hum of approval was immediate, a soft vibration that sent a rush of arousal through me, my pussy clenching with need. My emotions swirled—fear that this was too perfect, hope that I could be his forever, and a desperate ache to be enough.

"Fuck, yes, you are," he rasped, his forehead pressing to mine, our breaths tangling in hot, desperate pants. "My perfect girl. Now say *Mrs. Adler*."

"Mrs. Adler," I breathed, the name a fragile, shimmering dream that pierced my heart. It was a fantasy too beautiful to hold, a pipe dream I'd never dared believe could be real. Saying it out loud in front of him had me aching . . . aching with the hope that I could be his, truly his, even if it felt like reaching for the moon.

There was so much I was still hiding from him.

But if he could accept *this* . . .

Maybe he could accept . . . *more*.

His mouth crashed into mine, a kiss that was all fire and devotion, his tongue stroking mine with a sensual rhythm that left me dizzy.

His calloused hands roamed my body, tugging my dress over my head with a reverence that made my breath hitch. My bra followed, and my breasts spilled free, nipples tightening under his hungry gaze. He groaned, a primal, desperate sound that sent a fresh wave of wetness between my thighs.

"Fucking hell, Ophelia, these tits are fucking exquisite," he growled, his voice thick with lust as he cupped them, his rough palms squeezing with a pressure that made me gasp. "So beautiful, giving yourself to me like this. You're my whole fucking world, pretty baby."

He lowered his mouth, lips closing around one nipple, sucking with a hard pull that sent pleasure spiking through me. His tongue swirled, teasing the sensitive peak, while his teeth grazed just enough to make me arch into him, a moan spilling from my lips. "So perfect," he murmured against my skin, his breath a hot caress. "These nipples are so hard for me, aren't they? My good girl, dripping just from my mouth."

I moaned, my hands tangling in his hair, my body trembling with the intensity of his touch and the storm of my emotions. I felt worshiped, cherished, but also raw, like he was peeling back every layer of doubt I'd carried.

"Matty," I whimpered, my voice breaking with need and vulnerability, my heart aching with how much I wanted this, wanted *him*.

He moved to my other breast, sucking harder, his hand kneading the one he'd left slick and aching. "Fuck, I'm so obsessed with you," he growled, his words an obscene prayer that stoked the fire in my core. "You're such a good girl to let me worship you like this."

The word *obsessed* hit me like a lit match to dry tinder.

My breath snagged, and I pulled him closer to me.

I'd dreamed of being wanted, but obsessed?

It was my lifelong dream . . . laid bare and answered.

I tore at his shirt, revealing the chiseled planes of his body. I raked my nails down his abs, feeling him shudder, his control fraying. He laughed, a dark, ravenous sound that made my heart race, and fisted my hair, tilting my head back to expose my throat.

"You're fucking killing me, Ophelia," he rasped, biting my pulse point, the sting sending a jolt to my clit. "Feel how fucking hard you make me?" He pressed his cock against my hip, thick and rigid through the denim, a delicious promise that made my core clench and flood with an aching need.

"I love that," I panted as I fumbled with his belt desperately. I ripped it open in a frenzy to touch him. "I love *you*."

"That's my fucking girl," he praised, helping me shove his jeans and briefs down, his cock springing free—long, thick, veined, the head glistening with precum and that silver piercing. "Look at this, baby. All for you, because you're so fucking perfect."

I was aching at the sight, my emotions a tangled mess of longing and vulnerability. He guided my hand to his length, letting me feel the hard, pulsing heat of him.

"Stroke me, Ophelia. Show me how much you want me."

I moved slowly, my thumb circling through the slick at his tip, his low groans growing rougher with every pass. "Fuck, you're so good," he rasped, breath hitching. "Making me ache for you, my perfect girl."

Before I could answer, he caught my wrist, gently pulling my hand away. He urged me backward, and I stumbled until the backs of my knees hit the bed. I fell against the mattress, his gaze dark and consuming. For a heartbeat, he just stared . . . then shook his head, like he was trying to break whatever spell had taken hold of him.

"Take off those panties and spread your legs for me," he commanded, his voice rough with desire. "Show me that pretty pussy."

I obeyed instantly. My fingers hooked into the soaked lace, the fabric clinging to my slick lips before peeling away, leaving me bare.

My thighs fell open wide, and I reached down, parting my folds with two trembling fingers and exposing every glistening inch to his ravenous stare.

He groaned, a guttural sound that vibrated through the air. "Fuck, your cunt is perfection, Ophelia." His knees hit the floor hard, the impact echoing in the quiet room.

He gripped my thighs, spreading me wider, and buried his face between them. His tongue dragged up my slit, lapping at my dripping heat like he was starving.

I cried out, hips bucking as he devoured me—sucking my clit into his mouth, tongue flicking hard and fast, then plunging deep inside me, curling to taste every drop. His hands pinned my thighs open, fingers bruising, his groans muffled against my flesh as he ate me out.

Relentless. Messy. His nose ground against my clit with every thrust of his tongue.

"Fuck, you taste so good," he moaned, pulling back just enough to speak, his lips slick with me. "You're going to come all over my face."

He dove back in, sucking harder, tongue-fucking me deeper until my thighs shook. My moans turned to screams, my body arching off the bed as he claimed every inch of me with his mouth.

His stubble scraped my inner thighs, a decadent burn that made me whimper. He growled against my clit, the vibration shooting sparks up my spine, and I fisted the sheets, knuckles white.

"Matty— Fuck—" I gasped, my hips grinding shamelessly against his face, chasing the edge he was dragging me toward.

"Give it to me," he demanded. "Come on my tongue, baby. Let me taste every fucking drop."

He attacked again, his tongue lashing my clit in tight, ruthless circles, two fingers sliding inside me, rubbing that spot that made my vision blur.

"Yes, yes, yes," I chanted as he worked me perfectly, wet sounds filling the room, his mouth sucking my clit like he wanted to swallow me whole.

My back bowed off the bed, a scream ripping from my throat as I came hard. My walls clenched around his fingers as slick gushed over his hand, his chin, and the sheets.

He didn't stop.

He licked me through it, groaning like my release was the best thing he'd ever tasted, his tongue gentle now, lapping softly, drawing out every aftershock until I was trembling, oversensitive, and begging incoherently. Only then did he pull back and stand up.

I stared at him, dazed, my chest heaving.

His lips were swollen, glistening with me, his stubble dark with my wetness. Those blue eyes burned with raw triumph, like he'd just conquered something.

He was shirtless, inked skin gleaming with sweat, but his jeans still clung low on his hips, unzipped and shoved down just enough to free his enormous cock.

It jutted out, flushed dark red, slick with precum, the piercing glinting at the tip, seeping and throbbing in time with his pulse.

Matty crawled up my body, all muscle and ink and heat, caging me beneath him. His mouth crashed into mine, the kiss deep and dirty, letting me taste myself—salty, sweet, *us*—his tongue fucking my mouth the way he'd just fucked my core.

"You're fucking addictive," he whispered against my lips as he ground his cock against my soaked, throbbing center. I moaned into him, my hands clawing at his back, nails digging into his skin, needing more, needing *him*.

He pulled back. "Turn over," he ordered. "Ass up, Mrs. Adler. I'm taking *all* of you tonight."

CHAPTER 26

OPHELIA

My breath hitched at his words, a thrill sparking through me. I immediately obeyed, rolling onto my stomach and pushing up on my knees so that my ass was in the air, exposed and vulnerable. The cool air kissed my slick skin, and I shivered, my core still pulsing from my orgasm.

That's when I noticed it—a new full-length mirror propped against the wall by the bed, angled perfectly to catch every inch of us. My reflection stared back: cheeks flushed, lips swollen, eyes glassy with need, my body arched and waiting. The sight sent a fresh wave of heat through me, making me wetter.

Matty's gaze followed mine in the glass, a wicked grin curling his lips. "Like your new present, pretty baby?" he rasped in a lust-filled voice. "I wanted you to see exactly how fucking good you look while I ruin this ass. Every moan, every shake, every inch of you taking me."

He gripped my hips, spreading my cheeks wide. "Fuck, look at you," he growled, his thumb circling my tight hole, teasing, testing. "This ass is mine, too, isn't it? You're going to feel me every time you move."

I whimpered, pushing back against his touch, the forbidden heat of it making me drip. In the mirror, I watched my reflection—thighs trembling, breasts swaying heavy and full—and it made me bolder. "Yes," I gasped in a needy voice. "Please, Matty."

Matty leaned over me, his chest pressing against my back, his lips brushing my ear. "Good girl," he murmured, nipping my lobe. "I'll make it so good for you." I heard the rustle of his jeans as he pulled them all the way off. And then his fingers were back between my legs, scooping up my slick and coating them generously.

He brought them to my ass, and one finger circled my tight ring, pressing in slow until I relaxed, and it slid inside. I gasped, the intrusion strange but electric, my body tensing then melting as he worked me open, thrusting gently and letting me adjust. In the mirror, I saw his face over my shoulder. His eyes were dark, jaw clenched, lips parted as he watched himself sink into me.

"Fuck, you're so tight," he groaned as he added a second finger and started scissoring them, stretching me wider . . . the burn was intense but laced with pleasure. My moans grew louder, and I rocked my hips back, chasing the sensation as he prepared me.

The mirror showed it all.

It showed my face twisted in ecstasy and my lips parted in a silent scream.

It showed how I was dripping onto the sheets as his fingers worked me open.

This was so fucking hot.

"That's it, pretty baby," he praised roughly. "Open for me. You're taking my fingers so well, but I bet you'll take my cock even better." A third finger joined, and the stretch pushed me to the edge. My body was shaking, my slick dripping down my thighs as he fucked me with his hand until I was begging in broken sobs. I watched myself in the mirror—lips parted, eyes half lidded, body arching like I was made for this—and the sight made me clench harder around him.

Only then did he pull his fingers free. He sat back on his heels, his knees spread wide, and I twisted my torso so I could see him, too, in the mirror. His enormous cock jutted up, flushed dark and angry, veins pulsing, the piercing glinting under the low light. He slid his slick-coated fingers back through my core, gathering more of my essence, then wrapped his fist around his shaft.

He moved his fist up and down. Wet, delicious sounds filled the room as he coated every inch, his thumb smearing precum over the head, his abs flexing with each pump. The mirror gave me the perfect view: his hand gliding, his cock throbbing, his eyes locked on my stretched hole like he was already inside me again.

A second later, the blunt head pressed against me, and I forced myself to breathe, to trust him. I wanted this. I wanted him to own every part of me.

"Relax," he soothed, one hand stroking my spine, the other guiding himself. "Let me in."

He pushed slowly inside me, and the stretch burned, overwhelming me until my body finally started to yield and let him sink deeper. The piercing dragged against raw nerves that lit me up. In the mirror, I saw his cock disappearing into me, inch by inch, the sight erotic and mesmerizing, my ass stretching around his thickness.

"Fuck," he groaned. "You're so tight, but you're taking me like you were made for this. My perfect fucking girl."

He eased in with shallow thrusts, giving me time to breathe around the stretch. His hands clamped my hips, anchoring me, and the burn melted into a dark, pulsing pleasure that unfurled low in my belly.

I loved this.

Every inch of him filled me . . . claiming me in a way I'd never imagined. The mirror captured it all: his abs flexing, my back arching, the way my tits swayed with every movement.

"Matty—it's so good," I moaned, pushing back, meeting his rhythm, the sensation building fast and fierce. His hand slid around and found my clit. I screamed, the dual assault sending me spiraling.

"Love this ass," he rasped, thrusting harder, the bed creaking, his balls slapping against my slick core with every stroke. "Love how you swallow my cock with it, how you beg like my perfect, good girl. Every hole is going to be full of me, Ophelia."

His pace turned wild, the piercing hitting spots that made my eyes roll back, my body shaking with every thrust. I was lost in it, in him, my moans turning to sobs, my clit throbbing under his fingers. The mirror reflected the rawness—sweat-slick skin, my ass rippling with every slap of his hips, his face twisted in ecstasy.

"Come for me," he demanded in a voice breaking with need. "Come with my cock in your ass; let me feel it."

His fingers pressed harder, thrusts driving deeper, and I shattered. My body convulsed, ass clenching around him in tight, greedy pulses as waves of pleasure ripped through me, more of me dripping down my thighs.

He roared, slamming in one last time, spilling deep inside me . . . hot, thick, endless. His cum flooded my ass in powerful bursts, marking me from the inside out. Then he stilled, buried to the hilt, his weight pressing me into the mattress, his breath ragged against my neck.

We stayed like that, locked together, trembling. I soaked in the feel of him, his cock pulsing inside me, his cum warm and heavy, his sweat-slick chest sealed to my back, his arms caging me, his scent everywhere. Every inch of me was his, filled, claimed, and dripping with him. The mirror caught it all: my flushed, wrecked face and his possessive grip.

I never wanted to move.

He pulled out slowly, though, his cum leaking from me, and flipped me onto my back, kissing me soft and deep, his hands gentle now as he traced my skin.

"Don't hide from me, Ophelia," he murmured hoarsely, his forehead pressed to mine. "You're perfect. Just like *this*."

I melted into him, body sore, sated, his . . . and in the mirror's reflection, I wondered if maybe I could believe him.

And the real me, the one that had always been wrong, the *freak*, so to speak, could believe him, too.

Matty

Ophelia slept like peace had finally found her.

Her lashes brushed her cheeks, her mouth curved in the faintest smile, and it felt like the whole room had narrowed to just her.

Lamplight pooled over her collarbone, tracing the edge of her jaw, and I felt it in my chest like a fist. Everything I hadn't known I was searching for was right there, breathing soft and steady in my lap.

For someone so small, she was the most dangerous thing I'd ever touched.

We'd cleaned up—quick, quiet, with towels and whispered laughs—but she'd tugged my hand before I could pull away.

"I want you in my mouth when I fall asleep," she'd said shyly, already half asleep, her voice thick with afterglow.

I hadn't argued.

Now she lay curled against me, lips wrapped soft and warm around my cock, the head resting heavy on her tongue. No suction, no movement—just the steady heat of her breath, the velvet seal of her mouth, the slow pulse of her throat every time she swallowed in her sleep.

My fingers threaded through her hair, anchoring her gently, and I felt every tiny shift, every unconscious lick, like a promise she didn't know she was keeping.

I stayed half hard inside her, the ache sweet and endless.

Her body rose and fell with mine, slick skin pressed to slick skin, the sheets still damp beneath us. The room smelled of sex and her, and I let it sink into my lungs, into my blood.

She'd taken everything tonight, every inch, every drop . . . and still wanted more. Still wanted *me*.

I brushed my thumb across her cheek, tracing the swell of her lip stretched around me. She sighed in her sleep, a soft, content sound that vibrated straight through my cock and into my spine.

I dragged my hand lower, over the damp heat between her thighs, and I pushed inside her briefly so that I could spread *us* across her skin. Something dark and alive twisted through me as I stared at the shiny cum.

Possession. Worship. Whatever it was, it was her. Always her.

My obsession for her burned hotter.

I thought about how she'd freaked out earlier, crying like the world had ended just because I'd seen her journal. The pages had been filled with things she thought were terrible secrets . . . my name scrawled in her handwriting, her first name next to my last. Like it was some kind of crime to imagine a future that already felt inevitable.

I didn't think it was a big deal. Hell, didn't most girls do that at some point? I was sure Jace had a journal somewhere with Riley's name in it . . . and possibly mine, with how much he liked to snuggle.

Most people just didn't get caught.

She knew a lot about me too—stats, records, things only someone paying attention would know. But I didn't mind that, either. If anything, it made sense. We fit. We watched each other.

I mean, I'd had Jace change her emergency contact in her student file to my name and number, and I didn't think it was a big deal.

He'd also hacked the dining hall system so her meal card pinged my phone every time she ate. Also not a big deal—I just liked knowing she was eating.

Then there was the tracking app he'd installed onto her phone while she was in the bathroom at lunch. I hadn't ever thought I'd learn how to do it. But Jace had made an excellent teacher, and now I could be sure she was safe whenever we weren't together.

And the webcam thing . . . He had swapped it out for me so it streamed straight to my phone when she studied.

All of it felt . . . normal.

Just small ways to make sure she was okay.

We just really loved each other.

Matty, you kind of sound like a psycho.

Maybe I shouldn't have given Parker and Jace such a hard time about the things they'd done to get their girls . . .

I kept seeing Ophelia's face from earlier, though. The way her eyes had gone wide when I'd picked up her journal, the tears streaking down her cheeks like she thought I was going to end us. The sound she'd made when I told her to stop apologizing. Like she couldn't believe I wasn't angry.

The memory lodged somewhere deep, twisting.

She'd been so scared I'd run.

How could I help her to see I wasn't going anywhere?

Hmm. There was one thing I could do . . .

And even Jace would have agreed . . . it was a big-brain idea.

If she could see what she meant to me, if I could do something so she would know I wasn't going anywhere . . .

Then she'd stop being afraid.

I'd give her a tattoo.

Not flowers. Or initials.

I'd tattoo *Mrs. Adler* on her skin. Then she could look at it and know every day who she belonged to.

Fuck.

I'd have to do that in a few minutes . . . because her tongue had started to move. Slow, unconscious, sleepy licks along the underside of my shaft. She started suckling gently, her lips sealing around the head, soft, wet pulls that made my hips twitch.

Her breath hitched in her sleep, a tiny moan vibrating through me, and I felt it everywhere.

I didn't move.

I didn't need to.

She kept going, lazy and instinctive, her tongue swirling, her lips nursing slow and sweet like I was her comfort, her *home*. Each gentle suck pulled me deeper into her warmth, her throat fluttering when she swallowed around me.

My palm settled at her nape, a silent collar, keeping her exactly where she belonged.

I came with a shuddering groan, spilling into her mouth in thick, pulsing waves.

She swallowed in her sleep, throat working, lips never breaking the seal, taking every drop like it was the most natural thing in the world. A soft, satisfied hum escaped her, her body relaxing deeper into the mattress, still holding me inside.

Holy fuck.

She really was perfect.

Not just the way she took me, not just the way she trusted me completely, even unconscious, but the way she needed me like this.

Like I was her air.

Like I was her everything.

I eased out slowly, the wet slide of my cock leaving her lips with a faint *pop* as I slid off the bed.

She blinked awake, eyes still hazy, her voice small and raspy with sleep. "Where are you going?"

I leaned down, kissed her forehead, then her mouth, tasting myself on her tongue before pulling away.

She licked her lips slowly, chasing every last trace of me, tongue sliding over the plump curve like she couldn't let it go.

My brain short-circuited; I had to shake my head to focus.

"I'm not going anywhere, pretty baby," I murmured in a voice filled with certainty, my thumb brushing her cheek. "I'd never leave my good girl. Never." I sat on the edge of the bed, pulling her into my lap, her legs draped over mine.

"I had an idea," I said. "Something to help you feel more settled. Something permanent."

She tilted her head, still licking her lips, her eyes wide and trusting.

I grinned. "You're gonna wear my name, Ophelia. Right here." I traced a spot just above her hip bone. "*Mrs. Adler*. In my handwriting. So every time you look in the mirror, you remember who you belong to."

Her breath caught, eyes lighting up with a sudden, hopeful glow. "Yes," she whispered, eager and breathless, leaning into me. "I want that. I want *you* on me forever."

Her fingers curled into my shirt, tugging like she needed me closer, her voice trembling with excitement. "Please, Matty. I want it so bad."

I kissed her hard, swallowing her eagerness, then eased her off my lap and onto the bed.

"Stay right there," I murmured, standing.

She watched me the entire time, eyes never leaving me as I crossed the room to the closet.

I pulled out the small black case—my tattoo kit, needles, ink, everything ready.

Her gaze tracked every movement: the *click* of the latches, the *clink* of metal, the way I laid out the stencil paper, the black ink bottle glinting under the lamp.

She sat up straighter, knees pulled to her chest, lips parted, watching like I was the only thing in the world.

I set up on the nightstand, hoping it looked like I had done this more than the one time. When I snapped on the gloves and the tattoo gun whirred to life, the buzz filling the room, she froze.

Her eyes went wide, scared but shining. "Matty," she whispered in a small voice. "Are you sure?" She reached for my hand, fingers trembling. "This is going to mean *so much* to me. You have to be sure. Like . . . really sure. Because once it's there, it's forever. And I'll see it every day, and I'll love it, and I need to know you won't regret it."

I set the gun down, cupped her face, and looked her dead in the eyes.

"Ophelia," I said, steadily. "I've never been more sure of anything. You're my forever. This isn't a whim. It's a promise. I want my name on your skin so the whole world knows you're mine—and so *you* never forget it, either."

She searched my face, then nodded, her eyes brimming with tears, but she smiled through them.

"Okay," she breathed. "Do it. Make me yours."

Her hand squeezed mine, and I was awestruck for a second at her trust . . . her devotion. It hit me harder than any stadium roar ever could have.

"Good girl," I murmured reverently. "You're so brave." I kissed the hollow of her throat and heard the little catch in her breath.

I pulled back, eyes locked on hers, and picked up the stencil. My handwriting—*Mrs. Adler*—was already traced in as close to perfect as I could get on the transfer paper.

This had to be better than the messy letters I'd scratched onto Jace and Parker.

This was *her*. This had to be art.

I wiped her hip clean with alcohol, the harsh scent cutting through the sex-heavy air. She shivered, goose bumps rising, but didn't flinch. I pressed the stencil just above her hip bone, smoothing it down with steady fingers, peeling it back slowly to reveal the purple outline. Perfect placement . . . visible when she wore low jeans, hidden under lace when she wanted it private. Mine either way.

The gun buzzed to life in my hand, a low, hungry growl. I dipped the needle, black ink pooling, and leaned in.

Don't fuck this up, Adler.

"Deep breath, baby," I said in a voice that I hoped sounded calm. She inhaled, chest rising, eyes fixed on me—trusting and eager.

The needle touched skin.

She hissed, fingers digging into my thigh, but didn't pull away. I started the first line—*M*—slow, precise, the ink sinking clean and dark.

Better than Jace's crooked N. *Better than Parker's bleeding* L.

I angled the gun, shading the curve of the *R*, making it sharp, elegant, *permanent*.

"You're doing so good," I praised as I wiped off some excess ink with a cloth. "Look at you—taking my name like you were born for it."

She whimpered, a soft, needy sound, her free hand sliding up my arm, gripping tight.

Her eyes were glassy, like she was in that special space she sometimes went to during sex. Her lips were parted as she watched the ink bloom on her skin like it was the most beautiful thing she'd ever seen.

I worked faster now, building confidence, but every line was deliberate. The *S* curled just right, the *A* bold and unapologetic. *Mrs. Adler*—not a nickname, not a maybe. A vow.

Sweat beaded on my brow, but I didn't rush.

I shaded the final *R*, wiped it clean, and sat back.

The tattoo was flawless—crisp, dark, *mine*.

Honestly better than I could have expected now that I was on the other side of it.

I set the gun down, gloved hands framing her hips, thumbs brushing the fresh ink. "Look," I said. "Look at what you are now."

She stared at the *Mrs. Adler*, and I watched as a tear slipped down her cheek and she smiled the most radiant smile I'd ever seen.

"It's beautiful," she whispered. "It's *us*."

I leaned in and kissed just beside the ink, careful not to touch it.

"Forever, baby," I said against her skin. "You're mine. You're *home*."

CHAPTER 27

OPHELIA

The screen lit my face as I crossed the quad, the cold biting through my sweater, and the wind making little rivers of leaves chase one another across the bricks. I glanced down, and everything inside me went tight when I saw who it was.

Mom.

Oh my gosh.

I froze in the middle of the walkway, my breath puffing out in uneven bursts. That sick, dropping feeling hit before the thought even formed—

Dr. Whitaker.

I'd forgotten.

Again.

My stomach twisted.

I swiped to answer on the second ring, speed-walking toward the student center . . . my words spilling out too fast. "I'm sorry, I'm sorry— I forgot, I lost track of time—"

"Ophelia." Her voice came through thin and high, like a piano wire pulled too tight. "Do you have any idea how worried I've been? This is your *third* missed appointment. *Third.* The office called me. Your advisor emailed me. They could put you on medical leave if I push it. And then you'll be coming home. No arguments, no excuses . . ."

"I'm *fine*," I said quickly, my steps slowing as I tried to come up with the right words to convince her of that. "It's not a big deal. I just— Class ran over one day, and then I've had lots of practices, and—"

"And what?" The wire in her voice tightened. "You *promised* you wouldn't do this again."

"I know." The words scraped my throat on the way out. I stopped outside the building and leaned against the cold brick, trying to steady my breathing. "I know."

"Then what is going on?" Every syllable landed like a small slap. "You were doing so well. We had a plan. You and I and Dr. Whitaker had a plan."

I looked down at my shoes. Leaves stuck to the soles, wet and red like crushed petals. "Maybe I don't need to go anymore," I finally said, and even I heard how small it was. "I feel . . . good. Normal."

"Normal?" The word cracked, like she might laugh or cry and couldn't decide which. "You don't get to declare yourself *normal* and fire a treatment team, Ophelia. That is not how this works."

"I've been sleeping," I said quietly. "And eating. I—"

"And."

"I met someone."

The second the words slipped out, I wanted to scrape them back with my nails. The silence that followed sounded like a building holding its breath.

When she finally spoke, the wire snapped. "Oh, Ophelia," my mother said, and her voice was shaking now, not soft—angry. Scared. "Not *again*."

Wind sliced across the quad, and I tucked my chin into my scarf, people streaming past with takeaway cups and bright orange beanies pulled low.

"I know," I said, seeming not to have anything else to say to answer her. I took a deep breath, like I could pull bravery into my lungs with the air. "But this is different."

"It's always different, according to you." She talked right over me, the way she did when she thought she had to pour fear into me fast before I made a mistake. "You convince yourself of it. And then I'm the one driving to a facility at midnight because you haven't answered the phone in six hours and a boy's name is written eight hundred times in a notebook."

"Mom," I breathed, my cheeks burning in shame. "Please."

For a second my mind drifted, one of those bright flashes that made me dizzy with how real it felt. I saw the spiral of my notebook on his bedroom floor, my handwriting all messy and diagonal, his name looping through page after page until the margins were full. I remembered the exact way the light had hit the ink, how small the letters looked when he crouched down to pick it up. I remembered him closing the book and tossing it back on the bed, the sound a punctuation I could still hear. He hadn't yelled. He hadn't laughed.

I felt it now, how he'd cupped the back of my head, thumb pressing little circles into the place where my skull met my neck, the way his chest had risen under my cheek when I cried. He'd told me I was perfect, like it was a fact and not something dangerously fragile. For a beat, I almost believed it, and the shame that had been coiled in my ribs loosened enough that I could breathe.

"I'm not doing this again." My mother's voice cut through the memory. I blinked, shaking my head as if clearing water out of my ears, and forced myself back to the call.

I heard the sound of rustling papers in the background and the clatter of a pen. She was at her desk in her office, probably typing out an email to Dr. Whitaker as we spoke. "What about your medication . . . ? Have you been taking it?"

I hesitated for a half second, the honest answer skittering through my throat—I hadn't been bringing the meds with me to Matty's house because I didn't want him to see them, so I'd missed every dose this past week—but the thought vanished the second it arrived.

"Yes," I lied, because the last thing I wanted was her driving up. And the truth was, I'd felt fine without it; being with Matty smoothed the jagged edges in a way the pills never had, like he was fixing what the doctors only managed to bandage.

"Every day?"

"Yes."

"Show me the bottle when you get back to your dorm. I want to see the count."

"I'm not a child."

"You are *my* child," she snapped, her voice flaring wide like a lit match. "And forgive me for not trusting the version of you who thinks *falling in love* means she's cured. You want to stop therapy? Absolutely not. You know what your diagnoses are. You know what Dr. Whitaker said about structure. You don't get to just . . . opt out because you think you found a boy."

"He's not just a boy." The words slipped out before I could stop them. "He—"

"Does he even know you exist?" My mother pounced. "And don't lie to me."

For once, my breath didn't catch in my throat. I didn't have to twist or invent or pretend. "Yes," I said quietly, a tiny bloom of relief rising in my chest. "He knows."

It shouldn't have felt like victory. But it did . . . because for the first time in a long time, I could tell the truth.

Silence stretched across the line. I could hear my mother breathing, the faint *click* of her pen stopping.

Then her voice came back, slow and cold. "Just like Nico knew who you were," she questioned sarcastically. "Just like Tommy . . ."

The words sank into me, heavy and familiar, and a tear slid down my cheek before I could stop it.

"He knows me, Mom," I whispered. "And he *loves* me."

She laughed then, the sound humorless. "This so-called boy who loves you," she said mockingly. "What's his name?"

"Matty," I answered easily, a burst of warmth filling my chest just saying it. "His name is Matty."

"Full name."

"Matthew Adler."

For a moment, all I could hear was the faint clatter of typing on her keyboard, the sound of her pulling up whatever record she was about to use against me.

There was silence for a second. "The football player?" She gasped incredulously.

I closed my eyes, hating how shocking it was for her to hear that.

Even though I understood.

"Yes," I whispered.

"You expect me to believe that?"

Something in me snapped. With shaking fingers, I opened my camera roll and sent her the picture Matty had taken of us—his arm slung around me. He was staring at me with a soft smile on his face while I beamed at the camera.

Silence filled the line. For once, my mother didn't have anything to say.

For about half a second.

"How long?" she finally snapped.

I swallowed. "A while."

"How long?" she repeated, and I could imagine her eyebrows lifting, the tired, warning line of her mouth. "You missed your appointment today. You missed the one last week. You missed the *group* session on Sunday that you agreed to participate in. How long, Ophelia?"

"I don't know. We—we didn't make it official right away."

It felt like forever, though. Even though it hadn't been much time at all. Not compared to the months I'd spent watching him, memorizing the shape of his smile, tracing his name into the margins of my notebooks until it became part of me.

"You barely know him, and you're throwing away the scaffolding we spent *years* building." She laughed then, a low, joyless sound. "Of course you are."

"That's not fair."

"What's not fair is me being asked to watch you drown. Again."

I flinched, stung. A couple kissed as they passed by, laughing, and the wind carried their breathless happiness right past me like a taunt.

"I'm not drowning," I said quietly. "I'm . . . breathing for the first time in my life."

She didn't soften. "Who is his doctor?"

"What?" I asked, confused.

"His doctor. His therapist. There's no way that he isn't seeking mental help if he's dating you. I want names. I want to know he's not enabling you."

My throat closed. The world tilted cruelly, as if she'd just confirmed the worst thing I'd always suspected . . . that loving me meant there was something wrong with him, too. The sting hit so hard I couldn't breathe.

When I finally managed to speak, my voice was barely a whisper. "He loves me," I said again, shattered. "He really does."

I thought of his voice again. *It's not wrong, Ophelia. It's perfect.* You're *perfect.*

"He makes me better."

"No," she said quickly, like slapping a hand over my mouth. "He makes you *feel* better. That is not the same thing. You can be getting sicker while he masks the symptoms . . . until it's too late."

I stared at the scuffed toe of my boot. I could hear my mother riffling papers again, the *click-click* of her pen.

"Okay," she said, in that tight administrator voice, the one that meant a plan was forming into a weapon. "Here is what's going to happen. You are going to call Dr. Whitaker and beg for the next available slot. You are going to apologize to the group and show up this Sunday. You are going to text me a photo of your pill bottle with today's date and the count. And you are going to check in with me morning and night. If any of this is not done, I will push the issue with the school and make sure you are placed on medical leave."

Ice slid down my spine. "That's not fair."

"Why not?"

"Because that's—because—" Because it felt like letting her put a leash around my neck. "Because there's nothing wrong!"

"That boy is a trigger," she hissed. "You don't get to assign him a role that justifies whatever your brain wants next."

"He's not a trigger," I said, and the ache in my chest went hot and messy . . . anger, shame, love—all of it knotted together. "He's a person. He's *my* person."

"Stop," she snapped, and I heard the tremor then, the one she tried to hide under orders. "Stop talking like that."

I closed my eyes, another tear slipping down my face.

"You named me Ophelia," I said, and my voice barely carried over the wind. "You said it was because you almost died giving birth to me. Because love can kill you. I know. I know what you think I am."

Silence, except for her breathing.

"But I'm not walking into any rivers."

"You never think you are," she said, softer, and somehow that hurt worse. "You think you're standing on the bank, testing the water with your toes. You tell me you're sleeping better. You tell me you're eating. And then . . . everything falls apart."

I bit the inside of my cheek until I tasted metal. A couple of girls walked past me, talking and laughing like they didn't have a single worry.

The world seemed to keep moving for everyone else . . . while mine always telescoped down to this small, ugly place.

"I'm not that girl anymore," I said. "I swear. I'm not."

"Where are you right now?"

I swallowed. "Walking to eat."

"With who?"

"By myself."

"You shouldn't be by yourself when you're like this."

"Like what?" It came out harsher than I meant.

"Elevated," she said immediately. "Breathless. Defiant. That tone."

I laughed once, because if I didn't, it would turn into a scream and people would look. "That's funny, because you just told me that me being with anyone was wrong and unbelievable. So you would think that me being alone would be acceptable to you."

"That's it. You're coming home this weekend. We will reset. We will make a plan. I will drive up and get you tonight if I have to."

"No." My throat felt like it was closing. "I'm not leaving. I have the team's first playoff game."

"I think I'm beginning to understand why you tried out for the mascot in the first place," she said coldly.

My insides clenched. "I don't know what you're talking about," I replied, but it sounded weak even to me.

"You have twenty minutes to start working through the line items I gave you. If I don't hear from you, I will call the school for a wellness check or come up there and drag you home. Do you understand me?"

I stared at the black glass of my phone screen, at the tiny, distorted version of myself reflected there—pale and wide-eyed, hair shoved into a messy bun, the scarf I'd stolen from Matty's closet wrapped too tight around my neck.

"Ophelia."

"I understand," I said, feeling completely hopeless.

"Good," she breathed, and then softer, the wire loosening for a heartbeat. "I love you. Even when you hate me."

"This doesn't feel like love," I whispered.

She didn't answer that. "Twenty minutes," she repeated and hung up.

CHAPTER 28

MATTY

We were walking back into the facility after practice, our cleats clacking against the concrete. Out of habit, my eyes drifted toward the parking lot. To where that one familiar car still hadn't returned.

I didn't care. Not about that, at least.

What I cared about was Ophelia.

Something felt off. The way she'd looked this afternoon before practice, tired and distracted, like her head was somewhere far away.

Jace and Parker were arguing about the proper Taylor Swift song ranking when the words slipped out. "I think something's wrong with Ophelia."

They both glanced over. Parker frowned. "What do you mean?"

I rubbed the back of my neck. "I don't know. I think I might've . . . scared her."

Jace slowed, studying me. "Scared her how?"

I didn't answer right away. I knew exactly what I'd done—and that it might've been *a lot*.

"Well, I tattooed her," I said finally.

There was a beat of silence—Parker blinking, Jace's mouth parting in surprise. Then Jace grinned like Christmas had come early and lifted his hand for a high five.

"Matty, my boy," he said, grinning ear to ear. "You have officially leveled up."

Parker just stared at me, looking intrigued. "You tattooed her?"

"Yeah." I exhaled, running a hand through my hair. "And now I think she's freaking out about it."

"Did you do it while she was sleeping?" Jace asked, not seeming particularly concerned if I had.

I could feel the heat climb up my neck. For a second, my mind flashed back to how exactly she'd been sleeping right before I did it—with my cock in her mouth—and I had to clear my throat before speaking.

"She was awake," I said quickly, ignoring their amused, knowing stares at the weirdness in my voice. "And she seemed happy about it. I think."

Parker's eyebrows shot up. "You 'think'?"

"She'd seemed happy . . . but then she said she wanted to sleep in her room tonight," I added, and both of them froze like I'd just announced a death in the family.

"She *what*?" Jace demanded. "No. Absolutely not."

Parker shook his head, scandalized. "After the tattoo? That's . . . not good."

I let out a humorless laugh, dragging a hand down my face. "I mean, it's probably not a big deal. Normal couples have some space . . . especially when they've just started dating, right?"

They both stared at me like I'd just admitted to having eaten paint chips as a kid.

"Right?" I added weakly.

Jace blinked once. "Matty, that might be the dumbest thing you've ever said. Which is truly saying something."

I growled at the fact that Jace was the one confidently saying that.

Parker nodded. "Space is how relationships die, man. You're supposed to suffocate them—with love."

I groaned. "Yeah, you're right. I think I need to convince her to move in with me. Make sure she knows space is not allowed in this relationship."

Jace clapped his hands together. "Now *that's* the energy I like to hear. We'll help."

Parker grinned. "We could release a possum in her dorm. No one's staying after that."

Jace's head whipped toward him. "What the hell, Parker? That's *your* idea of help? You realize we'd be the ones catching the possum, right? Because I don't think Matty could do it. I'm not getting rabies for his romance schemes. There has to be a line somewhere. And I think it's at possums . . . and possibly sharks."

Parker shrugged. "Fine. Fire alarm? Maybe her window 'breaks' mysteriously, and she can't sleep there until maintenance fixes it."

Jace leaned in, nodding thoughtfully. "Or we stage a haunting. I've got a speaker and a fog machine left over from Halloween. Couple eerie whispers at three a.m., maybe a silhouette in her mirror—boom, she's out."

"Or we fake a campus mold infestation," Parker added. "Black mold. Gets 'em every time."

I stared at them both, torn between horror and admiration. "You two are actually insane."

Jace grinned. "Maybe. But we're not the ones letting our freshly tattooed girlfriend sleep somewhere else."

"Yeah," Parker said, crossing his arms. "You better fix that before she starts thinking she can, like, *breathe* without you."

Jace shivered, like the idea of that was terrifying to him. "How long have you two been together now? Feels like FiFi has been with us forever."

"Seventeen days, eleven hours, and twenty-three minutes," I said automatically.

Both of them side-eyed me.

Jace blinked, then let out a low whistle. "Matty Adler. A true Machiavelli."

Parker frowned. "Did you mean mathematician? Because what you just said makes no sense."

Jace tilted his head, considering it. "Maybe. Possibly. I'll let the big brains debate it." He pointed at me. "What I *do* know is that you just permanently branded a girl you've been with for exactly seventeen days, eleven hours, and twenty-three minutes. Probably twenty-four minutes now. That's definitely too long to go without moving her in."

Parker nodded. "You definitely need to escalate your wooing."

"The coffee cup he stole from me would say he's already escalated," Jace deadpanned.

Parker lifted an eyebrow in confusion, and I let out a silent *hallelujah* that Jace hadn't told him that little story yet.

My use of that coffee cup was another memory that gave me an instant erection, though, so I really needed to redirect.

Parker crossed his arms, leaning back on his heels. "So, what's it gonna be, then? It's best to go into these things with a plan. We would know."

They *would* know, the little psychos.

Although it was becoming very clear to me that I'd joined them.

"Ooh, I came up with a few more. We could file a fake maintenance request claiming a gas leak. Whole building gets evacuated; she's forced to stay with you. Easy," offered Jace eagerly.

Parker snapped his fingers. "Or you could sign her up for a campus pest control inspection. And we could order those bedbugs again."

I grimaced thinking of when Jace had opened the box and how they'd looked crawling around in the jar they'd been shipped in.

They'd been disgusting . . . but effective.

Jace shook his head. "That takes too long to ship. Matty-kins wouldn't last forty-eight hours before he started climbing the walls."

A week of space felt impossible. Fuck, a day did. The idea of her sleeping somewhere else had my pulse spiking.

I couldn't end up like Parker, snapping and committing a felony all in the name of love.

And I was too pretty for prison.

"Or," Jace said, his eyes lighting up like he'd just solved world hunger, "we flood her room. Burst a pipe, clog the drains, whatever. Whole floor's underwater by morning. Building gets evacuated. She's got nowhere to go but your place."

I stared at him. "You want to *drown* her dorm?"

"Not drown," he corrected, rolling his eyes. "*Displace.* Temporarily inconvenience. It would be very romantic."

Parker tilted his head, considering. "Could work. But if you want maximum chaos, I say we unleash a pack of dogs in there. Let 'em pee everywhere. Instant biohazard. RA calls it in, health department shuts the floor down for a week."

"Where the hell are you going to get a bunch of dogs?" I asked, thinking I actually liked that idea.

Parker grinned. "I bet Walker could help us out. Geraldine has a bunch."

I shivered at the mention of Geraldine. The eighty-something-year-old woman lived on the same floor as Walker's teammate Camden. I'd met her at Thanksgiving. She'd smiled at me over gravy and said dramatically as she'd sipped a weird, glowing cocktail, *I want you in my collection.* I still don't know what she meant, but it had made Ari Lancaster furious, so I didn't think I actually *wanted* to know.

Jace snapped his fingers. "Combine it. Flood *and* dogs. Wet dogs. Smells like wet dog piss. Uninhabitable. She'll be begging to crash with you."

I dragged a hand down my face, somewhere between laughing and genuinely concerned for their mental health. "I still can't believe we're talking about all of this with straight faces."

"Believe it, bubs," Jace said, clapping me on the shoulder. "The No Drama Llamas get results. And our girlfriends *do not* get away."

I had to agree with that one. No, they did not.

"If none of those sound good, you can always force her to marry you," Parker added, grinning.

I couldn't help it. A small, involuntary smile slipped out.

"Yeah," I said, deadpan. "Maybe I will."

We'd just stepped inside the building, the door clicking shut behind us, and both of them went dead quiet.

Jace's jaw dropped, eyes lighting up like I'd just handed him a winning lottery ticket. "Fuck, *yes*! Shotgun wedding, baby! I'm obviously the best man, Parkie-Poo. Sorry, but I look far better in a tuxedo, and we do have the pictures to think about . . ."

Parker looked like he was thinking hard. "What about instead of Vegas, we do it on the fifty-yard line, midnight, stadium lights on? Jace can hack the Jumbotron—'Matty plus Ophelia forever'—in neon. I'll get ordained online so I can officiate."

They were *vibrating*, already mapping logistics, voices overlapping, with pure, terrifying excitement.

I stared at them in awestruck horror for a solid ten seconds, then snorted, shaking my head.

"Relax, psychos. I think I can start with one of your other ideas first."

Jace skidded to a halt. Parker's grin faltered.

I shrugged, still smirking. "For now."

Sweat coated my skin, the sheets snagging my thighs as Ophelia's scent curled into my lungs. Her weight pinned me as she straddled my hips, squeezing tight as she rocked up and down.

Her dark blonde hair spilled like a curtain, grazing my chest, tickling my skin with every roll of her hips. Her copper eyes bore into mine as she rocked, each grind dragging a low groan from my throat. My hands dug into her hips, fingers sinking into the soft flesh as I guided her rhythm.

"Fuck, Ophelia," I growled as I urged her to move faster. Her breasts bounced, nipples tight, pink peaks grazing my chest, begging for my teeth. Her pale skin was flushed, and sweat was beading between her breasts, dripping onto me.

She rode me harder, her wetness coating my dick.

The slick sound of her pussy against my skin was driving me wild. "That's it, pretty baby," I rasped, hips bucking to meet her as the bed frame creaked. "Show me how much you want me."

Her fingers raked my chest, scraping over ink and muscle as sparks raced down my spine. She quickened her pace as her hands roamed my skin, tracing my abs, pinching my nipples, then gripping my shoulders, fingertips digging deep. Pleasure coiled tight in my gut, heat surging with every grind.

I thrusted up, hard, and she cried out, her hair whipping as she arched back, her breasts heaving.

"Fucking hell," I groaned. "Your pussy's choking my cock, it's so fucking tight." My fingers gripped her hips, guiding her faster. Her hand slid to my throat, fingers light but firm as her thumb pressed against my pulse.

"Feel that?" I panted as my dick slammed into her. "Every inch, baby. That's *me* inside you, stretching you open, owning you."

Her walls fluttered, a fresh gush of slick coating me, and I drove deeper, hips snapping, the wet *slap* of skin on skin echoing.

"Feel how hard you make me?" I moaned. "This cock's yours, but this pussy? *Mine*."

Her breath hitched, lips brushing my jaw.

And then her voice dropped to a chilling hiss that sent ice straight through my dick. "I told you I watch you when you sleep."

The words slithered out, sharp and eerie, her eyes glinting strangely. Her smile twisted, still hers but wrong, lips curling too wide, fingers tightening on my throat, just enough to prickle my skin. Her hips slowed, deliberate and torturous, her pussy still gripping me, but her gaze felt like it was peeling me open.

My hands froze on her hips, my chest heaving, confusion spiking through the pleasure. I tilted my head, staring up at her as she hovered above me. Her eyes were suddenly unblinking, boring into me with an intensity that wasn't human, wasn't *my* Ophelia.

"Ophelia?" I whispered, my dick still hard inside her, but the air shifted, heavy, wrong, her smile a slash of something too knowing.

I jolted upright, gasping, my cock pulsing against my briefs.

For one disoriented second, I thought I was still dreaming.

Until I saw her.

Emma.

Standing over my fucking bed.

Her pale eyes gleamed in the shadows, round and wide and so unblinking it made my skin crawl. Her mouth curved into a smile that was too wide for her face, teeth flashing like a row of knives.

"AAAAAAAAHHHHHHHHHHHHHHHHHH!"

The scream ripped out of me before I could stop it. Not a tough-guy shout. Not a football player's roar. No—this was a banshee shriek, cracking so high I was pretty sure dogs in the next county heard it.

Emma didn't flinch. Didn't even twitch. Just tilted her head, her brown hair somehow not moving with it.

"He's awake," she sang in a lilting, nursery-rhyme voice. "My Matty's awake. He screamed because he's so happy to see me."

"What the actual—*fuck*—Emma?!" I scrambled backward, sheets tangling around my legs, until my skull smacked into the headboard. Pain flared, but I didn't care. My heart was jackhammering, my skin crawling, and my dick—once alive in the dream—was now curled up somewhere in witness protection.

She rocked slightly on her toes, the way kids did when humming to themselves. "You were sweating. Moaning. Gasping. I wanted to see."

"Okay. No." I clutched the sheet tighter over my lap, like that would save me. "That was a dream, alright? You can't—you can't just stand there watching me sleep like some possessed doll!"

Her grin twitched, stretching wider. "I love watching you sleep." She sighed. "You breathe differently when you dream, slow at first, then it catches, like you can sense your death coming."

"Nope," I said quickly, voice shaking. "We're not doing this. We are *not* doing this."

Emma stepped closer, her bare feet whispering against the floor. She leaned down until her face hovered inches above mine. Her breath smelled like iced milk. I wasn't sure how I knew that, but if iced milk had a smell, it was like that. Her eyes were wide, pupils blown, and still—*still*—she didn't blink.

I whimpered. Actually whimpered.

"Blink," I croaked. "For the love of God, just blink once."

Her smile sharpened. "But then I can't see you, Matthew."

I slapped both hands over my eyes. "This isn't happening. This isn't real. I'm still asleep. This is a night terror."

Her voice slid under my hands, singsong and sweet. "Not a dream. I'm real. Real. Real."

I peeked through my fingers.

She was still there.

Of course she was.

But she was drifting away from the bed. Not leaving—oh no, that would've been too easy. She started *wandering around my room.*

My room.

Touching my things.

Her fingers traced the edge of my charging phone. "It lights up every few minutes," she murmured. "Little ghosts trying to reach you before I do."

My jaw dropped. "That's not a normal observation, Emma!"

She drifted to the desk where my playbook lay open, notes scrawled in my handwriting from team meetings. She bent over and trailed a finger down one of the diagrams.

"X's and O's," she sang. "Like kisses. Like bones."

I swallowed hard. "That's a *cover two*, not—" I cut myself off, dragging my hands down my face. "Why am I explaining football to you right now?!"

She ignored me, her eyes glittering as she picked up my shoulder pads from where they leaned against the wall. She cradled them in her arms like it was a baby.

"Armor," she whispered, rocking it gently. "My Matty's armor. Heavy and strong. But not enough."

I dragged my knees up to my chest, still clutching the sheet. "Stop rocking my equipment like it's Rosemary's baby!"

Her head snapped toward me, and my stomach dropped.

"Babies cry," she said flatly. Then, slowly, her grin returned. "You cry, too, Matty."

"I do not—" My voice cracked again. "I do not cry."

Her singsong cut me off. "Matty screamed. Matty whimpered. Matty—"

"Stop keeping a running commentary!" I shouted.

But she only giggled. High-pitched, melodic, and absolutely chilling.

Then she wandered to my dresser. Her pale hand traced over my trophies—the all-American plaques, the gold figures frozen mid-leap. She picked one up, tilting it toward the dim light, her reflection bending across the metal.

A muscle ticked in my jaw. Those trophies had always meant a lot to me, and now I was going to have to sanitize them about a million times to ever be able to touch them again.

In fact, my whole room was going to need to be fumigated.

"Shiny," she whispered. "Shiny like your eyes when you beg."

I slapped my palm to my forehead. "I don't *beg*, Emma."

"You begged in your sleep," she said simply, still rocking the trophy. "Ophelia's name. Ophelia's lips. Ophelia's body."

I made a sound halfway between a groan and another scream. "This is it. This is how I die. Death by . . . whatever you are. The coroner's gonna be like, 'Cause of death: creepy girl who doesn't blink.'"

Emma set the trophy down with care. Then she drifted to my laundry basket.

"No," I barked, pointing. "Do not touch that."

She ignored me, plucking one of my practice shirts from the pile. She lifted it to her nose and inhaled deeply, closing her eyes for the first time since she appeared.

And just like that, the sight was *so much worse* than her not blinking.

"Oh, fuck me," I whispered.

Her eyes snapped open again, back to wide . . . and unblinking. "Sweat. Grass. Fear." She smiled. "Delicious."

I gagged and shot off the bed so fast the sheet tangled around my legs, nearly toppling me. "Okay. Nope! We're done here. Get out. Get out of my room before I call—I don't even know who. Ghostbusters. The FBI. Somebody!"

Emma's smile never wavered. "You wouldn't call."

"I *would*."

"You wouldn't."

I froze, chest heaving.

Her grin tilted higher. "Because you like it."

My eyes bugged out of my head. "Like it?!"

"You like being watched. You like being wanted. And nobody wants like I do."

My knees almost buckled.

The door slammed open with a bang that rattled the wall.

"Matty, I'm coming. Don't go into the light!" Jace barreled in, shirtless in sweats, his long blonde hair sticking up like he'd run through a hurricane. His brown eyes were wild as he looked around.

He saw Emma and stopped dead.

"Oh . . . hell no."

"Yes!" I shrieked, tripping over the sheet still tangled around my legs. "Hell *yes*. She's just standing there! Not blinking! Look at her!"

Emma turned her head slowly, too slowly, like a doll on a rusted hinge. Her grin widened when her eyes landed on Jace.

"Two boys," she crooned in that high, singsong tone. "Two loud boys. Rabbits."

Jace's jaw dropped. "Did . . . did she just call us rabbits?"

"Yes!" I snapped, pointing frantically. "The *bad* kind of rabbits!"

Jace blinked at me. "There's a bad kind of rabbit?"

"Not the point!"

Emma rocked forward on her toes, humming. "Scared little rabbits. Hop, hop, hop. Eyes wide. Screams loud."

"Do something!" Jace hissed, flattening himself against the wall.

"Do *what*?!" I snapped. "Tackle her?!"

"Yes!"

Emma giggled.

"On second thought, don't do that. Because I think she wants you to do that," Jace choked out.

Emma swayed toward the bed again, her eyes unblinking. "Matty screams. Matty cries. Matty dies."

Jace's face went pale. "Nope. Nope, nope, nope. I think I've seen enough."

He grabbed the first thing within reach—a half-empty bottle of blue Gatorade—and flung it at her chest.

It splashed across her shirt.

She looked down. Then up. Then smiled wider. "Refreshing."

Jace's hands shot into his hair. "Okay. Plan B." He spun, snatched the silver chain off his neck, and brandished it. "Begone, demon!"

That obviously didn't work, either.

Emma drifted toward my dresser again, stopping at the photo of me and Ophelia. She picked it up, tilting her head at the glass.

"Pretty girl," she crooned. "But she blinks. She sleeps. She doesn't watch."

"Put that down!" I shouted, lunging forward. "Don't touch her!"

Emma giggled, tracing Ophelia's face with her fingertip. "I could watch her, too. While she sleeps. Would you like that, Matty?"

"What the fuck?" I bellowed.

Jace threw his hands up. "Okay, I'm out. You're on your own."

"Don't you dare leave me!" I shrieked.

"I already tried Gatorade and demon banishment. What else can I do?"

Before I could move, Riley burst in like a woman on a mission, hair wild, eyes blazing, holding a fire extinguisher that looked way too big for her.

"What the hell is—" I started, but she'd already pulled the pin.

A white cloud exploded across the room with a roar, coating everything—bed, trophies, me—in a choking frost. Emma shrieked, staggering backward as foam hit her full in the face.

"Get out of my house!" Riley screamed, spraying again for good measure.

Emma screamed louder this time, stumbling for the door, arms flailing, her pale figure disappearing into the hallway in a haze of cold mist.

Silence fell, the *hiss* of the extinguisher dying out.

Riley stood there panting, extinguisher still hissing in her grip, white residue clinging to her hair and lashes.

For a moment, none of us moved.

Then Jace took one slow, reverent step forward. “My hero,” he breathed with wide eyes, his voice dripping with awe. “Fuck, that makes me so hot.”

Before Riley could even blink, he scooped her up and slung her over his shoulder, her shocked yelp muffled against his back.

“You’re going to have to clean up on your own,” he said as he strode out of the room. “I gotta give this little legend what she deserves.”

“Thank you!” I called after them, still coughing through the lingering haze.

I heard his bedroom door shut with a dramatic *thud*, Riley’s muffled giggles echoing through the walls.

I sat down on the edge of the bed, staring at the foam-covered room, my pulse still sprinting.

I had no idea what the hell had just happened, but I did know one thing . . . Ophelia had never come over last night.

Before I could do anything about that . . . my phone rang.

I grabbed it without thinking. “Yeah?”

“Matthew,” my mom’s voice came through, tight and trembling. “It’s your dad. He’s in the hospital. You need to come—now.”

The room tilted, the cold chemical air suddenly too thin to breathe.

I froze, dread washing through me in a slow, suffocating wave. “I’ll be right there,” I said quietly.

CHAPTER 29

MATTY

I stepped into the hospital room, the steady beep of machines cutting through the stillness. My mom was by the bed, her head bowed, one hand gripping my dad's like she was afraid he'd slip away if she let go.

One look at him, and my stomach turned. His face was a ruin—swollen and mottled with deep purple bruises, one eye completely shut, a gash splitting his cheekbone. Dried blood clung to his hairline, and there were angry marks along his jaw and neck, fingerprints dark against his skin. His lip was split, his knuckles scraped raw, and even under the thin hospital blanket, I could see the stiffness in the way his ribs rose and fell.

It wasn't an accident.

Someone had done this to him.

My chest tightened. "What happened?" I asked, the words scraping out of my throat.

My mom jerked up like she'd been struck. Then she was in my arms, clutching at my hoodie, sobbing so hard it felt like the sound was tearing through both of us. "Oh, thank God you're here," she cried, voice muffled against my chest. "I didn't know if you'd make it in time. I didn't know what to do."

I kept my arms around her, comforting her as best I could, even while my eyes stayed fixed on my dad . . . on the bruises, the blood, the stillness that didn't fit him.

"Hey," I murmured finally, guiding her back toward the chair. "Sit down, okay? You need to breathe."

She sank into the seat, trembling, and I grabbed the half-empty cup of water from the tray, pressing it gently into her hands. "Drink," I said quietly. "Please."

She nodded, still crying softly, and I forced myself to look away from her . . . back to him. I couldn't stop staring.

The door creaked open behind us, and a man in uniform stepped in, hat tucked under his arm, his expression somber.

"Mrs. Adler?" he said softly. "I'm Officer Grant. I just need to ask a few questions about what happened tonight."

My mom blinked up at him, dazed, fingers still wrapped around the water cup like she didn't know what it was for. "I—I already told the paramedics," she stammered.

"I know, ma'am," he said gently. "But I need to get a clear timeline."

She swallowed, nodding once. "I was on shift. A double. The kids were at my mother's. When I got home . . ." Her voice cracked, and she glanced at my dad before looking away. "He was on the floor. I thought maybe he'd had a heart attack, but then I saw—the living room was . . . destroyed. The coffee table, the television, *everything*, broken."

She pressed a shaking hand to her mouth.

The officer nodded, jotting something down in his notebook. "Did anything appear to be taken? Wallets, electronics, cash?"

She blinked at him, confusion flickering across her face. "I . . . I don't know. I didn't look. I just called 911."

Her tone was thin, trembling, but there was something else under it, something small and off.

I studied her face, the way her eyes darted too quickly to the floor. My gut twisted.

She was hiding something.

A low sound broke through the steady rhythm of the machines—a rough, wet groan that made my head snap up.

"Ronnie?" My mom lurched forward, almost spilling the cup of water. "Ronnie, can you hear me?" Her voice cracked as she clutched his hand, brushing the side of his bruised face with trembling fingers. "Honey, it's me. Can you hear me?"

But his eyes stayed closed. His chest lifted once, then fell shallowly again, a soft moan slipping out that didn't sound like recognition, just pain.

My mom started to cry harder, whispering his name over and over, like she could pull him back just by saying it. The officer shifted awkwardly, clearing his throat.

"I'll get out of your way," he murmured, stepping back toward the door. "We'll be in touch once we know more." He nodded to me and slipped out quietly.

I was just turning to my mom—ready to ask what she wasn't telling me—when the door opened again. A doctor stepped in, clipboard in hand, his scrubs streaked with the kind of exhaustion you only saw at hospitals. He hesitated when his eyes met mine, the faint question clear in his face.

"It's okay," my mom said quickly, wiping at her cheeks. "He's our son."

The doctor nodded, then looked back at my dad, his expression tightening. "Your husband's stable for now," he said. "He has several broken ribs, a fractured wrist, and extensive bruising along his chest and abdomen. We're keeping an eye on his breathing and possible internal bleeding. There's swelling near his temple—we're watching for a concussion as well."

He hesitated, lowering the chart slightly. "Given the circumstances, we'll need to keep him sedated a little longer while we manage the pain and prevent further stress on his ribs."

My mom nodded, tears still streaking down her face.

I couldn't take my eyes off him—the bandages, the bruises, the tubes keeping him alive.

She wiped at her face, voice trembling. "Thank you, Doctor."

He gave a sympathetic nod and quietly slipped from the room, the door clicking shut behind him.

For a moment, the only sound was the soft, steady beeping of the monitors. My dad's chest rose and fell in a shallow, uneven rhythm, the bruises on his ribs shifting faintly with each breath.

I turned to her. "Tell me what you're hiding."

Her eyes flicked up, startled. "What?"

"Mom." My voice came out rough. "You've been holding something back since I got here. What aren't you telling me?"

She shook her head, voice breaking. "Matthew, please—not now."

"Now," I said firmly. "He's lying there half dead. Whatever this is, I need to know."

Her resistance crumbled all at once. She sank into the chair again, staring at her trembling hands. "He told me yesterday," she whispered. "He said he'd . . . messed up."

My pulse kicked hard. "Messed up how?"

"He said he had a sure thing." The words left her like a confession. "He said he had a big chance—some kind of game, something he was sure he could win. He said it would fix everything." She dragged in a breath, tears spilling down her cheeks. "But it didn't. He lost. Said it was too much, Matty. More than we could ever cover."

I stared at her, the words sinking like stones.

"He was devastated," she went on quietly. "Said he'd find a way to make it right, that he had an idea. He made me promise not to worry." She gave a bitter, shaking laugh and glanced back at my dad's broken body. "I guess his idea didn't work."

I stared at her, my pulse thudding in my ears. "Why didn't he just ask me?" I said. "If it was money—why not just come to me?"

She didn't answer right away. Her eyes dropped to her lap, her fingers twisting around one another. When she finally spoke, her voice was small, almost gone. "Because it was more than you could give him."

A cold feeling crawled up the back of my neck. "Did you know?" I asked slowly. "That he'd been hassling me for money?"

Her eyes flicked up to mine, guilt flashing through them before she looked away again. "Not at first," she whispered. "I didn't know until recently. We . . . we'd been fighting about it."

Her voice cracked then, and she pressed both hands to her face, the sound of her weeping filling the sterile room. "I thought it was over. I thought he'd stopped."

The words burned before I even knew I was saying them. "Why do you stay with him?"

Her head snapped up, eyes wide, but I didn't stop. I couldn't.

"He's done this over and over," I said, my voice rising, raw from everything that had happened—Emma, the hospital, all of it. "He gambled away everything we ever had. Every time we were close to getting ahead, he found a way to ruin it. You worked double shifts for years because of him. I paid bills he should've handled. He's the reason we never had anything, why we were always scraping by."

She was crying again, silent tears streaking down her face, staring at the floor like she couldn't bear to look at me.

"He's selfish," I said, the words loud and shaking. "He's never cared about anyone but himself, and now look at him. Look at what he's done."

Her shoulders trembled, but she didn't respond. She just sat there, weeping quietly, her hand pressed to her mouth like she was holding something in.

I took a step closer. My voice dropped, rough and tired. "Why do you stay?"

She drew in a deep, shuddering breath, her eyes fixed on the bed. For a long moment, she didn't move. Then, so softly I almost didn't hear it, she murmured, "Because, although you can't understand . . . he's my seven minutes."

The words hit like a punch—familiar, haunting, and completely foreign all at once.

She drew in another shaky breath. "When I die," she whispered, "he and you kids will be what I see."

I stood there, unable to move.

She kept talking, her voice soft and frayed at the edges. "I know you can't see it. I don't blame you for that. But he's my person, Matthew. Always has been."

She looked over at my dad then, her gaze tender in a way that twisted something deep in my chest. "You see what he is now. What he's done. But you don't see the other pieces. The man who used to sneak out of work early to make it to your games, even when we couldn't afford the gas. The man who carried all four of you kids to bed on nights I could barely stand from the double shifts. The one who stayed up for days fixing the car with his own hands because we couldn't afford a mechanic."

Her lips trembled, and she laughed brokenly. "You don't see how he still kisses my wrist every morning before I leave for work. Or how he hums the same stupid song when he cooks, just to make me smile. You don't see the way he cries when he thinks no one's looking."

She wiped at her cheeks, staring at my dad like he was both the wound and the cure. "He's not a good man, Matty. I know that. But he's mine. And I love him in a way that doesn't make sense—not to you, not to anyone. But when everything fades, when it all ends, he'll be the one I'll see."

The room felt too small then, the air too heavy. I wanted to argue, to scream, to tell her love wasn't supposed to look like this. But the words wouldn't come.

Because even through the pain and the blood and everything he'd done, I could see it—the truth of it shining in her eyes.

I crossed the room and pulled her into my arms. She didn't fight it, just collapsed against me, her sobs muffled against my chest. I pressed a kiss to the top of her head, breathing her in, the faint scent of soap and hospital air clinging to her hair.

"I don't understand," I said quietly. "Not any of it. But I do get that sometimes love doesn't make sense."

She nodded against me, shaking, her hands clutching the front of my hoodie like she didn't want to let go.

I eased her back gently, my hands still on her shoulders. "I have to go."

Her eyes went wide. "You're not going to stay?"

I swallowed hard. "I love you, Mom. I'll take care of the medical bills. Whatever insurance doesn't cover, I'll handle it. But I can't—" I glanced at the bed, at the man I barely recognized. "I can't look at him right now."

Tears welled in her eyes again, but I kept going before she could speak. "Keep the kids at Grandma's for a while, okay? Just until we know more. And I know you won't listen, but . . . try to stay safe."

Her lip trembled. "He'll change after this," she whispered, like she was trying to convince herself. "He has to."

I shook my head. "He needs real help, Mom. Not just time, not just promises. *Help*."

She looked at me helplessly, and I felt the weight of all the years between us—every fight, every lie, every forgiveness she'd given too freely.

"Seven minutes or not," I said softly, "you've got to try to make him get it."

She didn't answer, just turned her face away, her tears falling silently into her lap as I stepped out of the room.

I lingered at the doorway for a moment, the sound of the machines and my mother's quiet sobs tangling together behind me. My chest felt tight, every breath heavy and uneven.

There was nothing left to say—not to her, not to him.

I turned down the sterile hallway, my footsteps echoing off the tile. The fluorescent lights buzzed overhead.

There was only one person who could make me feel better right now. Only one person whose voice could cut through the noise in my head.

Ophelia.

And I was going to her.

CHAPTER 30

MATTY

I pounded on her door again, three sharp knocks that echoed down the hall like gunshots.

Still nothing.

Doors cracked open down the hall, and a few heads peeked out.

Whispers slithered down the hall.

"That's Matty Adler . . ."

"Holy shit."

"Why's he banging on Ophelia's door?"

A girl in fuzzy socks and a robe leaned out from next door, her eyes wide.

I flashed a lazy grin that I hoped looked unthreatening. A hard task with how feral I felt at the moment. Last night had been one of the worst nights of my life, and this morning wasn't looking up, either.

"Ladies," I tried to say charmingly. Apparently it wasn't charming enough, because they all popped back in their rooms like fucking groundhogs at the sound of my voice.

I knocked on the door one more time.

But she didn't answer.

For a beat I just stood there, palms on the wood, the cold of the metal handle under my fingers. "Where the fuck are you? It's five a.m.," I muttered to the door, the words more plea than threat.

Then—like a stupid little beacon in my skull—I remembered the tracker app.

I pulled my phone out, my thumb fumbling over the screen. Of course it took me three taps to get to the right app, because technology was the fucking worst.

I stared at it in disappointment.

There was no blue dot.

Just a grayed-out *Last known location*: *11:47 p.m.*

Her phone wasn't on. She'd probably forgotten to charge it again.

She hated her phone, never even glanced at it when we were together. She let it die all the time without a second thought.

I'd loved that about her, but at the moment, it was not my favorite thing.

I leaned back on the door, debating what to do.

I'd just have to wait inside her room. Which meant I needed to figure out how to get in.

I walked down the hall to the common area and stood in the shadow near the little desk, watching the RA like she was a sleeping animal I didn't want to spook. The girl behind the desk looked younger than I expected—hair in a messy bun, hoodie swallowed by the chair. She startled when I stepped forward, eyes going wide, but not with recognition, just surprise at seeing anyone on the girls' floor this early in the morning.

Thank fuck. She didn't seem to know who I was.

I forced an easy smile. "Hey, sorry to bug you. My girlfriend's downstairs trying to do laundry, and it's a mess. I think one of the washers exploded or something."

Her mouth parted. "You can't be— This is a women's residence—"

"I know, I know." I lifted my hands like I was trying to calm her down. "But I think you need to come help—there's water everywhere. Everything is flooding. It's already all over the floor, and my girlfriend's freaking out."

Her eyes went wide. "Flooding?"

"Yeah," I said quickly, adding a note of urgency. "Like, bad. I tried to turn one of the washers off, but I think it's still going. You should probably come take a look before it hits the hallway."

She glanced down the corridor, chewing her lip. "I—uh—I'm supposed to stay at the desk."

"It's five a.m.," I reminded her. "But seriously, if that water reaches the outlets . . ." I let the sentence hang, eyebrows raised.

That did it. She scrambled up, grabbing her lanyard and muttering something about maintenance.

"Thanks," I called after her as she hurried down the hall.

The second she disappeared around the corner, I reached over the desk and snagged the universal keycard from the holder, sliding it into my pocket. Then I headed for Ophelia's room, heart thudding, already half convinced this counted as an emergency, too.

I slid the card in, and the lock clicked. I was finally in Ophelia's room for the first time.

The air was faintly sweet, like her perfume lingered in the walls. I shut the door quietly behind me and flicked on the light. My hand brushed along the edge of her desk, over scattered notebooks and something that looked like a ticket stub. Then I turned—and stopped cold.

For a second, I just blinked in shock. My pulse stumbled, my mind trying to catch up with what I was seeing.

Now I understood why Ophelia had never wanted me to meet her here.

One entire wall was *me*.

A shrine.

Photos ripped from websites, news articles, grainy candids someone had snapped at practice . . . dozens of them, pinned in overlapping layers like a collage of obsession. Some were torn straight down the middle and taped back together, jagged scars running through my face like she'd rescued them from the trash, refusing to let go. Ticket stubs from every game I'd ever played. My name was circled in red, over and over, bold and possessive. Game programs, wristbands, a folded-up roster with my stats highlighted in neon yellow.

My breath caught.

There was the black beanie I'd lost two weeks ago. The silver chain I'd sworn was in my gym bag. A hoodie I hadn't seen in weeks, sleeves folded like it was waiting for me. And there, tucked in the corner, pinned with a single red pushpin, was the orange hat I'd worn after that press conference at the beginning of the season.

She'd *taken* them.

My pulse kicked—hard.

She's been watching me. Collecting me. Stalking me.

Every photo, every stub, every stolen piece . . . it wasn't just fandom.

It was *devotion*.

A secret altar to *me*.

And the longer I stared, the more the realization sank in: Ophelia was my stalker.

I *should* have been disgusted. Should've felt my skin crawl, my gut twist with fear. Any sane guy would've backed out, called the cops, burned the keycard on the way down the hall.

But I didn't.

I stepped closer.

My cock stirred, thickening against my thigh.

Fuck.

I yanked open the top drawer of her desk. There was more of me.

A stack of my practice jerseys—folded small, hidden under textbooks. A half-empty bottle of my cologne, the one I wore every game day. A single sock I'd lost after a practice.

My breath came faster, and I opened the next drawer. There were ten spiral notebooks, all labeled in her neat, looping handwriting.

Matty – Vol. 1

Matty – Vol. 2

Up to *Vol. 10*.

I flipped open *Vol. 1* first. The early pages were sweet, her handwriting smaller, careful, like she was whispering secrets to herself.

We're married in the stadium at sunset. He kisses me in front of sixty thousand people while the band plays our song. I'm Mrs. Adler in white lace, and he lifts me off the turf, spins me once, then carries me down the tunnel like I'm the trophy.

Our first baby's a boy, Matty Jr., born in the offseason, when the stadiums are quiet and he finally gets to stay home. The second's a girl with his eyes, and we name her after his mom. He teaches them both to throw spirals in the backyard while I watch from the porch, his jersey stretched over my belly, already carrying number three.

I swallowed, throat tight, scanning every word in disbelief. She's planned our whole damn life.

I turned the page. The fantasies shifted, becoming darker . . . hungrier.

He kisses me on the fifty-yard line after the championship. Not a peck. A full, filthy claim—tongue in my mouth, hands on my ass, crowd roaring. Then he drags me into the end zone, shoves me against the goalpost, and fucks me while the confetti's still falling.

We renew vows in the locker room. I'm in his jersey and nothing else. He ties my wrists with his armband, spreads me on the bench, and makes me come so hard I squirt across the team logo.

I groaned, cock throbbing.

I flipped to *Vol. 3*.

He pins me to the locker room wall after practice, rips my panties, and fucks me raw while the team waits outside, banging on the door, calling his name. He growls "mine" with every thrust, fills me up, then plugs me so I leak him all the way home.

I wear his jersey and nothing else, ride him in the back of his truck, and scream his name until the windows fog. He spanks me red, calls me his good little wife, then flips me over and takes my ass under the stadium lights.

He ties me to his bed and blindfolds me, making me come until I cry—fingers, tongue, cock, toys—over and over. Then he breeds me, whispering how many babies he's putting in me while I beg for more.

I slammed the notebook shut, breathing hard.

My dick was steel, leaking in my jeans.

I flipped through another. Dates. Times. Locations.

Oct 12 – listened to him shower after a workout. Came twice in the stall next to him.

Nov 3 – stole his hoodie from the dryer. Slept in it for three nights.

I should've been horrified. Instead, I was *throbbing*.

I dropped to my knees and opened the bottom drawer.

There was a lockbox in there, and I popped it open, blinking as I stared inside.

A used condom—*mine*—from who knows when, tied and labeled in Sharpie: *Matty–locker rooms*. My eyes widened as I briefly thought about the hookup I'd had one day.

How the fuck had she even gotten that?

A Polaroid of me sleeping, mouth open, sheets low on my hips. I could see her knee in the picture. She'd just taken that one.

A strand of my hair, tied with an orange ribbon.

I laughed, breathless and a little unhinged.

She's insane.

She's perfect.

I stood, cock aching, my heart slamming against my ribs.

I wanted to find her. Wanted to drag her back here, bend her over this desk, and fuck her while she stared at her own obsession. Wanted to make every fantasy real.

I was harder than I'd ever been in my life.

My eyes locked on the shrine again, at *me*, everywhere, every angle, every moment she'd stolen.

The torn photos. The circled stats. The orange hat. My name in red.

I couldn't wait.

I shoved my sweatpants down just enough, fisting my cock. It was hot and leaking . . . pulsing in my grip.

One stroke. *Two.*

The sight of her devotion burned into my brain.

She watches me sleep. She steals my things. She dreams of me breeding her.

I groaned, pumping faster. My thumb smeared precum over the head, hips jerking into my hand. I pictured her on her knees in front of this wall, mouth open, begging.

Pictured her watching me now—*knowing.*

"Fuck, Ophelia," I rasped. "You want me this bad?"

I stepped closer and aimed my cock at the shrine.

At the photos.

At the stolen pieces of *us*.

One final stroke—

I came with a guttural roar, thick ropes of cum spraying across the wall.

Splattering the torn photos.

Dripping down the ticket stubs.

Coating my name that she'd circled and highlighted and starred.

Marking *her* shrine with *me.*

I kept stroking through it, milking every drop, smearing it over the orange hat, the beanie, the hoodie sleeve.

My cum glistened on the collage, claiming every inch she'd claimed of me.

I leaned forward, forehead against the cool wall, breath ragged.

She's mine.

When she walked in . . .

She'd see.

She'd *know.*

CHAPTER 31

OPHELIA

When I opened my eyes, everything was dark except for the thin glow of a desk lamp flickering somewhere behind me. For a second, I couldn't remember where I was . . . then the smell of paper and dust hit me, heavy and stale, and my heart sank.

The stacks.

I pushed upright too fast, the corner of the table jamming into my hip, a tower of books toppling beside me with a dull *crash* that echoed through the underground room. My neck throbbed, and I could feel a faint imprint on my cheek from the spine of my notebook.

There were no windows down here. No hint of daylight. I had no idea what time it was, if it was midnight or morning or something in between.

"Oh no," I whispered, fumbling for my phone.

It was black. Dead. I hit the button anyway, over and over, like maybe I could will it to wake up.

Nothing.

My stomach twisted. I was supposed to go to Matty's after I was done studying. He'd probably texted and called . . . He was probably worried.

I pressed my hands over my face, breath catching. I hadn't meant to fall asleep. I'd just wanted to finish one more chapter, one more page, until the words started to blur together.

I'd come to the library feeling desperate. I thought that maybe if my grades were perfect, my mother would finally back off a little. Maybe she'd see that everything was okay. That *I* was okay.

But now, sitting here in the dark, neck aching, heart pounding, it didn't feel like I'd made progress in anything. It just felt like I'd failed . . . again.

He was going to think I didn't care.

The thought made my chest ache. Miserable didn't even begin to cover it.

Panic clawed up my throat. What if he thought I'd done it on purpose? What if he was angry, really angry, and decided he was done with me?

A small, reasonable part of me tried to cut through the noise. *Matty's not like that*, it whispered. *He wouldn't just give up on you over this.*

But reason had never been my strong suit. Not when it came to him. Not when the thought of losing him made my chest seize and my vision blur. Logic didn't stand a chance against the spiral already building in my head.

I pressed a hand over my chest, trying to breathe, but the ache there only deepened. I'd already been quiet yesterday, distracted after my mom's call. The sound of her voice, that cold mixture of disappointment and exhaustion, rang in my ears all day.

I'd spent the entire day jumping through hoops for her. Phone calls. Promises. Another appointment with Dr. Whitaker that I didn't want but couldn't refuse. By the time it was over, shame sat so thick in my stomach I could barely stand to look at myself in the mirror.

"You're not being honest with yourself, Ophelia." Dr. Whitaker's voice crackled through my laptop speakers—calm, clinical, unshakable. On the screen, she adjusted her glasses and tapped her pen against her notebook, the sound loud even through the mic.

"You keep saying you're fine, that you're managing," she went on. "But you've replaced one fixation with another, haven't you? You're tying your sense of safety to him."

I stared at the little square that held her face, at the tidy office behind her with its framed diplomas and neutral walls. I couldn't look her in the eye.

"That's not true," I whispered, though my voice wavered enough to make it sound like a question.

"Isn't it?" she asked softly. "When you talk about him, your breath spikes. Your hands tremble. You describe him like he's oxygen. That isn't love, Ophelia. That's dependency. And you know where that road leads."

The video lagged for a second, her face freezing mid-sentence, but the words had still crawled under my skin like a burn I couldn't scrub off, replaying over and over in my head long after the call ended.

Now, sitting in the dark stacks, her voice still echoed in my head. *Dependency. Fixation.* The words she'd used like diagnoses instead of feelings.

I'd told Matty I needed to study. That I'd come by later.

And that was true.

But I'd also needed some space. Time to gather myself . . . to stop hearing my mother's voice in my head, the one that said I was broken and dangerous and lucky anyone loved me at all.

I hadn't wanted him to see that version of me. Not when he looked at me like I was something he'd never let go of.

My throat tightened. I pulled my dead phone to my chest, whispering to the dark stacks, "Please don't leave me."

I scrambled to my feet and started shoving my books and notes into my bag with shaking hands. A few papers fluttered to the floor, but I didn't stop to grab them. I just needed to get out of here—now.

The metal stairs groaned under my boots as I climbed, the air growing warmer with each step until the door at the top burst open into blinding light streaming in from the floor-to-ceiling windows of the library's main floor.

I winced, throwing a hand up to shield my eyes. It was morning. Actual morning. I slept through the entire night.

"Shit," I breathed as I speed-walked through the library. The fluorescent lights were on, and students were already hunched over their laptops. I could feel every tick of panic crawling under my skin as I realized how late it was.

Matty was going to think I'd ignored him. Or worse, that I didn't want to see him.

I moved faster, heading for the exit, thumbing the power button like it might suddenly wake up, even though I knew it was useless. I tried shaking it, rubbing it against my sleeve . . . anything to coax a flicker of life from the black screen. I wasn't even watching where I was going until I slammed into something solid.

No—not something. Someone.

My breath hitched as my bag slipped from my shoulder and crashed to the floor, books and papers scattering across the tile. I froze, my pulse roaring in my ears, and slowly looked up at the broad chest I'd just run straight into.

"Whoa— Shit, I'm so sorry!"

The voice was deep, startled. I stumbled back a step. My stomach dropped when I saw I'd run into Garrett, Matty's teammate. The one who'd walked up to the car that day.

For a second, I couldn't move.

He crouched immediately, scooping up loose papers, muttering apologies under his breath. "Didn't even see you there," he said, his tone rough with guilt. "My fault, totally my fault."

"It's—fine," I managed, kneeling to help him, trying to keep my hair in front of my face.

He picked up my notebook and then glanced up at me, frowning slightly. Then again. Longer this time. His eyes narrowed, his brow furrowing like he was searching through memories.

I reached for my notebook at the same time he did, our fingers brushing . . . and that's when it happened.

His entire face changed. The confusion dropped away, replaced by something like shock. Horror.

"You're her," he said, his voice barely above a whisper. "You're the girl in the car."

I blinked up at him, stunned, my pulse hammering so hard I could barely hear myself think. "I—I don't know what you're talking about," I said, clutching my notebook to my chest like it could hide the guilty flush spreading across my chest.

But Garrett wasn't listening. He was staring at me like he'd just seen a ghost. His face had gone pale, his mouth parting as the words started spilling out fast and uneven.

"You're definitely her," he said, breathless. "Holy shit—shit, shit, shit."

My stomach flipped. "What car?" I tried in a voice too thin, too high.

He ran a hand through his hair, eyes darting around the library like he couldn't quite believe what he was seeing. "Does Matty know?" he asked, more to himself than to me. Then his expression twisted, and he answered before I could even breathe. "Of course he doesn't know. Oh fuck."

"Garrett—"

He shook his head, stepping back like he needed the space to think. "He's gonna lose his mind," he muttered, half under his breath, half to the world. "He's actually gonna— Fuck, I shouldn't even—"

"Please stop," I whispered, the words breaking, but he just stared at me, wide-eyed, horrified, and completely unraveling.

Cold prickled under my skin, crawling up the back of my neck. My fingers went numb around the notebook still clutched to my chest, the edges biting into my palms. Every muscle in my body screamed to move, to *run*, but my legs felt locked, rooted in place by the weight of his stare.

The nightmare that I'd imagined so many times was happening.

"Please don't—" I whispered.

But Garrett wasn't stopping. He was staring at me like he'd just solved a puzzle he wished he hadn't. "You're Matty's stalker. You're really her. I just— I just can't fucking believe it." He looked like he was about to pass out.

The word *stalker* hit me like a slap.

"I— What?" My throat closed. "No, that's not—"

He kept talking, half to himself, his voice rising with each word. "Holy shit. You're *her*. You're the one who's been sitting out there in that car every day. Fucking hell."

"Stop!" I shouted, but it came out strangled. Every nerve in my body lit up, my vision blurring at the edges. People were starting to look.

I backed away, shaking my head, clutching my bag so tightly my fingers hurt. "You don't understand," I choked out, but his face said enough . . . He'd already decided what I was.

Garrett took a step forward, still reeling. "Wait— Ophelia, I didn't mean—"

But I was already gone.

I turned and bolted, the sound of his voice chasing me down the hall. "Ophelia, wait!"

I didn't. I couldn't. My lungs burned as I tore through the doorway and into the blinding light outside, the world tilting around me as the word *stalker* echoed in my skull like it would never stop.

I ran until my legs screamed, until the air outside tore at my throat and my bag slammed against my hip with every step. The word wouldn't stop pounding through my head—*stalker*, *stalker*, *stalker*—each repetition worse than the last.

By the time the dorms came into view, I could barely see through the blur of tears stinging my eyes. I fumbled for my key, my hands trembling so badly I dropped it once before finally getting it into the lock.

The door swung open, and I stumbled inside, slamming it behind me with a hollow *thud* that echoed through the small room.

My forehead fell against the wood as I tried to reason through what had just happened . . . and then everything broke loose.

The sobs came fast and hard, shaking through me as I clutched the strap of my bag, tears running hot down my cheeks.

Garrett's voice kept replaying in my head, looping until I couldn't tell if it was his voice anymore or my own.

You're Matty's stalker.

I pressed my palms to my eyes, wishing I could scrub the words away, wishing I could make it all stop.

But nothing stopped. The words burrowed deeper, twisting into images I couldn't shut out.

Like Matty's face when he found out.

I could see it so clearly it hurt. The confusion first, then the horror, the betrayal. The way his mouth would harden, how he'd take a step back like I was something dirty. Like he'd never known me at all.

He'd leave. Of course he would. He'd probably get a restraining order or have someone from the team handle it, making sure I never came near him again.

My chest constricted. I slid down the wood until I was kneeling on the floor, the door the only thing holding me up.

I couldn't bear to see that look on his face . . . the disgust, the revulsion. I wouldn't survive it.

I pressed my hands over my mouth to muffle the sound of my crying, but it didn't help. The thought of him walking away, of knowing what I'd done and seeing me as nothing but the thing Garrett had named me—it split something deep inside me, like a seam tearing open that I didn't know how to stitch back together.

Freak.

That's what he'd think.

My mind spiraled, frantic, clawing for a way to keep him.

Chain him to the bed. Hide the key. Tell him it's a game until he believes it.

Drug his coffee. Just enough to make him drowsy, pliant. Drag him into his bedroom. Lock the door.

Get pregnant. Now. Before Garrett can talk to him. He'd never leave a baby.

Cut the brake lines on his truck. Not to hurt him—just to strand him here. With me.

Burn the dorm down. Force him to take me in. Forever.

I rocked on the floor, knees to chest, nails digging into my scalp.

He'll hate me. He'll leave. He'll never touch me again.

"What's got you so upset, pretty baby?"

An unmistakable voice cut through my spiral like a lifeline.

My whole body went still. The sob caught in my throat, my hands falling uselessly to my sides. For a second, I thought I was imagining it. I had to be. He couldn't be here—he *couldn't*.

I slowly turned . . . and there he was.

Matty lounged on my bed like he belonged there, back against the headboard, legs stretched out, one ankle hooked lazily over the other. His arms were crossed over his chest, his gaze fixed on me calmly.

He was lying right under my shrine.

The glossy corners of photos caught the light—the snapshots, the printouts, the scraps of newspaper clippings, the candid shots I'd thought were safe. Something white was streaked on the photos, dripping down the orange hat, sliding down the wall.

My breath hitched.

He tilted his head, watching me with a kind of quiet amusement that I didn't understand. His eyes were dark, unreadable, but there was a heat behind them, a dangerous calm that made the air feel too thin.

I couldn't make my mouth work. Couldn't force sound past the pounding in my chest.

Matty's gaze flicked toward the wall again, then back to me, and his lips curled into a dark, hungry smirk.

"Looks like we've got a lot to talk about."

CHAPTER 32

MATTY

I'd come again—thick, hot ropes splattering the shrine for the second time, streaking the torn photos, dripping off the orange hat, sliding down every red-circled *Matty*.

Still hard, I turned to her bed and somehow let a third load soak the sheets, claiming the mattress she'd slept on without me, the scent of sex and us thick in the air.

My pulse thundered, my skin was buzzing, and I wasn't sure it was possible to sate my lust. Finding out she was this obsessed, that she was my stalker, my secret worshipper . . . it evidently lit me up like nothing else.

Every stolen photo, every filthy notebook, every hoarded scrap of me wasn't creepy; it was perfect. I paced the tiny room, cock aching, eyes flicking to the door every few seconds, antsy and wild.

Come back, pretty baby.

I needed her here, needed her mouth, her tears, her screams, so I could pin her to that wall and make every fantasy real. I didn't know how I could wait another minute.

The buzz of my phone cut through the silence, vibrating against the nightstand.

I glanced over, irritation flashing through me when I saw the name lighting up the screen.

Garrett.

I almost ignored it, thumb hovering over the decline button, but the restless energy in my body needed an outlet, something to distract me from tearing the room apart while I waited.

I needed to save the rest of my cum for Ophelia.

I answered on the third ring, my voice coming out rough, the edge of a growl in it. "What's up?"

There was a pause, then Garrett's voice came through, uneven and rushed. "Matty— Shit. I— Look, I realized something, and I need to tell you."

A long pause, like he was trying to steady himself.

"Okay. Spit it out."

He rushed on. "It's Ophelia. I saw her at the library. She—she's the one that's been sitting in that car outside practice all semester. It's her. She's your fucking stalker!"

Silence stretched. My grip tightened.

"Have you told anyone else?" I asked finally.

"No—no, I swear." His voice was fast, pleading. "I haven't told anyone. I didn't even—"

"Good," I cut in, flat. "Because if you do and you embarrass her in any way, I'll kill you."

Another frozen beat. I could hear him swallow on the other end. "You . . . don't seem too upset. Did you—did you know she's your stalker?"

"Yes," I answered firmly.

"And that's, that's okay?" His incredulousness came out like a question and an accusation at once.

"Yes," I repeated, softer this time.

There was a strangled sound, part shock, part laugh. "You're a kinky motherfucker, Adler," Garrett said, stunned and oddly amused.

"Have I made myself clear about telling anyone?" I asked, annoyed now.

"I— Yes. Clear," he babbled. "I won't say anything, I promise. I won't. I won't—"

Then his voice dropped, guilty and small. "I might have scared her, though. When I realized it, I panicked. I didn't mean to—she ran. I feel like an asshole."

I let the line hang a second, listening to the little noises of him pacing. "Don't say anything," I said finally, before ending the call.

It was inconvenient that he knew, but Garrett was a good guy. He wouldn't say anything.

And if he did . . . I guess I'd have to get Jace and Parker to help me kill him.

Ophelia was going to be here any minute, though. I'd better let the guys know that she was moving in today.

Me: Ophelia's moving in today.

Jace: Wait. What? Which one of the plans did you use? Fog machine or bedbugs?

Parker: Or did you go full possum release? Because I really thought you were going to need us for that one.

Me: I didn't do any of that.

Jace: You didn't? She just . . . agreed??

Me: Well, not yet.

Parker: . . .

Jace: Okay, so does that mean you do need me to find some dogs?

Me: I'm good. I found out she's the one that's been stalking me. So if she says no to moving in, I'll just blackmail her or something.

Parker: . . .

Jace: . . .

I stared at the phone. Waiting for their reaction because *dot*, *dot*, *dot* could mean so many different things.

Parker: I think that will work well. Good job.

Jace: I can't say she has good taste, stalking you. But she has other traits that make up for it. So I'll let it pass.

I grinned. I knew I could always count on them for support.

Me: If you could clean up my room somehow, Jace-face. That would be great.

Jace: How did I know that was coming? Isn't it enough that my Riley-girl saved you?

Parker: What the hell are you two talking about? Riley saved you from what?

Me: Jace, can you catch him up? And then get to cleaning? I want it to be nice for when Ophelia gets there. I wouldn't want to start this off as anything but perfect.

Jace: . . .

Jace: Yes, when something starts with blackmail, you don't want to do anything to ruin the vibes.

Me: I would think you were being sarcastic, Bedbug Man, but we both know you would never do that.

Parker: I'm coming over for an explanation, Thatcher.

Parker: And if blackmail doesn't work, you can always use my basement, Adler.

Me: You're a man above men.

Me: No Drama Llamas UNITE!

I set my phone down, a no doubt insane grin on my face when I realized . . . I'd become just as crazy as those motherfuckers.

Outside, I heard movement, soft footsteps, and then the rattle of a key card sliding against the door. My pulse jumped, heat flashing through my veins.

I kicked off my shoes and pushed up onto her bed, ignoring the cum still drying on the sheets.

My muscles tensed with anticipation as I leaned back against the headboard, hands behind my head, eyes fixed on the door.

The handle turned.

My grin deepened.

She was here.

Ophelia

"How—how did you get in here?"

My voice came out thin and unsteady. I couldn't stop staring at him, at the impossible sight of Matty Adler sitting on my bed like he didn't have a worry in the world.

He smiled, almost lazily. "You're not happy to see me?"

"You know that's not it." My fingers clenched around the strap of my bag. "Matty . . . how long have you been here?"

"Long enough." His eyes flicked up, lingering on the wall above him . . . the wall I could barely look at. "So," he said quietly, almost conversationally, "how long have you been watching me?"

My stomach turned over. "What?"

"You heard me." His voice had dropped, and it was the kind of tone that left no room for pretending. "How long?"

"That's just . . . that's just a silly collage, and—"

His gaze hardened, the faint smile dying on his lips. "Don't lie to me, Ophelia."

My throat went dry. Every instinct screamed to run, to disappear, but my legs wouldn't move.

He shifted forward on the bed, elbows on his knees, eyes locked on mine. "Tell me the truth," he demanded. "All of it."

The words landed heavy between us. The air felt too thick, like it was closing around me. I wanted to speak, to explain, but nothing came out—just the sound of my heartbeat crashing in my ears.

Matty didn't move. He just sat there, waiting, gaze steady, like he could outlast every silence I had.

And the terrible thing was, he probably could. I didn't think I could deny him anything at this point.

Even if it destroyed me.

"I came here because of you."

The words slipped out before I could stop them. My pulse stuttered, but once they were in the air, there was no pulling them back.

His brow furrowed slightly. "What do you mean?"

"I mean . . ." My throat tightened, and I pressed a shaking hand to my chest, forcing the words out. "You're the reason I came to this school."

He didn't move. Didn't even blink. Just watched me with that still, unnerving calm that made my stomach knot.

"I was filling out college applications," I went on, my voice cracking. "And an ad popped up. I clicked the wrong button, and then a photo of you was on the screen—smiling, holding your helmet—and I just . . . I couldn't look away."

My laugh came out small and broken. "I know how that sounds. I know. But from the second I saw you, I *knew* . . . I'd never wanted anyone more."

There was still nothing from him. His face stayed impassive, eyes dark and fixed on mine.

"I started reading about you, watching every video I could," I whispered. "Highlight reels. Stats. Interviews. I memorized your favorite cereal, the way you tie your shoes, the brand of socks you wear. I learned to make chicken noodle soup because you once mentioned it was your favorite during an interview. I knew what your family looked like before I knew what campus looked like."

I looked away, wishing he would say something, *anything* . . . even if it was to scream at me.

"When I got here, it got worse," I said quietly. "I found your house. Your class schedule. I knew what time you left the gym, what table you sat at during lunch, which route you took to the library. I followed you every day—not close enough to get caught. Just close enough to breathe the same air."

His jaw flexed, but he didn't speak.

"I tried out for the tiger mascot so I could be on the field with you," I whispered. "I sat in the parking lot for every practice. I recorded your voice and played it on loop so I could fall asleep."

My chest ached. The words spilled faster.

"I transferred into the only class of yours I was allowed to. I stole your hat after a game, kept a mouthpiece in a Ziploc so I could taste you. I wore one of your practice jerseys under my clothes for a week straight—slept in it, showered in it, *came* in it."

His silence was suffocating.

"I tried to dress the way I thought you liked. I looked through photos and saw what kind of girls smiled at you, what they wore, how they talked. I tried to be that. I tried to be what you'd want. I even learned to throw a spiral just so I could imagine teaching our kids."

A tear slipped down my cheek, hot and humiliating. "But it didn't work. You didn't even look at me. Not once."

There was a frown on his lips now, but I still couldn't read it.

So I just kept talking.

"And then, when I'd finally given up on ever having you . . . you looked up and saw me in class."

The words hung between us—soft, fragile, and ruinous.

"That was it," I said. "That was the moment my whole world changed."

I pulled myself off the floor, never taking my eyes off him. I was afraid if I did, he would be gone.

"I love you," I said, the words trembling at first, then stronger, like they'd been waiting years to be spoken. "These past few weeks with you . . . they've been the best of my life. Every second, every breath, every heartbeat. I didn't say it before because love isn't big enough. It's too soft, too ordinary for what I feel. What I feel is a religion. You're my god, Matty. My altar. My everything. And no one, no one on this earth, will ever worship you the way I do."

For a heartbeat, the world went still. There was just the sound of my pulse thrumming in my ears and the sting of tears on my cheeks.

Matty's eyes closed. His jaw flexed once, like he was fighting something he didn't have a name for.

A shiver ran through him, barely there, but enough that I saw it.

When he finally opened his eyes again, they looked . . . wilder.

"Have you done something like this before?" he finally asked in an even, blank voice.

The question cut through the space between us, gentle but direct, and it made my stomach twist. My lip quivered. I wanted to lie—to shake my head, to say no. Because I knew how it looked. If I told him, he might think . . .

But his gaze didn't waver. "The truth, Ophelia."

I swallowed hard, my throat aching. "When I was fourteen . . . my parents sent me away. To a facility. For two years."

I hesitated, but when he didn't say anything, I kept going.

"They said it was because of a boy," I whispered. "Because I got too attached. I didn't understand boundaries. I couldn't let go." My laugh came out thin and cracked. "They gave me all these labels. OLD. OCD. BPD. Attachment disorder. Like they needed names to make sense of me."

I finally met his eyes again, desperate for him to understand. "But this—" I pressed a shaking hand against my chest. "This isn't that. I swear it's not."

I took a step closer. "With you, it's different. I don't feel broken when I think about you. I feel alive. You make everything quiet. You make everything make sense."

My voice dropped so low that I wasn't sure he could hear it. "My mother . . . my doctors . . . They all call this wrong. But I know they're wrong. There's nothing wrong with being obsessed with the love of your existence."

He cocked his head, watching me like he was trying to decide what kind of creature I was. The weight of his silence pressed down until I thought I might shatter just to fill it.

"Please," I whispered finally. "Say something."

He didn't. His jaw worked once, like he was biting back every word that wanted out.

The quiet between us roared.

"I know you probably want to run," I whispered. "And maybe you should." My chest rose too fast, my pulse fluttering against my throat. "But I don't know if I can let you go."

He exhaled roughly. "*Fuck*." The word suddenly tore out of him, and then he was shoving his sweatpants down in one violent yank, his cock springing free, thick, flushed, already leaking.

My eyes went wide. I watched as he fisted himself—once, twice—eyes locked on me, blazing and ravenous.

And then he *came*.

Heavy, white bursts shooting out, splattering the sheets on my bed. Some hit the waistband of his sweatpants, dripping down the fabric, marking it, too.

I stood frozen, mouth open, shock and heat flooding me all at once.

He groaned, hips jerking, milking every drop, continuing to paint my bed with his release.

When he finally stilled, breath heaving, cock still in hand, he looked at me . . .

Not with disgust.

Not with fear.

With *hunger*.

"Get over here, Ophelia," he growled. "You think you're the only one who's obsessed?"

CHAPTER 33

OPHELIA

My mouth fell open before I could stop it. "Are you . . . are you saying—"

He didn't even let me finish. "I'm saying," he said, "I love everything about you. Everything anyone else would say is fucked-up or obsessive. I think it's beautiful . . . perfect. The best thing anyone's ever done."

I just stared at him, the words tumbling around in my head without landing anywhere that made sense. My chest ached so hard I was a little afraid I was having a heart attack. He pushed off the bed, sweatpants still low on his hips, cum-stained sheets twisted behind him. His eyes, bright and almost fevered-looking . . . never left mine as he stalked toward me.

"I love every single thing about you," he said, like he was confessing a sin and a prayer at once. "Every photo. Every notebook. Every stolen sock. Every second you watched me sleep. It's the hottest, *best* thing I've ever heard in my life."

Tears welled up before I could stop them, slipping down my cheeks in hot streaks. I couldn't understand it . . . how he wasn't angry, how he wasn't already gone.

He reached out, not quite touching me, his hand hovering like he was afraid I might vanish if he did. "I don't know how I didn't see you before," he said softly. "But once I did? That was it. Game over."

Something inside me cracked wide open.

Matty held my gaze, his eyes unflinching. "You think you're the only one who'd do crazy things to keep the person they love?" He smiled then, and it seemed dangerous, full of something that looked like . . . everything I'd ever wanted from him.

"If I'm your god, Ophelia, then you're my goddess. There isn't anything I wouldn't have done to get you."

I swallowed, trembling.

"Tell me," I whispered, my fingers finding the hem of my shirt. "Tell me *all* the things you would've done."

I pulled it over my head and let it drop.

His eyes flared.

"I would've hacked your phone— I did hack it," he said, a small smirk on his beautiful lips. "I tracked every step. I knew where you were before you did."

I shivered and unhooked my bra, letting it fall.

"I would've broken into your room," he continued, stepping closer, his eyes flicking once to my breasts before they came back up to my face. "Left my cum on your pillow so you'd smell me when you slept."

My jeans slid down my hips.

"I would've swapped your birth control," he rasped. "Put my baby in you the first chance I got."

I stepped out of my panties, naked and shaking.

"I would've burned every bridge," he said in a raw voice, "so you had nowhere to go but to *me*."

I stood bare before him, tears streaming . . . my heart wide open.

"So you love me," I finally whispered, voice quivering. "You love *all* of me?"

He didn't answer with words.

Matty yanked me forward, one brutal, possessive pull, and crushed his mouth to mine. The kiss was fire and teeth and desperation, his tongue claiming every inch, swallowing my gasp. I melted into it, hands fisting his shirt, tears mixing with the taste of him.

When he finally pulled back, our foreheads stayed pressed together, both of us catching uneven breaths that tangled in the space between us.

"I love *all* of you," he said, his voice frayed at the edges like it could barely contain what he felt. "Every twisted, perfect piece."

His hands framed my face, thumbs wiping my tears. "Don't change a thing. Not one. You want anything—no matter how fucked-up it sounds, no matter who says it's wrong—I'll do it for you. You want to do it to me? *Do it*. I'm yours. Completely."

He grabbed me by the waist, hoisted me off the floor like I weighed nothing, and *threw* me onto the bed.

I hit the bed and bounced, the air rushing from my lungs as my legs fell open and my heartbeat kicked hard against my ribs.

Matty was on me before I could blink, his hands on my hips, hauling me up his body until my knees bracketed his shoulders. "Open," he demanded as his teeth scraped the inside of my thigh. I barely had time to gasp before his mouth sealed over my pussy—hot, wet, *ruthless*. His tongue speared inside me, curling, thrusting, lapping up every drop like he was starving.

I cried out as I bucked against his face.

He *groaned* into me, the vibration shooting straight through my clit. His hands clamped my thighs wider, fingers digging into my skin as he held me open for his feast.

It wasn't enough, though. I wanted to taste him. I wanted to feel him throb against my tongue while he kept wrecking me with his. I wanted us both undone, tangled . . . lost in each other.

I reached for him, tugging insistently on his shoulders. He got the message fast, and strong hands slid under my ass, lifting me effortlessly while he moved up the bed, turning us so his knees bracketed my shoulders. Now he hovered above me, his cock heavy and throbbing inches from my lips while his head dipped back between my thighs.

"Suck me," he begged, his voice muffled against my folds. "Now."

I leaned forward, hands bracing on his hips, and took him in. The head slid past my lips, salty and hot, stretching my mouth wide. He thrust up immediately, shallow but insistent, fucking my throat in time with his tongue inside me.

I moaned around him, and he *growled* back, the sound vibrating through my core.

His tongue flicked my clit mercilessly, and then plunged deep again, his nose buried in my wetness. I gushed over his chin, his cheeks . . . his throat. Matty *drank* it all, swallowing loudly as his fingers spread me wider so he could tongue-fuck me harder.

I took him deeper until I was gagging and tears were in my eyes. My saliva dripped down his shaft, and he hissed, hips snapping, his cock pulsing against my tongue.

"Fuck—*yes*—" he snarled as his teeth grazed my clit. "Swallow me, baby. Take it all."

I did. I sucked harder, hollowing my cheeks as my tongue swirled the piercing, my throat working around him.

His hips jerked, and then he was coming . . . thick, heavy bursts flooding my mouth, down my throat, spilling past my lips. I swallowed frantically, choking, moaning, *drowning* in him.

At the same time his tongue lashed my clit. His fingers plunged inside me, brushing against that spot . . . and I exploded. I screamed around his cock, my core clenching as more of me gushed over his face.

He devoured it, sucking and groaning until I was shaking and sobbing, grinding against his mouth mindlessly.

Matty didn't stop. He kept licking, kept thrusting into my mouth as we both rode the aftershocks. Only when I collapsed forward, trembling, did he ease me off. Cum and my juices were smeared across both our faces.

I glanced down, my eyes catching on the thick, flushed length of him. It was still somehow rigid, still leaking, pulsing against his stomach like it hadn't just come down my throat.

"I need more," he said hoarsely, and in the next second he spun me and slammed me down onto his cock.

I sank to the hilt, a sob tearing free as he filled me, thick and pulsing and perfect.

"Ride me," he commanded, his voice rough with want as his hands gripped my hips. "Ride your *god*."

I did, frantically, grinding down as he thrust up, the wet *slap* of skin echoing.

"I'd lock you in my room," he gritted out. "Chain you to my bed. Fuck you every morning before practice and every night after. I'd breed you until you were dripping, until you were round with me."

"More," I begged, my nails raking his chest. "Tell me *more*."

"I'd blackmail you into living with me," he said hoarsely. "Find every secret, every photo, every fantasy . . . hold it over you until you were begging to stay. I'd film us, every scream, every orgasm, and make you watch while I fucked you again."

I shattered. My pussy clamped down, milking him, waves of pleasure surging through me as I screamed his name.

He didn't stop.

He kept thrusting, kept *talking*.

"I'd sabotage every job, every friendship, every escape route," he rasped. "Make the world too small for anyone but me. I'd burn this dorm down just to carry you out in my arms. I'd kill for you, Ophelia. I'd *die* for you. You're not going anywhere. *Ever*."

I came again—harder, longer—a full-body convulsion that wrenched a harsh sob from my throat as I buried my face in his neck.

He flipped me and pinned me down to the bed so I couldn't move, his hips thrusting against me desperately before he followed me over the edge and spilled deep inside me.

I felt it seep out around him, warm and slick, dripping slowly down my thighs.

We collapsed against the bed.

For a long time, we just lay there, the world narrowed to skin and breath and the unsteady rhythms of our hearts trying to remember how to beat.

And then my tears broke loose before I could stop them. Happy tears. Disbelieving ones. They hit his shoulder, and he lifted his head, kissing me again, then again, like he couldn't stand to leave a single part of me untouched.

"Don't cry," he murmured, his voice rough with something that wasn't just exhaustion.

"I can't help it," I said, the words tumbling out of me. "I've never been this happy. It feels like my body doesn't know what to do with it."

His hand cupped my jaw and his thumb traced the corner of my mouth. "Then let it break you," he said softly. "If it's real, it should."

His forehead rested against mine, his breathing uneven. I reached up, meaning to touch his face . . . and froze when my fingers brushed damp skin.

He was crying, too.

For a moment, neither of us spoke. The world was just salt and skin and breath, the weight of something too big for either of us to hold.

It was the first time that *breaking* didn't feel like a curse.

The first time it felt like . . .

A miracle.

CHAPTER 34

MATTY

The wind stung like needles as I lined up for another drill, the December air cutting through my jersey and settling deep in my bones. The Tennessee cold wasn't supposed to hit this hard when you had an indoor facility, but Coach was on a "mental toughness" crusade and refused to let us practice indoors. "Playoffs aren't played in a dome," he'd said, which was rich coming from a man in three jackets and a heated hat.

By the time he finally blew the whistle for a water break, my fingers were numb inside my gloves. I yanked off my helmet and trudged to the sideline where Jace was crouched near the bench, grinning like he didn't even feel the cold.

"I'm still shocked you actually cleaned my room," I said, shaking my head. "After the . . . you know."

Jace blinked, all wide-eyed innocence. "You mean after Riley's heroic exorcism with a fire extinguisher to get rid of Emma?"

I glanced around, suddenly panicked. "Don't say her name out loud!"

"She's not actually a demon," Parker said as he jumped up and down a few times to try to warm himself up.

"Says the man who didn't wake up with her in his room in the middle of the night," I griped.

"You were giving me compliments," Jace reminded me, helpfully steering us back on track.

"Yes. I was thanking you for getting my room cleaned up so it was easy to move Ophelia in," I said.

Jace's grin was cocky. "Of course I cleaned. You think I'd leave your crime scene–looking room like that? I'm a good friend. The *best* friend." He pointed a thumb at Parker. "Way better than QB1 over there."

Parker was now jogging in place, and he snorted, bumping Jace with his shoulder. "Yeah, the best friend who *hired a cleaning service*. Don't let him milk it too much, Adler. He didn't even take out the trash himself."

Jace threw his hands up. "Excuse me, I *supervised*! That's emotional labor!"

"Yeah, I'm sure yelling 'get the demon residue off the posters' was real taxing," Parker said.

I huffed out a laugh, shaking my head as I tipped my bottle back for a drink. "I'll give you some friendship points for getting my room cleaned regardless of how it happened," I said, "but you only get a few. You scared away the home security company this morning by answering the door naked. And we really need those cameras and alarms. There've been way too many people entering our house uninvited lately."

I shivered again, picturing Emma touching my things. And talking. And being in my presence at all.

Parker barked out a laugh, nearly choking on his water. Jace turned, eyes wide with mock outrage. "Okay, first of all, *I didn't know* we were having company. That might have been a good thing to warn me about. Second, I was coming from the shower, so it was nice of me to answer the door at all. Third—" He paused, gesturing dramatically. "Did I *intend* to drop the towel? No. Did it happen? Almost no."

Parker snorted. "Those men were probably traumatized for life."

Jace nodded. "It would have been better for Matty to have done it. That extra inch was probably terrifying for them."

I was about to open my mouth to object, but then I glanced over at the parking lot . . . out of habit, and I forgot all about Jace's supposed larger dick.

A familiar white car was back in its spot.

A slow pulse started in my chest, something between relief and possession.

She was here.

Ophelia was watching again, just like she always did before. Only now, she didn't have to hide it. I'd told her she could. I'd told her I wanted her to.

She'd gladly taken me at my word.

"Why are you smiling like that? It's creepy," Parker said, before following my line of sight and squinting toward the lot. "That her?" he asked under his breath.

"Yeah," I said, still staring.

He gave a low whistle, then cocked his head. "I wonder if I can get Casey to sit out there with her," he mused. "I always play better when she's watching."

Jace popped up beside us, helmet tucked under his arm, his eyes bright with mischief. "If we're starting a spectator club, count Riley and Natalie in, too," he said. "They can get their girl time out there in the car—bond over snacks, matching blankets, whatever—and then Riley will have no reason not to spend all her free time with me afterward."

Parker barked out a laugh and then nodded. "That's actually a really good idea."

"I know. It's my big brain," Jace said. "It can be quality time for them and uninterrupted worship for us. Everybody wins."

As I turned back toward the field, my gaze caught on Garrett's across the line.

He was standing near the watercoolers, towel slung around his neck, following my line of sight out to the parking lot. His expression shifted—recognition, guilt, maybe both—and our eyes met.

I dragged my thumb slowly across my throat.

His brows shot up. Then he let out a snort, shaking his head like he couldn't believe me. A second later, he lifted one hand and gave me a lazy thumbs-up.

I nodded at him. Garrett and I were buddies . . . just as long as he didn't forget.

When practice finally ended, the sky had already shifted to that washed-out winter gray, the kind that looked like it couldn't decide between rain or snow. My breath came out in clouds as I jogged off the field, helmet under my arm, cleats crunching over the frost-stiff grass.

Her car was still there, and I didn't hesitate.

Ophelia's head was down, eyes fixed on her phone. Her mouth was slightly open, pink from the cold, a little smile curving there like she was seeing something she shouldn't love as much as she did.

When I got close enough, I realized what it was—an interview I'd done yesterday after practice. My voice came faintly through the cracked window, talking about playoffs, team chemistry, or whatever generic thing I'd said to keep the press happy.

I rapped my knuckles lightly against the glass.

She jumped, letting out a tiny squeak that hit me right in the chest. Her phone slipped, and she scrambled to pause the video as her wide eyes found mine.

I grinned, already reaching for the door handle.

"Hi, pretty baby," I said softly, pulling the door open before she could decide whether to hide or breathe.

"Matty," she whispered, her cheeks flushing pinker than from the cold.

I didn't wait for her to climb out. I just reached in, caught her by the waist, and tugged her against me until she was standing between my legs, pressed close enough to feel my heartbeat under her hands.

"I missed you," she murmured in a muffled voice against my chest.

I bent, kissing the top of her head. "You've been watching me this whole time."

"I've realized it's not the same," she said, looking up at me, her eyes glassy and unguarded.

My mouth curved. "No," I said softly. "It's not."

We stayed like that, her breath warm against my throat, my fingers tracing lazy circles on her back. For a second, the world went quiet. Just the two of us and the faint hum of traffic out on the street.

"Matty!"

I turned, jaw tightening automatically, but it was just Rachel—the team's media relations head--waving from across the lot, clipboard tucked under one arm. She had a serious look on her face.

"Hey, Adler!" she called. "I need to talk to you about something. It's important."

"Just a minute!" I called back, forcing a polite smile.

Ophelia's fingers tightened in my jacket.

I brushed my thumb over her cheek, tilting her chin up until she met my eyes again. "Want to meet me at home?" I asked, my voice dropping, the word *home* sinking between us.

Her flush deepened, remembering what that meant now. "Yes," she whispered.

"Good girl."

I kissed her then . . . slow, deep, and shameless right there in the parking lot, until her breath caught and I could taste the promise of later on her lips.

When I finally pulled back, she looked wrecked in the best way.

"Go home," I murmured against her mouth. "I'll be right behind you."

I watched her go, an ache in my chest because I was as addicted to her presence as she was to mine. The taillights of her car glowed against the frost, fading into the gray afternoon as she turned out of the lot. Only when she was gone did I let out the breath I'd been holding.

When I turned back, Rachel was standing by the entrance with her clipboard and her *I've waited long enough for this* expression.

"Took you long enough," she said, arching a brow. "I did say it was important."

"Sorry," I said, and I didn't bother to make it sound convincing.

She sighed, tucking a strand of hair behind her ear. "Come on. Let's go inside."

We headed toward the main building, the wind cutting down the breezeway. My cleats clicked against the concrete, echoing up the stairwell as we climbed to the second floor, where the conference rooms were lined with glass walls and too-bright lights hung from above.

Rachel's tone had gone clipped—professional in that way that always meant *something was off.*

"What's going on?" I asked, trying to sound casual, but the unease crept in anyway.

"What's going on," she said, pushing open the door to one of the meeting rooms, "is that we have a very big donor who's been waiting to talk to you."

I frowned. "A donor?"

She nodded toward the open doorway. "He requested you personally."

My stomach sank before I even stepped inside.

It was Kenton.

The same slick smile. The same expensive suit. The same faint smell of smoke and cologne that had clung to him at that dinner with my dad—the one where he'd leaned back in his chair and told me he had a network of people who'd pay for the right information.

He was sitting at the long table, legs crossed, phone in one hand, a Styrofoam cup of coffee in the other, like he owned the place.

"Matthew," he said smoothly, rising to his feet with a practiced grin. "Good to see you, son."

Rachel was already backing out of the room. "I'll give you two a minute."

The door shut behind her.

"Water?" he asked as he poured a glass from a crystal carafe.

"No," I snapped. "I don't think I'll be here very long."

Kenton huffed out a laugh like I was amusing him.

He slid a laptop around, pressing play on a highlight reel of me. My catches, my runs, my blocks. My name overlaid with statistics.

"I still think we can work out a deal," he said smoothly, setting the glass of water in front of me. "Unfortunately, I realized we never said specific numbers the other night. I think that would have made the evening go smoother."

I was already shaking my head. "I'm not—"

"We're prepared to offer you ten million up front, plus royalties. All in exchange for a few simple tips."

I froze. That amount of money short-circuited my brain for a minute.

"It's a lot of money, Matthew." He leaned back, smiling at my reaction. "And pro players do this all the time. It's not betrayal—it's business. Think what you could do with the money. Your father's debt wiped, your future secured."

"You motherfucker!" I lunged before I thought, fist flying, all the hot, ugly panic and fury that had been roiling in my chest since I'd seen my father in that hospital room roaring to the surface. Kenton stepped back, moving like he'd done this a hundred times before, calm and practiced, and the punch missed him by inches. The glass of water trembled where it sat, untouched.

He didn't flinch. He just gave me an oily smile. "Easy, Matthew," he said smoothly. "I had nothing to do with your father's unfortunate incident. I promise you that."

"Funny that you expect me to believe that," I spat.

"Believe what you want." He pushed the laptop away a little, palms up in the most casual surrender I'd ever seen. "But I do my homework before I work with anyone. I research people. I look at partners, associates, liabilities. Your father's name came up. His debt was one of the reasons I chose not to work with him." He shrugged, as if that explained everything. "Too many entanglements, too much risk. I don't like surprises."

"You didn't work with him," I said slowly, tasting the words. "Because he was already dangerous for you?"

"No," Kenton said. "Because he was a risk. Because if I'm going to move money, I need to know the ledger is clean. Ronnie Adler's book was . . . messy." He leaned forward, voice almost friendly. "That's business, Matthew. Not vengeance."

My laugh was a choke.

"I'm not here to talk about your father, though. Although, I do give you my condolences and I'm glad to hear he's on the road to recovery. What I'm here for is a way to get him out and help you. This deal gives you the money for both."

My thoughts flicked from my dad, who although down for the count right now, would no doubt be up to all his old tricks in a few months . . . and the money.

Ten million dollars.

For a second, I let the numbers eat me.

I saw it all in a flash: my dad's hospital bills paid without me having to stretch myself thin, a house for my mom that my father couldn't gamble away, a college fund for my siblings, and a pile of cash so tall it could give me time to bury the last of Ronnie Adler's mistakes while I worked on my football career.

I imagined buying time to fix things without looking over my shoulder.

The fantasy was stupidly clean, like a glossy ad: problems solved, futures secured. It made my chest ache.

Kenton watched me with that practiced patience. "Think about it," he said softly, as if he were offering advice instead of a mirror.

I felt the pull, vicious and stupid.

Then I let it go, because whatever the money could buy, it didn't buy whatever line I drew inside me.

"I'm not interested," I finally said. "I'm fucking not interested."

I slid back from the table and stood up.

Kenton sighed, a quiet, disappointed sound, and smoothed an invisible wrinkle from his cuff. "That's a shame," he said lightly, though his eyes were anything but casual now. "You know, Matthew, that reporter the other day, the one asking about that little rumor . . . that was just the start."

My stomach went cold.

He smiled. "People like stories. Tragic ones. Scandals. A boy with too much pressure, a family with debt . . . . You'd be surprised how fast whispers spread once the right people start them."

My pulse kicked hard in my throat.

"I'm giving you options," he said smoothly. "We can be friends, or we can be . . . adversaries. And I don't think either of us wants that." He leaned back in his chair, utterly relaxed, like we were just talking game stats. "Friends, Matthew, get protection. They get silence. They get freedom."

I shook my head and huffed out a dark laugh. I knew these weren't idle threats, but it had hit me sitting there. I could lose football. I could lose my reputation.

But I wouldn't lose Ophelia.

And that would make everything okay.

"Yeah, I get it, Kenton," I drawled. "You're threatening me. And just because your ears don't seem to be working . . . I'll repeat myself. I'm not for sale."

Something flickered behind his smile—irritation, maybe. He was about to respond when the conference door suddenly creaked open.

Both of us turned.

Standing in the doorway was a man I knew.

Tall, blonde . . . an expensive, fitted suit. An annoying smirk on his lips that was just like his brother's.

Jagger.

Jace's older brother leaned one shoulder against the doorframe like he had all the time in the world, his hair catching the overhead lights, brown eyes glinting with something amused. He gave me a lazy wink before turning that same expression on Kenton.

"Now, what's this?" he drawled, his tone smooth as honey and twice as dangerous. "Are you giving my friend Matthew here a hard time?"

Kenton froze. The color drained from his face so fast it was almost impressive. "N-no," he stammered, straightening in his chair. "Of course not. Just a miscommunication." His eyes darted to me in full-blown panic, as if I might save him. "That's all. Just a misunderstanding."

Jagger pushed off the doorframe, taking one unhurried step into the room, then another. "A miscommunication," he repeated softly, like he was tasting the word. "Is that so?"

Kenton nodded frantically. "Yes, absolutely. I was just leaving."

He shoved his chair back so fast it screeched against the floor, but before he could reach the door, Jagger moved, quick and smooth, blocking his path with a smile that didn't reach his eyes.

"You're never going to contact him again, are you, Kenton?"

Kenton's throat bobbed. "N-no."

Jagger tilted his head, still smiling. "No, what?"

Kenton's voice cracked. "No, sir."

"Good man." Jagger's grin widened, all teeth. He stepped aside with mock politeness, gesturing toward the open doorway. "See yourself out."

Kenton didn't have to be told twice. He practically bolted, the door banging shut behind him.

Silence fell for a second as I stared dumbfounded at Jagger. He straightened his cuff with a faint smirk. "That counts as your Christmas present, Adler."

My brain . . . and my tongue, finally started working again. "Holy shit, Thatcher. That was incredible. But I have so many questions."

Footsteps echoed from down the hall, and Jace strolled into the room, helmet hair still damp from practice, a grin already tugging at his mouth.

"Yeah, I bet you do," he said, clapping a hand on my shoulder before nodding toward his brother. "You're welcome, by the way. I told him what was going on, but I didn't tell him to, you know—go full James Bond about it."

Jagger rolled his eyes. "James Bond doesn't threaten people in conference rooms, Jace."

"Sure he does," Jace said cheerfully. "It's just off-screen. You're like . . . Bond with anger management issues."

"I don't have anger management issues."

"Yeah, you just scare the piss out of grown men for sport," Jace shot back. "Totally normal, totally . . ."

"Don't say it," Jagger growled.

"Don't say what?" said Jace innocently.

"Don't say mafia," he snapped before freezing and then wiping a hand down his face. "Fucking hell."

I was half laughing, half trying to catch up. "Wait, so how did you even know to show up today? I didn't even know about this meeting."

Jagger gave a nonanswer, straightening his tie with military precision. "Let's just say I have my ways."

"That's not comforting," I said. "What exactly is your job again? You're not CIA, are you? Or, like, an assassin? Because honestly, that would make a lot of sense."

Jace grinned. "Let's think. What kind of shady job has you disappearing for weeks, then showing up with a tan and bruises?"

"Those were vacations," Jagger snapped, glaring at him. "I like to do action sports when I vacation, and sometimes I get bruises."

"Uh-huh," Jace said, completely unfazed. "You took a vacation to Belarus, Jagger-meister."

Jagger's jaw flexed. "People do that all the time."

"What *action sports* did you do on your vacation?" Jace asked.

Jagger sighed again, pushing some hair out of his face. "I forget. It was a long time ago."

Jace looked delighted. "See? That was a shady answer. It was last month."

Jagger ignored him, turning back to me. "You're clear, Adler. He won't bother you again." Then, with a pointed glance at his brother, he said, "Try not to call me in for whatever soap-opera bullshit you three get into next time. I have an actual life."

Jace grinned wider. "An actual shady life."

Jagger shook his head and stalked out, vanishing down the hall as quietly as he'd appeared.

The door shut behind him, and I collapsed into the nearest chair, running both hands over my face as the adrenaline bled out of me. It hit me then—what Jagger had just done. What could've happened if he hadn't.

"Holy shit," I breathed. "That was terrifying."

Jace puffed out his chest. "Terrifyingly effective, you mean. You're welcome, by the way."

I let out a laugh, still in disbelief. "Thank you."

He grinned, clapping me on the shoulder. "Just as long as this earns me more bestilicious points. It obviously puts me ahead of Parkie-poo. What has he even done for you lately? Come up with a possum idea? That's terrible."

I shook my head, pushing to my feet. "He's definitely behind in points."

Jace did a fist pump as we both left the room, muttering something about rewarding him with corn dogs.

I was going to pick up Ophelia and then go to Costco right after this and get him some. Along with some milk. I'd even spring for the organic kind. He deserved it.

Steam still clung to the air, the scent of soap and disinfectant mixing with sweat as I toweled off fast, trying to get out of there so I could see Ophelia.

I slung the towel around my waist and yanked open my locker, grabbing for clean clothes. My phone buzzed on the bench beside me. I ignored it, already reaching for my sweats when movement flickered in the mirror behind me.

A figure stepped out from around the corner.

Tall. Black hoodie. Mask.

I jumped, and the towel slipped from my hand and hit the tile with a *slap*.

The masked guy groaned. "For fuck's sake, Adler. Haven't I seen enough of your dick?"

"Shit," I griped, snatching the towel off the ground and holding it in front of me as I shook my head. It would be my luck that my Sphinx handler, or whoever it was, would continue to catch me in compromising positions. Although in my defense, he was always somewhere he wasn't supposed to be.

It hit me then: If he was here, that meant . . . it was time for my third trial.

I groaned, thinking I'd been through enough today, as he flicked a crimson envelope at me with two fingers, the wax seal glinting under the fluorescent lights before it hit my chest and fell to the floor.

I snatched it up and ripped it open, holding the towel awkwardly in front of me so he couldn't see any more of my goods.

Inside was a single card, thick and heavy.

Welcome to the Sphinx.

I read it a few times, not understanding it. "That doesn't make sense," I muttered. "I haven't passed the third trial."

The guy tilted his head, voice muffled through the mask. "Sometimes life *is* the third trial, Adler. Good job on not taking the money."

Before I could say another word, he turned and walked out.

I stared after him in shock, trying to connect all the threads, Jagger and Jace and Kenton and my dad.

Eventually I just gave up and I shrugged. I wasn't going to look a gift horse in the mouth. It's not like Kenton hadn't been a fucking trial. And dealing with my father was just as bad.

It actually seemed fair.

I grinned, thinking the day hadn't turned out so bad after all.

I'd just become a member of the Sphinx. If I played my cards right, that might be worth ten million dollars right there.

CHAPTER 35

OPHELIA

The afternoon was soft and golden, the kind of Tennessee winter day that pretended it wasn't one—chilly enough for a jacket, bright enough to make you forget.

Matty's hand was warm in mine, his thumb tracing lazy circles against my skin as we walked down the sidewalk toward the row of coffee shops near campus. The world felt . . . quiet. Safe. Perfect, actually.

He was saying something about the playoffs, about practice that morning, but I wasn't really hearing it. I was too caught up in the easy way his voice rumbled, the way people glanced at him as we passed—smiles, double takes, whispers—and how he never noticed any of it. He just looked at *me*.

And then I froze.

The air around me seemed to disappear.

"Ophelia?" Matty's voice was gentle at first, confused. "What is it?"

I couldn't answer. My stomach had dropped straight through the pavement.

Coming toward us at a brisk, stiff pace were my parents.

My mother's posture was perfect as ever, her beige coat immaculate, her lips already curled up like everything she was seeing was shit. My father walked beside her, phone in hand, with the same distant half frown he wore whenever he wasn't looking at numbers.

They hadn't seen me yet.

But they would.

Matty followed my line of sight, his easy smile fading. "You know them?" he asked quietly.

I wanted the earth to just open up and swallow me whole.

I couldn't move. Couldn't breathe. My pulse roared in my ears. "They're my parents," I whispered right before my mother's eyes locked on me.

Matty's hand tightened around mine instinctively. I'd told him what my mother was demanding and of her threats to get me placed on medical leave.

He obviously hadn't been happy about that.

"Ophelia." My mother's voice cut through the noise of passing students, steady and cold as ever. "We need to talk."

Every muscle in my body screamed no.

"What are you doing here?" My voice sounded strange, too small, like it had gotten lost in my throat before it made it out.

"Don't take that tone with us." My mother's brows arched. "We drove all this way to help you. I warned you what would happen if you didn't cooperate, and look what you did. I got what, a day, before you were back to your nasty habits?"

"Don't speak to her like that," Matty growled.

It wasn't a request. It was a warning.

My mother's eyes snapped to him, startled, like she had just noticed him standing beside me. Maybe she hadn't. Maybe she'd thought it was a random student walking near me because I couldn't possibly have found someone to love me.

Matty stepped a little closer, just enough that I could feel the restrained fury radiating from him, his thumb still rubbing soothing circles against my hand even as the rest of him looked ready to tear someone apart.

"Matthew Adler," my dad said after a second, as though he knew him, as though the whole world knew him because his face was plastered across game-day posters. "We were just—"

Matty's gaze sliced through him like he didn't exist. "If you say anything to upset her, we'll be leaving," he announced, ignoring my dad's outstretched hand.

"She's fine," my mom said briskly, her chin lifting like she was staking claim over me. "We're her parents. We're handling it."

"Doesn't look like you're handling it," Matty said flatly.

My mom's lips pressed together in a thin, white line. "You don't know what you're talking about. You don't know her."

"Hmm. Is that so?" His voice went low, dangerous.

My mother scoffed. "She's been diagnosed," my mom said, like she had some kind of trump card. "I'm sure she didn't tell you. She's been diagnosed with obsessive love disorder, obsessive-compulsive disorder, borderline personality disorder, and an attachment disorder. Do you understand what that means? She doesn't feel things the way other people do. She's *sick*."

The words cut me open, even after hearing her say them for what must have been the millionth time. I wanted to crawl into the pavement and disappear into the cracks.

For one endless heartbeat, Matty just stared at them. The silence stretched.

"With absolutely no due respect, fuck off," Matty finally said calmly, wrapping his arms all the way around me and pulling my back to his chest.

"Excuse me?" my mother said, aghast.

"You don't get to decide what she feels," he snarled. "You don't get to tell me what this is. I don't give a damn what you call it in some office. What we have is real. You think it's obsession? Fine. Then I'm obsessed with her right back."

I stared up at him in awe.

Matty wasn't looking at me, though; he was staring them down like he'd never lost a battle in his life and wasn't about to start now. "You want to talk about symptoms? Here's one for you. I memorize the way she looks at me. I keep hearing her voice in my head when she's not around. I notice her before I notice anything else. I can't not. She's under my skin. She's in my lungs. I couldn't get her out if I tried."

My dad's face paled. "Son, you don't know what you're saying."

"The hell I don't." Matty's voice cracked like thunder. "I'm saying I choose her. Every broken piece, every diagnosis, everything you want to write off as sickness. She's mine. And I'm hers."

My throat closed, heat surging behind my eyes, because no one—no one—had ever said that for me. Not to my parents. Not against the weight of what they believed about me.

My mom shook her head, almost pitying him now. "You'll regret this. You don't know how bad it gets."

Matty turned his head slowly toward her, a humorless smile curving his mouth. "Oh, I know exactly how bad it gets," he said quietly.

My mother blinked. "What do you mean?"

"I've seen her school file," Matty said, disgust creeping into his voice. "And you know what I didn't see? I didn't see a single restriction. Nothing saying the campus was monitoring her or that they thought she was a danger. Nothing saying she couldn't live her life or do anything but be a regular college student."

I stared at my parents in shock. Tears burned at the corners of my eyes, and spilled down my cheeks. My throat went tight. All these months of worrying, of jumping through her hoops.

And none of it had been real?

"You made it all up," Matty said, each word angrier than the last. "You lied to her. You scared her. You used her medical record like a leash because it made you feel powerful."

He glanced between them, his expression pure hate. "Which means you're not just bad parents—you're conniving little assholes."

My mother's breath hitched, like he'd slapped her. My father's face flushed an ugly red. They both stared at Matty like they were seeing someone unhinged.

"And if you want a diagnosis . . . because the two of you seem to love them so much . . . I've got one for you. She's *mine*." Matty bared his teeth in something that wasn't a smile. "Write it down. Stamp it across my forehead. Because I won't stop thinking about her. I don't want to. She's in my head when I wake up. She's under my skin when I try to sleep. She's it for me. And you're out of your damn minds if you think I'm letting you hurt her ever again."

My knees nearly gave out. My heart pounded so violently I thought he'd feel it through his chest.

My mom's face softened into pity again, her eyes glistening. "Oh, Matthew. You'll destroy yourself trying to hold her up."

He shook his head slowly, never looking away from her. "You've got it wrong. She doesn't drag me down. She makes me stronger. You see her as fragile? I don't. I see a girl who survived everything you threw at her and still finds a way to stand here breathing. You think that's sickness? I think it's the bravest damn thing I've ever seen."

My breath caught, a sob clawing at my throat. I loved him so much.

"Get out of here," Matty ordered. "You're not welcome. Not until she says you are."

My mother's mouth opened, trembling around words she didn't quite know how to form. "Ophelia," she said softly, in that tone she used when she wanted to sound gentle but was really just trying to manipulate. "We were just trying to help."

Something inside me snapped cleanly into place.

I lifted my middle fingers, both of them, right there on the sidewalk. "Consider me helped," I said, my voice shaking—but not from fear this time.

Matty huffed out a quiet, disbelieving laugh beside me, the kind that sounded proud and wrecked all at once. Then he laced his fingers through mine, and we started walking.

We didn't look back.

I stirred the pot, the smell of chicken and garlic thick in the air as I made Matty's favorite . . . chicken noodle soup.

And for once I didn't have to feel guilty for doing it.

Riley sat on the counter, legs swinging, her blonde hair pulled into a messy bun that somehow still looked perfect. She was scrolling on her phone with one hand, sipping iced coffee with the other.

"That smells so good," she said. "You're going to let me have some, right?"

"Of course," I said shyly. I was still getting used to the fact that I now had three roommates . . . and that they wanted to hang out with me. I smiled a little, tucking a strand of hair behind my ear. "It's Matty's favorite. His mom used to make it before every big game in high school."

Riley grinned. "That's adorable. It's nice having someone in the house who can cook."

I laughed softly and turned to the cabinet above the stove. "He said he likes a ton of pepper, so I'm just going to—"

The second I opened it, a dozen orange pill bottles tumbled out like hail. They clattered across the counter, a few bouncing onto the tile floor and rolling under the island.

"Oh my gosh," Riley squeaked, diving forward. "I'm so sorry! I didn't put that away very well."

She crouched to scoop them up, muttering under her breath as she gathered the bottles into her arms.

I bent down to help her, my eyes catching the labels, vitamins, supplements, and a few prescriptions I didn't recognize. "Are these all yours?" I asked gently, handing her one.

Riley nodded, cheeks pink. "Yeah. I have chronic fatigue syndrome," she said quickly, like it was something she'd had to explain before. "I take a bunch of stuff to help. Or . . . try to help. Some of it's prescriptions, some of it's just vitamins. My system looks like a science experiment half the time."

She gave a small laugh, embarrassed, but I could hear the edge underneath it—the exhaustion of living with something no one else could see.

I leaned against the counter. "That must be hard. Having people not really get it."

Riley's mouth twisted. "Yeah. They see you standing there, smiling, and think you're fine. They don't see the mornings where you can't lift your head off the pillow or the way it feels like your bones are made of lead." She hesitated, fingers brushing the label on one of the bottles. "For a long time, I thought there was something *wrong* with me. Like my body couldn't keep up with the rest of the world."

I looked at her, my throat tight. "I get that."

Her eyes flicked to mine, curious and kind. "You have something, too, don't you?"

I hesitated, then nodded. "Yeah. They've called it a bunch of different things. It's hard to explain, but it's like my brain gets stuck. I try to let go of things, but I can't. It loops and loops until it feels like I'm going to crawl out of my skin."

Riley was quiet for a second, then she smiled softly, understanding, not pitying. "I used to hate myself," she said. "And then I met Jace, and he made me realize maybe I'm not broken. Maybe I'm just wired differently. And that's okay."

Her voice softened, warm as the steam rising from the pot. "He doesn't try to fix me. He just . . . shows up. Even when I'm at my worst. Especially then."

I swallowed hard, an ache in my chest because that's what Matty did for me too. "He sounds like he really loves you."

She nodded, eyes shining. "He does. And it helps. Having someone who sees all your cracks and decides to love you *because* of them, not despite them."

I stared down at the soup, watching the noodles swirl in the golden broth. "Yeah," I whispered. "It really does."

Riley leaned her shoulder into mine, her voice teasing now. "So, what you're saying is . . . we both hit the jackpot and lucked out with hot guys that worship us."

That made me laugh, a real one, light and unguarded. "Something like that."

"Perfect," she said, bumping me again. "Although, I'll state for the record that they lucked out, too. Not everyone could handle their crazy asses."

I blushed thinking of exactly how crazy Matty could be.

She side-eyed me knowingly and held out a hand. "Now, pass me a spoon before I start drinking this straight from the pot. It's not chicken noodle soup if it's not burning your tongue. Or at least I think that's what they say."

Riley and I both turned as the front door swung open and the new security system beeped.

Matty appeared first, hair damp from a quick shower at the facility. Jace trailed behind him, grinning like he'd just gotten away with something.

"Hey—that's mine," Matty said, pointing accusingly at Riley, who was midway through a second bite of soup.

She froze, spoon halfway to her mouth, her eyes wide with mock guilt. "Oh no," she said solemnly. "I've been caught red-handed."

Matty stalked closer, sniffing the air like a bloodhound. "That's *my* chicken noodle soup. My favorite. Ophelia made that for *me*."

I rolled my eyes, smiling as I stirred the pot. "I made plenty," I said.

"Yeah, for *me*," he said, already leaning down to steal a quick kiss before swiping a spoon from the counter.

"Unbelievable," Jace said, slipping between them and reaching for a bowl. "I'm *bestilicious number one*. Riley literally saved your ass with a fire extinguisher! That means, by association, I get soup privileges. Not to mention all the other times I've saved you lately."

Riley giggled. "He's got a point."

Matty huffed but relented, ladling out a bowl and handing it to him with exaggerated reluctance. "Fine. But you better thank your girlfriend for your continued existence."

Jace grinned, clinking his spoon against Riley's. "Already do every fucking day."

I watched them, Matty pretending to scowl, Jace stealing another piece of bread, Riley laughing into her bowl . . . and something soft unfurled inside me.

The kitchen was warm, alive with small sounds—spoons clinking, Matty's low laugh rumbling through the air, Riley humming under her breath.

And I just stood there for a second, taking it all in.

The noise, the warmth, the way Matty looked at me every few seconds.

Looking back now, it was obvious to me that it had been a long time since I'd had a real family, people who lifted me up rather than tearing me down.

But that's what Matty had given me.

He'd given me people who accepted me for who I was.

He'd given me a home.

"You okay?" Matty murmured, staring down at me in concern.

I grinned and nodded. "Yes," I answered. "I really am."

CHAPTER 36

MATTY

The stadium roared around me, a hundred thousand voices folding into one as the ball hit my palms and I broke through the line. I barely felt the hit that came too late or the grass tearing under my cleats.

Touchdown.

I spiked the ball, adrenaline searing through me like fire. My teammates tried to swarm, giving me slaps to my helmet and shouts in my ear, but I made them wait until I did my celebration dance.

The one that perfectly matched the moves Ophelia had just performed for the crowd, of course.

I made her teach me the tiger's dances every week so I had them ready.

And then it was time for the next part of my celebration.

Kissing her.

I jogged toward the sideline, looking around with a grin until I spotted the orange tiger mascot—*my* tiger—jumping up and down.

My chest warmed.

Then the warmth curdled.

Because it took me half a second to realize that the jersey she was wearing, the one stretched over that tiger suit, wasn't mine.

It was Parker's.

My breath stuttered. The grin died on my face.

The noise of the crowd blurred into a dull, roaring hum as a strange ringing sound filled my ears.

She was jumping up and down, pom-poms shaking, completely oblivious. And all I could see was the bold number on her back—his number—flashing every time she moved.

My vision went red.

I wasn't even aware I'd stopped moving until Jace's hand hit my shoulder. "Hey, man. You good?"

No. Of course I wasn't good.

"She's wearing his jersey," I growled.

Jace blinked, confused. "Who?"

"Ophelia."

I sprinted straight for her, cleats pounding the sideline, the roar of the crowd turning into a distant wave. She saw me coming and froze mid-jump.

I didn't slow.

I reached her in four strides, grabbed the tiger head with both hands, and ripped it off. Her hair spilled out in a wild, sweaty tangle, her face flushed, lips parted in shock.

Before she could speak, I crushed my mouth to hers.

Hard.

Possessive.

A kiss that said *mine* in every slide of my tongue, every bite of my teeth.

She melted into me, a soft whimper vibrating against my lips.

I broke the kiss only long enough to yank Parker's jersey over her head, tearing the fabric at the seams and tossing it into the grass like trash.

"What are you—" she started, breathless.

I stripped my own jersey off in one motion, the crowd exploding behind us.

Then I grabbed her wrists, forced my jersey over her head, and tugged it down until my number stretched across her chest.

"There," I said happily. "That's better. You're only allowed to wear *my* name, pretty baby. Only mine."

Her eyes were wide as she glanced down at the jersey and then back up to me.

I kissed her again, slower this time, sealing the claim.

"Keep it on, Ophelia. I'll see you after I win this fucking game."

I spun and jogged back to the team, the crowd losing their minds, her taste still burning on my lips, my name blazing across her back . . .

And the wrong catch finally in my hands.

EPILOGUE I

OPHELIA

The roar of the stadium had faded to a low, distant hum, swallowed by thick concrete and steel. The team was still out there celebrating, but the locker room door could swing open any second.

Matty had me bent over the bench, my tiger costume shoved down to my knees, orange fur bunched and clinging, soaked through with sweat and us.

He knelt behind me, tongue buried deep in my core, lapping at me greedily like he'd been starving for days. His lips sealed over my clit and sucked hard, then let go with a slick *pop* before plunging back inside. He flicked his tongue in tight, relentless circles, tasting every inch. I moaned loudly as my palms smacked the wood, nails clawing as my hips bucked helplessly against his face.

"Matty." I gasped.

He growled into my pussy, the vibration ripping straight through my core. His tongue lashed over my clit, slow circles that built the ache, then dipped lower, thrusting inside me, his breath hot and ragged against my slick skin. His hands slid up, and he spread my cheeks wider, exposing me completely. One thumb brushed my tight hole, pressing just enough to make me whimper and my legs shake.

His free hand snaked around, two fingers plunging inside me alongside his tongue, curling hard against that spot that made my vision blur.

"This," he rasped, his voice muffled against my folds, "was in one of your journals. *Volume Ten*. 'Locker room. After the championship. He eats me on the bench until I scream.'"

I whimpered, my thighs trembling as slick dripped down his wrist.

He sucked my clit hard, fingers pumping faster.

I *detonated.*

Screaming his name, I clenched around his fingers, sobbing as I pushed against his mouth, chasing the pleasure.

A second later he was on his feet.

His cock, thick and dripping, slapped heavy against my ass. He gripped my hips, lined up, and *slammed* into me in one brutal thrust, filling me to the hilt.

I cried out, back arching, hands scrabbling for purchase on the bench. He didn't give me time to adjust. He fucked me hard, hips snapping, balls slapping my clit with every thrust, the bench creaking under us. His hand fisted my hair, yanking my head back, forcing me to arch deeper.

"Mine," he demanded. "This pussy. This body. This *life*. All fucking mine."

He pounded into me, one hand sliding around to rub my clit. I came again, *harder*, my pussy milking him, tears streaming down my cheeks as my whole body convulsed.

Matty followed, driving deep until he finished and the excess was dripping down my thighs and then onto the bench.

We collapsed forward, my cheek pressing against the cool wood, his weight heavy and perfect on my back.

He kissed the back of my neck. "Fantasy number forty-three, check."

I laughed, breathless and wrecked. "There are still four hundred and twelve to go."

He grinned against my skin. "Good. We've got forever."

Then he nipped my ear, his voice dropping to a dark whisper. "Want to hear more obsessed things I want to do to you?"

I shivered, still impaled on him. "Yes," I said instantly, because Matty telling me every obsessed, insane thing he could come up with was my favorite game.

He pressed deeper, rutting in and out slowly as he talked. "I'm going to marry you, Ophelia. Even if you say no. I'll drag you to the altar, put my ring on your finger, and fuck you in the vestry while the priest waits outside."

I grinned, clenching around him.

He kept going. "I'll breed you in every room of our house. Make you wear my jersey to every game, pregnant and glowing, so the whole world knows who you belong to."

I moaned, pushing back against him.

"It's going to happen, Ophelia. All of it," he murmured as his fingers brushed against the *Mrs. Adler* on my hip, making me shiver in ecstasy.

"Now there are only four hundred and eleven to go," I whispered, blissed-out and on the verge of falling asleep on the bench . . . despite our precarious position.

He laughed, happily, and thrust again.

"Challenge accepted."

EPILOGUE II

MATTY

Our first class since the championship, and the lecture hall felt like someone had crammed a stadium's worth of noise into four walls. People were still riding the high of the win. There were lots of orange hoodies, phones flashing clips from the final seconds on repeat, and half the class looked like they'd been celebrating nonstop, judging by the hungover pallor to their skin.

Garrett dropped into the seat beside me, still smelling faintly of beer from last night's festivities. His hoodie was half zipped, baseball cap pulled low. It was the same one he'd worn through the entire season. His superstition.

He had his phone out before his ass even hit the chair, scrolling fast through another mock draft thread. His name kept showing up in the *top ten* in every one. He'd already been called "the next great running back" on ESPN twice this week.

"You realize the draft's four months away," I muttered.

Garrett didn't look up. "Four months is forever in draft years," he said, flicking his thumb across the screen. "Scouts are fickle. I sneeze wrong at the combine, and I drop three slots; I'll never hear the end of it from my brother."

I grinned. Garrett's brother was a star quarterback on the New York Predators. I could see that being a lot to live up to. "Yeah, you'll survive, Top Ten."

He smirked, finally glancing up. "You mock me now. Let's see how you act next year when you're the one having to wait."

I chuckled, tapping my pencil against my notebook. "We'll see."

The door at the front of the lecture hall opened, and Garrett's phone hit the floor.

Garrett followed it a second later.

He didn't trip. Didn't stumble. He just *collapsed* straight out of his chair, knees folding, hitting the tile with a dull *thud*.

I blinked, leaning over the desk. "Fucking hell, man—what are you doing?"

He wasn't listening. His eyes were wide, fixed on something at the front of the room.

I followed his gaze to the woman stepping up to the podium. She looked like she'd walked straight out of a commercial for expensive perfume. Auburn hair pinned up in a sleek twist. Sharp black blazer hugging her waist. Heels that clicked like punctuation.

She looked young, too young to be a professor, but I was pretty sure that's what she was.

"Aubrey," he breathed.

"Do you know her?" I asked.

He nodded, his eyes still locked on her even though he was still on the floor and she was going to notice any second. "That's my wife."

My jaw dropped. "Your what?"

He swallowed hard, face pale. "My wife. I married her in Vegas. The night we celebrated the championship last year."

I still was having trouble understanding the words coming out of his mouth. Because I was pretty sure he'd just said he was married.

I glanced to the front of the room again.

Down at the podium, she smiled tightly and picked up a marker, writing her name across the whiteboard in clean, looping script.

Dr. Aubrey Bro—.

Her hand froze halfway through the *O*.

Because her eyes had found Garrett.

The color drained from her face, and for a second she looked like she might bolt. Then her professional mask slid back into place.

"Good morning, everyone," she said, her voice just a touch too bright. "Welcome back. For anyone who missed last class, I'm Dr. Browning, and I'll be teaching Intro to Shakespeare this term."

Garrett looked like he might throw up.

I leaned back, fighting the grin threatening to take over my face. "Holy shit," I muttered.

He turned to me, whispering harshly, "Don't. Say. A. Word."

"I didn't say anything," I murmured, still grinning. "Just— Wow. Didn't expect the semester's first scandal to come from *you*."

He dropped his head into his hands, groaning. "She disappeared the morning after. I had no idea how to find her. I never thought I'd see her again."

"She looks *found* now," I whispered, nodding toward the podium. "But what was your plan? Just to be married to her forever?"

He made a sound like he was choking, and I clapped him on the back as he finally staggered back into his seat.

Dr. Browning cleared her throat and launched into the syllabus, eyes darting back to him only once—long enough to confirm that, yeah, this was really happening.

I stifled a laugh, shaking my head.

First class after a championship, and my teammate had just discovered his Vegas wife was his new professor.

There was no way this wasn't going to blow up spectacularly.

I couldn't wait.

BONUS SCENE

Want more Matty and Ophelia? Come hang out in C. R. Jane's Fated Realm for an exclusive BONUS scene! Get it here: https://www.facebook.com/groups/C.R.FatedRealm

MATTY'S FAVORITE CHICKEN NOODLE SOUP RECIPE

ERVINGS: 8

NGREDIENTS

TABLESPOON BUTTER
RIBS CELERY, DICED
WHITE ONION, DICED
-4 LARGE CARROTS DICED
CLOVE GARLIC, MINCED
CUP FLOUR
CUPS CHICKEN STOCK OR BROTH
TEASPOON SALT, TO TASTE
TEASPOON FRESHLY GROUND BLACK PEPPER
TEASPOON DRIED ROSEMARY OR MORE, TO TASTE
TEASPOON DRIED THYME
TABLESPOONS ORGANIC BETTER THAN BOUILLON
CHICKEN FLAVOR (OR MORE, AS NEEDED)
BOX EGG NOODLES (OR GLUTEN FREE
JOVIAL BRAND EGG NOODLES
CUP HEAVY CREAM
CUPS COOKED ROTISSERIE CHICKEN

NSTRUCTIONS

DD BUTTER, CELERY, ONION, AND CARROTS TO A LARGE STOCK POT OVER MEDIUM-HIGH HEAT. SAUTÉ UNTIL SOFT. ADD GARLIC AND COOK OR ANOTHER 30 SECONDS. ADD FLOUR AND MIX UNTIL COMBINED.

DD CHICKEN STOCK AND SEASON THE BROTH WITH SALT, PEPPER, ROSEMARY, AND THYME. TASTE AND ADD SPOONFULS OF CHICKEN OUILLON CUBES OR GRANULES AS NEEDED.

RING BROTH TO A BOIL. ADD NOODLES AND COOK JUST UNTIL NOODLES ARE AL DENTE. BE CAUTIOUS NOT TO OVERCOOK YOUR NOODLES! EMOVE POT FROM HEAT AS SOON AS THEY ARE JUST BARELY TENDER. THE NOODLES WILL CONTINUE TO COOK ONCE YOU REMOVE THE OT FROM THE HEAT.

OUR IN HEAVY CREAM SLOWLY AND THEN MIX.

DD THE ROTISSERIE CHICKEN. TASTE THE BROTH AGAIN AND ADD MORE SEASONINGS, IF NEEDED.

ACKNOWLEDGMENTS

Dear Reader,

To every single one of you who's ever fallen for the wrong person, made the wrong choice, or loved a little too hard . . . this book is for you.

Matty and Ophelia were never supposed to be a love story. They were obsession and ache and need, a tangle of everything you're told not to want. But somehow, they found their way through the dark. Writing them was like bleeding and breathing at the same time.

Thank you for letting me tell stories that are messy and unhinged and far too much. Thank you for understanding that sometimes love isn't gentle; instead it's consuming, terrifying, and utterly impossible to walk away from.

If you've read every "Wrong" book, you know by now: The goal is not perfection. It's about finding the one person who looks at your pain and calls it home.

So, from the bottom of my heart, thank you for letting me keep breaking rules and hearts right alongside you.

For Matty and Ophelia.

For all of us who love too much.

For everyone who knows that sometimes the *wrong* catch . . . is the only one that feels right.

XOXOXO,
C.R.

P.S. I didn't get the name Ophelia from Taylor Swift.

A few thank-yous . . .

To Raven: Moons forever.

To my beta readers, Crystal and Blair: Thank you for being some of the first people to believe in me and in these stories before anyone else did. Your faith, your feedback, and your friendship have meant more than I can ever say. You've been with me almost since the beginning, and every word I write carries a piece of that belief.

To Stephanie, my editor: Thank you for diving headfirst into my stories with such care. You make every book sharper, stronger, and more fearless than it was before. Thank you for understanding my characters even when they make terrible decisions . . . and for never once flinching when I said, "Okay, this one's going to get dark." I'm endlessly grateful.

To my PAs and BFFs, Caitlin and Sarah: Love you forever.

To my publisher, Podium: To everyone at Podium, and especially Cassie and Victoria, thank you for believing in this world and in me. For your passion, your vision, and your commitment to bringing my stories to life. Every collaboration reminds me why I love what I do.

To my agent, Stephanie: Thank you for your fierce advocacy and your unwavering belief in these stories (and in me).

To my husband: You're my favorite plot twist, my safest place, and the best kind of forever. Thanks for being mine.

And to you, the readers who make this dream a reality: You are the heartbeat of every book I write. Thank you for falling for these characters, for screaming with me, crying with me, and believing that love, no matter how dark, messy, or unhinged, can still be beautiful.

ABOUT THE AUTHOR

C.R. Jane is a *USA Today*–bestselling author of romance, fantasy, and whatever else she feels like writing. Her stories are designed to make readers cry, scream, and eventually . . . swoon. Welcome to her world, where heartbreak and happy endings rule.